# MONTANA

## ✦ ⟨ COUNTRY LEGACY ⟩ ✦

# THE RELUCTANT RANCHER

—— ⚒ ——

## Donna Alward

## Mary Sullivan

Previously published as *The Cowboy's Homecoming*
and *Rodeo Father*

ISBN-13: 978-1-335-50011-3

Recycling programs for this product may not exist in your area.

Montana Country Legacy:
The Reluctant Rancher
Copyright © 2020 by Harlequin Books S.A.

The Cowboy's Homecoming
First published in 2015. This edition published in 2020.
Copyright © 2015 by Donna Alward

Rodeo Father
First published in 2017. This edition published in 2020.
Copyright © 2017 by Mary Sullivan

All rights reserved. No part of this book may be used or reproduced in any manner whatsoever without written permission except in the case of brief quotations embodied in critical articles and reviews.

This is a work of fiction. Names, characters, places and incidents are either the product of the author's imagination or are used fictitiously. Any resemblance to actual persons, living or dead, businesses, companies, events or locales is entirely coincidental.

This edition published by arrangement with Harlequin Books S.A.

For questions and comments about the quality of this book, please contact us at CustomerService@Harlequin.com.

Harlequin Enterprises ULC
22 Adelaide St. West, 40th Floor
Toronto, Ontario M5H 4E3, Canada
www.Harlequin.com

**Printed in U.S.A.**

# "Come on, I'll walk you home."

Kailey laughed. "News flash, Duggan. You're on Brandt land. I'm already home. Maybe I should walk you back, huh?"

She was so quick, a little feisty, and he liked that about her. A lot. "If you want to kill my reputation with a single blow, sure. Big bad rodeo star needs an escort home in the dark."

Not that he couldn't find a few things to do in the dark with her.

He had to stop thinking that way.

"I guess we'll just part ways here, then," she replied, pushing herself to her feet.

"I guess." He'd taken maybe half a dozen steps when she called out to him.

"Hey, Rylan."

He turned and faced her, and the image of her standing in the twilight among the waving grass did something crazy to his pulse.

"I'm glad we cleared the air." Kailey turned and started walking away, her hips swinging a little with each step.

He was glad she was happy about it, because to his mind things had just become a whole lot more complicated.

# CONTENTS

**Donna Alward** lives on Canada's east coast with her family, which includes her husband, a couple of kids, a senior dog and two crazy cats. Her heartwarming stories of love, hope and homecoming have been translated into several languages, hit bestseller lists and won awards, but her favorite thing is hearing from readers! When she's not writing, she enjoys reading (of course), knitting, gardening, cooking...and she is a *Masterpiece Theatre* addict. You can visit her on the web at donnaalward.com and join her mailing list at donnaalward.com/newsletter.

## Books by Donna Alward

## Harlequin Romance

### Destination Brides

*Summer Escape with the Tycoon*

### Marrying a Millionaire

*Best Man for the Wedding Planner*
*Secret Millionaire for the Surrogate*

### Holiday Miracles

*Sleigh Ride with the Rancher*

### Cadence Creek Cowboys

*The Last Real Cowboy*
*The Rebel Rancher*
*Little Cowgirl on His Doorstep*
*A Cowboy to Come Home To*
*A Cadence Creek Christmas*

Visit the Author Profile page at
Harlequin.com for more titles.

# THE COWBOY'S HOMECOMING

## Donna Alward

# Chapter 1

Crooked Valley Ranch had changed since Rylan had last been here.

He drove slowly up the driveway, the Ford 4x4 and hybrid camper he towed behind moving easily over the gravel lane, not a pothole to be seen. Duke must have had it leveled this spring, he mused.

Ry touched the brakes and stared at the house. A fresh coat of white paint was on the front porch and flowers bloomed in a profusion of color in front of criss-cross lattice skirting. The barns could use a new coat of paint as well, but there was an air of neatness and organization that had been missing before, too. It looked as if his sister hadn't been kidding. Crooked Valley Ranch was on its way up.

"I'll be damned," he breathed, a smile touching his lips. He never would have thought his dyed-in-the-wool military brother, Duke, would turn out to be a rancher. But if outward appearances meant anything, Duke was doing a damned good job revitalizing their granddad's spread.

Rylan scowled a little, chafing against the demand-presented-as-a-request he'd received from Lacey. Duke was staying on at Crooked Valley. Hell, he was married and had a baby on the way—a family to support. Lacey had taken over the administration aspect of the operation, and she and the ranch manager, Quinn Solomon, were planning a June wedding. Joe Duggan's will required all three of his grandchildren to take their place at the ranch before the year was up or else the place would be sold. Lacey had totally guilted him into coming "home," as she'd put it.

"It's not forever," she'd assured him. "Just use this as your home base. That's all we ask. We've never asked anything else of you, Rylan. Please help us keep it in the family. Once everything's settled, Duke and I will find a way to buy out your third."

Roots. He tried to avoid them whenever he could. Still, it kind of stung that Lacey had just dismissed him as having no interest in the ranch. Not that he wanted his part of it, but that they hadn't expected it of him. No one ever expected anything of him, did they? He should have been used to it by now.

He pulled into a big vacant spot next to the horse barn and cut the engine, which also cut out the comforting sounds of the music he'd had blaring on the radio during the drive from Wyoming.

Truth was, he'd known since February that this day was coming.

His arrival must have made some noise, because a

little girl came rushing out of the barn, brown curls bob-
bing. Amber, Quinn's daughter. Rylan grinned. Little-
known secret: he liked kids. Kids were easy, and honest,
and thought being a grown-up meant doing what you
wanted to do and not what someone told you. At least
with kids, he never had his choices judged. To them,
he was "cool."

"Hey, short stuff!" He hopped out of the cab and
slammed the door.

"Hi," she offered, but stopped short, tilted her head and
stared at him. "Are you going to be my Uncle Ry now?"

Yep, blunt honesty. He grinned back at her. "Looks
that way. I'm okay with it if you are."

She nodded. "I gots a dog. Her name is Molly."

"Congratulations."

With a happy giggle, Amber turned around to run
back to the barn, but stopped when she saw Quinn coming around the corner. Rylan liked Quinn, and he was
happy for his sister. They'd make this work out somehow… He knew his brother and sister didn't realize it,
but he actually did care about their happiness. That was
the only reason he'd come back.

That and the heavy sense of inevitability that told
him he probably should face his demons at some point.

And then a blond head appeared, the streaky strands
of hair twisted back in a braid. His gut clenched. Maybe
it wasn't her. Maybe he could be that lucky. He wasn't
ready for the confrontation he knew would be coming.

The woman came around beside Quinn, both of them
talking, and he recognized the long legs, curvy figure
and slight sway to her walk. Kailey Brandt. He held
back a groan. Why did she have to be here right at this

particular moment? Why couldn't he have had time to prepare, to work out something to say?

He hadn't spoken to her since Valentine's Day, when she'd hopped into his truck and had gone back to the motel with him after the benefit dance at the Silver Dollar. He'd slipped out the morning after, before she woke. It had been a coward's move and one he wasn't proud of. He figured he deserved whatever she would sling his way. He'd just hoped to avoid it for a little while longer.

"Daddy, Uncle Ry's here!" Amber's sweet voice broke the silence and both Quinn and Kailey looked up. Quinn's face broke out into a smile while Kailey's...

Damn. His gut twisted again. She looked ready to commit murder.

"Rylan," Quinn greeted him, holding out a hand. "Glad you're finally here."

Rylan shook his hand. "Me, too, Quinn. Congratulations on your engagement. Glad my sister isn't marrying some pansy-ass."

Quinn laughed. "To the point. And a compliment, I think."

"It is."

His gaze slid over to Kailey. Her lips were set in a thin, unrelenting line, her eyes as cold as January ice.

"Hello, Kailey."

She looked down at Amber, who was within earshot, then pasted on the falsest smile he'd ever seen. "Why, hello, stranger."

Quinn frowned, looking from Rylan to Kailey and back to Rylan again. "Okay, I'm just a guy and even I can tell there's some friction here. What's going on?"

Kailey patted Quinn's arm. "Nothing. Nothing at all. I'd better get back home now. Chores to do and stuff."

Without so much as a nod goodbye, Kailey marched off in the direction of her truck. Rylan noticed it was a year or two newer than his, a V8 with a crew cab and lots of power to tow a trailer full of stock. He had no doubt she could do it, too. She was the prettiest girl he'd ever seen. And one of the toughest and most capable.

Quinn's voice was low. "That have something to do with Valentine's Day?"

No sense making excuses. Rylan met his gaze evenly. "Probably," he admitted.

Amber bounced away to play with Lacey's pup, Ranger, and Quinn blew out a breath. "You know, Lacey insisted that you guys were adults. That I needed to let things be. But let me tell you this. That girl is one of my best friends."

"Warning received," Rylan acknowledged. "I'll make things right. I don't have any intention of hurting her, Quinn."

"Intentions are funny things," Quinn replied. But he let the matter drop, thankfully. "Have you been inside to see your sister yet?"

"No."

"She's thrilled you're here. Just so you know."

Unease settled over Rylan again. He'd come to Crooked Valley as requested, but he fully intended to do his own thing and on his own schedule. That was the agreement. None of this convincing-him-to-stay crap. He'd be on the road most of the summer anyway, hitting as many rodeos as possible in his run for the National Finals title. He had a real chance this year and he wasn't about to blow it.

"I'll park the trailer and make my way up in a bit."

Quinn nodded. "I'll see you later then."

He gave Ry a clap on the shoulder before moving on toward the rambling farmhouse. Rylan looked after him, vague memories stirring in his brain. He'd been little but he still remembered. He remembered Grampa Joe and Grandma Eileen and learning to ride the horses and the sound of his dad's laughter. Grandma had made the best chocolate cake he'd ever had, and Grampa Joe had bought Ry a pony to ride since he was younger and smaller than Duke. The pony's name had been Daisy and he'd doted on her from the first moment, feeding her treats of apples and carrots, and brushing her every day.

His early childhood had been absolutely perfect.

There were other memories, too. He remembered how it had felt to hear the news that his father was never coming home. It had been incomprehensible to imagine a world where Dad wouldn't come thumping in, dropping his duffel and looking so tall and important in his uniform. Ry had spent hours in the barns, sitting with the horses, smelling their warm, pungent hides and trying to make sense of it all. He'd told Daisy all his feelings, burying his face in her coarse mane when things got to be too much for him to understand.

And then even that had been taken away when their mother had moved them to Helena and that small house on a postage-stamp lot. The city, for God's sake. No fields, no chocolate cake and no Daisy.

He would never invest that much of himself in a place again. No commitments meant no disappointments, and that was just how he liked it.

He got back in the truck and found a nice level spot to park his camper.

\* \* \*

Kailey had thought a lot about what she'd say to Rylan Duggan the next time she saw him. She'd also known that Lacey and Duke had asked him to come to Crooked Valley. His presence here would ensure that the ranch stayed in the family, and with two of the three Duggan siblings invested in it now, his agreement was especially important. She understood that.

But to her knowledge he hadn't agreed, and he certainly hadn't advised anyone of his arrival. He'd just shown up, wearing those faded jeans and a cocky grin that had made her traitorous body stand up straight and pay attention.

She hated him for that. Almost as much as she hated that she was just that weak to fall for a sexy smile and fine ass. Well, falling for it and acting on it were two different things. He wouldn't get the chance to burn her again.

Dust puffed up in clouds behind her tires as she drove along a dirt road parallel to the Brandt ranch. Just beyond the next ridge was the bend in the Crooked Valley Creek, where the water slowed, creating the perfect summer swimming hole. She needed some peace and quiet, some tranquility, before she went home. The last thing she wanted to do was take this mood inside.

Sometimes it really sucked being in her late twenties and still living with her parents. Yet it made no sense to do otherwise, when she spent 90 percent of her time working the ranch. The ranch that was going to be hers someday. That had always been perfectly clear. She was an only child. Without her, the ranch would have to be sold.

She loved Brandt Ranch. She truly did. But having the weight of it on her shoulders had come with a price.

Finally, she slowed and pulled off the dirt road, driving carefully down a path that was no more than two tire tracks through the grass. It opened up into a wide, grassy knoll that led to the water. As she climbed out of the truck, she could hear the comforting warble of the creek and the sound of the birds in the nearby trees and bushes.

She picked her way down the bank to the edge of the water and dipped her fingers in. "Brrr." She shivered and pulled her hand back out. It was only May and the creek was higher than usual, fed by the runoff from the mountains. There'd be no swimming today.

But the sun was warm and there wasn't a soul around for miles. She closed her eyes and rolled her shoulders, trying to ease the tension out of the tight muscles, but she could only see Rylan in her mind, his weight resting on one hip, looking calm and sexy and as if he didn't have a care in the world.

It was her own stupid fault. She'd anticipated a no-strings night of fun when they'd hooked up a few months ago. She'd needed it after putting on an "I'm so over it" show for Colt Black. No one had known how serious their relationship had been, or how hurt she'd been when he'd rebounded so quickly and found another girl. Newly single and at the benefit for Quinn and Amber, Colt had danced with her and asked if they could be friends again.

And to demonstrate how very over him she was, she'd flirted with Rylan, danced with him, fallen under his spell despite herself. By the time she'd awakened in an empty bed the next morning, she'd fallen for him.

Hard. And she'd seen Rylan Duggan for who he really was.

A heartless bastard.

Worse than that, she hated herself for her moment of weakness. Maybe Rylan had left her high and dry, but she'd put herself in that position all on her own. She'd rather just forget that whole night had ever happened.

Letting out a huge sigh, Kailey sank into the warm grass and lay back against the ground, letting it cushion her body as she turned her face up to the sun. The water was cold, but the sun's rays were gloriously hot. She unbuttoned her plaid shirt, letting the fabric fall away from her chest and abdomen, exposing her skin to the sun. She let the rays soak in, restoring her calm and her confidence. It made her feel feminine, when so often she felt like one of the guys, smelling like the barn and sweat. She loved every second of it, but once in a while a woman liked to feel like a woman.

She'd definitely felt like a woman in Rylan Duggan's arms. After he'd left her at the motel, she'd come to the conclusion that she not only didn't need Rylan, but she didn't need anyone at all. Maybe someday the right man would come along and sweep her off her feet, treat her the way she should be treated. Like an equal. With respect. Someone who wouldn't mind that she already was tied down—to her ranch.

Kailey sighed heavily, a deep, cleansing breath. And if her Prince Charming never showed up, well, that was all right, too. She was fine just the way she was.

Except she sometimes wondered if that were true. First it had been Carrie, now Lacey. Both deliriously happy. And somehow Kailey felt as if she was missing out on something important.

One thing she knew for sure, she thought, as she stretched out in the sun. Rylan Duggan was *not* the thing she was missing out on. She'd learned her lesson there.

If she had her way, he'd be hitting the road for his next rodeo before any of them had time to catch their breath. In and out of her life as quickly as he had been the last time.

On Rylan's first night home, Lacey pulled out all the stops, just as Ry had known she would. Duke and Carrie came for dinner, and Quinn and Amber practically lived at the ranch, though the official move-in wasn't until after the wedding in June. Lacey had made potato salad and Caesar salad, and Quinn was grilling rib-eyes for the prodigal celebration. It was nice but unnecessary. He didn't want any fuss made.

Good luck with that.

They had asked all sorts of questions about Rylan's latest rodeo conquests and were well into the meal when Duke brought up the subject of Rylan's camper.

"I noticed you set up your RV," Duke said as he cut into his steak. "That's a great little rig. You must like it when you're traveling."

Rylan nodded. "It's smaller than some, but there's only one of me. Doesn't take long to set up and suits me just fine." Truthfully, he'd had something bigger but it had been a pain in the ass, heavier to haul, more space than he'd needed. He'd sold it in February and had bought the smaller set-up. On the heels of his latest win, he'd been flush with cash for a few weeks.

Including over Valentine's Day.

"I made up the spare room with fresh sheets," Lacey

broke in, handing a basket of buns to Quinn. "Same one you slept in at Christmas."

Rylan put down his fork. "Not necessary, sis." He smiled. "I'm happy in the camper."

"Rylan Joseph Duggan. You are not sleeping in a camper!"

He raised one eyebrow as all eyes turned to look at her. "Wow," Quinn said. "You've got the mother voice down cold."

"Can I sleep in your camper, Uncle Ry?" Amber speared a piece of steak that her father had cut for her. "I's never been camping."

"We'll see, pumpkin."

Lacey regarded him with disapproval. "Rylan, really. There's no need to sleep in the yard when there's a perfectly good room here with your name on it."

Right. Just what he needed. To horn in on her relationship with Quinn. Maybe the manager hadn't formally moved in yet, but it was clear as the nose on Rylan's face that the three of them had a cozy little vibe going on. Besides, the wedding was in less than a month. The last thing he wanted was to be smack in the middle of their newlywed love nest.

"I like it," he contradicted mildly. "I've got my own space. My own privacy. And I won't be invading your privacy either."

"There's a much better mattress on the bed upstairs." Lacey frowned. "You surely didn't come all this way to sleep in that contraption."

"I prefer it."

"What if you have to go to the bathroom in the night?"

Rylan couldn't help it. He burst out laughing and

smiles bloomed on faces around the table. "Really? What am I, five?"

Amber lifted her chin. "You can't be five, Uncle Ry. I'm gonna be five in two weeks." She rolled her eyes.

"See?" He reached over and ruffled Amber's hair. "Five, huh? Guess that means you start school in September."

"Real school," she replied importantly.

Amber's insertion into the conversation had mollified Lacey a little bit. "You're sure?" she asked. "There's lots of room."

"I'm sure. I also know how to do my own laundry. Make food."

Quinn stepped in. "You're going to want to take advantage of the food thing. Your sister's a heck of a cook." Rylan watched as Quinn turned a tender gaze on his fiancée. "Even when you don't want it, she's going to press food on you. You might as well accept it and enjoy."

Lacey turned pleading eyes on him. "Yes, Rylan, please eat your meals here."

"I can probably do that," he conceded. The small concession would get her off his back, and he'd eat a lot better than if he cooked for himself.

Duke joined the conversation. "You're always welcome at the bunkhouse, too, Ry. Carrie and I have room. At least until the baby comes."

Which would be in a few months. Carrie was already glowing with motherhood, her hand resting on her rounded belly. And Rylan smiled through it all, feeling incredibly claustrophobic and smothered.

"I'll stick to the camper for now, but thanks for the invites." His jaw felt tight and he forced himself to relax it. "Heck, I'm going to be rodeoing a fair bit of the time anyway. Easier to just hook up and go, you know?"

This would be his home base. No commitments, no ties. He was still going to run this life the way he had for the past several years. On his terms, coming and going as he pleased.

He knew at times it must have seemed as if he didn't care for his family, but nothing could have been further from the truth. That he was here was proof of that. He wanted this for them, if it was what would make them happy, and he was strangely happy that he could finally do something right rather than merely being an afterthought.

He just hoped they could accept that he needed to run his life his own way, too, and understand when the time came for him to leave again.

## Chapter 2

Kailey stared in the boutique's mirror and had to admit that Lacey had fantastic taste.

The bridesmaid dress was turquoise blue, a slightly brighter shade than a robin's egg. The light material draped and flowed in an utterly feminine way, fluttering to a hem just above her knees. It was strapless, leaving Kailey's shoulders bare, and she realized she was going to have to rectify the farmer tan she had from working outside in T-shirts by employing some self-tanner. But she loved it. She completely and utterly loved it.

Lacey came back to the dressing room with a box in her hands. "Oh my gosh! That's so beautiful on you!" She put the box on a padded seat and put her hands to her mouth. "Oh, Kailey. You're stunning."

Kailey felt a blush climb her cheeks. Not that she didn't like dressing up for a night out, because she did.

Occasionally it was nice to feel like a girl. But this was different. It felt so formal. So…foreign. The only wedding she'd been in before had been Duke and Carrie's, and that had been so low-key that she'd just worn a pretty red dress from her closet and a flower in her hair.

"It's not too much?" Kailey looked down, hitched up the bodice just a touch. She had to admit, she liked the way the fabric crisscrossed her breasts and waist.

"It's perfect." Lacey beamed at her. "And don't worry about wearing heels you'll break your neck in. Here. I got you these. My present to you."

Lacey picked up the box again and handed it to Kailey.

Kailey opened the lid and found a gorgeous pair of cowboy boots nestled inside, with matching blue accents inlaid on the boot shaft.

"Wow. Just…wow."

"I figured you might not wear the dress again, but you might find some use for these."

Kailey took the first one out of the box and slid it on. It was a perfect fit. "There is nothing more comfortable than a good pair of boots," she decreed, looking up at Lacey and smiling.

"I'm going to be wearing a pair, too," Lacey replied. "Under my dress."

Kailey had seen Lacey's dress. It was sweet, in a similar style to Kailey's only long and white and with frothy light material on the overskirt. Simple and very, very sweet—just like the bride. "The boots can be your something blue," Kailey suggested, and Lacey grinned.

"I might have thought of that." She looked at Kailey. "So what do you think? Alterations? Or is it fine as is?"

It fit perfectly. "I think we can take this home today, don't you?"

Lacey nodded. "I can't believe it's only a few weeks away. Sometimes it feels like it's all happened so fast, and other times it seems to be taking so long!"

Kailey smiled in return, though it felt forced. She kind of understood what Lacey meant but in the totally opposite way. Valentine's Day seemed like ages ago, yet the time from then to now had gone so fast. Quinn and Lacey had been busy falling in love and she'd…

She'd been busy, all right. Thinking she'd seen something in Rylan Duggan that didn't exist. Thinking he was…different.

"I should change," she suggested, annoyed that she'd allowed Rylan to sneak into her thoughts. "We still have errands to run, right?"

With two and a half weeks until the big day, Kailey was spending more time than usual away from the ranch, fulfilling her maid of honor duties. Not that she minded, but it was a busy time of year. They'd be making the first cut of hay soon, not to mention rodeo season picking up. She didn't often travel with the stock, but she had the final say on which animals traveled and she was in charge of making the arrangements.

"Right," Lacey replied, taking the boots from Kailey as she reluctantly removed them. "K, you're going to knock Rylan's socks off in that dress."

Kailey scowled. "That is so not the objective."

"Oh, of course not." Lacey's face looked a little too innocent to be believed. "But you have to admit it's a nice little side benefit."

"Whose side are you on, anyway?" Kailey turned

her back so Lacey could undo the hook and eye at the top of the zipper.

"Hey, I love my brother. Don't get me wrong." Lacey's fingers were cool against Kailey's skin as she undid the clasp. "But that doesn't mean I agree with everything he does. Like hurt my new best friend."

Kailey swallowed thickly. She loved it in Gibson, had lived here all her life. And she and Carrie had been good friends for years. But she had to admit, that with the exception of Rylan, she was very, very glad that the Duggan siblings had come to live at Crooked Valley. Duke and Lacey's friendship had become really important to her.

"That's sweet," she said, trying to make her voice sound breezy. "But you don't have to worry about me. That's water under the bridge."

"I'm glad to hear it."

Ouch. Not that she mistook Lacey's meaning. Clearly the family was aware of what had happened on Valentine's Day. And she knew that all Lacey meant was that she was glad Kailey had moved on. But it stung a little, too, that Lacey was glad there was nothing between them. It felt as if the Duggans wouldn't support her having a relationship with Rylan… After all, blood was thicker than water. Maybe they thought she wasn't good enough for their little brother.

She locked herself in the changing room and frowned. What the heck was wrong with her, thinking like that? She didn't *want* a relationship with Rylan, for Pete's sake! What she wanted was for him to satisfy his inheritance requirement and then just leave again.

And good enough? She pulled on her jeans and zipped them, her movements quick and efficient. Jeez, she let one guy catalogue all her faults as a girlfriend and suddenly she doubted herself. Honestly, there were days she wished she'd never met Colt Black and his charming face. Or Rylan and his charming face, too. Boy, she was a sucker for the lookers, wasn't she?

But today that didn't matter. Today was about Lacey's wedding, so after she put the dress in the garment bag and paid the balance at the counter, she and Lacey started back to Gibson for lunch. This afternoon they had appointments to put in the final order for the cake and flowers. Lacey was the perfect blushing bride-to-be, radiant and happy during the preparations. There hadn't been a single bridezilla moment, and for that Kailey was eternally grateful.

The Horseshoe Diner was doing a bustling business over the lunch hour, and Kailey and Lacey found themselves at a table near the back, close to where the ancient jukebox sat. Lacey, being ever conscious of fitting into her wedding dress, ordered a salad with dressing on the side. Kailey didn't worry so much about what she ate, considering the physical labor she did each day. She ordered a cheeseburger with bacon and hot peppers and then, at Lacey's horrified expression, asked for a side salad instead of fries.

She would not look at her watch and worry about chores. She deserved a day off. This was Lacey's wedding after all. Things could run without her for a few hours.

Their food came as they were discussing the merits of having both a white and chocolate layer in the wedding cake. Kailey was just considering the best way to pick up her cheeseburger when the front door swung open and Rylan and Quinn strode through.

Lacey had her back to the door, so it was Kailey who saw them first, and her heart sank as she watched Quinn scan the room for an empty table. There weren't any that Kailey could see, and she looked down, hoping the pair wouldn't see them sitting there. Not that she'd mind Quinn, but Rylan? No thanks.

No such luck. A quick glance showed her that they were on their way over, Quinn leading the way with a big smile. Of course he was smiling. Lacey was there. Rylan didn't look quite as pleased. Apparently he wasn't looking forward to seeing her any more than she was looking forward to seeing him.

"Is there room for two more here?" Quinn asked, and Lacey's head snapped up in surprise, her face flushing with pleasure.

"Of course there is!" She patted the chair next to her. "Our food just arrived. I'm sure yours won't take long."

Quinn gave her a quick kiss and sat while Rylan stood by Lacey's chair. "May I?" he asked quietly, politely. Unenthusiastically.

"Be my guest," she answered coolly, wishing now that she'd gotten the fries. And a big soda. And a hot fudge sundae to bury her head in.

"Thanks," he murmured and took the seat beside her.

He and Quinn ordered and Kailey noticed that Lacey wasn't eating, instead saving her salad for when everyone had their food. She looked longingly at her burger, still hot from the grill, the scent of the beef so delectable her stomach growled in anticipation. With a little chuckle, Rylan leaned over. "Eat it. It won't be as good cold."

"That would be rude," she replied, trying to ignore

the delicious shiver that skittered down her spine at the quiet words uttered so closely to her ear.

"Not if we say it's not." He sat back, picked up his glass of water and took a sip. "Seriously. Eat. Don't let us interrupt your lunch."

She still felt awkward, but she picked up the burger—she needed both hands—and took a first delicious bite. Closed her eyes and simply enjoyed the explosion of flavor happening inside her mouth.

When she opened her eyes again, Rylan was watching her, a look of fascination on his face, and something more, too. Hunger. For her? Or for her lunch? She grabbed her paper napkin and scrubbed it across her lips, looking away from him.

"It's that good, is it?" he asked, the note of teasing slightly strained.

"Always," she replied, taking a drink of water. "I'm afraid I'm not one of those fancy dish people with the fresh this and that, and herb and goat stuff and whatever. A good beef burger with bacon and cheese and some jalapenos and I'm a happy girl."

"Not champagne tastes then."

She met his eyes evenly. "Not really. My tastes tend to be rather…ordinary."

She could see in his eyes when he got her meaning, and she felt a little bit small for implanting the barb in such an innocuous way.

She hid by taking another bite of her burger while Quinn and Lacey chatted about wedding stuff.

Moments later Quinn's and Rylan's meals arrived, and she watched with envy as Rylan picked up a crispy fry and dipped it in a little dish of ketchup. He'd ordered a club sandwich, and didn't waste any time helping himself. Likewise, Quinn picked up his pulled-pork bun and took a hearty bite. Out of sorts, Kailey wondered why men could order such meals and it was all manly and if a woman did the same thing, she got sideways looks. It was a stupid double standard. Especially considering what her daily calorie burn tended to be. Scowling, she took another huge bite of her burger.

"You should see Kailey's dress." Lacey's sweet voice interrupted the meal, and Kailey nearly dropped the half of the burger she had left in her hands while she chewed what had ended up being too big a bite. "She looks beautiful. The color is just perfect."

Kailey struggled to finish chewing and finally swallowed the mouthful, feeling as if she had no table manners at all. "Lace, I'm not sure the guys are interested in bridesmaid dresses, you know?"

Quinn put his arm along the back of Lacey's chair. "Aw, there's nothing wrong with being excited about the wedding," he replied, looking at Lacey with such devotion it was nearly sickening.

Kailey wasn't usually so cynical. Maybe it was because Rylan was beside her. And Rylan had been the one to leave her alone in a motel room after what was the most romantic night of the year—Valentine's Day. Perhaps if it had been underwhelming, it wouldn't be so difficult to put in the past. Trouble was it had been amazing. Rock-her-world amazing.

Kailey had often wondered if she should trust her own judgment with men, and the incident with Rylan pretty much had cemented the answer.

She was better off sticking to horses and bulls.

"What color is it?"

Rylan asked the question and she really, really wished he hadn't. "Blue," she answered. "It's blue."

Lacey laughed. "You can't just say blue. There are lots of blues out there." She turned her attention to Rylan. "It's kind of a turquoisey sky blue. It looks great with her hair and tan."

Kailey put her forehead on her hand. Her tan? Really? Because she was only tanned around her neck and from the biceps down…like every other rancher in these parts.

"Sounds nice," Rylan answered.

Lacey and Quinn started talking about something to do with Amber, leaving Rylan and Kailey silent on their side of the table again.

"Sorry," he offered quietly, eating another fry. "If I'd known you guys were here, I would have suggested somewhere else."

"It's just awkward, that's all. We're going to run into each other occasionally. We might as well get used to it."

She wiped her fingers on her napkin, then picked up her fork and speared a slice of cucumber from her salad.

"Kailey… I'm sorry."

"For?" She crunched the cucumber, determined to ignore the weird flutterings in her tummy.

"For being such a jerk that morning."

She looked up quickly, checked to see if Quinn or Lacey had heard. Luckily, they were still engrossed in their own conversation. "This isn't the place to discuss it."

"I get the feeling you don't want to discuss it at all, and that's fine. But I do owe you the apology."

Dammit. It was easier to hate him when he wasn't doing the right thing.

Scratch that. The right thing would have been sticking around, at least until coffee. They could have agreed to go their separate ways or…whatever.

"Noted." She stuck her fork savagely into the lettuce.

"Noted, but not accepted?" he asked. "I mean it, Kailey. I was totally in the wrong. Wouldn't it be better if we could get along? As you said, we're going to run into each other. And possibly more than occasionally. I'd like to put it behind us."

She would, too, but she wasn't sure she could until she understood why. Why had he felt the need to rush out before sunrise? Or was he really just a love 'em and leave 'em kind of guy? She'd certainly seen that type before…though she hadn't pegged Rylan as that kind. On top of Colt's rather quick moving on, it had left her feeling, well, *disposable*. Not worth the trouble of sticking around, even for breakfast.

Sitting in the diner with a lunchtime crowd audience didn't seem the right time or place to ask him why. But he was right. Their ranches were side by side. She was good friends with Carrie and Quinn, and Rylan's brother and sister.

Then there was the fact that he wasn't planning on staying at Crooked Valley forever. He was here to fulfill the terms of his grandfather's will, so Lacey and Duke could keep the ranch in the family. Surely she could suck up her personal feelings for a few months. Couldn't she? She'd gotten pretty good at hiding her feelings over the years. She'd had to when she'd taken a bigger role at the ranch and had become the boss of a largely male workforce.

"Consider it behind us," she replied, pushing away her salad. She really wished Lacey would get a move on. Not that she was in the mood for more wedding details, but it would get her away from Rylan.

Rylan, whose gaze she could feel glued to the side of her face. When she couldn't stand it anymore, she sighed.

"What?"

"Thank you," he said simply.

She looked at him and felt her animosity threaten to abandon her. He didn't look cocky or insincere in any way. In fact, his eyes were completely earnest and his lips open just a little, so she could get the full effect of their bowed shape. The bottom one was just a little fuller than the top, and she remembered them being surprisingly soft and...capable.

He was as attractive as ever, but she'd learned her lesson and learned it well. Rylan Duggan was trouble, and trouble was the last thing she needed.

"You're welcome."

Lacey was finally finishing up her salad and Kailey figured she might escape without having to speak to him again, but once more Rylan picked up a new thread of conversation.

"I could use some advice," he said, pushing away his plate. All that was left on it were the four toothpicks that had held his sandwich together, and the little dish that had contained his ketchup.

"Advice about what?" she asked. She hoped to God it wasn't anything personal. An apology was one thing. But they hadn't made that many amends yet.

"On the stock situation at Crooked Valley."

That made her sit back. "Oh?"

He kept his voice low. "Quinn and I have been talking. He's doing okay, but really, Quinn's a cattle man.

The little stock we've sent to competition has been handled by Randy. And I know Brandt stock. It's top-notch. I wanted to run some ideas past you."

Nothing he might have said would have surprised her more. On one hand, it was nice to know he respected her knowledge and opinion.

On the other hand, it made her wonder if the apology had really been meant to soften her up into giving him free advice.

Well, either way, it wouldn't hurt to state the obvious. "What Crooked Valley needs is some new breeding stock. A new stud, a couple of mares. But mostly a good stud that you can make some money off of breeding fees. That'll help pad your program so you can grow it."

"That's what I thought." He frowned.

"And Quinn probably knows that, too, but truth of the matter is Crooked Valley can't afford to outlay that much money right now. It's risky, even if the money was in the account. Am I right?"

He nodded. "Yes. According to Duke, our grandfather thought it would be fun to breed some rodeo stock. But it was more of a side thing than a focus, and it's never paid its way or lived up to its potential."

"I know Quinn and Duke have talked about selling it off." Kailey made herself smile. What she'd said about potential was absolutely correct. There were a few mares in the stables that she'd love to get her hands on, breed them with Big Boy. If the Duggans did decide to call this side of the operation quits, she hoped she could get first dibs on some of the unrealized potential in the barn before it went to auction.

"I don't think we're at that point yet."

Did he realize he'd said *we*? He was a temporary addition to the Crooked Valley operation, wasn't he? Or perhaps he used the concept as cavalierly as he used his women.

And maybe she hadn't quite accepted his apology. She bit down on her lip. It wasn't like her to be this nasty, even in her thoughts. She didn't like it. She didn't like anything that Rylan Duggan made her feel.

Quinn coughed, interrupting their conversation. "Sorry to break this up," he said. "But, Ry, I've got to get back."

"No problem," Kailey replied. "It wasn't anything important."

Rylan got up and reached back in his hip pocket for his wallet. She watched as the muscles in his shoulders and back shifted beneath his shirt, remembering what those very muscles looked like without the covering of cotton. He took out some bills and threw them on the table. "Lunch is on me, ladies. Enjoy the rest of your afternoon."

Kailey's face flamed. He was smiling his charming smile and smoothing everything over, wasn't he? And it would be so easy to fall for that again.

Instead, she reached inside her purse, took out a twenty and dropped it on the table before picking up one of his bills and handing it back to him.

"I can pay my own way," she said quietly, and without looking back, headed for the exit.

Kailey strode to Lacey's car, anxious to get going and away from Rylan but trying to look more purposeful than actually running away. That was what he did, not her.

Her breath hitched a little, surprising her, and she gulped, trying to shut down the flood of emotion. She wasn't acting like herself. The Kailey she knew was able to let things roll off her like water off a duck's back. She took things in stride, put them in perspective.

That she couldn't in this one particular instance bugged the hell out of her.

"Hey, wait up!" Lacey's quick steps sounded behind her and Kailey, almost to the car, slowed.

Lacey was slightly out of breath. "Did someone light your tail on fire or what? And what was that whole deal with the bill, anyway?"

"I'm sorry." Kailey looked at Lacey and wanted to confide, yet held back. This was Rylan's sister. Blood did run thicker than water, or so she'd heard. "I shouldn't let it get to me so much."

"You really don't like Ry, do you?" Lacey put her handbag over her shoulder and studied Kailey.

It was probably the opposite—that she'd liked him too much. "It's not that…" Her voice trailed off, unsure of how to explain.

Over Lacey's shoulder, she saw Quinn and Rylan hop into Quinn's truck and pull away from the curb.

She sighed. "How much do you know about Valentine's Day?" Kailey asked her friend.

Lacey grinned. "I know that as I was leaving with Quinn, you were leaving with Rylan."

That's right. There'd been another, more successful, romance budding back in February. One that had ended with a far better result. "You went home with Quinn, and I had a romantic night at the Shady Pines Motel. With your brother."

Lacey blushed a little. "I know, I know," she said, flapping her hand as Kailey lifted an eyebrow. "I asked."

"I won't go into the gory details." Kailey would spare

Lacey that trauma. No one wanted to think of their brother that way! "But here's the thing. I met Rylan at Christmas when he spent the holiday with your family. He's a good-looking guy, Lace. Charming, too. I'd be lying if I said I hadn't been interested. I'd been seeing someone off and on, but that had gone south in a big way. So when he was back less than two months later, and we were both at that Valentine's Day dance…"

"One thing led to another."

"It certainly did. It wasn't something I'm in the habit of doing, either. I was more interested than I probably let on." She gulped. It had sort of been…revenge sex. It just hadn't been with someone random. She'd chosen. She'd chosen Ry.

"He didn't return the sentiment?"

Kailey looked her friend straight in the eye. "Maybe we can finish this conversation in the car? Away from public consumption?"

At Lacey's nod, they got inside the little sedan. Kailey turned in the passenger seat and faced her friend. She had to be honest here, even if Rylan was Lacey's baby brother.

"Okay," she continued. "When I woke up, he'd taken his things and checked out. His truck was gone…it was like he had never been there."

Now Lacey frowned, a wrinkle forming between her perfectly groomed eyebrows. "He ran?"

"Like he couldn't get away fast enough. And he hadn't left enough cash with the room key, so I had to pay the difference."

It had been the singularly most humiliating moment of her life. If he'd hung around, she might have been able to avoid going to the office and seeing Lyle Tucker behind the desk. The small smirk on his face had only added insult to injury as far as Kailey was concerned. It was enough to turn her off romance for a good long while.

"Oh, ouch," Lacey said, frowning. "Hey, I love Ry. He's my brother. But that was pretty crappy behavior."

"Yeah, it was." Kailey sighed. "And I know I should get over myself and just… I don't know, put it behind me. Not let it get to me."

Lacey looked far too hopeful for Kailey's liking. "Could it be you still care for him?"

There was a very real chance of that, but Kailey would never admit to it. "I barely know him," she replied. "And I'm very aware of how that makes me sound considering what we shared." And what they hadn't shared. Her shoulders slumped. "I made a mistake, that's all. And I'm trying, really I am. We were chatting about the stock and stuff and doing fine until he insisted on paying the bill." She sent Lacey a sheepish half smile. "I'm afraid it set me off, since he stiffed the motel, you know?"

"Maybe if you just talk to him—"

Kailey cut her off before she could finish the sentence. "No way. What's done is done. It'll be fine. I just need to put on my big-girl panties."

Lacey laughed. "Well, if it makes you feel any better, Duke is Quinn's best man. You won't be paired up for the day or anything."

It didn't. Because that was just for the ceremony, and maybe a few pictures. The rest of the night Duke and Carrie would be pasted together. And Kailey, the maid of honor, would be the old maid of the group.

Ugh.

"Speaking of…" She changed the subject. "Let's get

these errands done. We're supposed to be focusing on your wedding, not my romantic drama."

The mention of wedding errands was enough to set the efficient Lacey into action, and they talked about lace versus satin ribbon for the flowers and cake flavors as they headed down Main Street.

It was just too bad Kailey couldn't get Rylan's gray-blue eyes out of her mind, or the sound of his voice. She knew Lacey and Duke needed him to keep the ranch in the family, but honestly she hoped he wasn't around much. Then life could get back to normal.

# Chapter 3

Rylan pulled into the Crooked Valley yard at quarter past seven. Too late for dinner—though if he asked, Lacey would probably have leftovers—and still with enough daylight left that he could chill for a bit before falling into bed.

It would be good to move around for a while, loosen up the tight muscles that came from driving the better part of the day. The past two weekends he'd competed, both times in the money, once at the top. But it hadn't been easy, either. He'd twisted his knee a little yesterday during an awkward dismount, and the rides had been tough, beating his body around enough that he felt it through his ribs and shoulders.

But he was home now. And while he wouldn't admit it to Lacey, it was nice to have a home base. Not that working in Wyoming had been bad. His boss had been good to him. Paid him well.

Ry's needs were simple and he'd been careful with his money. As a result he had a rather nice little nest egg built up for a rainy day.

A rainy day that might have arrived. He still had some thinking to do before making any firm decisions. Still, it didn't hurt for a man to have his ear to the ground.

But first he had to get unhitched. He could hear the dogs, Molly and Ranger, barking inside when he hopped out of the truck and moved to disconnect the camper. It took very little time for him to have it level and ready, just the way he liked it.

No one was home, so he went in the back door and emptied his dirty clothes from his duffel into the washing machine. After petting the dogs and putting some water in their bowl, he took a quick scrounge of the fridge and found leftover meatloaf. Ry sliced a huge hunk and put it between two slices of homemade bread for his dinner, then grabbed a beer from the fridge before heading back outside.

It was quiet. Almost too quiet. What he'd really like to do was go for a swim, let the cool water soothe his tired muscles. With more than an hour of daylight left, he shoved the last crust of bread into his mouth, washed it down with the beer, and struck out for the western edge of the property.

He'd discovered the bend in the creek quite by accident a few days after he'd arrived at the ranch. He'd been out riding, familiarizing himself with the place, and he'd started following the creek toward the property line. He knew at some point the land became Brandt property, but he didn't know when and where. It took him a good half hour to make his way to the spot he'd found before, where the rushing, burbling sound faded to a soft lapping. It was wide enough, deep enough to swim. With the warm sun bathing his face, he stepped through the tall grass to the edge and prepared to strip to his briefs.

And halted, with his hands on the button of his jeans. There was already a pile of clothes on the ground, a heap of denim and a pale green T-shirt next to running shoes. Women's running shoes.

He snapped his gaze to the water at just the right moment to see a woman surface in the stillness, parting the water with a soft splash and then swiping her hair back off her face.

Kailey.

His body reacted in a typical way and he shifted his weight to the other foot, unsure of what to do. What were the chances of him getting out of here without attracting her attention? Slim to none, he would imagine. Standing here staring was another ill-advised move... Damn. It didn't really matter what he did, it would be wrong. After leaving Kailey the way he had, he'd come to expect it from her.

He took a step backward and dry grass crackled beneath his feet. Maybe she wouldn't hear. He'd approached after all, and she hadn't been the wiser. But no such luck this time. Her head snapped around and she saw him standing there, next to her mound of clothing, and he could see her blush even though they were several yards apart.

"Sorry," he called. "I'll go."

He'd turned halfway around when her voice stopped him. "What are you doing here, Rylan?"

He hesitated and faced the pool—and her—again. "I was going to go for a swim. I saw this place a few weeks ago and thought it would be perfect."

"It is. Don't go. I'm done anyway. If you don't mind turning your back for a few minutes, I'll leave you in peace."

He swallowed, hard. Looked down at her clothes. He didn't see any underwear, and he let out a relieved breath. He wasn't sure his body, or his imagination for that matter, could take knowing she was skinny dipping.

"Don't get out on my account. Really, I'll just go back home."

He'd taken two more steps when she called after him. "Are things going to be this awkward between us forever?"

Forever was a long time. He called back, "I'm not staying forever, so I doubt it."

She didn't answer, but he heard a splash and dared to look over his shoulder.

She'd disappeared again. Lord, but the woman knew how to get under his skin. Far more than she realized.

The water parted and she popped up again. *Screw it*, he thought. He was tired and hot and achy, and he wanted a swim. She could stay or she could go, but she didn't own sole rights to the swimming hole.

He went back to where her clothes were and began unbuttoning his shirt. Kailey had switched from treading water to floating on her back. Only little bits of her were exposed. The tips of her breasts in a white bra and he could just see the edge of matching white underwear.

He took off his jeans and was suddenly very self-conscious. Tighty whities left nothing to the imagination. At all.

There was only one thing to do. He jogged to the water and splashed his way in up to his thighs before diving under.

He surfaced with a bellow. "Janey Mac, that's cold!"

He scrubbed the water away from his face and saw Kailey floating nearby, an amused smile on her face. One thing was for sure, the cold water had gone a long way in helping his uncomfortable situation. He shivered as goose bumps popped up on his skin.

"Janey Mac?" she asked, the surface swirling around her as she tread water.

He grinned. "Something I remember my grandfather saying when I was just a little boy. And my gram would always give him this strange look and call him Joseph."

She nodded. "I remember that. I miss them, you know."

He knew it would be strange for him to say "me, too." He hadn't seen his grandparents in years. He'd avoided this place like the plague, had written it off as simply a part of his past. Being here again, though, had brought back a lot of memories. "You knew them better than I did. Of course you miss them."

He gave a little shift of his body and used his arms to propel himself around, not really swimming, but not treading water either. "It's a bit better when you get used to it," he observed, and Kailey nodded.

"I'm kind of dreading getting out. The air is going to be cold."

"Do you come here a lot?" he asked.

"This is my first time swimming this year. It'll be warmer in the middle of summer. Unless we get a really dry season. Then the creek goes down and there's not much good swimming at all."

"I just got back from Washington. Felt like a dip would blow some of the dust off."

She leaned back, let her toes pop out of the water. "You haven't heard of a shower?"

"This sounded nicer."

They were quiet for a few minutes and Ry decided it was one of the strangest silences he'd ever encountered. On one hand, it was surprisingly comfortable. And on the other, he knew she had a zillion burning questions. Probably starting with asking why he'd run out on her that morning. He hoped to God she didn't actually ask.

"How'd you do?" she said finally, as she started to push herself off in a breast stroke.

"Huh?"

"At the rodeo. How'd you do?"

He shrugged, the air cold on his shoulders. "I did all right. In the money."

He'd won, but he wasn't going to brag.

"You're really good. I've seen the standings. And a couple of our guys are pretty excited you've shown up next door. You could probably come over and sign autographs."

Maybe she really was warming up to him after all. Maybe she'd gotten over whatever had been bugging her that day at the diner when she'd refused to let him buy her lunch. "That's pretty generous of you to say," he observed. "Considering."

"Considering what? That I think you're a jerk?"

And just like that she was beneath the water again. The girl could swim like an otter.

She emerged at the other side of the swimming hole. "Maybe it is time for me to go," she said, and struck out for the edge.

"Kailey, I get that you're mad, and you have every right to be. I'm sorry. I have no excuses for my behavior."

Her feet touched bottom and she started walking her way in. "It says something when a guy can't even hang around for breakfast." She was stomping now, making an unholy racket as she splashed her way toward shore. "Or when you stiff the motel on part of your bill."

"Wait, what?" He put his feet on the bottom and stared at her. What was she talking about?

"You underpaid. I had to drop off the room key, which would have been humiliating enough. But there was still twenty bucks owing."

He'd been sure he'd counted out enough twenties before leaving the money on the desk in an envelope he'd found in a drawer in the room.

But it had also been five in the morning. And dark.

She was standing on the edge now, in her white bra and panties. Which theoretically covered as much as any two-piece bathing suit, maybe more. But then there was the issue that it was white. And soaking wet.

And see-through.

"Kailey," he said, his voice rough. "For the love of God, I hope you have a towel."

She stared at him for a few seconds before what he'd said registered. But it was long enough for him to get a good long look at what was beneath the transparent fabric. And long enough for him to remember what it had been like with her back in February in the dim light of the motel room.

Amazing. Incredible. Scary as hell.

It was that last part that kept him grounded, tempered the need pounding through him to have her again. Cold water or not, he knew it was best for both of them if he stayed submerged right now.

She spun away and trotted off to where she'd left her clothes, then bent over to retrieve a towel she'd brought. He groaned a little, wondering if she'd bent over like that on purpose just to torture him.

When she turned around again, she had the towel

wrapped around her. Well, around her middle, anyway. It was short and only went to the tops of her thighs. He could still see the lovely, long expanse of leg beneath it.

Kailey Brandt was trouble. And he was starting to believe she didn't realize that about herself.

She was also angry. And beneath that he suspected she might be a little bit hurt. That's what bothered him most of all. He hadn't meant to hurt her. Hadn't known he actually could.

"I'm sorry," he repeated. "Kailey, me leaving that morning was all on me. It had nothing to do with you."

"Really?" Skepticism was ripe in her tone.

"Really," he insisted. What could he say that would be close to the truth but not *the* truth? He was scrambling and the moments strung out until Kailey let out a huff.

"You're a liar, Rylan Duggan. What was it, anyway? Was I too clingy? Too sweet? Did you think I'd expect a proposal in the morning? Was I unsatisfactory as a lover? I mean, I haven't had that complaint before, but sometimes people don't gel for whatever reason and—"

"No!" He cut her off, ran a hand over his wet hair. "Shut up, Kailey. Just shut up."

He started walking out of the water and as he got closer he could see her eyes swimming with tears. "Aw, Kailey…"

She held up her hand. "Just don't. I cry when I'm angry. And right now I'm really wound up."

He reached her and tried not to shiver as the cool evening air touched his wet skin. "You want to know the truth? I liked it. A lot. Too much. And I was afraid that if I didn't get up and leave that morning that I'd end up staying for breakfast. Or longer."

"And would that have been so bad?"

"At the time? Yes."

"Why?"

God, he hated these kinds of conversations. He'd learned long ago that there was no right answer to her kind of question, so he was as honest as he dared to be. "Because I didn't have anything to offer you. I still don't. I'm not the kind of guy who hangs around, Kailey."

"You're here now. At the ranch, I mean."

"But only temporarily. Remember?" He didn't stick around any one place for long. He liked it much better being free to go where he pleased, when he pleased. He called the shots and made his own choices. It had been a long time since anyone had made them for him. His choices, his consequences. It was easier that way.

He scooted past her and grabbed his shirt from the ground, gave it a shake and pulled it on. His shorts still dripped and there was no way he could put his jeans on over top. If she hadn't been here, he would have simply stripped to the skin and gone for a dip. Now his only option was to stand here and be cold or to take them off and pull on his jeans commando.

"Turn around," he ordered.

"What?"

"Turn around."

He could tell the moment she understood his meaning because her cheeks flushed bright pink. Despite it, she lifted her chin a little. "It's nothing I haven't seen before."

He could mention that he'd pretty much seen everything of hers, too, through that wet underwear, but he didn't. If she was determined to prove a point, he'd oblige. With a shrug he pushed down his shorts and stepped out of them, then reached for his jeans and tugged them on awkwardly. His skin was still wet and the fabric clung to his legs. He finally got them buttoned and carefully zipped.

When he looked up her face was bright red, but she hadn't looked away.

It was better now that he was dressed, and he reached down and grabbed her T-shirt, handing it over. "Here. Get warm."

She dropped her towel and he caught a glimpse of her abdomen, lean and pale compared to the worker's tan on her arms and face. Immediately the green shirt got dark, damp spots on her chest.

What he really wanted to do was spread out his shirt or that towel and lay her down on it. That part hadn't changed. He still found her beautiful, intriguing and sexy as hell. Probably because of her confidence. Or bullheadedness. Two sides of the same coin, he figured.

And then she stripped off her panties and pulled on her jeans and he had to look away. Whatever point she was trying to prove, she'd done it.

"Kailey, I don't want things to be strained. I can't apologize forever. I meant it when I said I was completely at fault. I don't know how else to make amends. What do you want me to do? I'll do it. The last thing I want is to disrupt anything here."

She wadded up her underwear and rolled them into the damp towel. "There's nothing you can do. I don't actually want to keep punishing you for it. I can't seem to help myself."

"I'm not trying to push your buttons."

"I know that. You've gone out of your way to be nice. I just…don't want you to be nice. I don't know what I want, Rylan. I have too much pride for my own good."

He chuckled then. "No wonder we seem to butt heads. All that pride getting in the way."

"What can I say? I have a bit of a chip on my shoulder. I've had to."

He didn't doubt it. He knew for a fact that Kailey was heavily involved in raising Brandt stock, and that took strength and a good amount of backbone. There were still some good old boys who didn't appreciate a woman running ranch operations and didn't like taking orders. It was a load of garbage, in his opinion.

But he guessed that what had happened on Valentine's Day probably also had gotten around town. He sat down on the grass and patted the spot beside him. "Sit for a minute, instead of looking like you're ready to throttle me."

She hesitated but then sat, pulling her knees close to her chest and wrapping her arms around them. The pose made her look almost childlike, especially with her tawny hair falling over her shoulders in wet ribbons.

"Did what happened with us make things difficult for you?" he asked quietly.

She frowned. "What do you mean?"

"I mean, stiffing the guy for the room was unintentional, but Gibson is small. If what happened got around…" He let the thought hang for a few seconds before continuing. "I know you're a woman operating in a male-dominated world. The last thing you need is rumors about your personal life undermining that."

"I'm not sure if I'm touched by your concern or infuriated that it's even an issue. I'm sure your reputation wouldn't suffer for such a thing. You'd be given *atta boys*. Am I right?"

"It's a stupid double standard, and I hope I didn't play a part in it."

She met his gaze. "Rylan, I'm no angel. I'm in my late twenties and definitely not some delicate, virginal flower. But I certainly don't make a habit of catting around, and I keep my personal life discreet." She sighed. "Or at least I try to."

Rylan hadn't considered this side of things before, and a pang of regret made his heart heavy. When was the last time he'd truly liked someone enough to care what happened the morning after? He honestly couldn't remember. He moved around. Got used to the buckle bunnies who followed the circuit and were looking to put another notch on *their* belts. Up until this year, he'd obliged now and again.

Not since February though. Not since he'd awakened in the dark to find Kailey sleeping beside him. Something had happened. Something that had made him feel wonderful and extremely uncomfortable at the same time.

The urge to stay.

He'd half figured that by leaving the way he did, she'd get a good old-fashioned hate on for him and that would be that. He'd come back to Crooked Valley expecting a cold shoulder. Over and done with, move on.

He could see now his thinking had been flawed. Because Kailey was more hurt and embarrassed than angry, and knowing it brought out every single protective and possessive instinct he had. He wanted to fix it, explain. He wanted... Crap. He wanted to be able to forget about her the way he'd expected her to forget about him. And he couldn't.

That wouldn't do anyone any good, and neither would sitting in the middle of a field in semi-darkness.

"Come on. I'll walk you home," he suggested. "It's getting dark."

"Newsflash, Duggan. You're on Brandt land. I'm already home. Maybe I should walk you back, huh?"

She was so quick, a little feisty, and he liked that about her. A lot. "If you want to kill my reputation with a single blow, sure. Big bad rodeo star needs an escort home in the dark."

Not that he couldn't find a few things to do in the dark with her.

He had to stop thinking that way.

"I guess we'll just part ways here then," she replied and pushed to her feet.

"I guess." He got up and brushed the dirt from the seat of his jeans. "Um, I'll see you around. I guess."

"Yup."

He'd taken maybe half a dozen steps back toward the horse trail that ran along the creek when she called out to him. "Hey, Rylan."

He turned and faced her, and the image of her standing in the twilight among the waving grass did something queer to his pulse.

"It was good to say my piece. Clear the air, so to speak."

"Good. It's probably better if we can be civil."

She nodded. "Well, see ya."

Kailey turned and started walking in the opposite direction, her hips swinging a little with each step, her towel and underwear balled up in her hand. Rylan looked down at the cotton in his hands and let out a huge breath before tucking his shorts half into his back pocket, the end trailing out like a handkerchief.

Civil. Clearing the air.

He was glad she was happy about it, because to his mind things just had gotten a whole lot more complicated.

## Chapter 4

Kailey looked in the mirror and frowned. The dress fit perfectly. The boots were cute. Her hair was pulled back a little from the sides, but the curls were left in corkscrews over her bare shoulders. Thanks to Lacey's self-tanning cream, they'd managed to mostly blend her tan lines with her darker skin, though she could still tell where they were, particularly around her neck. Oh well. Hazards of being a farm girl and she wouldn't change that for anything.

Her makeup was perfect. The happy little bouquet of yellow and white flowers was on the bed behind her. Lacey was currently having her makeup done in the next room, and then Kailey would help her get dressed and calm the bride's frayed nerves.

There was a lot to do. A crazy day during a manic time of year for ranchers. There was no reason at all for her to be thinking about Rylan.

But she was.

All the damn time.

Now she was wondering what he'd think of her in this dress and hating herself for it. Was it wrong that she hoped it knocked out his eyeballs? It would serve him right…

And then there was that niggling knowledge that she wasn't entirely blameless in what had happened that night.

She turned away from the mirror and grabbed her bouquet. Might as well go to Lacey's room and focus on getting the bride ready for her big day rather than fret about what couldn't be changed.

She opened the door to the bedroom and nearly chucked her flowers as Rylan stood there, his fist poised to knock.

"What are you doing here?" she blurted out, and then let out the breath cramping her lungs. "Sorry. You just startled me."

"Quinn and Duke sent me over. I'm supposed to pick up Mom and David and take them to the church, then come back for you and Lacey."

"I thought Duke was going to do that."

His expression changed, as if he was trying to look nonchalant but was hiding something. "They ran into a slight snag. And that's all I'm going to say because I'm not equipped to deal with wedding-day drama. I'm to tell you that we're just saying that Duke is driving Quinn and Amber, and I'm driving you two like one big happy family."

He smiled at her. When he smiled at her that way she knew she'd agree to just about anything. She was such a weak woman where Rylan was concerned. Not that she'd tell him that. Like ever.

"Mum's the word. I don't know if Lacey is a nervous bride or not, but I'm not going to be the one to tempt fate." Worried, she looked fully into his face, trying to read it. "You're sure it's nothing major?"

"Major is relative on wedding days. Quinn's handling it. Don't you worry. By the time we get to the church, it'll be right as rain."

"I'm going to trust you."

"There's a first."

But the words were said in a teasing manner, not with an edge of sarcasm or hostility. She couldn't help it, she grinned back at him and in that shared moment she was reminded all over again why she'd found him attractive in the first place.

"I'm about to check on Lacey. You can go chill for a bit. We'll be ready soon."

He checked his watch. "Schedule says I need to have Mom to the church in twenty-five minutes. Can you tell her to meet me downstairs in fifteen?"

"Of course."

He turned to go back down the stairs and she got a good look at him. Black trousers and dress boots, a crisp white shirt and a tie. No jacket, but then he wasn't in the wedding party either, and it was June. He'd had his hair cut, the hint of dark auburn curls that were usually at his temples and neck clipped off in precise lines.

He was gorgeous—even if she did secretly prefer the bits of curl that added a roguish look to his rugged face.

"Ry?"

He turned around. "Yeah? Did you need something else?"

She shook her head. "N-no," she stammered. "I just wanted to say that, uh, you look nice today."

"So do you, K. So do you."

He threw her a wink and went down the stairs.

Kailey took a calming breath and opened the door to the master bedroom.

Lacey was sitting on a little stool in a lovely satin robe waiting to put on her gown. Her mom, Helen, was behind her, hooking a set of creamy pearls around Lacey's neck. Lacey had the Duggan coppery hair, and right now it was pulled back in a lovely romantic top knot with a simple circlet of white flowers around it.

"Is there a blushing bride in here somewhere?" Kailey asked, stepping inside.

God, Lacey looked happy. Her cheeks were flushed but not unnaturally. She was simply radiant, and calm, and so, so sweet looking. Helen couldn't stop smiling either. "We're nearly ready. Just the dress and boots to go."

"Kailey, you look beautiful. Thank you so much for doing this today."

"Of course I'd be here. Don't be silly." She put down her flowers and moved to the closet to get the dress. Together she and Helen unzipped the garment bag and withdrew the soft material. Kailey draped it over her arm. "Okay, are you ready? I'll unzip and you step in."

It took no time at all for them to get Lacey zipped and hooked into the simple but stunning dress.

"Honey, you're beautiful."

"I know I said no to the whole veil thing, but you don't think white is, well, you know…"

Kailey gave a little snort. "That whole wearing white thing has been out the window for years. So what if this isn't your first trip down the aisle? We all know it's your last."

"Amen," Helen said, taking Lacey's hands in hers. "You've got a wonderful man in Quinn and a daughter to love now, too. I couldn't be prouder of you, sweetheart."

"Even though I'm here at the ranch?" Lacey looked troubled. "I know how you feel about the place, Mom."

"Ranch life wasn't for me, at least not without your father. But the nice thing about being an adult is being able to make your own choices. This is a good one. And I can tell because it's written all over your face."

Kailey's nose stung a little, the emotion of the day getting to her a bit as Lacey and Helen hugged. She wasn't sure if it was Carrie marrying Duke or Quinn finding Lacey or what, but Kailey had been chafing against her own life a little bit lately. Wanting more. Particularly since Colt had asked her that important question and then withdrawn it again once he'd understood how things would have to be.

She loved running the ranch with her dad. But she wanted her own life, too. Maybe… She bit down on her lip. Maybe even her own family. Colt had changed his mind because he'd wanted her to leave Gibson behind, and she couldn't bring herself to say goodbye to the ranch and the business her dad, and now she, had built. He'd wanted her to choose him. And for Kailey it just wasn't that simple.

But it had worked out for Quinn and Lacey, and Kailey was thrilled for them. "You just need your bouquet." Kailey went to the box containing the flowers and withdrew them from the tissue. "These are so pretty, Lacey.

And, Helen, your corsage is in here, too. Maybe Lacey could pin it on you."

While Lacey did the honors, Kailey snapped a few pictures with her phone that she'd send Lacey later. Then she handed Helen the boutonniere for David and let her know her ride was waiting to take them to the church.

It seemed in no time at all and Rylan was back to take them to the ceremony.

"Wait, I thought Duke was picking us up?" Lacey frowned at the sight of Rylan unfolding his legs as he got out of the car.

Kailey could tell that Lacey was getting nervous. There was no way she'd mention an emergency of any sort. Keeping Lacey calm and radiant was job number one, so she fudged a little. "I think it's nice. He doesn't have a part in the wedding, and I bet Quinn did it so Rylan would be involved, you know?"

"Do you think?" Lacey looked so pleased that Kailey knew she'd taken the right tack.

Kailey couldn't take her eyes off him. "Sure I do. Now your whole family has a role to play in your big day."

Rylan had borrowed Helen and David's sedan for the occasion, so that Lacey didn't have to get in and out of a half-ton truck in her gown. Sunglasses shaded his eyes as he held the car door, first for Lacey, and then the other side for Kailey, once she had finished tucking the mini-train in around Lacey's ankles.

"Forget what I said about you looking nice," he said in a low voice, his hands resting on the window. "You look beautiful, Kailey. Really, really beautiful."

Surprise and pleasure had her throat tightening. "Thank you, Rylan," she murmured.

"You're welcome," he answered. Then he shut the door behind her and went around to the driver's side as if he'd done nothing more important than comment on the weather. The compliment had gone straight to her heart, though, because she knew it had been sincere.

It was a perfect day for a wedding. The early summer sun was warm but not too hot, and a light breeze ruffled the hems of their dresses as they got out of the car at the church. Duke was there, holding Amber's hand. Kailey grinned when she saw Amber's face. She was as proud as anything in her white flower-girl dress with a sash that matched the color of Kailey's. A little basket was in her hands, and once more, the brown-and-blue boots on her feet. She was adorable. Even more so when she ran forward, pulling her hand out of Duke's grasp.

"Lacey! You look like a princess!"

Ignoring her hem, Lacey squatted down to Amber's height. "So do you, pumpkin. You ready to do this?"

"Heck yeah."

Kailey burst out laughing at the slightly inappropriate answer from a five-year-old. Confused, Amber looked up, but then Duke bade them goodbye as he went to meet Quinn at the front of the church, and Rylan sent her one parting look before giving his arm to Carrie—they'd sit together with Helen and David throughout the service.

They were waiting in the vestibule, nearly ready for the walk up the aisle when Lacey spoke. "Amber, do I have bride brain? I thought we got you a yellow and white bouquet like Kailey's. Not a basket."

Amber turned troubled eyes on her nearly new step-mother. "Oh. Um. Well."

"Um well?"

"Molly and Ranger ate them."

The dogs. Quinn had taken both puppies to his house so that they'd be away from the bridal trappings. But apparently flower-girl flowers weren't immune to their antics.

"They what?" Lacey's expression was horrified.

Amber's lip quivered. "I'm sorry. I just put them down for a minute. Daddy put the dogs on the porch and Uncle Duke went to the store. That's why Uncle Rylan came to get you. Duke was getting me new flowers."

Lacey raised an eyebrow in Kailey's direction and Kailey tried to adopt an innocent look. "I see," she said, and Kailey shrugged.

"I think they're pretty," Amber continued. "Don't you like them, Lacey?" Her big eyes were worried.

Kailey had to admit that they were lovely. For a rush job, the sunflowers, daisies and baby's breath were a pretty close match to the other bouquets.

Lacey smiled down at Amber. "Don't worry. I think they're very pretty. Maybe prettier than the ones we ordered. Now, are you ready for your walk up the aisle?"

Amber nodded. "Lacey, I'm glad you're going to be my new mommy." She wrapped her arms around Lacey's hips for a quick hug, and Kailey saw Lacey's eyes mist over.

Moments later Kailey watched from the front of the church as Lacey walked down the aisle to where Quinn was waiting. For the first ten steps she had her gaze locked on Lacey, looking so happy and stunning in her dress. But then she looked at Quinn and her heart turned over. He was watching his bride walk toward him with pure, naked adoration written all over his face. She'd seen him happy with his first wife, Marie, had seen him devastated when Marie died. No one she knew deserved a second chance at happiness more than Quinn.

But more than that, she wondered if anyone would ever look at her that way. As if she was the entire world. As if she was the sun that brought all the light and warmth to his life. Because that was exactly how Quinn was looking at Lacey. And for the first time, Kailey wanted that for herself.

She wanted to matter. She wanted to be more than Kailey Brandt, rancher. Kailey Brandt, friend.

She wanted to be Kailey Brandt, *everything*.

She turned and focused on the minister and what he was saying as the ceremony got under way. And she definitely didn't sneak looks at Rylan, sitting with a very pregnant Carrie in the second pew. Because Rylan Duggan was the last man on earth who would ever want her to be that person.

The reception was held at a golf course just north of town. Tents were set up outside the club house, and guests mingled around sipping punch and nibbling on snacks as the wedding party arrived after pictures. Kailey hadn't minded the photos much. The photographer had been efficient and funny, and in no time at all they'd been on their way. Now they were at the country club where there'd be a sit-down dinner and a dance. It still all added up to a long day.

She was already tired. Haying would start in a few days if the weather held. What she really wanted to do now was get out of this dress, put on some pajamas and get a good night's sleep.

The bride and groom began mingling with the guests in the minutes before the meal was served, and Kailey found herself at the punch bowl, filling a cup and hoping the cool drink and sugar hit might perk her up. She'd taken a cautious sip when Rylan came up behind her.

"Is it any good?"

She looked up at him. "Is it very bad of me to say it would be improved by a shot of vodka?"

He chuckled, his gaze warm. "You look like you've put in a full day. Everything okay?"

She nodded. "I swear, I could spend a whole day working on the ranch and not find it as exhausting as this."

"Who knew getting pretty could be so tiring, huh?"

She made a face at him. "Smart aleck."

Rylan poured himself some punch. "It's a crazy time to have a wedding, but I don't think they wanted to wait. It all came together pretty fast."

"Don't I know it." She smiled a little. "And I'm happy for them. You didn't know Quinn before, but he's had a rough time. They're good for each other."

"How come you've never gotten hitched?" They'd moved away from the punch bowl and were now ambling around the fresh-cut grass. The scent of blossoms from the tidy flower beds perfumed the air.

"Me?" She tossed him what she hoped was a saucy grin. "Why, sir, no one would have me." Despite the light tone, it was the absolute truth.

"I'm surprised."

And that surprised her. "You are?"

"Sure," he replied. "You're pretty, smart, strong and successful…"

"Gee, Rylan. I never knew you thought so much of me." She couldn't resist teasing him a little. Things *had* been a little easier since their talk at the swimming hole. Not that she didn't still notice him. A blind woman would notice those bedroom eyes and that muscled body. But their chat had cleared the air considerably. They both knew what and what not to expect.

"I take it back. I know why you haven't been asked."

"Why?" Intrigued, she stopped and looked up at him.

"Because you're pretty, smart, strong and successful. I bet most of the guys around here are intimidated as hell. You make them look bad, sugar."

Her temper flared so quickly she wondered if puffs of steam were coming out of her ears. "So, what, I should dumb myself down to snag a husband?" Or perhaps abandon the business she'd put her heart and soul into so her husband's pride wouldn't take a dent?

Hmm. Maybe it wasn't really Rylan she was mad at. Maybe she was still furious with Colt for giving her such a ridiculous ultimatum.

Rylan looked appropriately horrified, and his lips twitched as he tried not to laugh. "Absolutely not. You keep those standards right up high where they belong." He lifted his hand and twined a finger inside one of her long ringlets. "You need someone who's able to go toe-to-toe with you, Curly. Or else you'll be bored to death."

Funny how she seemed to go toe-to-toe, as he put it, with him quite regularly. But he was not the man for her. Rylan Duggan went where the wind blew him and certainly wasn't looking to be tied down.

She stepped back, aware that she could get sucked

into his charm without a whole lot of effort on his part. "There's something to be said for boredom," she replied tartly. "At least you know where you stand."

Damn man, he just grinned at her, his blue eyes sparkling. "Touché."

"Maybe we should talk about something else."

"Good idea. I think Crooked Valley needs a stud."

She coughed, felt the sting of the punch in her nose. She bent over a little and her eyes watered as she had the unholy urge to laugh. Why was it he seemed to be able to do that to her without even trying? A napkin appeared in front of her face and she took it, dabbed her lips and eyes, the whole time aware that Rylan was standing there with a smirk on his too-handsome face.

"You did that on purpose," she accused.

"Maybe. But I am serious, you know. Can you breathe now? Everything okay?"

"Besides you driving me nuts? Perfectly fine." She offered an angelic smile. With teeth.

"Okay, so back to business. I've been thinking about what you said a few weeks back at the diner."

"About your program."

He nodded, and she noticed he looked semi-serious now. Rylan pretty much always looked as if he were privy to some sort of inside joke, but she was starting to realize it was just who he was. Part of his innate charisma.

"We've got some solid stock, but nothing spectacular, nothing that's creating any buzz or fuss. Not like you. You've built up your breeding program so that you've got some great bloodlines running through yours. It's been smart."

"You've checked?"

"Of course I have." As if oblivious to her surprise, he continued on. "Crooked Valley doesn't have that. According to Quinn, about five years ago Joe took it in his head to *dabble* with the idea."

"Yeah. He came to my dad for advice."

"And he made a decent start, I'll give him that. But it's not growing and it needs to. Right now it's costing Crooked Valley far more than it's making."

She agreed with him. "But where are you going to get this stud savior?" she asked. "I can't see Duke signing off on that kind of purchase. To get what you're looking for…we're talking a minimum of ten grand. Probably more like fifteen or twenty."

"I'm working on that. I guess my question to you is would Brandt consider using our stud in your program? If we had one?"

She stopped and looked up at him. He was dead serious now. Was he really taking that big of an interest in the ranch? How much did he have at stake?

It was easier to talk to him with her work hat on. "Rylan, you know as well as I do that it would depend on the horse, and what you'd charge."

"But if you did like what you saw, you'd consider it?"

"I consider everything."

"That's all I needed to know."

The guests were called to dinner then, and Kailey and Rylan parted ways. He sat with his parents and Quinn's mother while Duke, Carrie and Kailey sat with Quinn, Lacey and Amber. Throughout the meal Kailey thought about what Rylan had said about Crooked Valley. He didn't talk like a man who wasn't invested. Instead, it sounded very much like planning for the future.

Then again, he was one-third owner, at least technically. She supposed making the bucking stock operation profitable would pad his bottom line, too. Help fund his expenses. She'd seen his results. The NFR was a definite possibility this year if he kept on the way he'd begun. Shoot, he'd said that he'd been in the money on the last rodeo. He didn't say that he'd won top spot. She'd only seen that when she'd checked the standings.

She looked over at him, saw him laugh at something Quinn's mother said. Something in her heart softened. This wouldn't do, not at all. She couldn't be starting to like him. Not after he'd been such a jerk.

Which he'd apologized for. Sincerely.

Maybe she should be better at holding grudges.

After dinner the tables were cleared to make room for the dancing to come later. Lacey and Quinn cut the cake and fed each other while people snapped pictures. The band tuned up and they had the first dance, then David danced with Lacey while Quinn danced with his mother, and then Lacey danced with Duke while Quinn danced with Helen. Once the family dances were out of the way, Kailey was called upon to dance with Duke. Finally the slow songs ended and the band sped up for some boot stomping music. Kailey wondered how much longer she had to stay.

Then she felt guilty for wanting to leave. How often did she get to dress up and party? A year ago, heck, even six months ago, she would have really cut loose at something like this. Danced until last call.

At some point she'd changed. Decided life should hold more meaning than the daily grind. She'd…grown up. Problem was, she hadn't yet found that extra meaning and it seemed as if there was a big hole where it was supposed to be.

It was around the time that Lacey was going to throw the bouquet that Kailey realized she hadn't seen Rylan in a while. The girlfriend of one of the ranch hands caught the flowers, and the evening began to fade into purply twilight. Still no Rylan. Had he gone home?

She finally caught up with Lacey at the bar, where her friend was ordering a plain tonic water with lime. "Hey, Lace, have you seen Rylan?"

Lacey took a sip of her drink and fanned her face, which was pink with the exertion of dancing. "He left."

"Left?" Now why on earth should she be feeling disappointed? Still, he just up and took off from his sister's wedding?

"Quinn's mom wasn't feeling so well, and Amber was getting tired. Duke was going to take them back to Great Falls, but Carrie…" Lacey grinned. "I think they're just Braxton Hicks contractions, but she's a bit worried with a bit over a month left to go, and Duke was getting on her case about overdoing the dancing. Rylan offered to drive instead."

"Oh. That was nice of him."

"It was. You know, Kailey, I'm not excusing his behavior before. But he really is a decent guy. He didn't have to come back here at all. He did it for Duke and he did it for me. He won't admit it, but in his way he's trying to help. I really do believe that."

"Me, too," she admitted.

"You do?" Lacey sipped on her straw, her eyebrows lifting at Kailey's unexpected agreement.

"We've talked about bucking stock a few times. He might not stick around, but I get the sense he does actually care what happens to the place. I think he'll do what he needs to so you and Duke can keep it."

Kailey got a glass of ice water from a pitcher to the side of the bar and Lacey followed her there. "You know he was like that when we were kids, too."

"Like what?" She tried to picture Rylan as a child. It wasn't that hard. Hair a little lighter—perhaps a true redhead—and with a devilish twinkle in his eye.

"Devil-may-care, like nothing mattered. Things rolled off him like water off a duck's back. But when the chips were down, he'd come through. Like the year I lost my purse when we were Christmas shopping. I'd saved my allowance for weeks to be able to buy presents for Mom and him and Duke. I was probably ten years old. Duke gave me a lecture on responsibility. Rylan reached into his wallet and gave me half his money, which was more than I'd had to begin with."

"How sweet."

"He really was." Lacey smiled with fondness. "We kind of thought he'd outgrow his fascination with rodeo as he got older. Instead, he graduated high school and took off the next day. Found a job, then another, started competing and ended up at a big place in Wyoming."

"And now here."

Lacey nodded. "I don't pretend to understand him. I understood Duke's need to follow in our dad's footsteps with the military. And me…" Her face softened a little. "I just wanted a home and family with a mom and a dad and a perfect little life."

"And you got it."

"I do now." Her smile was beautiful. "But I've never quite understood what drives Rylan. He just goes from place to place like he's searching for something."

"Or running away."

"Or that. Either way, I'm enjoying spending more time with him. I'll take it for as long as it lasts."

Quinn came over to claim his bride for a dance. "Are you ready to leave soon?" he asked. Kailey felt that little bit of longing in the pit of her stomach again. Clearly Quinn couldn't wait to begin married life with his bride.

She hated that she was jealous.

Lacey gave Kailey a quick hug. "Looks like we're heading out in a bit. I just want to say thank you, for everything. It's been a perfect day."

"Yes, it has," Kailey agreed.

She stayed until they drove away in Lacey's car, headed to a resort in the mountains for a few days of privacy and an abbreviated honeymoon. It wasn't until they were gone that Kailey realized she'd been left without a ride back to the ranch, where her truck was parked. Duke had taken Carrie home, being the concerned dad-to-be. Once more she chafed against circumstances; she was going to have to ask her parents to give her a lift.

Maybe it was finally time for her to find a place of her own. On her own.

## Chapter 5

The porch light was off and the house was dark when Kailey retrieved the spare key from under a flower pot and let herself in. Her jeans and T-shirt were upstairs, along with her makeup bag and curling iron. She'd grab them and head home and to bed. Tomorrow was Sunday, but there were still chores to be done.

She was halfway down the stairs when she heard the front door open.

"Duke? That you?"

Footsteps paused. "Kailey?"

It was Rylan. Damn.

"I just came back to get my stuff. And my truck." She went the rest of the way down the stairs. She could do this. It didn't matter that they were alone. It changed nothing.

And then she turned the corner and saw him standing in the kitchen, still in his wedding clothes but with his tie untied and hanging around his neck, the top buttons of his shirt undone.

Trouble. Times ten and then some.

"I just got back. Came in for a beer before heading to bed. You want one?"

"I've got to drive home."

He didn't argue with her or make a smart comment like "you don't have to." She appreciated that. It was the sort of thing he might have said a few months ago. In fact, she was pretty sure it was close to verbatim what he'd said at the Valentine's Day dance.

"Do you want something else? Ginger ale? I think I saw some of that in the fridge."

Actually, it sounded good. "Sure. I guess."

He reached in and got a can, handed it to her without the benefit of a glass. She popped the top and watched as he opened his beer. "Want to sit on the porch for a few minutes?" she suggested. It would be better than staring at each other here in the kitchen. "I could stand a few minutes of peace and quiet."

They made their way outside to the veranda, settled into the deep wooden chairs that lived there during the summer months. Kailey let out a sigh. "It's nice to sit. In the stillness, I mean." She could still hear peepers chirping from the ditches, and a cool breeze fluttered the leaves on the trees. Up on the porch, though, they were sheltered from the wind.

"I thought you liked music and commotion."

"I do. I don't know why, but I was just tired today." Dissatisfied, really, she realized. And had been for a while now.

Silence stretched out.

"It was nice of you to take Mrs. Solomon home."

He took a long pull of his beer. "It was no biggie. It

was a long day for her. Plus Amber was getting tired. She fell asleep on the drive."

"She sure looked cute in her flower-girl dress."

"Yes," he said, his voice deep and smooth. "She sure did."

Kailey had just taken a long, cool drink of ginger ale when Rylan added, "And you looked pretty, too, Kailey. That color suits you."

She was still wearing her dress. She'd figured she'd jump in the truck, head home, maybe take a bath before bed. "Lacey chose it," she said, and somehow her voice sounded strangled in the peaceful night.

This was probably a mistake. Right now all she was picturing was the sight of him changing back into his jeans after swimming, his body corded and muscled and the scar on his left hip from a long-ago injury. She should leave. Take her bag and get in her truck and go as quickly as possible. He was no good for her.

Yet she couldn't seem to make herself get out of her chair.

He was right beside her, close enough that she could smell his aftershave, sense the warmth of his body. Her right leg was crossed over her left knee, and she watched, transfixed, as Rylan reached over and touched the skin just below her hem with a single finger. Her eyes fluttered closed as all her senses went on high alert. Warning bells crashed through her brain, but she didn't hear them. She was so focused on the delicious feel of that single finger lightly grazing the skin right above her knee. No higher or lower. Just back and forth, a lazy caress, sending her hormones into overdrive.

"Ry," she whispered, a warning wrapped in a sigh.

"I know," he answered softly. "I know I shouldn't. But you're so damned pretty."

She swallowed against the lump in her throat.

"I can't seem to stay away from you," he lamented, all the while the rough pad of his finger slid back and forth on her skin. "I know I should. I know I'm not the kind of man you want. Hell, I don't want to be. And yet here I am, wondering if I dare kiss you again."

How was it that one innocent touch could send her body into a nuclear meltdown?

"Why'd you have to come back, anyway?" She closed her eyes, losing herself to the sensation of being seduced. By his voice, by his touch, by simply being here in the dark with him.

"I ask myself that a million times a day," he answered, and now it was his hand on her knee, sliding beneath the light fabric of her dress, running over her thigh. "I don't know, Kailey. I just don't know."

"Me either," she said, and opened her eyes. Her whole body was at attention. "Ry, you either have to stop or kiss me because I'm dying over here."

It was all she had to say. Slowly, so slowly it was sweet torture, Ry slipped his hand away from her leg and pushed himself up out of the deck chair. Then he leaned over her, his hands braced against the arms of her chair, and touched her lips with his.

This was what she remembered. What she'd hungered for. The memory had been accurate but not nearly as good as the reality, and she put her hands on his shoulders, kissed him back. When he lowered himself farther, kneeling in front of her chair, something flashed through her mind, a remembrance of how good, how intense, how consuming it had been making love to him. They wouldn't go that far tonight. Couldn't. But she'd waited three and a half long months to touch him again.

He let go of the chair and put his hands on her hips,

pulling her forward a little so that her legs parted and he knelt between them. She leaned forward and kissed him back, his head just slightly below hers. A gasp sounded in the stillness—hers—when his lips slid away and trailed down her neck to the hollow of her throat.

Yet something didn't feel right. It wasn't even the way he'd left her before that was sticking in the back of her mind somewhere. It was the knowledge that he'd leave her again. And recognizing that, at least for her, there was more at work than sexual attraction.

He was fun, he was charming. He cared for his brother and sister and was good with kids. If they played with the fire that was desire, she would be the one who got burned the worst.

"Stop," she breathed, torn between knowing they had to cease this craziness and never wanting it to end. "We can't do this, Ry. We can't."

"We already are," he murmured, his tongue sliding behind her ear and sending shivers down her spine.

"No." She put her hands on his arms and gripped them firmly, pushing him away. "I don't want this."

He stopped, but he met her gaze boldly. "You're a liar. You do want it. You want it as much as I do, Kailey."

Damn him for making things so difficult. "Yes. I do. Physically. But it's more than that for me, and it'll never be more than that for you. Do you understand?"

He frowned. "You make it sound like I don't care about you at all."

Kailey sighed, wished he'd move so she didn't feel pinned in her chair. But at least he'd stopped, moved back so that he wasn't right in her space anymore.

How could she explain that everything had changed the morning she'd woken alone, without making him think that she was in love with him? She wasn't. But it had been the kick in the pants she needed. A cold-water slap of reality.

"Ry, neither of us can deny that there's a certain... attraction between us. But something changed in February, the morning I woke up and you were gone."

She met his gaze, hoped she wasn't blushing. Confession and unloading her feelings wasn't really her style. "It was a wake-up call to me. I know what I want, and it's not what you want, and I'd only be setting myself up to get hurt."

He finally sat back on his heels. "Jeez, Kailey."

"Ry, you're not a bad guy. You're funny and charming and fairly kind. You'd have the power to hurt me, and I can't walk into that. This really isn't about me being angry about what happened then. It's more...understanding what would surely happen now, and being smart enough to avoid it."

Rylan sat down on his rump and pushed back the few extra inches until his back rested against the veranda railing. "You know, in my experience most women see that as a challenge. That I'm a project that needs to be fixed."

Kailey understood that, too. Heck, she'd been there. Attracted to the unattainable guy, so sure that she was the one who could change his mind and tame his bad-boy ways. Colt Black had been a prime example. She'd taken her time, certain he'd come around and reconsider, and then he'd found someone else. On Valentine's Day she'd started dancing with Rylan just to make Colt jealous. Make him see what he'd given up...

"I'm not interested in fixing anyone." She let out a sigh and then a little laugh. "Shoot, do you think this means I'm getting old?"

He chuckled a little, too. "Not old. Wise." He held her gaze, his eyes nearly black in the moonlit evening. "Look, I'm not going to deny that I'm disappointed. You do something to me, Kailey. But I also appreciate you shooting straight with me."

"I don't want to be angry at you," she replied. "I just want…"

That was just it. Part of her still wanted to throw caution to the wind and fall into his arms. The other part wanted them to find a way to coexist for the next few months until he left Crooked Valley behind.

"I just want us to be friends. Do you think that's even possible?"

"I don't see why not."

"Okay. Good." Yet agreeing to keep things 100 percent platonic caused an awkward silence to fall over the evening. "I'd better go. Mom and Dad will be wondering where I am."

He grinned and she rolled her eyes. "I know. Don't say it. I'm too old to live with my parents."

"No judgment," he replied, the smile still on his face.

"Cool." She got up and went inside to get her bag. When she came back out, Rylan was still sitting with his back against the veranda railing, his arms resting on his knees. He looked a little sexy and a little bit sad at the same time. Definitely lonely.

She looped her keys over her index finger and went down the steps, her boots sounding extra loud in the stillness of the night. She paused at the bottom and looked back up at him.

"Rylan? For some reason, you seem to sell yourself short. Maybe if you stopped doing that, you wouldn't feel the need to keep running."

He spun to look at her, and she shrugged. "Just a suggestion."

She drove back to the ranch, her body still humming from his touch, but sure in her head that she'd done the right thing.

It was just unfortunate that her heart took a little more convincing.

This time when Rylan rolled into Crooked Valley, it was midafternoon and he was pulling a horse trailer behind him. The latest rodeo had taken him north, and he'd come out on top again. The side trip he'd made yesterday had turned out to be worth it, and the prize money had come in handy.

Very handy. He whistled as he pulled up next to the corral outside the horse barn and carefully backed the trailer toward the gate.

He parked and hopped out, then checked the doors and gates to make sure the corral was secure. Only then did he swing open the gate behind his trailer and prepare to let out Rattler, the newest addition to the Crooked Valley stock contracting business.

He could hear the stomps and crashes of hooves in the back and he grinned. This stallion was full of piss and vinegar for sure. Getting him into the trailer had been interesting, but Rylan knew how to be patient. Just as he'd be patient now.

Rattler could be a pussycat if he wanted to. At least with no one trying to sit on his back.

Randy, one of the hands who worked mostly with the horses, came out of the barn and ambled up to the fence. "Whatcha got in the trailer, Ry?"

"A present. Do me a favor and stand over here, will ya, Randy? I'm going to let him out."

A thump echoed against the side of the trailer. "Sounds like a bruiser," Randy mused.

"We'll find out when I get him in the chute," Rylan answered. He was pretty sure he'd made a sound investment. And even Duke couldn't argue about the price because Rylan had a plan for that, too. Just because his plans didn't include sticking around in the long term didn't mean he couldn't help invest in the ranch's future.

"Ready?"

Rattler thundered out of the trailer with a clatter of angry hooves, charging down the ramp and straight through into the corral. He was off like a shot, kicking up his legs in a tantrum-like statement. The equivalent, Rylan figured, of giving him the finger for keeping him closed up for so long. He chuckled, impressed and, to his surprise, quite excited. Rattler could make all the difference to Crooked Valley if Duke could hang tight for the investment to pay off.

"He's a pretty one." Randy nodded.

"Don't let him hear you say that. You'll offend his manhood." But he was secretly inclined to agree. "Close the gate, Randy. I'm going to pull the trailer ahead."

By the time he'd moved the truck, a small crowd had gathered by the fence. Carrie had come down from the house, bringing Lacey with her. Duke and Quinn came into the yard as supper time drew close. Unconcerned, Rattler trotted around the fenced circle, his mane streaming and eyes bright.

"What in the world?" Duke asked, a deep frown marring his face.

"Meet Rattler, the newest stud for your bucking stock." Rylan kept his voice deliberately upbeat and light.

"My what?"

Duke looked anything but pleased, and Rylan saw him exchange a look with Carrie. A look that set Rylan's teeth on edge. *Uh-oh*, it said. *What's Rylan gone and done now?*

"Rylan. Where on earth did you get this horse?"

"At Mack Rigden's place outside Dickinson. Mack's thinking about retiring soon. I heard a rumor that he was going to take some stock to auction, so I made a detour on the way home."

"Why on earth… Did it occur to you to run this past me? Or Quinn?"

Rylan held his cool. He'd expected some resistance, after all. "We all know what you need to keep the program going is a good sire. One that others will pay stud fees for."

"And it'll take a long damn time for him to earn his keep! What were you thinking, doing this without consulting me? Forget upkeep, there's no way we could afford this right now."

He'd expected Duke to be mad. He looked at Lacey and saw hope on her face. Things didn't really change, did they? Duke was the oldest and figured he should have the final word on everything. And Lacey was the tenderhearted one who believed in him even when she shouldn't.

He hated the thought of letting them down. He'd avoided putting himself in this position for a lot of years. He'd hated the idea of coming back here, facing all the old hurts, irritated that Grandpa Joe was yanking them around like puppets on a string even after his death. If he had to be here, he was going to do it his way. At least some of the time, anyway.

"I knew what you'd say."

"For Pete's sake, Ry. Lacey's been trying to trim

some costs since she came on, and we've both got families to support."

Ouch.

"Duke," Carrie admonished quietly.

But Duke was well and truly irritated. "Well, it's true. Rylan's been going wherever the wind takes him without a care in the world, and now Lacey and I both depend on this ranch to support our spouses and children. Meanwhile, he can blow in like a tornado and leave again just as quickly."

Ry's temper flared, and he struggled to measure his words. He didn't ask for this. He was trying to help, for God's sake. But clearly his brother had some issues he needed to get off his chest.

"Crooked Valley isn't on the hook for a red cent, so don't get your panties in a twist." Ry lifted his chin. "Rattler's mine. I bought him with my own money."

Duke's jaw dropped. Lacey stared. "Your own money?" she asked. "But, Ry, you said before that a good stud horse would be expensive."

"How expensive?" Duke asked, an edge to his voice.

Carrie and Quinn remained silent, as if sensing this was between the siblings.

"Seventeen and a half."

Duke cursed. Carrie's eyes widened. Even Quinn let out a low whistle.

"You're going to ask, so I'll save you the trouble. I've had a good year. And I've been working for years. My last place, my board was covered in the winter and in the summer I stayed in the RV. My only expenses were my truck and the clothes on my back. I managed to put some away. Then when I sold the camper and bought the smaller one I still had money in the bank."

Not only in the bank. He'd never been much of a

spender, kept things simple rather than extravagant. He'd actually taken the step of investing some of his salary every payday. If he told them how much, they'd never believe him. He wasn't even thirty yet and he had a nice little nest egg.

Duke ran his hand through his hair. "You should have come to me. We should have talked about it."

"I was trying to do something good here. The opportunity came up and I seized it. Yeah, I paid a good price for him, but I would have been on the hook for more if I'd waited for him to go to auction."

The fire in Duke's eyes was starting to mellow.

"Look, Duke, here's the deal. For all intents and purposes, Rattler is part of Crooked Valley. We can use him to breed our mares. He'll earn his keep with breeding fees. He's going to be in demand, I promise you. And all the money will go into ranch coffers. The only thing I ask is that his ownership stays with me."

It felt like a big step. Owning Rattler tied him to Crooked Valley in a bigger way than he cared to be, but he also knew it was the only way Duke would agree to the purchase.

"I don't know, Ry."

"Trust me," he entreated. "I've been doing this a long time, Duke. Hell, if you don't trust my judgment, trust Kailey's. Have her come over and give her opinion."

He thought about it for a moment and took it a step further. "I'll make you a deal. If Kailey comes over and says I made a mistake, I'll take him to auction."

He looked at all of them. Quinn's gaze held a glimmer of respect and even Duke looked uncomfortably resigned to the idea. It was an impulsive suggestion, and things were hot and cold with Kailey, depending on the situation. But he trusted her horse sense. Brandt's stock was top-notch. He also trusted her to be honest—even if she didn't like it.

Hmm. It had been quite a while since he'd really trusted anyone that much. And that included Duke and Lacey.

Quinn stepped forward. "I think that's a fair idea, Rylan. Kailey's been helpful with advice for me over the past several months and there's no question she knows what she's doing. What do you say, Duke?"

Duke gave a short nod. "I'll agree to that. I'll hear what she has to say before making any decisions."

Rylan bit his tongue, knowing he had to choose his moments. And he realized that Duke had taken on the bulk of the day-to-day operations of the ranch. But, dammit, they each owned a third. They each had equal say. He looked over at Lacey, who was now looking uncomfortable, probably because she was caught in the middle. He knew if it came down to it, she'd go with whatever Duke wanted. Duke, the natural leader. Not Rylan, the baby of the family.

Meanwhile, Ry went to the truck and retrieved an apple from a bag he had on the seat. He applied just the right pressure to break it in half, and he took a bite, crunching into the white flesh while holding the other half on the palm of his hand.

All he had to do was hold his hand over the top of the fence for about two seconds and Rattler started trotting over. Hide glistening and eyes bright, he lipped the fruit from Ry's palm and chewed contentedly, bits of apple and juice flying.

"Atta boy," Ry soothed quietly, rubbing his hand along Rattler's neck. "The ladies are gonna love you."

Quinn interrupted the moment. "Kailey says she can come over after supper."

"Thanks, Quinn," Ry said. He got the sense that Quinn was an ally and was actually relieved someone had stepped up with the stock program. But maybe the ranch manager wasn't saying much because he didn't want to put himself in the middle of a family issue. Couldn't hate a guy for that.

While Quinn and Duke went to do evening chores, Carrie and Lacey headed to the house. Ry stayed behind, watching Rattler become accustomed to his new surroundings. There was a particularly big stall at the near end of the barn that he could claim, though for right now what the stallion really needed was to be turned out to pasture. That was something Ry would have to talk to Quinn about, since they had a number of open mares and the last thing Ry wanted to happen was some unplanned breeding.

He skipped the family dinner and instead parked the trailer, cleaned it out and unloaded his stuff in the camper. Then he went back out and took a good look at the brood mares. If Kailey was on board, if he could get her to hold true to her promise to use a new stud for Brandt's stock, it would be a big boost for Crooked Valley's reputation.

He'd like to breed one or two of their own mares, too. Like Candyfloss, an Appaloosa with some Clyde blood in her. She had a size and attitude that Rylan liked to see in a horse. Manageable and friendly when not in the chute, but a natural bucking instinct that he thought would work well with Rattler's temperament. With her strength and Rattler's high spirits, he figured there was a chance of breeding a good saddle bronc.

After Rylan had gone through the barn, he went back to the corral and leaned on the fence, watching as Rattler stood in the sun, his hide twitching now and again.

And swallowed against a lump in his throat.

When he'd been little, he'd loved this ranch. He'd loved the horses and the cows and Grandma Eileen's cooking. He'd wanted to run through the fields and pastures all day long, climb on the huge, round bales of hay, pick up garter snakes in the grass. He'd ridden his pony every opportunity he'd had, and when he wasn't doing that he'd nagged Duke to play rodeo with him. It usually had involved lassoes and some sort of mock calf Grandpa Joe had set up for them behind the barn. Duke, if Rylan remembered correctly, had done it grudgingly. At first Ry had thought it was because Duke didn't want to be saddled with a younger brother. But now, Rylan realized something important: Duke had always wanted to be a soldier. Out of all the kids, it had been Rylan who'd missed the ranch the most.

When they'd moved to Helena, Rylan hadn't fit in anywhere. In his ideal world, he was back on the ranch, with the horses and the cattle, currying Daisy's coat and feeding her carrots. Not in a city school where kids teased him if he wore his boots and hat. Even the week or so in the summer that they'd used to visit hadn't been fun, because it only served to remind Rylan that he had to say goodbye and go back to the city he'd hated.

Rattler wandered around the corral and Rylan sighed. He'd put off coming back here because it hurt too much. Because he resented being ripped away from it in the first place. He wished it didn't feel so much like home again. Wished he could stay detached. But he knew that his biggest fear had already come to pass.

He was going to hate leaving again.

# *Chapter 6*

Kailey thought about taking her truck over to Crooked Valley, but it was too nice of a night. She was bone-tired from haying all day, but the before-supper shower had felt heavenly and the beef roast and mashed potatoes her mom had made for dinner had perked her up considerably. What she really wanted was to enjoy some peace and quiet rather than feel rushed from place to place. She saddled one of the geldings and went cross-country in the soft evening, the rhythm of being on horseback soothing and familiar and far preferable to sitting on tractors all day long.

Rylan was standing at the corral, his elbows on the fence. He didn't seem to hear her approach, and she frowned. He was usually quick to smile, but right now his body language suggested he was lost in thought. Tough thoughts. His shoulders hunched and his head drooped a little as he rested his weight on the fence rail.

"Hey, Duggan," she called out, realizing she'd assessed the situation accurately when he jumped in surprise.

"I was looking for your truck," he said, flashing a smile that erased the troubled expression from his face. Whatever thoughts had been dogging him, he'd pushed them aside. She was starting to realize he was very good at that.

"This was more relaxing. I've been haying all day."

"I just got back this afternoon."

She dismounted and tied her horse to a nearby fence post. "So I heard," she answered, crossing the yard, moving toward him. "Caused quite a hubbub with your cargo, too."

His gaze warmed. "Come see."

She stood beside him at the fence and gave a whistle. The horse's ears perked up at the sound and he turned his head. He sure was a beauty. Heavily muscled, strong hindquarters, broad chest and standing seventeen hands or more if she was any judge.

"He can buck?"

"I certainly hope so." Together they watched as the horse caught wind of something and lifted his head before trotting to the opposite side of the corral. "Previous owner retired him from competition a few years back. He was becoming valuable from a breeding standpoint."

"And he sold him why?"

"Retiring. You probably know him. Mack Rigden."

"I know Mack. Good guy." She narrowed her eyes. "He selling off more of his stock?"

Rylan laughed then. "You interested?"

"If they look anything like this big lad, I might be." She hesitated. "I'd have to look at the bloodline, but I'd say there's a little draft horse in there somewhere. Percheron, maybe. You breed him with Candy and you'll have a horse like a tank."

He chuckled. "I was thinking the same thing."

Kailey kept her eyes on the stallion as she pondered the question on her mind. "Ry, I don't know how to ask this delicately, so I'll just come out with it. I didn't think Duke would approve an expenditure this big. Not now. What changed his mind?"

"He didn't change his mind. That's why Quinn called you."

Her face must have looked shocked because Rylan started to laugh. "You should see yourself," he joked. "You look horrified. Don't worry, Kailey. I didn't rip off Crooked Valley funds. I paid for him myself."

She thought about that for a moment. First of all, there was the surprise that he had enough money for a really good stud horse when he was living out of a tiny camper. More than that, though, she thought about how this marked an interesting step in his involvement at Crooked Valley.

So much for no ties. He had the horse. He had already mentioned one potential pairing. Did he realize he'd just made an investment in the family bucking stock business?

"I take it you live below your means, then," she said quietly, resting her arms on the fence.

"Not hard to do. My needs are pretty simple."

She looked over at him, surprised. This was a different side to Rylan she hadn't seen before. She'd always had the impression he didn't take things very seriously. That he was...impulsive. Despite what Duke might have thought, this wasn't an impulsive purchase.

He'd asked her before what she thought. Asked if she'd consider helping him out. He'd been planning this. Looking for the right horse. He'd had money put aside.

It was completely opposite from the man who'd thrown his cash down for a custom-made saddle at the Valentine's Day auction, who'd danced with her and propositioned her to something outrageous…

"Who are you, Rylan?"

She didn't realize she'd asked the question out loud until she heard him sigh. "I just am," he answered, avoiding the question. "No sense trying to dig too deep with me. What you see is what you get."

"Oh, I don't think so." She looked at him, examined the firm set to his jaw, the tightness of his lips. He didn't like talking about himself much, did he?

"Come on," she prompted. "You like this place more than you'll admit. You came back here. You've gotten yourself involved in this part of the operation… Why do you fight it so hard?"

He turned his head and met her gaze, though he kept his emotions shuttered away so she couldn't really read his face. "I never said I hated this place. I probably love it the most out of the three of us. So don't you question that, Kailey."

"Then why are you so determined to leave?"

His lips thinned further. "Just because I care about the ranch doesn't mean I want to come back. Doesn't mean I belong here. So get that out of your head, okay? I get enough of that from Lacey and Duke. I don't need it from you, too."

"Sheesh. Sorry." He was so touchy about it. "Did something happen to drive you away? I'm just trying to understand, Ry. Things just don't add up."

"Well, that's life," he replied bitterly. "And for the record, I wasn't driven away. I was taken away. Big difference."

She would have asked more, but the screen door slammed up at the house and both of them turned to see Quinn and Duke coming down the driveway to the barn. Just the men. Carrie and Lacey didn't join them.

"Hey, Kailey," Duke called out as they approached. "Thanks for coming over."

"No problem. Ry and I were just talking about this guy here. What's his name, Ry?"

"Rattler."

She grinned. "I like it. Strikes fast and a little bit dangerous. Just like you want."

Quinn smiled. "Well, the problem is we can't really take him at his name, you know?"

Duke nodded. "You're a good judge, Kailey. What do you think of Rylan's purchase?"

She looked at Rylan. Saw defiance in his eyes, but something else, too. Hope. He really wanted this to work. And she wanted it, too. For Crooked Valley. And, on a more unsettling note, for him.

"Well, at face and name value, he's great. I was just telling Rylan that if you bred him with Candyfloss, you'd have a horse like a tank. But the bigger question is bucking ability. I'd like to have a look at his papers. Ry says he competed for a while until he became too valuable as a stud. That natural bucking ability is important. I'd like to see someone get on him. Try to stay on."

Ry's eyes lit up. "It'd give us a chance to see him in the chute, too."

Duke looked his brother in the eye. "You're dying to get on him, aren't you?"

"He hasn't competed in a few years. But yeah. I'd like to see what he's made of. That instinct doesn't just go away."

"Let's do it," Quinn said.

Kailey was usually right in the mix back at her own place, but tonight she stood back and watched, just for this once. She wanted to get a good look at how Rattler handled, his temperament, how he was in the chute. She and Duke went to the small arena and stood at the rails as Quinn and Rylan prepared horse and rider for the main attraction.

"You really think this horse was worth the money?" Duke asked. "Because it's a hell of an impulse buy. Rylan can be so reckless."

It scared her how quickly she wanted to leap to Ry's defense. "Time will tell, Duke. But he didn't buy some old nag, I can tell you that. If I were in the market I would have given him a second look. And I can guarantee you he would have gone for more at auction. If this ride is anything at all, your brother just brought home a bargain."

Duke's jaw dropped a little. "You think so?"

"You need to have more faith in your brother, Duke. He's a pro rider. He knows what he's doing. And it wasn't nearly as impulsive as you might think."

"What do you mean?"

She watched as Quinn and Ry got Rattler in the chute, as Ry perched up on the rails, waiting for the right moment to ease his weight into the saddle. "I mean Rylan asked me about the program here not long after he first arrived. I agreed with him that the place needed a boost to your breeding program, but we both knew money was an issue. He's trying to help, Duke. And he's the one bearing the financial risk. Don't be too hard on him."

She held her breath as Rylan positioned himself on Rattler's back, and then gave Quinn a sharp nod to open the chute.

Rattler burst forth with strength and aggression, bucking with a power that surprised and delighted Kailey. A grin spread over her face and her eyes were glued to the spectacle as she said to Duke, "Retired my patootie. Look at him go!"

And it wasn't just Rattler. Rylan spurred him on, gorgeous form as he gripped the rope with one hand and held the other aloft. He was a beautiful rider, and while the two were at cross purposes—one trying to rid himself of his cargo and the other trying to stay on—it was almost as if they were working as a team to provide the best ride possible.

Rattler gave a quick and sudden lurch to the side and she saw Ry slip a little, but then he purposefully dismounted, landing on the soft loam of the arena. He got up and brushed off his jeans, a huge smile on his face as Rattler continued around the circle, smaller, quick bucks punctuating his gait.

"Did you see that?" Rylan called out. "Whooeee!"

"He didn't get rid of you," Duke pointed out.

Rylan swaggered over, his hat in his hand. "That has more to do with the quality of the rider than the horse, bro."

Duke rolled his eyes while Kailey chuckled. "Nothing wrong with your ego," Duke muttered.

Ry's face still glowed with excitement, but he became more serious as he met Kailey's gaze and then Duke's. "Let's be honest. A less experienced rider wouldn't have stood a chance. And he's been out of competition for a few years now."

Duke nodded. "And you think he'll earn his keep?"

Kailey looked at Rylan, not Duke, when she cut in. "Brandt can get the ball rolling on that score," she said.

Rylan's gaze was warm. "Thank you, Kailey."

"Don't thank me. This is business, remember?"

But she knew he was thinking—as she was—about that night at the creek, when he'd first asked for her help.

Rylan looked at Duke and held out his hand. "We have a deal then? Ownership stays with me and Crooked Valley reaps the proceeds."

It was a hell of a gift. Kailey hoped Duke realized how much.

"We have a deal," Duke replied, taking his brother's hand.

Rylan stayed true to his word. While ownership of Rattler was in his name, as far as he was concerned, nothing had changed. He'd given his ideas to Quinn, and then he'd hooked up the camper and the highway had become his home.

June became July. July morphed into August, hot and dry, and he was getting tired of the travel and the fair ground and diner food. What he was really craving was a batch of Lacey's fried chicken and a slice of her apple pie. He collected prize money and stayed at the top of the rankings, but at night, when everything was quiet and he was in his camper alone, it was Kailey he thought of most. Kailey swimming in her underwear, challenging him. Kailey in that pretty blue dress from the wedding, smelling like flowers and tasting like summer.

It was better he stay on the road. And away from her. When he was with her, he forgot a lot of things. Like why he didn't want to settle down in the first place. If anything, his feelings for her drove the point home.

He flipped over on the hard mattress and punched his pillow.

He had too much damned time to think, that's what. And he could blame it all on Duke and Lacey and their stupid summons. He was such an idiot. He'd liked the idea of being needed for once in his life, and the chance to prove to his brother and sister that he wasn't just a screwup who'd hit the highway as soon as he'd been old enough. He'd always been the youngest, the tagger-on, the one people felt they had to take care of but never bothered asking what he wanted.

He flipped again. Wondered where all the control he'd managed to attain over his life had fled.

Control.

He sighed, giving up on sleep and staring at the ceiling. That was what this came down to, wasn't it? A need to control his life. He absolutely hated being at the mercy of anyone else.

And now that control wasn't working so well. Because he'd made it a policy never to get too close to anything or anyone who could hurt him. And he'd done both in his return to Crooked Valley by caring for both Kailey and the ranch.

And damn, he was lonely.

Before he could change his mind, he picked up his cell and dialed. It took three rings, and then Kailey picked up. "This had better be good, Duggan."

He hadn't thought about caller ID. Or the time. It was after midnight.

"I'm sorry. Go back to sleep."

She sighed. "I haven't been to sleep yet. Though I was almost there."

"Me, too."

"How's things?"

He wondered how to answer. "Good," he said. "Real good."

"Some of our stock was in Cody last weekend. Heard you put on quite a performance."

"It was okay." Truth was, it had been a hell of a weekend with some very tight competition. And he'd come out of it with a sore shoulder and a bruised rib.

"So why are you calling me in the middle of the night, Ry?"

Her voice was soft, the way lovers spoke late at night, in the dark. What was he doing? He should be staying far away. He didn't need to get wrapped up in her, too.

Too? He pinched the bridge of his nose. It wasn't just Kailey; it was the ranch. It was all of it.

"I needed to hear a familiar voice," he replied. "Look, I really am sorry I called so late. I didn't realize the time. I'll let you go."

There was a long pause while neither of them hung up.

"The thing is," she said quietly, "I can't stop thinking about that night of the wedding."

He couldn't either. Or the sight of her in a wet, white bra and panties. But having her admit it took his libido and kicked it into overdrive. Why did she get to him so easily?

"Kailey—"

"That is why you called, right? Because of this thing we have going on that we keep trying to ignore?"

She was so forthright. It was one of the things he really liked about her. She didn't play games. Didn't beat around the bush. She just said what she meant. Even when it wasn't what he wanted to hear. Or when it was what he wanted more than anything. Or both.

"I don't want to think about you as much as I do." He held the phone close to his mouth, as if it made his lips closer to hers.

She laughed, a sexy little ripple in his ear. "Ditto. The big question is why? Why is thinking about me so bad?"

How did he answer that?

"Come on, Rylan. You think I don't see, but I do. You have this face you show to the world but underneath there's a whole lot of complicated stuff going on. You don't want to be at Crooked Valley. You don't want to be tied down to anyone or anything. Does that seem normal to you?"

He was so surprised by her insight that he couldn't answer. But there wasn't time anyway as she forged on. "Why does the idea of belonging somewhere scare you so much?"

"It's easy for you," he blurted out, wishing he didn't feel so defensive. "You've been in the same place your whole life with the same people. You've always belonged somewhere."

"And you haven't?"

"I did once."

There was silence down the line. And then Kailey asked the simple question with the difficult answer.

"What happened, Ry?"

"It doesn't matter."

"Of course it does. Talk to me, Rylan. Trust me."

Couldn't she see that was part of the problem? He didn't trust people. "I think I've made a habit of only trusting myself, K."

"And you shut other people out."

"I don't get hurt that way."

"Except you're hurting yourself. And you're missing out on what could be important relationships. I don't just mean romance either, Rylan. But with your sister, your brother. Your mom. People who care about you."

His temper flared. "Oh, you mean people who end up leaving?" He sighed. "God, I did not want to get into this tonight. I just wanted to…to…"

"Make a connection," she whispered. "You don't have the corner on feeling alone, you know."

Her? Alone? She was adored by all, the life of the party. How was she alone?

"Kailey, my dad was killed in action. One day he was alive, the next I was told I would never see my father again. It was hard to wrap my head around that concept, because I was used to him being gone on deployment. But it was different, knowing he'd never walk up the driveway again or throw a ball in the yard or take us riding. He wouldn't laugh or smile or kiss my mom, even in front of us. He was just…gone. It was so final."

"I know, Rylan."

"I had the ranch, though. And Joe and Eileen and all the things I loved, until that was taken away, too. My mom never asked what I wanted. She just decided that we were leaving and moving to Helena. I hated it there. I was a square peg in a round hole. Once I even tried to run away and go back to the ranch."

"How old were you?" she asked, her voice gentle.

"Seven."

"Oh, Rylan."

"Everything was completely out of control. Lacey didn't miss the ranch like I did, and Duke was far more interested in being like our dad to worry about me and what I wanted. So, I got through it. I was the after-thought tagged on the end of the family. And when I was old enough, I did what I wanted. What I'd always wanted."

Wow. He took a deep inhale. He'd never told anyone all that before. Maybe it was because it was Kailey. Maybe because they were on the phone and not face-to-face, and the bit of distance helped.

"So, why didn't you just go back to the ranch?"

Why hadn't he? He'd asked himself that question several times, and all he could come up with was because it was a reminder of his worst memories. "Because it hurt too much. I just wanted to forget the past, leave it behind me and make a new future. But thanks to Joe I got dragged back home anyway."

He could hear her breathing. It was so still. Finally, gently, she spoke.

"Do you realize that you just called Crooked Valley home?"

He hadn't.

"Rylan, I understand that you're hurt. You were so young to lose a parent and to be uprooted. Then to feel like you didn't fit in… I understand, too, that you made a choice to live your life on your terms. There is nothing wrong with that. Just…think about why you're doing things. Is it because it's what you want or because you're trying to protect yourself?"

"No one gets to call the shots in my life again." His voice was firm.

"But you're not calling the shots either," she reminded him. "Fear is. That doesn't sound like a fun way to live."

"It was until the past two or three months."

"Like having a one-night stand in a budget motel?"

Embarrassment flooded through him. "I thought we weren't going to mention that again."

"I wasn't. Except I'm starting to realize that your life on your terms probably isn't making you all that happy."

This was not how he'd wanted this conversation to go. "Listen, I didn't call to get in to all this. I was just by myself and thought…"

Lonely, he reminded himself. Dammit.

"Rylan, I stopped hating you for that night a while back. I had to get over my pride and feeling humiliated. That's all. But I think since then we've started to become friends, you know? I'm only saying these things as a friend who cares. You can't live your life in a bubble without letting anyone in."

Friends. Not that he'd say it, but he had a hard time thinking of Kailey as just a friend. Perhaps it would work better if he could stop wanting more. But she'd put an end to that. She also wasn't the only one with some pride, and he resented the way she made it sound as if she had it all together.

"Really, Kailey? Because I think you do a pretty good job of living in a bubble, too. The only difference is you hide behind your ranch. Hell, you still live with your parents. Talk about putting the kibosh on anyone getting too close. How about lack of privacy as a convenient excuse?"

Silence.

He hadn't meant to lash out. It was just…he hated

that she was right, even a little bit. And, he admitted to himself, he was a little bit frustrated. Because Kailey seemed perfectly able to think about them as friends when he couldn't. Couldn't think of her in a solely platonic way. Couldn't get her off his mind. Couldn't go through a whole day without thinking about kissing her again. Seeing her smile.

His head was starting to ache now.

"I'm sorry," he murmured.

"No, I deserved that," she said back. "If I'm going to judge and give free advice, I should expect the same in return."

He'd say this for her. She was fair.

"I've never met anyone like you, K."

"Of course you haven't."

He laughed in spite of himself, resting his hand on his forehead, half out of frustration and half from amusement.

"Hey," she said softly. "I wasn't trying to pick a fight. It's just that the more we… I mean, the more I see you, the more I realize that you're not exactly the person you show to the world. Maybe it's time for you to stop running, Rylan. The way I need to stop settling."

He swallowed hard. He knew he put distance between himself and people he cared about. It was a self-preservation mechanism he'd perfected long ago. It wasn't something he could just stop doing. But what did she mean, settling? Did she mean settling for him? Because she was right on that score. A woman like Kailey deserved better than a rodeo drifter with no fixed address, a camper and one horse to his name.

"Listen, I really do have to go," she whispered. "You gonna be okay?"

"Sure. I'll be home next week anyway. Heading down to Oklahoma before taking a bit of a break."

"Drive carefully."

"I always do."

"And good luck."

"Thanks."

There was an awkward silence for a few beats. "Kailey, thanks for the talk. I don't think I've ever told anyone that before, you know?"

"You're welcome, Ry. Be safe."

In his head he knew the words could be a simple goodbye, but as he clicked off the phone it felt like they were something different. An endearment, two words that meant someone out there was waiting for his return, cared if he made it back in one piece.

## Chapter 7

Crooked Valley Ranch was a beehive of activity. As the end of July approached, so did Carrie's due date. When she went into labor ten days early, no one was entirely prepared. Duke disappeared to the hospital. Quinn manned the ranch, while Lacey cooked and cleaned and baked and kept everyone updated as Duke texted her with their progress.

Kailey had been too busy working to spend much time with the Crooked Valley crew, but this morning she came over, both to bring a baby blanket that her mother had knitted and also to put a proposition to Quinn.

She dropped off the blanket to Lacey in the big house, taking a moment to inquire about Carrie and long enough to accept a fresh doughnut still warm from the grease. Quinn came in for a cup of coffee, and Kailey took the opportunity to speak to him about his house, which was newly renovated and sitting vacant now that he and Amber were living at Crooked Valley. She was just walking across the yard with a second doughnut in her hand when she heard an engine and saw a puff of dust. Rylan's truck came into view and her heart gave a little thump.

She'd thought about him often since his late-night phone call. And she kept picturing a cute little boy who'd lost his dad and who had been forced to move away from the only life he'd ever really known. Rylan always seemed so confident, even cocky. But it was all an act. Deep down, he was afraid of being hurt. Of letting himself care for anyone who might let him down.

He'd been right about her, too. She'd focused on work for so long that she'd forgotten that she had a life outside the ranch that she needed to live. She wondered what he'd say about the latest development.

He stopped. She saw the driver's side door open and a pair of dusty boots hit the gravel.

She couldn't help it. A smile broke out on her face. She was glad to see him. Besides, he probably didn't know about Carrie if he'd been driving all morning, and…

He came around the hood of his truck and she halted in her tracks.

A navy sling cradled his right arm close to his body. His gait had a hitch to it, and when her gaze darted to his face she saw scrapes running down one cheek and a dark bruise around his right eye and eyebrow.

All the things she'd said about keeping her distance faded, and she rushed to greet him, concern sending chills down her body. "Oh, my God! What happened to you?"

He smiled, and she noticed his lip had a split that kept him from opening his mouth wider. "Nothing too serious. Minor motor vehicle accident."

"Minor? Look at you!" Gingerly she put her arms around him and held him close. "From the looks of it, you might have been killed. You're okay, right?"

"Easy," he cautioned, his voice gruff. "I hurt all over, Kailey, and I've been sitting in that truck for the past four hours."

His truck. Frowning, she cast a quick look behind him. The truck appeared unscathed.

"Your truck is okay. Did you get it fixed already?"

He shook his head. "Not my truck. I was a passenger, catching a ride back from the bar on Saturday night."

A passenger. Kailey tried to ignore the sharp stab of jealousy and disappointment that rushed through her. She had no claim on him whatsoever. If he'd hooked up with someone after the competition, who was she to judge? After all, wasn't that basically what the two of them had done?

But still. It stung, and the fact that it did made her mad at herself.

"Kailey," he said gently, and she met his gaze. What there was of it, anyway. His left eye was swollen enough that it was half-shut. "I was in a cab. I don't drive after I've had a few."

There was relief, and a little guilt at assuming the worst, but mostly just concern for his injuries. "Are you okay?" she asked again.

He shrugged with one shoulder only. "Not really." His lips formed a bitter line. "I'll heal. But this pretty much ends my season."

His run for the NFR. Kailey's shoulders slumped as

she felt the depth of his disappointment. He'd worked hard and she knew he'd coveted a title since he'd started riding broncs. "I'm so sorry," she said. "I know how much you wanted it this year."

"Not your fault." Frustration underlined his voice. "You know, I always thought that if I got injured it would be in competition. Not in a cab on the way back to my stupid camper. Stupid kids out joyriding and hit us broadside. A little bit of fun with a whole lot of consequences."

Before she could say anything, he bit out, "I'm aware of the irony. Ry Duggan, likes a good time, sounding like an old fogy."

"You're angry and frustrated and disappointed. I'd say you're entitled to a little bit of a rant." She peered up into his bruised face. "Truly, though, Ry. The most important thing is that you're okay. What's wrong with your shoulder and is anything else hurt?"

"My shoulder was dislocated. It's back in now but it hurts like the devil, and I'm going to have to do physical therapy, of all things. The doctors weren't sure if I'd need surgery or not. I got a good knock to the head, which gave me this lovely shiner, and the glass from the window left a calling card on my face. And I'm bruised. Down my ribs, which miraculously weren't broken. And down my hip and thigh. I swear the whole right side of my body hurts."

"You need an Epsom salts bath," she decreed. "I'm surprised they let you out of the hospital so soon." It was only Monday.

"They didn't have much of a choice." Again he sent her a slightly crooked grin, and she knew he'd probably checked himself out of the hospital. "Look, do you think you could help me set up the camper?"

"Camper?" She stood back. "You know Lacey isn't going to let you do that. You should be in the house, in a decent bed. This is not a time to be stubborn, Rylan Duggan."

"I'm not up to her fussing and fluttering around, okay? I just want my own space." He seemed to weave on his feet a little and alarm rushed through Kailey at the sight of his suddenly pale face.

"You dumb ass," she chided, going to his left side. "You shouldn't even have been driving today. Here, get back in your truck on the passenger side. I have a plan, but it means we have to scoot out of here before Lacey realizes you've arrived. I can buy you a couple of days of peace and quiet."

"What the heck...?"

"Get in. I'll explain on the way. Unless you want your sister out here."

He obeyed, getting gingerly in the truck as she hopped into the driver's side. In seconds they were headed back down the driveway toward the main road, and less than ten minutes later she pulled into the driveway of a cozy bungalow surrounded by a stand of pines.

"What is this place?"

She reached into her pocket and withdrew a key. "My new home as of this morning. Partially furnished, rent is good." She grinned. "It's Quinn's house. He's been trying to decide what to do with it, and I offered to rent it on a month-to-month basis in the meantime."

Rylan turned slowly to face her. "Kailey, if this is about what I said on the phone the other night..."

"I've been thinking about it for a while, anyway,"

she admitted. "What you said just gave me the nudge I needed. It's time I got my own place."

She got out of the truck and was around to his side before his feet had even hit the ground. Oh, he was moving slowly. Not like Rylan at all, who she suspected would power through most injuries without letting on he was hurt.

"Come on. Let's get you settled inside. I'll make a run back to my house to pick up some necessities, but you can at least take a load off."

He walked slowly behind her as she went ahead and opened the door, then walked through the house and opened windows, letting the fresh summer breeze inside. She'd always liked Quinn's house. When Marie had been alive, she'd put her stamp on the décor. But the fire earlier this year had meant renovating, and as a result the main areas of the house were freshly painted and devoid of any personal touch. Kailey didn't feel as if she was walking into someone else's home. She felt as if she was walking into a new possibility. It was quite exciting and long overdue.

The insurance had paid to replace the furniture, so a brand-new sofa sat in the living room. Rylan sank into it, his breath hitching as his muscles protested, and Kailey knelt down before him, helping him take off his boots. She knew what it was like to bruise ribs or anything in the core area. Simple things such as getting out of a chair or bending to take off boots were painful. Muscles a person took for granted suddenly made themselves known. She slipped the boots off his feet and put them beside the sofa. "Lie down. I bet you didn't sleep much last night."

"Not a lot," he admitted. "This is a nice place."

"It's time I did it. I kept telling myself it was money I didn't need to spend, but we're doing well enough now that I think I deserve it."

"Of course you do."

"You're okay here for a while?"

"Peace and quiet. Why wouldn't I be?"

She paused. She'd already told her parents about her idea of renting Quinn's house. She'd gotten the feeling they were almost relieved, though they'd never say so. But she wasn't sure how they'd feel about Rylan staying, even for just a few days as he recuperated. She'd just pick up what she needed to make him comfortable. There was no rush to move all her things in, too. Besides, in a day or two Rylan would be back at Crooked Valley, sleeping in his camper again. Once the soreness eased he'd feel more like himself.

"I'll be back in a while. The power's still on, but there's no phone hooked up, so if you need anything you'll have to reach me on your cell."

He stared up at her with glassy eyes. "Be careful with my truck."

Right. She'd nearly forgotten they'd brought his rig over. "I'll unhook the camper. Don't worry about a thing."

As she left he eased himself down on the cushions. The long drive really must have sapped all of his energy. She unhooked the camper and leveled it before heading back to her parents' house. She packed toiletries and a few cleaning supplies, a handful of new towels they'd kept on hand for the barn but had never used. She didn't want to take her mom's groceries, so she decided a quick trip into town was in order. By the time she got back to the house it had been two hours, and Rylan was still asleep.

She put the bags down quietly and stared into his face. One other time she'd been awake and watched him sleep. It was no less personal now. After everything he'd said during their late-night phone call, she knew he had to hate being sidelined, being at the mercy of his injuries and forced to stay at Crooked Valley. He looked so vulnerable, so young. Sometimes she forgot that he was the youngest of the Duggans, not even thirty.

Deep down he had an old soul.

Gently, she smoothed a lock of reddish-brown hair away from his brow. He must have been sleeping lightly, because he opened his eyes, his right one still squinted but the left iris was a deep, intense blue.

She slid her fingers away. "Hello, sleepyhead."

"Hey." He moved to sit up and grunted as the muscles protested. "You're back already?"

"I've been gone over two hours."

Rylan moved to stand up, but she heard the gasp of pain as he levered himself off the sofa. "I swear, I get stiffer by the hour."

"I brought salts. I'll run you a bath and fix you something to eat."

"Don't you have work to do? I don't need a babysitter."

She shrugged, knowing she could always find work to do. Knowing she often did just to avoid other stuff. "I think the ranch can survive without me for one day. Besides, I needed to pick up some groceries and cleaning supplies."

"Kailey—"

"Shut up, Rylan, and let someone help you for once.

You don't have to be so fiercely independent all the damned time."

She left him muttering in the living room, and went to the bathroom to run water in the tub. She added a good dose of Epsom salts to ease his muscles, and got out one of the new towels for when he was finished. As the tub filled, he went to the camper and found clean clothes. It was all good until it was time for him to get undressed.

He got the sling off okay, if somewhat awkwardly, using his left hand. The problem came with taking off his shirt. He couldn't use his right hand to pull the cuff off his left arm or shrug the fabric off his shoulders as he normally would. After watching him struggle and hearing a few choice curse words, Kailey stepped in. She pulled his left sleeve off his arm and then moved to his right side, easing the freed fabric over and off his shoulder and down to his wrist.

"Better?" she asked, her throat tight. With his shirt off she could see the tight curves of his muscles as well as the shocking amount of bruising down his right side. How he must be hurting right now. The desire to lean in and kiss the purple spots was strong, but she held back. Friends only. That's what she'd said. That was what was best for both of them.

"Thanks," he murmured. "I think I can get the rest."

"Call if you need anything. Towel's hanging on the towel bar."

She escaped before he started unbuttoning his jeans, half hoping he wouldn't need help, half hoping he would. But all she heard on the other side of the door were a few scuffling noises and then the soft sound of him sinking into the water of the bath.

She'd been holding her breath and hadn't even realized it.

While he was soaking, she emptied out his duffels and sorted the laundry into piles. The first load was in the washing machine when she went to the kitchen and began unpacking the groceries and supplies she'd bought.

It had been fun and a little bit exciting, knowing that the purchases were for her own place. She literally had nothing, but with what Quinn had left behind, she could make do. It was midafternoon but neither of them had eaten lunch. When the fridge and cupboards were filled with groceries, she started cooking what she'd picked up for a simple but hearty meal: pork chops and baked potatoes and a salad kit.

The chops were sizzling when she heard the squeaky sound of Ry's feet on the bottom of the tub as he got out. She took out butter and sour cream for the potatoes and listened with one ear in case he got into trouble. Minutes ticked by until she heard the bathroom door open.

"Did you manage okay?" she asked, turning around, and then every other thought fell clean out of her head.

He looked good, so good. His hair was wet and tousled around the tanned skin of his face, and he had on a light cotton shirt and clean jeans. The only problem was he hadn't buttoned either, and he held his right arm close to his chest while the sling dangled from his left hand.

"I had help this morning," he confessed. "One of the nurses at the hospital."

"I just bet you did." She teased him, hoping it would dispel the feeling she got in the pit of her stomach just from looking at him.

He grinned. "Apparently some women actually can resist me, you know."

Right. Maybe not everyone looked at Rylan Duggan and got flushed all over. Which meant it might just be her who was crazy.

"It's been almost twelve hours since my last pain pill," he said quietly. "I could use a hand. If you don't mind, that is."

"Of course. Just a sec."

She turned down the chops and met him in the living room. He'd put his sling on the back of the sofa and had sucked in his stomach, trying to manage the button on his jeans with one hand. Heart in her throat, determined to not make a big deal of it, Kailey silently went to him and reached for the waistband of his pants.

His sharp intake of breath pulled his stomach in, but not enough. The backs of her knuckles still touched the soft, warm skin of his belly as she put the rivet through the buttonhole.

"I can zip," he said, his voice strangely husky.

He pulled the zipper to the top and then Kailey went to work on his shirt buttons. One by one she fastened the buttons, staring at his chest rather than into his eyes. But it didn't matter. The swirl of intimacy still surrounded them. She studied the hollow of his throat, the ruddy color of the little bit of chest hair that curled at the center of his collarbone, the way his Adam's apple bobbed when he swallowed. As she got to the second-last button, she realized that her fingers had slowed, taking their time in covering the distance from waist to neck.

"There," she murmured, her voice cracking a little.

"Can you help with the sling?"

"Of course."

What on earth was wrong with her? She cleared her throat and reached for the sturdy brace, helping him position it just right and making sure it was fastened securely. She stood back. "Nearly good as new," she stated.

"Something smells good," he said, looking over her shoulder. "Are you cooking?"

"We missed lunch. I made an early dinner. It won't be much longer, I don't think."

"I don't know how to thank you."

"Don't thank me yet. I can't cook like your sister. Besides, you're going to be on your own after dinner. I've got a lot to do."

She headed for the kitchen and he followed her. "I know you do. I really appreciate you giving me a place to stay. You're right. The camper isn't the most comfortable, not now, anyway. And Lacey would hover. Not to mention Duke riding my ass."

Kailey slapped her palm against her forehead. "Oh, my gosh! How could I have forgotten? You haven't heard the news."

Rylan frowned. "What news?"

"Carrie was in labor this morning. Duke texted while I was grocery shopping. They have a bouncing baby boy. A few weeks early and a little under seven pounds. You're officially an uncle."

She was surprised by the look of pleasure that transformed his face. "I already consider myself an uncle to Amber," he confessed. "But Duke has got to be over the moon. Hard to imagine my big brother a father."

"I've only had the one text, but he sounded pleased as punch. Lacey probably knows more if you want to call."

He reached into his back pocket. "That reminds me.

I thought I heard my phone buzz while I was in the tub. Maybe it was her." He checked the call log with a few swipes of his thumb. "Yep. One missed call, and it was the ranch. I'll call back in a bit, get more details."

"Do you like kids, Ry?" He was really good to Amber and seemed pleased about the new baby. It would be a surprise, though. Rylan didn't seem the type. He was too much of a free spirit.

"I do, actually," he said. "Kids have generally got it right. They're not old enough to complicate stuff with personal agendas."

Lacey thought about that for a moment. "But, Ry, kids aren't really old enough to understand that life comes with consequences." She turned the burner back up, checked on the potatoes.

She was just reaching for the bag of salad when he spoke again. "I don't think kids are oblivious to consequences," he said, sitting down at the little table and chairs in the eating area. "I think…well, I think they aren't afraid of them yet. Until we make them that way."

It was an interesting thought. She considered the idea for a moment. She agreed children had a wonderful sense of innocence and simplicity. It wasn't until they got older that they understood fear. That they made decisions based on being afraid rather than taking chances and doing the impossible.

But then there were children such as Amber. Such as Rylan.

"You might be right," she agreed and poured lettuce into a bowl. "But you learned fear early on. When your dad died. When you had to move. And Amber has, too. She lost her mother when she was just a toddler. You know things like that shape who we become. You said so yourself."

She looked up, drawn to his gaze. Maybe he'd think her silly but one of the first things she'd noticed way back last Christmas had been his eyes, thickly lashed, a stunning, clear blue. Her mom would call them Paul Newman eyes. Kailey had seen enough of the older movies to agree.

"That's true," he admitted. "But answer me this. If you took a survey of six-year-olds and asked them what they wanted to be when they grew up, and then asked a room full of thirtysomethings, how would the answer differ?"

That made her stop and think. She vaguely remembered being six. But she remembered friends and classmates talking about being movie stars or sports figures or astronauts. There were no limits. Most thirtysomethings she knew were thinking about kids and bills and making the mortgage payments.

"Is that why you don't settle down, Ry? You're avoiding those responsibilities and consequences for as long as possible?"

He lifted one shoulder. "Maybe. There's a TV show I like and one of the guys has this saying: *I reject your reality and substitute my own.* I like to think I've been making my own reality. Calling my own shots." He frowned. "Up until this point, at least. Now I can't ignore consequences and complications. I've wanted that title for as long as I can remember, Kailey. I gotta be honest and say it hurts knowing I'm not going to get it."

"Maybe next year," she suggested. "You'll heal. Be good as new."

"Maybe," he agreed, but his heart didn't sound in it. "For right now I could use one of those pain pills."

She retrieved the bottle, noticed that they were just over-the-counter strength. "No prescription?"

"I don't like taking that stuff. Makes me dopey. Give me two of those, though. It should take the edge off."

She shook a couple into her hand, gave them to him along with a glass of water. "Dinner shouldn't be long."

"Thanks. I appreciate it."

"I started a load of laundry for you, too. Figured you've been gone a while and could use some clean clothes."

"You don't have to look after me, Kailey. I'll be fine. Really." He popped the pills into his mouth and chased them with a big swallow of water.

"It's nothing I wouldn't do for any other neighbor," she protested. "Seriously."

But the intensity of his gaze said something different. They both knew he wasn't just another neighbor. If he had been, her fingers wouldn't have hesitated over his buttons. She wouldn't still be thinking about kissing him, or about his long legs folded into the steaming bathwater, or wondering how he was going to manage later tonight.

As she served the meal, she told herself she couldn't let it be her problem.

# Chapter 8

Rylan tried to roll over and nearly cried out from the pain.

The bed was comfortable enough, or would have been if he didn't ache all over.

The night after the accident, the hospital had kept him doped up on some primo narcotics. Tonight, the acetaminophen wasn't cutting it. He couldn't get comfortable. Moving positions meant engaging core muscles and shifting ribs. He tried lying on his left side but even then, his right hip pained as gravity pulled it down toward the mattress.

He managed to doze off and on, but by the time the sun came up he was sore, exhausted and honestly felt as though he'd been hit by a truck.

Which, of course, he had.

There was no sense in staying in bed. He got up, tried

a warm shower to loosen his muscles, searched for coffee and found none. Kailey had called her dad for a ride back to the ranch after dinner so she could get her own truck. Technically, it was her place, but she'd lent it to Rylan rather than staying here herself. She was still determined to keep space between them. Not that he'd be any threat to her anyway.

He checked his watch. Lacey would be up by now, getting breakfast for Quinn, doing all those housewifely things she did nowadays in addition to her accounting business. Heck, she'd even put in that vegetable garden. He'd never pictured her as a farm wife, but he supposed it wasn't that far a stretch. She'd always been a nurturer, wanting children and a home.

She'd definitely have something to eat. Besides, he hadn't called her back as he'd told Kailey he would. Yesterday the idea of hiding away to lick his wounds had been perfect. Today, though, he knew he should face his family. At some point he had to stop being a coward and start having difficult conversations.

He popped a few more pills, but wasn't too hopeful they'd help. He felt every bump and pothole on the drive to the ranch, relieved when he finally crawled his way up the driveway.

He didn't expect to see Kailey's truck in the yard.

Gingerly he climbed out of the truck and made his way to the house.

Lacey met him at the door, a dusting of flour on her cheek and an apron covering her front. "Rylan! You're home! Carrie has a boy!"

He grinned at his sister's enthusiasm. "I know. Have you spoken to Kailey?"

"Not this morning. Did you drive all night?"

"Actually… I stayed at Quinn's—I mean Kailey's—last night."

He took off his hat, and then she noticed his bruised eye.

"Oh dear." Her face fell with dismay. "That's not from a bar brawl, is it? Oh, Rylan."

It irritated briefly that his family was so quick to assume the worst about him. In February, she'd been suspicious of where he'd gotten the money to bid on the saddle at Quinn's benefit. Duke didn't trust his judgment. Of course, he hadn't really given them reason to in recent years.

Yet the one person who really had a reason to distrust him was the one person who truly seemed in his corner. Kailey.

"I haven't been in a bar fight in…" He did a mental check. "Years." He smiled at her, trying his charm. "I was, however, taking a cab last Saturday night and we got broadsided."

"What? Are you okay?"

He sighed. "Yes, and I'm dying for a cup of coffee. Can I come in and fill you in on what happened?"

"Of course." She stood back and let him in, and he hesitated before deciding to take off his boots. It wouldn't do to wear them in the house, but damn, it hurt taking them on and off.

He sat on the stairs and by the time the boots were off his feet he'd broken into a cold sweat.

When he finally made his way to the kitchen, Lacey's eyes were dark with worry. She had a fresh cup of coffee waiting for him and was putting a plate in the microwave to reheat. He eased himself into a chair at the table, picked up the cup and took a first, fortifying sip.

Delicious.

"I thought about hiding out at Quinn's for a few days. Kailey told me yesterday that she was going to be renting it, and I wasn't ready to face you and Duke and answer a lot of questions. Or be fussed about."

"What changed?"

He grinned. "No coffee in the house. And realizing that I can't just run away from awkward situations all the time."

She simply waited for him to explain. Which he did, making sure he added the part about Kailey going home last night. "I asked her to keep it a secret. I was kind of licking my wounds, literally and figuratively."

"This means the end of your championship hopes, doesn't it." Her face was sympathetic.

"Yeah, it does." He watched as Lacey went to the microwave and took out the plate she'd put in. When she brought it back the scent of apple pancakes and fried ham hit his nose, and he was glad he'd decided to visit this morning.

She put syrup down beside him and he poured on a generous helping before picking up his fork. "You spoil me," he admitted.

"Maybe it's time you got some spoiling," she observed, taking a seat at the table.

He thought about Kailey last night and her simple but lovely dinner, and how he'd enjoyed talking with her. Normally a scene such as that would have sent him running for the hills. So why wasn't he?

The obvious reason was that he couldn't, not in the shape he was in. But that would be a big fat lie.

"Lacey, when you came back here, you had no intention of staying. What changed your mind? Quinn?"

"Hmm." He chewed and swallowed a mammoth bite of pancake while she considered. "Part of it was Quinn, and part of it was Amber. But there was a time when I was sure we weren't going to work out and I knew I was going to stay in Gibson anyway."

"Why?"

He kept feeding his stomach, hoping to dislodge the weight that seemed to settle right in the pit. He had a feeling he knew what she was going to say.

"I suppose it's because this place has a way of getting into a person's blood. No one could have been more surprised than me, Ry. But there's something about this town, this ranch, that just grounds a person. At first I couldn't imagine staying, and then I couldn't imagine leaving it behind."

Just as he'd thought.

Then again, it was no surprise. He'd had the same feeling when he was five years old. Like this was the best place on earth. And leaving it had left him feeling...

Bereft.

He looked at Lacey and finally grasped what he'd always known in his heart but hadn't been able to quite describe. He'd grieved the loss of his dad. But he'd also grieved the loss of Crooked Valley as much, if not more. It had been perfect. He'd belonged here. He'd felt safe and loved and understood. And then it had been gone.

And by staying away all these years, he'd never had to truly deal with that grief. Until now.

"Ry? Are you okay?"

He swallowed, his throat thick. "Not really. I'm just tired, I guess. I didn't sleep much last night."

"Do you want to stay here?"

He shook his head. "You're newlyweds and a new family. You deserve your honeymoon period."

She grinned and patted his hand. "Well, that's quite a romantic notion, for a rodeo bum."

He smiled back. "I have my moments. Anyway, seriously, a few days at Kailey's and I'll be right as rain and back in my camper."

"Kailey, huh?" Lacey's gaze was sharp.

"It's not like that. Believe me. She made sure to stay at her mom and dad's last night rather than move her stuff in. Kailey's not interested in me that way."

Lacey burst out laughing. "Right. Okay. Whatever." Her tone said that she didn't believe him in the least.

"Hard as it may be to believe, she's pretty determined not to give me another shot. We're just friends." He didn't quite believe that, but there was no other way to describe their relationship when they both felt the pull of attraction and were nothing about it. He raised an eyebrow. "After what happened in February, that in itself is a miracle."

"She must believe in you on some level. She took your side with the Rattler issue."

"Horses are a different matter." Very different from gambling with hearts. "That's business."

Right on cue, the front door slammed and he heard Kailey's voice call out. "Halloo, is the coffee on?"

Lacey grinned and called back, "Of course. And I have cake."

Rylan frowned. "You never said anything about cake."

"You needed a good breakfast."

Kailey stomped into the kitchen in her stocking feet and stopped short when she saw Rylan. "Oh. Hi."

"Hi, yourself. I was filling Lacey in on what happened."

Recovered, Kailey went to the cupboard for a coffee cup. "I came over to get the goss on the new baby." She smiled at Lacey. "When are mama and baby headed home? Maybe I'll make a run in later today to visit."

"Tomorrow, if all goes well. We're going to have a family dinner here, quiet-like. You should come."

Kailey shrugged. "I'm not family."

"The hell you aren't." Lacey sent her a firm look. "I know for a fact you and Carrie are like sisters. She'd be hurt if you weren't here, Kailey."

"I'll try. Things are pretty busy."

"It's showery today and it's calling for rain all day tomorrow. You won't be haying. There's no reason why you shouldn't be here," Rylan added. It would be better if things weren't weird between them, wouldn't it? After all, they'd been much better yesterday once they'd sat down to dinner. Platonic. Polite. And then she'd said "see you later" and left him to his own devices.

The phone rang, and Lacey disappeared to answer it. Rylan looked up at Kailey. "In the end, I figured telling her was probably better than hiding out or having her hear from somewhere else." He sent her a winning smile. "Plus there was no coffee at your house."

"Did she freak out?" Kailey took a sip of her brew and watched him over the rim of her cup.

"Not as much as I expected. But the offer to stay was made right away. Do you mind if I stay at yours for another few nights? She and Quinn are newlyweds. It's awkward. Even staying in the camper is pushing it, because I'm in their hair all the time, you know? But at least there's a little privacy."

"Afraid you might get some of that love stuff on you?" She chuckled, then shook her head. "I don't mind. It's so busy right now that I was thinking I'd just take a few things over each time I go by. I won't be ready to really move in until, well, probably the weekend."

"Thanks. I appreciate it. By then I should be fine to move back into the camper again."

She went to the cookie jar and lifted the lid, searching for a treat. Rewarded, she took out a chocolate chip cookie and started to munch. "I see you managed to get dressed all by yourself this morning," she observed, her eyes glinting with mischief as she chewed the cookie.

"It was not a quick job," he admitted. Indeed, he'd struggled most with the button of his jeans. He'd made a quick movement without thinking, and his shoulder had seized and his eyes had watered from the pain. The shirt, though, that had been easier. Time consuming, but easier.

He wiggled the fingers of his left hand, gesturing for a cookie, and she retrieved him one from the jar. "So, are you really thinking of heading to the hospital later?" he asked.

"How would it look if I didn't visit my best friend when she had a baby?" Kailey asked. "I didn't go last night because I thought it was too soon. But if she's in another day… I should take her flowers or something."

He shoved the cookie in his mouth, washed it down with a gulp of cooling coffee. "Duke's my only brother. I should probably put in an appearance, too. Want to drive together?"

Lacey's muffled voice coming from the office was the only sound in the relative silence.

"For Pete's sake. I'm staying at the place you're supposed to be renting. We run into each other all the time, and you have a vested interest in my new horse." He looked into her eyes. "There is nothing weird about an uncle and honorary aunt visiting the hospital together. Unless you make it weird, in which case I'm going to start thinking this isn't as platonic as you let on."

Boom! It was a good shot, but it didn't have the oomph he thought it might. Maybe because he wasn't thinking platonically about her at all either.

"Fine. We'll save the gas and drive in together. Happy?"

"Immensely. How about I pick you up at four? That way we don't lose the whole workday."

"You're working? Like that?" She nodded toward his sling.

"I want to stop by the barn. Talk to the guys. Check on Rattler. I've been gone awhile. I need to get caught up."

"I guess that'll be okay then."

"We can visit and then stop for a burger on the way back."

"But this isn't a date," she confirmed.

"A man's gotta eat."

She checked her watch. "I gotta run. I came for the update but really I wanted to drop off the first month's rent to Quinn. I didn't expect him to give me the key yesterday, and I don't want to take advantage."

"You might possibly be the most responsible person I've ever known," he said, grinning. "Wait, scratch that. Duke is. But you're a close second."

"Gee, thanks."

She gave his good shoulder a jostle on her way by. "Catch you later."

"Four o'clock. Sharp."

"Yeah, yeah," she called back, and a few seconds later he heard her go out the door.

Lacey was still on the phone, and Rylan took a few moments to think about what was happening. More than that, he wasn't sure what he wanted to do about it. He'd come back to Crooked Valley with the intent of simply using it as a place to park. His goal always had been a run at the championship. In the absence of that goal what was he supposed to do? Part of him wanted to run away. Not let himself get attached again.

The other part told him to stay and see this through. That he couldn't go on running forever. At some point he had to deal with stuff. At some point he had to...

Grow up.

Deep down he knew what he really wanted, and it scared him to death. But he'd known it from the moment he'd loaded Rattler in the trailer and had headed for home.

Home.

Hell of a thing.

Lacey and Duke had been right after all. He'd sworn up and down that coming back wouldn't mean they could count on him to stay. But that was exactly what he was going to do.

Stay.

## Chapter 9

Kailey knew it was just a trip to the hospital, but she didn't want to show up in jeans and a T-shirt. At three she called it quits and left the barn in favor of a shower. Now, wearing a sundress and sandals, she put the last twists on the single French braid and wrapped the elastic around the end. For some reason her hair braided easier when it was damp, and she checked the mirror briefly, satisfied with the neat plait. Her freckles were starting to stand out thanks to days in the sun, and a swish of mascara made her eyes seem bigger and a swipe of lipstick highlighted her lips. She hoped it looked like she was trying—but not trying too hard.

Her mom had made cheese biscuits and had packed a half dozen in a zipped plastic bag in case Carrie was getting nasty hospital food. Kailey wasn't the crochet type, so the blue gift bag in her hand held store-bought clothes. Her favorite was the Onesie that said Handsome

Cowboy across the front with the picture of a mustache beneath it. She knew Duke would get a kick out of it. There was also a pair of the tiniest jeans she'd ever seen, paired with a soft red-and-blue plaid shirt.

This little guy was going to be a rancher all the way.

"Rylan's here!" her mother called.

"Thanks, Mom." Kailey made her way toward the front room. She rather hoped to get out before her mom had the opportunity to say anything, but no such luck. Her mother met her in the entry, holding out Kailey's purse.

"Don't forget this. And have fun."

"I'm visiting a hospital, Mom."

"With Rylan Duggan. He's very handsome, you know."

"Yes, I know." She took the purse.

"And you look very pretty, honey."

Kailey smoothed her hand over the skirt of the dress. "Is it too much? I didn't want to look like I'd gone right from the barn or smell up the hospital."

"No, it's not too much. Give Carrie and Duke our love. And take a few pictures with that phone of yours."

"I will." On impulse she leaned over and kissed her mother's cheek before opening the door and stepping out onto the porch.

Rylan had shut off the truck and was walking across the yard, but he stopped when he saw her. A low whistle sounded from his lips. "Shee-oot," he said, grinning at her. "You dressed up and everything."

She scowled. "I do own clothing other than jeans and shirts."

"Yes, you most certainly do, Miss Brandt." He back-tracked to the truck and opened the passenger-side door.

She hoped she wasn't blushing as she climbed into the cab and he shut the door behind her.

On the seat beside her was a tote bag and a teddy bear with a blue gingham ribbon around its neck. "You went shopping?" she asked as Rylan got in and started the truck by reaching around the steering wheel with his left hand.

"Just a stop at the store in town. Lacey went to visit before lunch and said that Carrie had put in a request for some clothes. I guess they weren't quite ready to leave for the hospital when Carrie went into labor." He chuckled as they started out the driveway. "Duke's only been home long enough to get a few hours sleep and have a shower, and he was so anxious to get back, he forgot to pack what she'd asked for. Lacey says he is one proud papa."

"Of course he is. Especially since this is his first baby."

It seemed Rylan was true to his word about the platonic thing. On the way to the hospital they chatted about Crooked Valley, the changes Rylan wanted to implement in the program, things Kailey had done with Brandt stock and the plausibility of implementing similar practices at the Duggans'. Nothing personal, no innuendos. It was nice, she realized. As Ry sang Rattler's praises, she discovered she'd missed this kind of chat in recent months. She and Carrie had often shared work talks, but since Duke's arrival, her friend had been preoccupied with love and babies. So, too, with Quinn. His focus was on Lacey now and a brand-new family. Not Rylan, though. No romance and babies for him.

Her relief was tempered by a slight thread of disappointment, which was absolutely ridiculous. Romance and babies weren't what she wanted from him. She really didn't want anything, besides peace.

They arrived and made their way to the maternity wing, treading softly as they approached the correct room number. Kailey peeked around the corner of the door and saw Carrie sitting up in bed, flipping the pages of a magazine while a nursery bassinette sat beside the bed.

"Knock knock," she called softly.

Carrie looked up and a smile lit her face. "Hi! Come on in." Her voice was clear but hushed. "He's sleeping right now. Perfect time for visitors."

Kailey stepped in, feeling as if she was in another world. Sure, she'd been around babies now and again. She'd babysat occasionally growing up and she'd always been close to Amber, Quinn's daughter. But her best friend, as a mom...it did something to her. Made her happy and sad and a little bit broody. Had her dedication to Brandt Ranch cost her something important? What might have happened if Colt hadn't withdrawn his proposal?

"You look wonderful," Kailey said, and Rylan trailed into the room behind her. "Mom sent you biscuits and honeyed butter. And Rylan brought you your clothes."

Ry held up the bag. "Lacey packed it. I didn't go through your delicates."

Carrie choked on a laugh. "Oh, God, the very idea of delicates right now is...well, comical."

Rylan blushed. Kailey grinned.

"Where's Duke?"

"On a sandwich run. I'm dying for a turkey sub and a glass of cold milk."

Kailey peered into the bassinette. The junior Duggan was sleeping, his tiny lips sucking in and out, a pale fringe of red hair peeking around a stretchy blue cap. He was swaddled in a flannel blanket, and looked so tiny and fragile that Kailey caught her breath.

"He's beautiful, Carrie. Just beautiful. Ry, come see."

Rylan dutifully peeked at the baby and Kailey watched as his face softened, mellowed. What kind of father would he make? Kind, she figured. Probably patient.

But restless. And whoever married him would have to get used to his itchy feet. He didn't like to stay in one place for long, didn't like to be fenced in, did he? It would be like permanently stabling a bronco who longed to run wild in a pasture thick with rich grass. A punishment.

"Have you named him yet? Lacey never said."

"Evan Joseph." Duke's voice came from the doorway and he stepped inside as they turned to look at him. He was grinning from ear to ear, puffed up as any proud papa would be, carrying a paper sack of sandwiches, a can of soda and a bottle of milk.

"After our father and his father," Rylan said softly.

"Do you mind?" Duke met his brother's gaze, his face losing its joviality and turning serious.

"Of course not." Rylan held out his left hand to Duke. "It's a fine name, Duke. Congratulations."

Kailey watched as Duke put down the food and shook Rylan's hand, their gazes holding. Something was different tonight, something in the way they were with each other. More…equal. It didn't really make sense, as she didn't think anything had really changed. Heck, Rylan had been gone for weeks. When had there been time for them to hash out their differences? Last she'd seen, Duke was still ticked at Rylan for buying Rattler without his input.

"Sorry to hear about your accident," Duke said, nodding at the sling. "Glad you're all right, though. Guess this changes a few things, huh?"

Rylan nodded. "Unfortunately. If it's all right with you, I'll stay through until Christmas. Work with the bucking stock. That way the terms of the will'll be met and Crooked Valley will be in the clear. All yours."

Duke looked at Carrie, who smiled encouragingly, and then back at Rylan. "Wow. I appreciate that, Ry. Big-time."

"I know it's what you want. What Lacey wants. That's why I came back, after all. It's not your fault I can't compete for now."

Kailey tried not to let her mouth drop open. Rylan was staying? For at least another four months? When he'd been traveling while competing it had been easier to deal with the temptation he presented. He was only around now and again. But four months... Sixteen weeks. Hoo-boy.

Carrie spoke up from the bed. "We'll have to decide what to do with your third, Rylan. We can maybe put together enough money to buy you out, if that's what you want."

He nodded. "We can talk about that when the time comes. No need to worry about that now." He looked down at the baby. "Seems to me we have something here a little more important that takes priority."

Duke reached into the bassinette and picked up the baby, holding him by the bottom and cradling his head in his big palm. "You're right," he agreed. Even though the baby was sleeping, Duke spoke to him. "Evan, meet your uncle Ry and your aunt Kailey."

Kailey's face heated. Had Duke paired up their names on purpose?

Duke held out his hands, offering Evan to Kailey first. "Do you want to hold him?"

She did. She blinked, thinking about how she'd had a chance to have a family of her own and had passed it up. Logically she knew there was still a chance. She wasn't exactly old. But it definitely felt as though her options were limited, and seeing her friends marry and have families just drove the point home.

She'd made her choice. It wasn't likely that situation would change, either.

But for now she held out her arms and accepted the small, warm bundle into her embrace. Evan's tiny head rested in the curve of her elbow as she looked down into the angelic face. He'd awakened, not fussing, but with dark, unfocused eyes staring at her.

"Well, hello there," she said softly, feeling her heart turn over. Babies were so innocent, so helpless. So... precious. "You and me, we're gonna have some fun. I'm gonna teach you to climb that old oak tree behind the big house, and we'll catch tadpoles in the pond and get good and dirty. Just you wait."

She looked up at Carrie. "You did good, hon. He's awesome."

"We think so. At least for now. Talk to me in a few days when I haven't had any sleep."

Any jealousy Kailey might have felt was short-lived. Carrie had no family left. She was an only child and her mother had died of cancer a few years earlier, and her father had taken off. It was so good to see Carrie happy and contented. "You are going to be spoiled rotten. Lacey and I are going to see to it that you get some downtime to sleep. We'll be fighting over who gets to babysit."

"I feel very lucky," Carrie replied, patting the bed.

Kailey went and sat beside her on the mattress, Evan still snuggled in her arms. "I never expected this. And I don't feel so alone. It's nice to know that you're close by, and Lacey, too. Helen is even coming for a week to help out."

The baby felt very right in Kailey's arms. She leaned back against the pillows and nudged Carrie. "Look at that. I thought Duke was still mad at Rylan."

The brothers were sitting in two vinyl armchairs, chatting away effortlessly.

"I know it sounds terrible, but I'm almost glad that Rylan was in that accident," Carrie said.

"What? But why?" Kailey recalled all the bruising down Rylan's side and cringed. "He's really banged up, you know. Lots of bruising you haven't seen."

"And you have?" Carrie's words were laced with delighted curiosity.

"Not like that. I helped him get his shirt off yesterday, that's all."

"Sounds like enough to me," Carrie responded, grinning.

"You still haven't told me why you're glad this happened?" Kailey frowned, trying to keep the conversation on track. "Ry's incredibly disappointed. He really had a shot, you know?"

Carrie met her gaze. "You really care about him, don't you?"

She hoped she managed to keep her poker face. "I don't hate him anymore, and that's a big step."

"Well, Duke and I think that Rylan's been running from something. Maybe this accident is what will make him stop running and think about settling down."

"I've had the same thought myself. But what would

he have to run from?" Kailey shifted the baby a bit, getting more comfortable.

"Duke doesn't know. He just knows that once Rylan turned eighteen he was gone. He's done nothing but move around since. Ranch to ranch, place to place, rodeos every other weekend. Avoiding anything that might be construed as a commitment."

Kailey looked up and found Rylan's gaze on her. Something warm and feminine curled through her insides, having him look at her like that.

She shifted her attention back to Carrie. "Maybe he just wanted a different adventure than Duke. You know, Duke was in the army for a lot of years. He got to move around, see different things, different people. I'm not saying it was easy…not at all. But maybe we're all a little quick to judge."

Carrie nudged her. "Oh, girlfriend, you've got it bad. You're defending him now."

Kailey shook her head. "What he did in February was wrong. I don't defend those actions at all. I'm just saying maybe people shouldn't be so quick to dismiss him."

And maybe that had been the problem all along. He'd said something about always feeling like the tagger-on, either in the way or invisible. Maybe Carrie was right. Maybe staying on at Crooked Valley was just what Rylan needed for his family to take him seriously.

Except she'd distinctly heard him say the words *until Christmas*. Nothing long term or indefinite.

She'd monopolized Evan for long enough, so she got up off the bed and walked over to where Rylan was sitting. "You want to try, Uncle Ry?"

"I've only got one arm," he cautioned. "Maybe I shouldn't."

"Your left one works fine and he's just a little thing. I'll help. You can't visit and not at least hold him for a few minutes."

He curled his arm into position and Kailey slid the baby into the strong curve, making sure his head was supported and he was held nice and tight. Rylan adjusted his shoulder and posture. "Well, would you look at that," he murmured. "Gosh, he's just a little mite. Hardly weighs anything."

"Until he cries," Duke said. "Then he gets real big, real fast."

They all laughed. Rylan settled back in the chair while Duke handed Carrie the milk and unwrapped her sandwich. The talk was much lighter as they visited, and when the food was gone, Kailey went to work and brushed and braided Carrie's hair as a treat.

"Lacey packed real pajamas for you in there," Kailey said, nodding toward the tote bag. "Tomorrow you'll be home and you can have a shower in your own bathroom and sleep in your own bed."

"That sounds heavenly."

By that time Evan was really awake and unhappy, looking for his next meal. When Carrie blushed, Kailey understood that she was going to nurse and that she wasn't quite comfortable doing that in front of people— in particular her brother-in-law.

"We should probably get going anyway," Kailey suggested. "Rather than outstay our welcome."

"I'm awfully glad you came," Carrie said, and Duke gave Kailey a quick hug. Rylan leaned over and kissed Carrie's forehead in a tender gesture that softened Kailey's heart even further.

"We'll see you in a day or so. Call if you need anything, okay?"

He really had to start being not so nice.

They headed back toward Gibson, making a pit stop along the way for supper. True to his word, Rylan sprang for burgers and fries, and they sat in his truck and ate them with the windows rolled down, Rylan manhandling his sandwich with one hand. It was about as un-date-like as Kailey could imagine, yet there was something rather intimate about sitting there with a surprisingly humid breeze pulling through the cab. The showers that had been forecast hadn't arrived yet, but as Kailey ate her fries she knew rain was coming. There was a smell in the air, a taste that she'd experienced many times over the years.

They didn't talk. There'd been a lot of talking the past few days, and instead they simply sat and ate, and enjoyed the fresh air and greasy food.

Finally, when the last fry had been eaten, and Kailey took a long pull on her soda, Rylan spoke.

"Thunderstorms are rolling in."

Indeed, the sultry air had gone cold, and the wind shushed through the leaves in a telltale whisper of impending bad weather. Through the windshield, Kailey saw dark clouds towering in the sky, gray and menacing. "Damn," she murmured. "I hope everything was dried and baled this afternoon. I probably shouldn't have gone tonight."

"Not much you can do about it now," Rylan said reasonably. They watched through the window as the cloud built and shifted, drawing nearer. A spear of lightning forked toward the ground, and despite the noise from traffic on the highway beside them, they heard the rumble of distant thunder several seconds later.

"Do you want to try to head back now, or sit through it and wait?"

"Let's drive," she said. "Rain's forecast for tomorrow, too. The showers could last for hours."

"You got it."

They were almost to Gibson when the sky darkened and the thunder could be heard over the rumble of the engine. A gust of wind grabbed at the truck, and Rylan's lips formed a grim line. "Damn, I think we're in for it now."

He no sooner got the words out of his mouth than the sky opened up, hammering down huge droplets of rain that sounded like gravel hitting the truck. Rylan turned on the wipers full blast, but the road ahead was a wall of water, reducing visibility to a few feet. He slowed, put on his four-way flashers, and when a dirt range road appeared on the right, he turned off the main drag away from other traffic.

"Wow," Kailey said, frowning. Rain was a welcome sight in summer, but not this kind, not such a downpour that it caused crop damage and run-off and flash floods.

"Wow is right," he replied, pulling off on the wide shoulder. "We might as well ride the worst of it out. You don't have a deck of cards or something in that bag, do you?"

She snorted out a laugh as he cut the engine. Without the purr of the motor, the rain was a rhythmic pounding that sheltered them from the outside world.

"Afraid not. But I have a pad of paper. We could play hangman."

His sideways grin was back. "I know who you'd like to hang," he said acidly. "Me."

"Eh, not so much these days. I'm getting used to you." She raised her eyebrow, arched it at him saucily. "That doesn't mean I like you, by the way."

"You did offer your house," he reminded her.

"Because I felt sorry for you," she replied.

"Damn," he said softly. "This is why I like you, Kailey. You never give an inch and you make me laugh."

She wanted to say likewise, but he didn't need the encouragement.

The noise on the roof of the truck intensified, and their smiles faded. "Hail," she breathed, knowing it could cause so much damage. Even with their limited vision they could see the white balls of ice bouncing off the windshield and hood.

The first storm cell eased, and Kailey thought for a minute they were going to be able to leave. But then a second cell came right behind it, complete with flashing lightning and cannon-like thunder. The safest place for them right now was exactly where they were.

She looked over at Rylan, who was staring grimly out the driver's side window. "Mind if I ask you something?"

He shrugged. "Would it matter if I did mind?"

"Probably not," she answered honestly. "There's a consensus among your family that you've spent your adult life running from something. Is there any truth in that?"

He snapped his head around to stare at her. "Is that what they're saying?"

She nodded. "That there has to be a reason why you left as soon as you were done high school. Why you haven't settled anywhere. In fact, I think you surprised the hell out of them by coming back at all."

"I like what I do. That's all."

She wondered if he'd open up if she opened up first. "I get the not wanting to be vulnerable, Ry. At the wedding when you asked why I wasn't hitched? I had a real answer that I didn't want to tell you."

"Yeah?"

"Colt Black asked me last fall. We'd been seeing each other for a while. I thought we were crazy about each other. He works in a feedlot up around Cut Bank. When he realized I wouldn't just up and leave the ranch behind, he changed his mind."

"He withdrew his proposal?" Rylan's eyes widened. "Are you serious?"

"Very." She twisted her hands in her lap. She didn't like talking about it, which was why the only person who knew what had happened was her mom. It had been impossible to hide her distress the night he'd broken it off.

"But...cripes, Kailey. You run the ranch. It couldn't run without you."

"That's what I said." She shook her head. "According to Colt, a woman followed her husband, not the other way around. I had no idea he was so...shortsighted."

"Not to mention sexist," Rylan added. "You're better off, trust me."

"I know," she whispered, her voice barely audible above the racket of the storm. "But it still hurts sometimes. I know I come across as Fun Kailey. And up until the past year or so, that was enough. But seeing Carrie so happy and Lacey... I realized I want those things, Rylan. And I almost had them."

He turned in the seat, unbuckling his seatbelt so he could face her better. "Listen," he said firmly. "Having it doesn't matter if it's with the wrong person."

She knew he was right.

Just as she knew he wasn't the right person either.

"I know that. Deep down, I do. Anyway, that's why I'm not hitched. I'm pretty much married to Brandt Ranch, and it comes with the package."

Rylan nodded. "It's a hell of a legacy. Of course you want to stay there."

She was puzzled now. "Okay, so Crooked Valley is *your* legacy. Why fight taking on your third? You always wanted to be a cowboy. You loved it here as a kid. I know you said it hurt too much to come back, but now you're here. What's keeping you from going all the way?"

He sighed, slumped in his seat. "I don't know. Fear? Stubbornness? I made myself a promise the day we drove away from here and moved to Helena. I promised myself that when I was old enough I would always, always call the shots in my own life. That no one could make me go anywhere I didn't want. I cried every night for months, wanting to come back here. My best friend was a fifteen-year-old pony named Daisy, and everyone treated me like she was a stupid pet who didn't matter and I should just get over it. I had no say. My opinion was brushed off because I was a little kid."

"Are you still angry at your mom?"

His brows pulled together as he thought. "No, not really. The ranch was my dad's family's place, and without him she didn't feel at home. She wasn't a farm girl. And she had a family to support after he was gone. She did what she had to do. I understand that. She made her decisions and I've made mine. The thing is…"

He paused then. Looked at her and then looked away. "Never mind."

For him to stop so suddenly, she knew what he'd been going to say was important.

She reached over and put her hand on his knee. "What is it, Ry?"

His gaze met hers. "I didn't want to come back here

because I was afraid I'd turn into that scared little boy again. God, that sounds silly."

"No," she answered, squeezing his thigh. "No, it doesn't. Our memories shape us into who we become. Sometimes we embrace them. Sometimes we wish we could leave them behind."

"I hate fear, do you know that?" His jaw was clenched. "My dad died and I was so scared that something might happen to my mom and we'd be left alone. Then Duke joined the army and I was afraid he'd be killed. I hate that helpless feeling."

"And yet your passion is doing something that has the potential to hurt you."

He pondered for a moment. "You know, it's my way of giving fear the finger. I will never, ever let myself be so vulnerable that I turn into that frightened little boy again."

Such as staying in one place too long. Such as forging meaningful, long-term relationships. The pieces came together for her now. It was all about self-preservation for Rylan. And damned if she didn't understand it. Wasn't that what she'd been doing for the past year?

"We end up doing some strange things in the name of protecting our hearts," she mused. "Like Valentine's Day. After we broke up, Colt moved on so fast he nearly gave himself whiplash. It stung. But when you showed up at the dance… I guess I thought it would be a good idea to show him what he'd tossed away."

Rylan's jaw dropped. "You mean I was revenge sex?"

Her cheeks heated. "This is where I owe you the apology, Ry. I was so hard on you for running out that morning, but my motives were far from pure where you were concerned. I own part of the blame for what happened."

He put his left hand to his chest. "Oh, my God. You've just shredded the last bit of my pride."

A small smile crept up her cheek. "I'm sorry, okay? I should never have gotten up on my high horse and been so rough on you. It was pride, pure and simple. Humiliation. I wasn't proud of myself, and when I woke up I had to face the music."

"I seriously think my feelings are hurt."

She patted his knee. "If it's any consolation at all, once we hit the sheets Colt Black was the furthest thing from my mind."

She'd meant to make it sound like a joke, but once the words were out there they were really out there.

Rylan let out a soft curse. "You need to warn a guy before you say something like that, K. Because if you're trying to make me forget that night, that's not the way to do it."

And neither was saying that. The rain still poured, and their minutes spent inside the truck had steamed up the windows. They were in their own little world, on a side road in the middle of a storm and nothing to do but fight the temptation that was getting heavier in the air by the second.

"Why don't you come over here," he suggested softly, locking his gaze with hers. "Come over here and kiss me like you know you want to."

"Rylan…"

"No revenge, no promises, no skipping out in the morning. Just you and me, Kailey. I'm not sure how much longer we can do this dance without something giving."

## Chapter 10

Kailey debated for all of two seconds before she tossed caution to the wind. He was right. They'd been fighting this ever since his return. And this time they both knew what they were walking into. And what they weren't.

Desire…it took over and rendered everything else irrelevant. With her gaze locked on his, she unbuckled her seat belt while Ry reached for the lever to push the bench seat all the way back. Her heart pounded and her blood raced as she crawled over the upholstery to straddle him. Everything about him was muscled and hard and sweat pooled at the base of her spine, both from the humid air in the cab and how her body heated just being close to him like this.

She cupped his jaws in her hands and lowered her mouth to his.

His lips were soft, pliant, beguiling. For long moments she simply enjoyed kissing him, tasting him, the textures of his mouth and the way his left arm came around and pressed her closer to him. Her knees were on either side of his hips and without thinking she shifted her pelvis, rubbing against him, until their breath came hard and fast. Need pounded through her, and she found herself thankful that she'd chosen the light sundress over jeans. The cotton skirt pooled around them and the only fabric that stood between her and the denim of his jeans were the silky white panties she wore.

His hand pulled on the sundress strap, sliding it roughly off her shoulder, exposing her breast.

"You didn't wear a bra," he marveled, cupping her in his hand.

"There's one built in," she breathed, and gasped as he replaced his hand with his mouth.

"Rylan," she murmured, overwhelmed. "Ry."

Need took over and she slid a bit backward, fumbling with the button and zip of his jeans, sliding them down and setting him free. Removing her panties proved a little more challenging, but they were both highly motivated now.

Lightning flashed and thunder boomed as she slid back on top of him.

"Be sure," he murmured, putting his palm on her cheek and looking her dead in the eye. "Be really sure, Kailey."

"Shut up, Ry. I don't want to talk. I just want to feel."

He peeled down the other side of her dress and they rode out the storm together.

The windows were thick with steam as the storm eased, both inside and outside of the truck. Kailey reached for the straps of her dress only to find Rylan's gentle fingers there, helping her put her clothing back in place. She retrieved her underwear from the floor and slid it over her legs while Rylan tugged at his jeans with his one good hand.

"Let me help," she murmured, and together they got his pants back on and she had him buttoned and zipped again.

"I think the rain is letting up," he said. He turned the key so that the battery was on and rolled down the window. It was nothing but a light shower now, the violent storm cells moving off to the east.

Kailey moved to her side of the seat and rolled her window down, too, clearing the moisture from the inside of the pane.

The windshield was another story. Rylan turned the key all the way and fired up the defrost. He looked over at her with a lopsided smile. "You okay, Curly?"

The nickname should bother her, but it didn't. "Better than okay," she replied, resting against the back of the seat. "I think I really needed that."

"Me, too."

She chuckled. "Hey, I bet it's been longer for me."

His eyes were so blue that she thought she might drown in them. "Let me guess. February fourteenth?"

She was pretty sure she was blushing. "Uh, yeah."

"Me, too."

That was a surprise. Her head came away from the back of the seat as she stared at him. "Really? Even with all your travel and the, uh, buckle bunnies?"

"Even with." His gaze softened. "That surprises you?"

"Well, yeah." It gave her a warm, fuzzy feeling,

knowing that she'd been the only one since the winter. "You're Rylan Duggan. Sexy bronc rider. Charming drifter."

"Charming, huh?"

"Maybe a little. Mostly a pain in my ass."

The smile he sent her was so sweet her heart ached with it.

"What happens now, Ry? No pressure, okay? I just want to know where we stand. No confusion. No… surprises."

The windshield was starting to clear, and Rylan rolled up his window most of the way to keep the light rain from getting in the cab. "I like you, Kailey. I like you a lot. I like being with you and arguing with you and God knows I like…the sex. I just can't make promises. If you're looking at me like you were looking at this Colt guy—as a settle down forever kind of thing—you're setting yourself up for disappointment. But if you know that going in and you're still interested, I want to see you again. I'm not ready for this to be over."

She'd known before tonight ever happened that this would be the outcome if they ever gave in to their desires. Knowing it didn't stop the little bit of disappointment from hearing him say it, though. If they carried on, it was with the full knowledge that it was short term. An affair.

The big question was how badly did she want him? Enough to agree to this kind of an arrangement, knowing the conclusion in advance? Would it be worth it?

Then she got the strange stirring deep in her pelvis simply from the memory of making love to him. Being with Ry was like having the earth shift beneath her feet, like fireworks, like nothing she'd ever experienced. Could she really let that go so soon?

"I'm not ready for it to be over either," she whispered. "I don't know what you do to me, Ry, but I'm not going to be satisfied with just tonight."

He shifted on the seat, scooting over to be closer to her. She turned her face up to his and he kissed her, long and deep.

"I love your honesty," he said, his lips by her ear. "I swear to God, it turns me on."

"You're crazy."

"You're just figuring that out now?" He nibbled on her earlobe, teasing.

If he wasn't careful, she was going to start climbing all over him again.

"You want to stay at the house tonight?" he asked, and to add a little persuasion, he slid his tongue down the tendon of her neck.

She shivered. "I'd better not tonight. I don't have a change of clothes, and my parents will wonder if I don't come home. Not that I need their permission, but I'd rather avoid that awkward conversation tomorrow morning."

"It's your house."

"And they know I haven't moved in yet." She touched her finger to the tip of his nose. "Don't be so impatient."

"Can you blame me? I just had my mind blown. I'd like for that to happen again." He winked at her. "As soon as possible."

"Tomorrow night," she suggested. "I'll bring a load of stuff over after dinner. It might take me a while to get back home again."

"It's a date."

They were doing this. Embarking on an affair. It was all terribly exciting, yet she couldn't quite rid herself of the nagging feeling that it wasn't going to turn out happily in the end. Would they be able to walk away unscathed?

Could she truly let go and just enjoy the moment for once?

Now that the steam was gone from the windows, Rylan put the truck in gear and they pulled a U-turn, headed back toward the main road and Gibson. The road was washed clean from the rain, and the sky was lightening to the west, little lines of peach and purple marking the sunset.

He dropped her off at home. Drops of rain still clung to the flowers and shrubs surrounding her porch. "Thanks for dinner," she said softly, picking up her purse. "I, uh, had a really nice time."

"Me, too, K. Me, too."

There was an awkward moment where she was undecided about whether or not to kiss him good-night. He put the truck in Park and faced her, his eyes twinkling.

"Is this one of those 'do we or don't we' moments?"

She laughed, her breath coming out in a soft, feminine sound she hadn't known she was capable of making. "Kind of," she replied.

"I vote for do. Then I can take the taste of your lips home with me."

Had she really called him charming earlier? It was more than that. Rylan knew how to be sweet. And if he wasn't sincere, he definitely had a knack of appearing convincing.

She leaned in partway, he did, too, and they kissed

goodbye, a sweet, lingering kiss that ended with a soft parting of lips and a sigh. At least on her part.

"Good night, Kailey."

"Good night, Ry."

She opened her door and hopped out of the truck, then slid her purse strap over her shoulder. At the bottom of the porch steps she turned around and gave a little wave, and he lifted one finger off the steering wheel in a casual acknowledgment. Then he put the truck in gear and headed back out the driveway.

It turned out that having a relationship with Rylan wasn't as fraught with difficulty as she'd expected. Work on the ranches kept them busy during the day, and Rylan moved back to Crooked Valley after the single night they spent at her house. She wondered if it was because staying at her house would have felt a little too much like something permanent, but she tried not to dwell on it. For right now, living their own lives with their own purposes seemed to be working well.

Rylan's shoulder improved and his bruising faded, and he dutifully went to his physical therapy appointments, wanting to be completely healed and healthy to return to competition.

The haying was mostly finished for the season and on her visits to Crooked Valley, Kailey spent time with Carrie and little Evan, and helped Lacey in the kitchen during her first year of putting up garden harvest. Kailey had been doing it with her mom for years, so she spent fun evenings helping Lacey can tomatoes, green and yellow beans, carrots, beets and dill pickles. When they were done, she and Rylan often would go for a walk in the moonlight. Sometimes they'd miraculously end up at his camper, satisfying their hunger for each other that never seemed to go away.

One of Kailey's mares came into heat and they bred her to Rattler, hoping for a healthy foal the next summer. During a particularly hot dry spell, they met at the swimming hole after quitting time and made love in the cool, refreshing water, laughing at some of the awkward logistics but totally enamored with the feel of the cool water on their hot skin. Afterward, they lay on the grassy bank on soft towels, and Rylan made love to her again, slowly and thoroughly, so that when they parted ways she was sure she gave off a glow the whole way home.

In September, Brandt was taking a fair number of stock to a rodeo in Lewiston. The foreman who normally traveled with the stock was taking a little vacation since his wife had just had their fourth baby, so Kailey decided to make the trip herself. A few days before, she asked Rylan to go with her.

They were over at the Brandt spread, walking back from the east pasture when she put forth the invite.

"So… Lewiston coming up this week."

"Weather looks good. You're traveling with the crew?"

She nodded, but her heart was pounding like crazy. Why was she so nervous about asking him, anyway? "Have you missed it?"

"Missed what?" He looked over at her, his eyes shadowed from the sun by his hat. Truth be told, she never got tired of looking at him. The sexy quirk to his lips, the strong jaw, the little bit of reddish-brown hair that curled just above his collar… Rylan Duggan was as sexy as they came.

"The show. I mean, you lived it every weekend up until a month ago." He'd stopped wearing his sling after the first two weeks, and was slowly working on getting strength and mobility back.

"I do," he confessed. "Don't get me wrong, working with the horses at home has been good. But yeah, I miss it." He grinned. "Maybe I have an addiction."

*Just ask him*, a voice in her head said.

"So…why don't you come with me? We're leaving Tuesday at noon and coming back Saturday night. It'll be busy, but you can take in the competition, see some of the guys, and I'll have some company other than Dan and Jim." She named the two hands who would be traveling with her. "Not that there's anything wrong with them, but, well, there's generally just chew, spitting and monosyllables."

He stopped and looked at her. "You're asking me to spend four nights with you in a motel?"

Her courage started to wither. "Too much?"

"I don't know."

At least he was being honest. She tried hard not to be disappointed, and most of the time she tried not to think about where their relationship was going or what was around the corner. But it was hard. She wanted to spend time with him…real time, not just sneaking in romantic rendezvous every few days.

"If it would make you more comfortable, I could book you your own room," she offered. "And you don't have to come. I just…thought I'd put the offer out there in case you wanted to get away for a few days." She offered a bright smile. No big deal.

"Kailey." He came up beside her again and took her

hand. "Believe me, there is nothing I'd like more than four days locked up in a motel room with you."

She swallowed. That was how they'd started, after all. In a motel room. She actually hadn't thought of that until just now. But this wasn't February, it was September. And clearly this wasn't a one-night thing. They'd been seeing each other for weeks. Then again, if he went with her and stayed in the motel with her, their secret relationship wouldn't be so secret anymore.

"Well, think about it. The offer's open, but my feelings won't be hurt if you say no."

It was a complete lie, but she wanted it to be true. That should count for something, right?

"I'd like to go," he said, squeezing her hand. "You're right. I have missed the scene, a lot. It'll be strange not competing, but it'll be fun, too. And I can give you a hand now and again."

"Great," she said, relieved and a little bit excited. "Come over on Tuesday. The guys can take the trailers and I can drive with you, if that's okay."

"Sounds just fine," he agreed.

They were in sight of the house now and he dropped her hand. Kailey held back a sigh. At first the sneaking around had been exciting. Now, though, it was starting to feel old. Instead of a secret it was something different. Something…less. She discovered there was a big difference between wanting to keep something to yourself and wanting to keep it from other people.

"Thanks for the walk," she said, slowing her steps. "I suppose I should get inside and give Mom a hand. Her migraines have been acting up, and she's been trying to keep up with the last of the garden."

"Do you ever stop?" he asked. It wasn't a criticism.

One thing she could say about Ry, he didn't seem threatened by her drive and work ethic. Maybe that came from being raised by a single mom who'd had to work hard to support her family.

"Occasionally," she replied.

They stopped by his truck and he opened the door. Before he hopped in, he pulled her close and kissed her, his soft lips melded to hers.

She wished she hadn't noticed that the truck and open door hid them from any eyes that might see what they were up to.

"G'night, beautiful," he said, hopping into the cab and throwing her a wink.

"Good night, Ry."

He drove off in a cloud of dust, leaving her standing in the yard.

She'd walked into this with her eyes wide open, so she couldn't expect too much. Instead she turned around and headed for the house, prepared to help her mom and keep busy so she didn't spend any more time thinking about what their relationship was…and wasn't.

## Chapter 11

To say that Ry was having second thoughts was a massive understatement.

He pulled into the Brandt yard, duffel bag beside him on the seat, ready for four days of rodeo and four nights with a beautiful woman.

To anyone else, it had to look as if he had life right by the tail.

To Ry, it was an uncomfortable realization that he'd agreed to this even though he knew it meant a giant step forward for their relationship. A relationship that was supposed to be based solely on enjoying each other with no plans beyond the here and now.

But even Rylan knew that you didn't spend four whole days with a woman without it meaning something.

The yard was a hive of activity. The hands were in the throes of loading stock into trailers, ready to make the drive to Lewiston. Kailey's dad was there, too, supervising alongside his daughter, who had her honey-streaked hair pulled up in a ponytail and sunglasses shading her eyes. She lifted her hand to her forehead as if the sun was in her way, and he accepted the truth: he was far more involved with Kailey Brandt than he'd ever wanted to be. Not far behind that little nugget of honesty was a second. It wasn't caring about her that was freaking him out. It was the fact that he *wasn't* freaking out about it that had him panicking.

He should just come up with a good excuse and make his apologies. They could distance themselves slowly, ease away from each other and just be friends again.

Then he thought of Kailey's sharp tongue and hot temper and realized that would never be an option. She was too much of a firecracker.

A smile bloomed on her face the moment she saw his truck, and he saw her lean over and say something to her dad. The senior Brandt had a stern face that Rylan couldn't read, but he could take a pretty good guess. Kailey was his only child and a daughter, no less.

He hopped out of the truck. "Looks like you're in the thick of it," he called out, crossing the yard.

"Nearly done. Jim's loading the bulls now. We should be on the road in the next thirty. Your timing's great."

They walked back over to where Mr. Brandt was standing with his arms folded across his chest. Formidable. Rylan couldn't help but respect him for it.

"Afternoon, Mr. Brandt." He held out his hand. "Good to see you again."

Brandt shook his hand, a firm grip that held just a little bit of threat. "Duggan. Heard you're traveling with this circus this afternoon."

"Yes, sir. The accident sidelined me and I have to

confess, I've missed it. I'm looking forward to watching some events, lending a hand when I can."

Kailey had started chewing on a fingernail, but she dropped her hand as if she'd suddenly realized she was doing it. "Oh, Rylan, I booked your room for you."

"Thanks for looking after that," he said, understanding. Perhaps they weren't as far apart on this relationship thing as he thought. She was certainly making an effort to make it appear as though they weren't together.

There was a shout and Kailey trotted off to see what the fuss was about, leaving Rylan beside her dad.

"Rylan, I'm not a stupid man. I can see how things are."

"Yes, sir." He'd half expected to get some sort of "talk" this afternoon. Brandt wasn't going to beat around the bush. Rylan figured that was where Kailey got her direct nature.

"I don't need to say anything more, do I, son?"

Rylan shook his head. "No, sir. That's your little girl out there and she's also the person who's going to run this ranch. In other words, she's not a woman to trifle with."

"You might be smarter than I gave you credit for," Brandt said gruffly.

Rylan looked Kailey's father in the eye. "Begging your pardon, sir, but you know Kailey better than me. So I'm sure you know that she's made her wishes and thoughts crystal clear. She is one of the most forthright women I've ever known."

Brandt chuckled a little. "That doesn't scare you?"

"Of course not. Women are hard to understand. One who says exactly what she means? That's like breaking the secret code right there."

There was silence again as they both watched Kailey shut the trailer and latch it, then dust off her hands.

"Just for the record," Brandt said, his voice firm once again. "I'm not entirely happy about this situation."

"Yes, sir."

"But she's a grown woman. She's got to make her own choices and I respect that."

"Me, too," Rylan agreed.

"All right then," Brandt said.

A few minutes later the convoy was rolling out the yard, Kailey perched on Rylan's truck seat, her eyes alight with excitement. "So," she said, her tone a little too conversational to be natural. "You and my dad. Talk about anything interesting?"

Rylan looked over and then back at the road. "The weather."

"Right." She laughed a little. "Try again."

"Let's just say we understand each other and leave it at that."

"He's not going to show up at the motel tonight with a shotgun?"

Rylan shook his head. "I doubt it. After all, I'll be in my own room."

When Kailey didn't offer a smart remark, he glanced over at her. Damned if she wasn't blushing. "Kailey?"

She bit down on her lip. "Well, there isn't exactly another room. I just said that so Dad would think we weren't staying together."

He wasn't sure if he was relieved or disappointed. "You don't think his spies will fill him in the moment we get back?"

"Maybe, but then the trip's over and done with." Her grin flashed again. "If you asked him what I was like as a kid, he'd tell you I was a great one for asking forgiveness rather than permission."

"I bet."

"You want to share driving? We'll probably gas up in Missoula and then go straight through." She changed the subject.

"We'll see. I'm used to long drives, K. And I'm not even hauling anything this time. Six hours is nothing."

"Well, let me know then. It's a pretty drive. I haven't gone for a few years, but you can't beat it for scenery."

They were content not to talk for a long time. Instead the music on the radio and the sweeping foothills leading to the mountains kept them content. In Missoula they stopped for gas and a quick snack. Dinner would be later in the evening, as they'd have to get the stock settled before any of them could head to the motel for the night.

At one point Rylan looked over and realized that Kailey had fallen asleep, her head tipped to one side, bolstered a bit by the strap of the seat belt on her shoulder. She was so beautiful, but so wrapped up in the ranch and everything going on that he was pretty sure she didn't realize how incredible she was.

He had some decisions to make and soon. He was enjoying Crooked Valley more than he expected. In Wyoming, he'd been a hand on a cattle ranch. It had been good work and he'd had a great boss, but working with the rough stock at Crooked Valley was surprisingly fulfilling. He knew he'd told Duke that he would stay on until Christmas so that the terms of the will would be fulfilled, but the thought of leaving the ranch made him feel a little bit empty inside. Who would care for Rattler and the other horses? Where would he be next summer when Candyfloss foaled? Quinn was doing an okay job, but he'd been happy to leave the decisions to

Rylan, saying a smart man played to his strengths and acknowledged his weaknesses. Plus, with Carrie and Duke starting a family, Quinn was taking on more of Carrie's foreman duties.

And then there was the woman sleeping beside him. This was the longest he'd ever stayed with anyone. He'd gotten very good at picking out women who were only out for a good time so he could avoid romantic complications. That hadn't worked with Kailey. He was in it up to his neck.

And finally, there was the rodeo. It was in his blood. He couldn't deny that he was looking forward to the next few days because being on the fairgrounds, listening to conversations, smelling the food booths' savory offerings and watching the events would feel like being home. Heck, it had been his home for the past few years.

Kailey woke up about a half hour from Lewiston. He figured she must have been tired from the long work days. Once she rubbed her eyes her energy was renewed and she was raring to go. "Oh, my gosh. We're almost there! I slept a long time."

"Yes, you did. Missed the prettiest part, too. But I didn't have the heart to wake you."

She smiled. "There's always the drive back."

They made it to the fairgrounds in good time, and everyone worked together to get the stock unloaded and cared for for the night. When Kailey told Dan and Jim she'd hang around for a while to make sure things were okay, they shook their heads.

"No, ma'am," Jim said. "One of us will do that. We all usually take turns anyway, and I ain't got a damned thing going on tonight."

"You arguing with the boss, Jim?"

Rylan chuckled down low. Jim had to know that was a battle he'd lose.

"No, ma'am. Just suggesting you enjoy tonight 'cause it's gonna get real busy around here." Rylan figured Kailey had been right about the chew when Jim spat off to the side. "You and Rylan should go get a nice dinner or something."

That she didn't automatically contradict him surprised Rylan. Finally she gave a shrug. "You're sure?"

"Sure I'm sure. We can handle things. We would've if you hadn't come, wouldn't we?"

"Yes, I guess you would. Everything's taken care of at the motel. I guess I'll see you in the morning."

"Yes, ma'am." Jim had done the talking, but Dan touched the brim of his hat and grinned.

They were back in Rylan's truck and Kailey frowned. "You really think everything's okay?"

Rylan laughed. "Gosh, you really haven't traveled with the crew in a while, have you? Look, they'll make sure everything's fine and then they'll grab a few beers and head back to the motel. Could be that having the boss lady along is cramping their style a bit."

She looked at him, her worry deepening the crease between her eyes. "Hey," he added, "that doesn't mean they won't do their jobs. It just means that they'll be extra careful about being well-behaved. You're their boss. And you're a lady. There are…sensibilities."

She snorted. "Rylan, I've been working with ranch hands since I started walking. I think I've heard it all."

"Yep," he agreed. "And those men respect you. So they'll step up and go the extra mile for you this week. You didn't have to come along. You could have sent someone else. But they know that they work with you, not just for you. And I'm guessing they admire that about you a lot."

He knew he did. She was some woman. Tough and strong when she needed to be, and soft and tender, too.

"So, where do you want to go to eat? Any ideas? I'm starving."

They ended up heading through town and stopping at a Mexican place, but instead of sitting to eat, they ordered takeout, stopped for a six-pack of beer, and took it all back to the motel. Kailey insisted she was too dirty and smelly to be in polite company, and what she really wanted was some chow and a hot shower. That suited Ry just fine, and before long they were checked into their room and sitting at the little table with takeout trays of enchiladas and Spanish rice spread over the top and two semi-cold beers ready to wash it all down.

After their messy but tasty meal, Kailey disappeared into the bathroom for a hot shower and Rylan shoved all their garbage into a paper bag and put it in the waste basket. He cracked open another beer and parted the curtains, staring out the window at his truck parked in front of the room and the rather dreary lot across from the motel. He still wasn't convinced he should have said yes to the trip. In all his years of traveling to rodeos and fairs he'd managed to stay free of the relationship trap. Sometimes he'd indulged in what was offered, sometimes not, but never had he let his heart get involved. And never had he given any woman false hope for the future. He was terrified that that was what he was doing right now. And hurting Kailey was the last thing he ever wanted to do.

She came out of the bathroom, letting out a cloud of steam and floral scent. He turned around and his fingers tightened around his beer. She was wrapped in one of the motel's white towels, nothing more, her wet hair slicked back from her face like a mermaid's.

He shut the curtains.

She was fresh-faced, radiant, devoid of makeup or perfect hair. Just a woman in a towel. He swallowed, his throat thick with truth. Not just a woman. His woman. He'd been trying to deny it for some time now, but it was no use. He was falling for her and hard. She was going to make leaving Crooked Valley so difficult, but he wasn't going to think about that right now. Couldn't. Right now there was just her, and him, and eight hours before they had to be up and at the roundup.

Kailey turned the top on her bottle of water and took a long swig. Early September could be cool or it could be blistering hot and today it was hot. She could see the waves of heat shimmering in the air as competition got under way in the afternoon. Today one of their bulls, Brandt's Boilermaker, would be in the lineup. This was the first year they'd put Boiler in the arena, and so far he'd done well. She had her fingers crossed for an exciting show today.

Rylan came up beside her carrying two hot dogs. "Hey, you've got to eat. I brought some more water, too." A bottle bulged out the left chest pocket of his shirt. "It's a hot one for sure."

"Thanks," she answered, taking the hot dog and giving him a smile. Rylan had been different the past few days. Sometimes she got the feeling he was distant, as though his mind was somewhere else. But then other times she was the center of his focus. She'd never felt as cherished or loved as she had these past nights. There

was a care in his lovemaking that hadn't been there before. The fire still burned as hot as ever, but there was
more, and she knew she was falling in love with him.

In her head she knew she should stop. That it was no
good. But then another sort of logic reminded her that
you couldn't just dictate feelings and turn them on and
off. They were what they were. And with the change in
Rylan…well, maybe he was feeling it, too. Maybe they
stood a chance…if they just took it slowly.

"You having fun?" she asked after chewing and swal-
lowing a mouthful of bun.

"I am. It sucks being up here instead of down there."
He nodded toward the chutes. "But it's fun to watch, too,
and not have to worry about competing." He balled up his
napkin. "I kinda miss the prize money, too, but what's
done is done. I can't change it. Might as well accept it."

He took a big drink of water. "Besides, it's been kind
of fun, working with the stock back home. I like it better than what I was doing before."

That was good, wasn't it? There were still a couple
of months left before the anniversary of Joe's death.
Maybe Rylan would change his mind. Stay on. He still
could compete next year, when he was back in shape.
And since that night at the hospital, he'd never once
mentioned his leave-by date. He'd only talked about
the business and his ideas for it.

"You've started implementing some good strategies,"
Kailey agreed. "Have you had any requests for Rattler's
DNA? That would help your bottom line a lot."

He nodded. "I've been talking to a few people here
that I know. To be honest, they were just sort of polite
about it. Until I mentioned where I got Rattler and that
we'd already bred him to one of Brandt's mares. That

made their ears perk up a bit. I hope that's okay. I know I'm just along to enjoy the rodeo..."

"Don't be silly." She smiled over at him. "You'd be foolish not to take advantage of connections while you're here. Wasn't that one of the reasons you wanted my help to begin with?"

He nodded, then reached over and squeezed her hand. "I just didn't want you to think I was using you," he said.

His low voice made everything in her go warm and squishy. "Of course not." The announcer called the next event and she nudged his arm. "Bull riding's about to start. Boilermaker's in this round."

They watched the events together. Kailey didn't go down to check on the guys until things were winding up for the day. She'd learned very quickly that not only were Jim and Dan fully capable, but the smartest thing for her to do was to step back and trust them to do their jobs. She stepped in when needed, and was always around to answer questions, and she also had a good chat with the on-site veterinarian. But mostly she enjoyed the week, the energetic atmosphere and being with Rylan.

Thursday night's dinner was take-out pizza. They'd started to enjoy taking their meal back to the motel, where they could kick off their boots and chill with a beer after the hot, dry days. Kailey looked at Ry over her slice and felt a wave of love wash over her. There was no denying it. She was in love with Rylan. No turning back, no reasoning it away. She loved how he looked, how he smiled, the way he teased his sister, the way he was patient with Amber, how he sat a horse and how he cared far more about things than he ever let on.

"What?" he asked, putting down his pizza and wiping his fingers on a napkin.

"Just this," she murmured, getting up from the chair. She went to him and he turned to face her, an expectant look on his perfect face. She put her hands on his shoulders and leaned down for a hot, searing kiss.

"Miss Brandt," he whispered. "I do declare."

"Declare what?" she asked, nibbling on his bottom lip. She heard the sharp intake of his breath.

"Declare that you're about to seduce me."

"You could be right."

A smile spread across his face, an expression of delight and with that ever-present teasing light to his eyes. "By all means," he said, sitting back in the chair. "I'm most willing to be seduced."

Another thing about Rylan. He was perfectly okay with not always being the one in control.

Slowly, as slowly as she could stand it, she slipped the buttons out of the holes of his shirt, then pushed the fabric off his shoulders. His chest was broad and strong, with a small swatch of reddish brown hair at the base of his neck and around his nipples. She unbuttoned the cuffs and slid the sleeves off his arms, then dropped the shirt on the floor without taking her eyes off his face. She loved him, wanted to kiss him everywhere, but she knew the number one way to drive him crazy was to show him what was in store.

So she stood just out of his reach, and slipped off her jeans. Then she unbuttoned her shirt, dropped it to the floor, and stood before him in a pale pink lace bra and a matching pair of bikinis that didn't really cover much of anything.

"Kailey," he uttered, his voice hoarse as he sat up straight in his chair.

But she took a step backward, letting him know it wasn't quite time. Instead she reached behind her back, undid the bra and let it fall down her arms to the floor. The panties followed suit, until she was naked before him.

Her gaze met his. Not just naked. Bare. In every way she could be without actually saying the words.

Slowly he got up from the chair. Took the two steps required to stand in front of her, but still he didn't touch her. He waited, as if he knew this time was for her, and she saw his chest rise and fall with the effort of standing perfectly still.

She reached for the waistband of his jeans. Undid it, then the zipper, then knelt and slid them down his legs until he could step out of them. Only his shorts remained, and she let her hand brush strategically against them before grabbing the waistband and disposing of them to the growing pile of clothing on the floor.

She reached for his hand. Lifted it, kissed it and placed it on her breast.

It was silent permission, and for long moments they kissed and touched until Kailey was sure she couldn't stand much longer. They moved to the bed, but if she'd thought things would move faster now, she was greatly mistaken. With more care and tenderness than she thought possible, Rylan made love to her so thoroughly her body hummed with satisfaction and her heart was so full she thought it might overflow.

She looked up at him, braced above her, and felt tears gather in the corners of her eyes. The words sat on her tongue but she couldn't bring herself to say them, too afraid they would ruin everything.

So she said them in her heart instead, wondering if he could feel them through their connection.

*I love you, Rylan. I love you.*

# Chapter 12

She lay asleep beside him, naked between the plain white sheets, her hair spread on the pillow like a gold wave of summer wheat.

He was wide awake.

Rylan was still reeling from what had happened. From the moment she'd abandoned her food and walked over to where he'd been sitting, something had been different. Electric. It had just been...more.

Seeing her undress, offer herself like that to him, it had shaken him to the core, both sexually and emotionally. Until tonight he hadn't known what it really was to make love, but when they'd come together that was exactly what it had been. Love. Not just bodies but hearts.

God help him.

He turned onto his side and watched her sleep, reached out and tucked a piece of hair behind her ear so it didn't fall over her face. How had this happened?

Yet he'd known it was possible. Of course he had, in his hesitation to even come here with her this week. Things had been getting a little too comfortable. Too serious. It had been like this from the beginning. He'd just been pretending otherwise.

He loved her. It scared him to death. Almost as much as it scared him to think about staying at Crooked Valley indefinitely. Making that commitment to Lacey and Duke and investing so much of himself in any one single thing went against everything he had wanted for himself.

He sighed. But Kailey never moved. He'd discovered she was an incredibly sound sleeper. In the mornings he almost had to shake her awake since she merely slapped away at the snooze button on the clock radio, all without waking.

In the silence of the night there was a buzzing sound.

He reached over to the nightstand and grabbed his phone, frowning at the lit display. It was definitely his that was buzzing, and the number that came up was Duke's.

He slid out of bed and scooted into the bathroom to answer.

"Hello?"

"Rylan?"

"Carrie?"

"Yeah. I'm sorry to bother you, but…"

It was after midnight. If that weren't reason enough, something in her voice sent warning bells screaming through his head. "What's wrong?"

"It's Rattler. There's…been an accident."

His stomach seemed to plummet clear to his feet. "What happened?"

Carrie's voice was shaky. "We think it was a mountain lion. The vet's out here now, but I thought you ought to know."

He sat on the edge of the tub and pinched the bridge of his nose. Seventeen grand. The hopes for the whole program at Crooked Valley. But more than that, he felt sick at the thought of the pain and fear his horse was going through. "How bad," he breathed.

"Bad enough." She choked up a little. "Duke's with him now. They've got him sedated." He heard her gulp. "I've never heard a horse scream like that in my life."

There was nothing else to do. He had to head back to the ranch…tonight. As it was, he wouldn't make it back until early morning, and that was driving straight through. But Rattler was his horse. He was the biggest investment they'd put into the ranch and his responsibility, not Duke's or Quinn's.

"I'm coming back," he said to Carrie. "Go ahead and do what needs to be done to help him, okay? I'll hit the road in the next thirty."

"You're sure?"

"I'm sure. It's not like I'm competing or anything. This is more important. Tell Duke I'll see him as soon as I can."

"Okay, Rylan. Whatever you say."

He hung up, feeling slightly surprised at Carrie's response. *Whatever you say.* As if he was in charge of anything…

He ran his hand through his hair. He'd think of that later. Right now he had to get his stuff together and get going.

As Kailey slept on, he packed up his jeans and shirts and toiletries, shoved a few pieces of forgotten pizza in a paper bag and grabbed an unopened bottle of cola, thinking he could use the caffeine hit on the road. When he was all ready to leave, he went to the side of the bed and sat on the edge.

"Kailey," he said gently, putting a hand on her bare shoulder.

Nothing. He smiled softly, loving this little quirk about her. The woman, as she was about everything else, was serious about sleeping. Efficient. He gave her shoulder a little shake. "Kailey, wake up."

"Mmm," she murmured, but that was it. She rolled away from him and let out a deep breath.

"Kailey," he said again, but nothing.

He could really press matters and wake her. But she looked so soft and peaceful he didn't have the heart to do it. Still, he couldn't just leave. Not after what had happened between them before.

He grabbed the complimentary motel notepad and pen and wrote out a quick message.

K, there's been an accident with Rattler and I had to rush back to Crooked Valley. I'm sorry to leave in the night but it doesn't look good and it's my job to look after him. If you can't get a ride back with the guys call me and I'll come back to get you on Saturday night. I'm so sorry...thanks for this week. It's been amazing.

He hesitated over how to sign it. In the end he decided on a breezy, See you soon, Ry.

He ripped the sheet off the tablet and propped it up against the lamp on the dresser next to his room key. He shouldered his bag, grabbed the packet of pizza and gave her one last, lingering look, imprinting the image of her sleeping face on his mind before opening the door.

A cold front had come in during the evening and the stiff breeze that came with it caught the door, nearly pulling it from his hand. He stepped outside and then closed the door as gently as he could, hoping the sudden gust hadn't awakened Kailey. Seconds later he was in his truck, his bag on the seat beside him, backing out of the parking space and making his way through town to the highway that would take him home.

Kailey rolled over, squinted at the clock radio beside the bed. Seven forty? Surely Rylan would have gotten her up by now?

And then she realized that the other side of the bed was empty. And had been for some time. The sheets were cool.

"Ry?"

The shower wasn't running. And it didn't sound as though anyone was in there, either. Kailey was in the motel room all alone.

She crawled out of bed stark naked and hastily pulled on underwear and a shirt from a pile on the floor. She peeked through the curtains and saw that his truck was gone. Maybe he'd been up early and had just run out for some breakfast. He'd come back with coffee and sausage biscuits, and it would all be okay. She'd be a little late to the roundup but it would be fine.

She had a quick shower and dressed and when she came out of the bathroom he still wasn't back. A little beat of warning pulsed through her brain.

And then she realized his bag was gone. And so

was his toothbrush and shampoo and anything that said Rylan Duggan had been here. It was seriously as if... he hadn't been there at all. All except the room key card, left propped up against the base of the lamp on the dresser.

He'd run.

The first sensation she felt was numbness, taking over her whole body, including her brain. For a few minutes the only words that would form in her head were *not again*. He wouldn't, couldn't have snuck out in the middle of the night as he had the last time, could he?

Could he?

She shoved her bottom back on the bed, pulled her knees up to her chest. Oh God. Oh God oh God oh God. Her breath started coming fast and shallow, her heart beat fast. She wouldn't panic. She'd hold herself together.

Only she couldn't. Because the last time it had just been one night. One single night, not weeks of caring for each other, not months. In February she hadn't been *in love* with him.

Like she was now.

Oh God.

Like she was now.

The tears she didn't want came anyway, streaking down her cheeks, forced out by sobs that choked her throat. "Why?" she cried softly, dropping her head to her knees. Why now? Why did he have to leave without a word in the middle of the night like a coward? Why did he have to break her heart just when she'd decided to trust him with it?

All the while the room key stared at her, accusing her of being a fool. Not just once, which had been difficult enough, but twice now. With the same man. The man who'd told her he was not permanent. Who'd made it clear from the beginning that he was just passing through.

Just who was the idiot here?

That was them. The idiot and the…she filled in the blank under her breath, the initial numbing pain transitioning to righteous anger.

He'd left her in a motel room six hours from home. When everyone knew he was there with her this week.

She thought of his face last night as he'd held her in his arms. He'd looked deeply into her eyes. Whispered her name. She'd been so sure. So very sure that this was a giant step forward for them. That he felt the same way for her as she did for him. Remembering that moment caused something deep inside her to shrivel up and die.

For some reason, men loved her. But they didn't ever love her enough. She was never their everything. Their reason for breathing. The light in the darkness. Not like the way Quinn looked at Lacey. Or the way Duke smiled at Carrie as she held their baby son.

Kailey fell back among the sheets and finally let it out. All the disillusionment, the heartache, the humiliation and pain. She cried into the sheets until she was spent.

When she finally blinked her painful eyelids, she checked her watch. Eight-thirty. She couldn't show up like this. She had to get herself together. First thing to do was text Jim and let him know she was running late, ask if there was anything urgent and she'd catch up with him in a bit. She frowned and decided she'd pick up some doughnuts and coffee on the way as a peace offering.

Next she got out of bed and went to the bathroom, ran a sink of cold water, retrieved a washcloth from the towel bar and laid the cool cloth over her face, hoping to minimize the redness and puffiness. What she really wanted to do was collapse on Carrie's sofa with a bottle of wine and bawl out her troubles.

But Carrie didn't live in her little house anymore, and it felt awkward crying on her shoulder now that she was married with a family of her own. Lives changed…

At least some did. Some didn't, even when a girl tried.

She let the cold water work before patting her face dry and surveying the damage. It wasn't pretty. Defiantly she reached for her makeup bag. She usually didn't wear much to the rodeo grounds, but desperate times called for desperate measures. The only way she could get through today…and tomorrow…was to put Rylan Duggan at the back of her mind. Not spare him a single thought. She was Kailey Brandt, general manager of Brandt Ranch. Strong and capable. Maybe she'd been stupid to chafe against her commitment there, because one thing she could say about the ranch: never once had it let her down.

Moisturizer, concealer, foundation, powder. She used them all to smooth out her complexion, and then added a swipe of clear lip gloss and a coat of mascara on her lashes.

She examined herself in the mirror. Not perfect, but perhaps fixed enough that it looked as if she'd not had much sleep versus a ginormous crying jag over a man who wasn't worth it.

She scowled. "You are not going to think about him," she instructed her reflection in a stern voice.

The other issue right now was transportation. She'd traveled with Rylan, and the guys were already gone, so she'd have to find another way to the rodeo grounds.

Her lower lip quivered in a moment of weakness; she bit it and stopped the trembling.

Rylan's key sat defiantly on the dresser and she left it there. This time she wouldn't deliver his key or anything else to the motel office. It could damn well sit there until the end of the world for all she cared.

The taxi she'd called arrived and stoically she got inside, gave the address to the driver and prepared herself to face the day.

Rylan Duggan was not the end of the world.

She wouldn't let him be.

The rest of the rodeo seemed to drag on twice as long as the first two days. Kailey let go of her hands-off approach and dug in and worked side by side with Jim and Dan, getting her boots and hands dirty. Friday night she went back to the room and took a long bath and opened a bottle of wine she'd grabbed when Jim had stopped for some beer on the way back to the motel. Normally she wasn't for self-medicating, but she could still smell Rylan in the room and she shifted between anger and sadness depending on the moment. Three glasses in she brushed her teeth and crawled beneath the sheets, hoping for eight hours of oblivion. Tomorrow afternoon they had a horse in the finals, and after that they'd be packing up and making the long drive home, arriving sometime close to midnight. The idea of being home in her own bed was soothing. She only had to make it twenty-four hours and she could stop this pretense.

The only person who'd asked about Rylan had been

Jim. Dan was working away behind him and Jim had asked where Rylan was. She'd tried to keep her expression and voice neutral as she explained briefly that Rylan had needed to return to Crooked Valley, and would Jim mind if she hitched a ride back with him? He couldn't exactly say no, and she wasn't about to share personal details with an employee, no matter how friendly they all were.

On Saturday morning Kailey was up and ready to go by seven-thirty, and she and Jim drove to the grounds together. Her heart was still hurting, and she was still angrier than she ever remembered being. But she was holding it together. At some point she'd let everything out, but not now. She let the anger feed her composure until she was a model of efficiency and straight-up business.

The finals began right after lunch and Kailey put her personal feelings aside and focused on Lucifer, their bareback entry into the competition. He was smaller than Crooked Valley's Rattler, and compact, well-suited to bareback competition and with a glistening jet-black coat that made him a treat to watch.

When the time came, he was loaded into the chute, his hooves stomping as he tossed his mane. The cowboy who'd drawn him was a twenty-five-year-old out of Oklahoma who had the highest score going into the final. Kailey crossed her fingers as she waited for the door to open. A good ride for both cowboy and horse would mean good things. Brandt stock was in demand; Kailey wanted to keep it that way.

The horn sounded, the chute opened and horse and rider burst into the arena. Lucifer lived up to his name, bucking like the devil, throwing in a few turns and twists trying to unseat his rider. Eight seconds later it was all over, with a clean ride and the wait for final points. When the board lit up, Kailey grinned from ear to ear. An eighty-seven…a damned good mark, and good scoring for both competitors.

Lucifer was their last competitor, so Kailey took a long breath and exhaled it. She wished they could simply load up and leave right now, since their part of the competition was over. But Jim and Dan had spent the whole week following standings and performances. The extra hour and a bit to let them watch the finals wasn't too much to ask.

One good thing about it was that they'd checked out of the motel that morning. For the first time since he left, Kailey had picked up Rylan's key card, only to return it to the main office with her own. Her bag was in Jim's truck. The dried-up pizza and box were in the trash and she could start putting this behind her. For good. She'd given Rylan a second chance, but she wouldn't be giving him a third.

The bull-riding had just started when her phone buzzed. Surprised, she immediately pulled it out of her back pocket and looked at the screen. A text message… from Rylan. In a split second she went from surprise to traitorous excitement to red-hot anger at his presumption that a text message would be an acceptable form of communication at this point.

You coming home tonight?

What the heck? He'd left her high and dry and then wanted to know when she was getting home? As if nothing had happened? Lips pursed, she shoved the phone back into her pocket, leaving the text unanswered.

It buzzed again. And once more when the third competitor was having the ride of his life. She blindly took the phone out and shut off the power. She was not going to give him the satisfaction of an answer. If they talked at all, it would be at a time and place of her choosing. It would be when she decided what she wanted to say and not before. She definitely wasn't going to engage in a text argument when they needed to speak face-to-face. She wasn't going to be a coward and take the easy way out. Not like he had.

The rodeo finally ended and Kailey headed straight for the truck, ready to load their stock on the trailer and make the long ride home.

Right now, that was all that mattered.

## Chapter 13

Rylan checked his phone one more time and frowned.

Six. Six text messages since yesterday afternoon and she hadn't answered a single one. Plus two phone calls that had gone straight to voice mail. He had moments of worrying about her but then told himself she was with Jim and Dan and if anything were wrong, someone would be aware of it. So he worried that she was angry at him for leaving, though he'd explained everything in his note.

Surely, she could understand his needing to come home during an emergency. He rubbed his hand over the stubble on his chin, realized he hadn't shaved since Thursday morning. It was nearly a beard, and he should probably take the time now that he knew Rattler was going to be okay.

For whatever reason, she wasn't answering his calls,

and he was getting tired of it. His patience wasn't endless, and he dialed the number one more time, willing her to answer.

Straight to voice mail.

He ran his hand through his hair and stared at the wall of his camper. When the tone sounded, he left a message. "Kailey, I don't know why you're not answering your calls or texts, but I'm starting to get annoyed. Please call me back. Clearly we need to talk."

He hung up, knowing deep down she wouldn't call. But now he was really spooled up and he dialed the other number he knew now by heart: the main line at the Brandt ranch.

Her mother answered the phone.

"Good morning, Mrs. Brandt. How're you? It's Rylan Duggan."

There was a disapproving pause. "Hello, Rylan. What can I do for you?"

*You can tell your pigheaded daughter to start answering her messages*, he thought irritably, but instead he forced his voice to be pleasant. "I was just wondering if everyone made it back from Lewiston okay."

"Sure did. Rolled in around eleven-thirty last night."

He was relieved…and then annoyed all over again. "Is Kailey there?"

"I'm sorry, but she went home after they finished up here. I'll tell her you called."

*In a pig's eye*, he thought. As he hung up the call, he frowned and felt like kicking something. Dammit, the Brandts were ranchers. If they couldn't understand him leaving to take care of his own stock in an emergency…

He thought back to the note he'd left in the motel room along with his key. Had he not explained things sufficiently? Maybe if she'd pick up her stupid phone or answer a text, he could clear things up.

But the truth slapped him in the face. Kailey didn't want to clear things up. If she had she'd be over here talking. Asking him what had happened. But she wasn't. She was acting as if he didn't even exist.

And to think he'd fancied himself falling in love with her.

He flopped back on the bed, put his hands behind his head. That was the problem, wasn't it? He'd gone and done the one thing he hadn't wanted to do. He'd fallen in love. It had been coming for a while now, but last Thursday night had really cemented it. It had been different. All his barriers had been broken down when he looked into her eyes. Hell, he'd almost told her he loved her.

He was glad now he hadn't.

When he was sure he'd wallowed enough, he headed to the house for the breakfast he'd missed. Lacey was in the kitchen, pouring Quinn a midmorning cup of coffee now that Amber had gone off to school for the day. Quinn took one look at him and raised an eyebrow. "Wow. You do not look like you're in a good mood."

"I'm not, particularly," he answered, opening the fridge. "Lace, you got any leftovers I can heat up or something?"

"For breakfast? Sit down. I'll get you something."

"I can make my own."

"I know that. But I'll be faster. And you can get some coffee in your system. Maybe that'll help your sour mood."

She elbowed him aside and he stomped to the cupboard for a mug. In no time at all she'd fried up a piece of ham, sliced up a potato for home fries, and had made him a couple of fried eggs. Quinn hadn't said much as all this was going on, but when Ry finally sat down with his plate of food, Quinn pushed away his cup and sat back in his chair.

"Everything okay with Rattler?"

Ry nodded and sliced into the flavorful ham. "He's doing better. Some of those gashes are going to be a long time healing. No permanent damage, though, I don't think."

"Good. Lucky, too. Everyone's on alert now. For a cat to come this close…you have to be on the lookout. Especially with kids and pets."

Rylan nodded again. "You have trouble with cats before?"

Quinn shook his head. "Not so much. Last winter it was coyotes."

"We didn't much either at the last place I was at." Rylan finished his eggs and sat back. "Much as I hate to say it, if it's not captured…"

"I know," Quinn replied, his face solemn. "None of us likes the alternative."

Rylan got up and took his plate to the sink. "Thanks for breakfast, sis."

"Anytime, Ry." Lacey smiled at him. "I like having you around."

He jostled her elbow, a gesture of brotherly teasing, and then turned to Quinn. "You got a few minutes? There's something I want to run past you."

"Sure. I'll walk with you down to the barn."

The air was cooler in the mornings now, and some of the leaves were beginning to turn a telltale gold that marked the advent of autumn. It was one of Rylan's favorite times of year, when the heat was less brash and the colors of everything—the sky, the grass—seemed more vivid. He let out a big breath.

"Something on your mind, Ry? And I don't think this has anything to do about Rattler."

Since Kailey wasn't answering his texts, he figured one of her best friends might be a help. Particularly a guy friend. "So… Kailey's not answering my texts or taking my calls."

"What did you do?"

"I don't know. I came back here, but…" He wondered how open to be and figured he didn't have much to lose. "I didn't wake her before I left. I tried, but I swear a freight train could've gone through the room and she would've slept right through it. Instead I left my key and I wrote her a note explaining what had happened."

Quinn nodded. "A good note?"

"I thought so. I mean, I don't think I left anything out."

"And what happened?"

They stopped outside the corral, watched a group of mares standing in the sun, their hides flat and gleaming. "That's just it," he replied. "Nothing happened. I was so busy with Rattler and then so tired that it wasn't until Saturday morning that I realized she hadn't called or even sent a text to see how things were. And when I tried to reach her…no answer. I even tried calling her folks' place this morning and they put me off. What do I do, Quinn? Do I go over there? Or do I wait?"

Quinn looked over at him, his lips curved up the slightest bit on one side of his mouth. "You got it bad, Rylan?"

"The worst," he confirmed readily. "Swore I wouldn't.

Couldn't. But there it is. I promised you I wouldn't mess with her, Quinn, and I haven't. I love her."

"I'm glad to hear it. You're a good man, Rylan. I don't pretend to understand all your motivations for how you've lived your life, but I know a good guy when I see one."

"Then what do I do? What's your read on the situation?"

The semi-smile slid off Quinn's lips. "I think that even if Kailey says she forgives you for February, it's always going to be in the back of her mind. And you leaving her in another motel room is probably hitting her right where it hurts. Even if you did have a good reason."

"But not to answer a single text? I don't get it. I mean, aren't women supposed to be all about the talking? The silent treatment is freaking me out."

Quinn frowned. "Ry, figuring out why women do anything is a mystery man will probably never solve. But maybe she chose the silent treatment because she knew it would freak you out. Maybe this is her way of showing you how it felt. I don't know, man. But you should talk. If you love her, you have to try."

"I think so, too. I think I was just hoping she'd come to me, you know?"

Quinn grinned. "You wanted her to make it easy on you? Oh, brother, you picked the wrong woman for that. But after knowing Kailey for a lot of years, I can tell you that she's worth it. Don't throw in the towel yet."

Ry felt marginally better, but he spent the better part of the day alternately checking his phone and pondering how exactly he should approach her. At the ranch? At Quinn's house? Ask her over here? What would he say?

Would he be welcome or walking into a rattlesnake's nest?

In the end Quinn was the one who came up with the solution. He knocked on Rylan's camper door around seven and stuck his head inside when Ry called out.

"Hey, Ry? Kailey just called. She said there's something going on with the washing machine and wondered if I'd take a look."

"Really?" Ry met Quinn's eyes. "Kailey seems the type that could handle a repair on her own."

Quinn's eyes glinted with humor. "I agree. I'm guessing she wants to ask me the same questions you did this morning. I was thinking I'd send you instead. Cut out the middle man."

Rylan thought for a minute. He wanted to talk to her. Needed to, but he was scared, too. Like he was walking into unknown territory full of traps.

"I guess I can do that."

"Take a toolbox. Look official, and say I sent you because I was busy."

"You think she'll buy that?"

Quinn chuckled. "Not a chance."

He ducked out again, then popped back in with one last encouragement. "Good luck, Ry."

Even though it was just for show, Rylan shoved a little handyman box he kept for simple repairs into the truck. He considered having a second shower but then decided he didn't need to procrastinate and instead changed into a clean shirt and ran a comb through his hair.

The drive seemed to take hours rather than a few minutes.

Kailey's truck was in the yard and the butterflies

in Rylan's gut went from fluttering to ferocious. She mattered. No one had mattered this much to him for as long as he could remember. He really didn't want to screw this up.

Heart in his throat, he got out of the truck, grabbed his toolbox and headed for her front door.

She met him on the step, standing in front of the doorway to prevent him from entering. "I sent for Quinn. My landlord," she emphasized.

He kept his voice even, though seeing her right now both thrilled him and scared him to death. She'd clearly showered earlier, because her hair was soft and damp and smelled like the shampoo he now recognized, and she was wearing sweats and a soft hoodie. She looked utterly snuggly.

"Quinn said to tell you he's busy and that whatever you need fixed, to have me take a look at it."

She frowned. Sighed. Which might have been bad enough but then he looked her in the eye and what he saw startled him. Finality. And he didn't understand why.

"There's nothing wrong with the washer. I made that up. You can go home now."

His patience was thin, but he told himself to keep calm, try to get to the bottom of what had created such a change. "See, the thing is, Quinn figured you wanted to talk. And since I already put him in the middle today asking his advice…he figured he'd just get out of the way." Rylan tried a small smile, attempting to soften that hard look that she kept giving him.

"And what did Quinn say?"

There was a sarcastic edge to her words that Rylan

didn't much care for. "He said he'd never been able to figure out women. He really wasn't much help."

"And do you need help, Rylan?"

Anger, so much anger in her tone. And pain, too. He heard bits of it bleeding through her words and he reminded himself to be patient. To get to the bottom of what was going on without losing his cool.

"Kailey, what happened? Why are you so angry? You didn't answer any of my texts and phone calls… I know I left in a hurry, but Rattler was in a real state and I had to get back as soon as I could."

Her mouth dropped open. "Angry? Why am I angry? Are you serious?" Her voice lifted and Rylan looked around. The next house was a couple of acres away, and normally that would be lots of privacy. But not if Kailey really let loose.

"Of course I'm serious," he replied carefully. "K, we're talking about you and me here. That's something I take very seriously."

She burst out laughing, but not the amused kind. The harsh, incredulous kind that was like knives. "Rylan, one thing I can say for sure. You don't ever take anything seriously."

Well. Now he knew what she really thought about him, didn't he? And it stung. More than he expected it would.

She shook her head, as if she couldn't believe what he'd said. "What was I supposed to think, when I woke up again and you were gone? Not only gone, but you left me high and dry with no vehicle. Six hours from home. You know what, Ry? Fool me once, shame on you. But fool me twice? That's shame on me. I should never have given you a second chance."

The words whipped at him and for a moment he was so stunned he didn't know what to say. When he finally figured it out, he gave back as good as he got. Because she was accusing him of something he didn't do.

"Fool you? For God's sake, Kailey. Rattler nearly died from that attack and he's my responsibility. Mine. I couldn't expect Quinn and Duke to just handle things when I wasn't even competing. I was along for the ride last week. Enjoying the time with you. I was needed at home."

"You could have just explained that!" she shouted.

"I did!" he shouted back. He tempered his voice a little. "I did and you know it. I explained it all in the note I left with the key card on the desk."

"What note?"

His heart froze. "What do you mean, what note? I tried to wake you up, but you're a sound sleeper. So I wrote you a note and put it by the lamp, right by my key. I explained that Rattler got attacked and was really injured. That I was heading back home to take care of things, but that I'd come to get you on Saturday if you needed me to. And when I texted you, I got nothing. I tried to call you, and it went right to voice mail."

"There wasn't any note, Rylan," she snapped. "And you expect me to believe you got this sudden attack of accountability?" She laughed.

He was starting to get worked up. "You know what? I get damned sick of people telling me how irresponsible I am. How I don't care about anything. I made a pretty big investment in Crooked Valley and he's my horse. Would you have rather I didn't care enough to look after him? What would you have done, huh? What would you have done if that had happened to one of your stock?"

Her eyes were wide. "Look. The key card was there, but there was no note. I swear it."

"And I swear I wrote it." He thought back, trying to remember leaving that night. He'd packed his things. Written the note. Grabbed some pizza and soda and gone out the door...

"It was windy," he said, quieter now. "The weather front was coming in. When I left, maybe it blew off the table. That's all I can think of, Kailey. I swear to you I wrote you a note. After last winter, did you really think I would just leave you in a motel room again?"

She looked down, and everything inside him suddenly felt heavy.

"You did. You really thought I had left you there. After all we shared this summer. After going with you to Lewiston, after making love to you...you thought I had just up and abandoned you without an explanation."

She lifted her chin. "I never saw any note. What was I supposed to think?"

So many answers rushed through his head. "I don't know, but the benefit of the doubt might have been nice. Or maybe answering my text. Or taking one of my many phone calls and giving me the chance to explain." He clenched his jaw. This wasn't going as planned.

"You really don't get it, do you?" she asked. "You hurt me. You humiliated me—again. This time in front of my employees. In front of a lot of people who knew you were there with me last week!"

"So, this is about your pride?" He cursed, frustrated and angry. "You know what, Kailey? I think I deserve a little portion of the hurt and anger that's being handed around. I was really starting to care for you. Do you think I would have gone to Lewiston with you otherwise? Really? But maybe this was more one-sided than I realized. Maybe you're so damned worried about appearances and being right that you can't see something when it's right in front of your face. I ran, yes. I ran to take care of my responsibilities. I left you to be with a horse that was ripped to shreds by a mountain lion and, by some miracle, survived. I wrote a note explaining my quick exit. I followed up with a text as soon as Rattler was treated, and I'd managed to get a few hours sleep after driving all night and then being with him all day. And what do I get for my trouble? Being told what a rotten human being I am and how your stupid pride took a beating. Just who is the coward, anyway?"

Her lips fell open and he half regretted being so harsh and the other half of him was relieved he'd gotten all that off his chest.

"You're putting this on *me*?"

He swallowed. The lump in his throat was growing, but he was tired of being the bad guy simply because of a bad judgment call six months ago. "I heard a saying a long time ago. I never knew what it meant until now."

"Oh, and what's that?"

He met her gaze evenly. "The real courage isn't in loving someone. It's allowing them to love you back. I know I made mistakes, Kailey, but I put myself out there. It's not me running away right now. It's you. You're the one who's scared. You're the one running in the other direction, and I'm the convenient scapegoat."

"You left me," she whispered hoarsely. "You left me there like I meant less to you than a stupid horse."

He made a disgusted noise and took a step back. "Kailey, would you listen to yourself? You, who should understand most since you were asked to make that choice not that long ago. You told me Colt didn't understand why you couldn't leave the ranch. That it was an impossible choice to make. And now you're accusing me of caring more for Rattler than I do for you?"

She lifted her chin in response. He stepped forward now, cupped her saucy little chin in his hands. "Do you think that if you were hurt somewhere that I wouldn't move heaven and earth to find you?"

"I don't know that for sure."

He dropped her chin. "All this time I thought we could just take it slow and see what happened. I thought we could figure it out. That you'd forgiven me for my stupid mistake. That you could trust me again. But you don't. It's not just about trust, either. If you have that many doubts, you really don't know what kind of man I am at all."

No one had ever had any expectations where he was concerned. Or perhaps he hadn't expected enough of himself, either. Of course, by holding everyone at arm's length, it kept him from being hurt.

There just came a time in a man's life, he realized, where he had to make a stand. And that time was now. It was time he decided what he wanted, time he stopped settling, time he started having his own expectations. For himself and for the people he cared about.

Kailey was still standing on the porch, barring the door, her arms crossed against her chest. Stubborn, stubborn woman. His anger was fading and in its place was disappointment. In their relationship. In her. That hurt most of all.

"At some point, Kailey, you're going to have to stop putting up walls and blaming everyone else. Ask yourself what you're really afraid of. Take it from someone who knows. Because I was like you. Never let anyone too close. Never show my hand. Until you. I fell in love with you. Are you brave enough to do something about it?"

Her face paled and her eyes glistened, but she didn't say anything. Disheartened, Rylan picked up his toolbox, turned around and went back to his truck. He shut the door and looked up, and she had gone back inside.

He backed out of the driveway and started toward home. Only one other time in his life did he remember feeling this heartbroken. And that was when they'd driven away from Crooked Valley, leaving their old life behind.

Well, maybe Kailey had broken his heart, but he could definitely do something about the second.

It was time he came home. Really came home, the way he'd been afraid to all these years.

# *Chapter 14*

Kailey hung up the phone, her hand shaking and her heart heavy.

After Rylan had gone, she'd called the motel in Lewiston. It had been less than forty-eight hours since she'd checked out, and she knew housekeeping would have gone through the room. But if there was a chance the note still existed, she wanted to find out.

The room had been cleaned, the clerk had said, but they'd send someone to check to see if a slip of paper had been missed behind the desk or something, and they'd call her back. And they did, only twenty minutes later, with Rylan's note in hand. They read it to her over the phone and she'd closed her eyes, feeling sick about how she'd treated him.

She stared at the phone, wondering if she should call him and apologize, but she didn't. She sat on the sofa, her legs crossed and her elbows on her knees, thinking. This wasn't about missing a note he'd written. It was about faith and trust and fear, and she couldn't fix those with a simple phone call. Because that was about her, not Rylan.

And that was work she had to do on her own.

She threw herself into working at the ranch, and went along to two more rodeos during the month just to get away and clear her head.

But no matter how much she tried to sort out her feelings, she was reminded that Rylan, for all his declarations, hadn't even hinted at anything permanent. He had no plans to stay on at Crooked Valley, so where would that leave them even if they could work things out?

Setting herself up for more hurt, that's where. It would just be better if she kept her distance and worked at getting over him.

The days were getting shorter and the nights cooler, and she was spending a quiet Friday evening at home rather than heading out to the Silver Dollar. The bar didn't hold much allure these days, and her busy schedule made her appreciate a night to stay home in comfy leggings and a soft sweatshirt. But she was lonely, too. She was just contemplating putting in a DVD when there was a knock on the door.

Her heart leaped. Maybe Rylan had been as miserable as she'd been and wanted to talk. She'd avoided Crooked Valley altogether since their breakup and hadn't seen him. She ripped the ponytail holder from her hair and gave her head a brisk shake, squared her shoulders and went to answer the door.

It was Lacey and Carrie. Carrie was holding Evan in her arms, and had a diaper bag over her shoulder, while

Lacey carried a bottle of wine, a box of chocolates and a bag of potato chips.

She held up her loot. "I have all the bases covered. You asking us in or what?"

Kailey stepped aside. "What is this? A pity party?" It was shameful how happy she was to see her friends. She really had isolated herself the past few weeks, hadn't she?

"An intervention. And since Carrie's nursing, she gets to play sober driver."

"Indeed," Carrie said, sliding the diaper bag off her shoulder. "My treat of the evening is some sort of fizzy lemonade that Lacey bought."

They went straight through to the living room, and Kailey stopped in the kitchen to retrieve two wineglasses, a corkscrew and a pretty glass for Carrie's beverage. In those few moments, Lacey had put all the food on the coffee table and Carrie was sitting in a cozy chair, Evan on her lap, his little fingers clutching a toy that looked like red, blue and yellow keys.

Lacey waggled her fingers for the corkscrew and Kailey handed it over. "Okay," she said. "What sort of intervention are we talking about?"

"A romantic one," Carrie said, her knee bouncing just a bit to keep Evan occupied. "Something happened between you and Rylan the weekend Rattler was attacked, and it occurred to us that both of you are miserable."

Kailey snorted. "I wouldn't say miserable." The wine opened with a pop and Lacey went straight to work, pouring two glasses. She handed one to Kailey.

"Miserable," Lacey confirmed. "Nothing else would explain you totally avoiding Crooked Valley for two solid weeks and never calling your best friends."

"It's been busy…"

"Sure," Carrie and Lacey replied in unison.

"It has. I've been to two rodeos, too. Out of town."

"Interesting. Since you rarely travel with the stock."

It was true. There was no sense in trying to fool either Carrie or Lacey. "Fine. I've been avoiding your place. It would just be awkward."

She took a sip of wine. Then another. Lacey poured the lemonade for Carrie and handed her the glass, then opened the box of chocolates and tore open the bag of chips. "Pick your poison," she stated.

Kailey reached for a dark chocolate truffle first. It went very nicely with the rich merlot and she leaned against the back of the sofa.

"Look, you guys, Rylan and I had a misunderstanding. Some of it was his fault. A lot of it was mine. But when we talked, I think we both realized there's a lot more wrong with us than we thought. Yeah, I've done some thinking, and it's just better this way. I mean, come Christmas Rylan will be gone to wherever, and it won't be an issue anymore."

Carrie and Lacey looked at each other, then back at Kailey. "Is that what you think? That Rylan's temporary and you'll just be able to forget him?" Lacey put her hand on Kailey's knee. "Honey, I was there the day he offered to pay for lunch at the diner. Things have never been easy for you. And one thing's for sure…you've never been indifferent to each other."

Kailey's heart hurt just talking about it. "Like I said. It doesn't matter. He'll be gone soon enough, right?"

Carrie's gaze was sympathetic. "Um, not exactly. He's staying on at Crooked Valley."

The second truffle seemed to catch in her throat and she took a quick gulp of wine to wash it down. "What do you mean?" she asked, her voice shaking a little. "Staying on how?"

"As in taking on his third," Lacey replied. "He told us nearly two weeks ago. He's going to take over managing the rough stock side of the ranch. I'm staying on as administrator, and Quinn and Duke are going to run the cattle operations."

"I'm going to pitch in whenever and however," Carrie added. "With Evan being so small, I'm really focusing on being mom right now. Plus—" she smiled a little bit "—we're thinking we'd like to have more than one."

Kailey blinked quickly and reached for another chocolate. Her friends were so happy. Why could she not find that? Or was what Rylan said true? Was she the one standing in her own way?

Rylan. Staying on at Crooked Valley. Which meant she'd never be able to truly forget him because they'd be neighbors. Neighbors in the same line of work. The idea of seeing him to talk business darned near gutted her. How could she face him, knowing how she felt about him?

"But…" She looked up at both women. "He always said he wasn't one for settling down in one place. That he doesn't want to be committed to anything or anyone."

*I fell in love with you*, he'd said. Had he really meant it? Then there was the whole thing with Rattler. It wasn't just that it was his horse. He'd used words like responsibility and courage and home. Did that sound like a guy on the verge of running?

"He didn't," Lacey confirmed quietly. "Until now. He told us how difficult it was for him as a kid, being uprooted from here after our dad died. How he never fit in, never belonged anywhere. But he feels like he does now. Like he's part of something important, like he's where he's meant to be."

Bully for him and all his belonging and completeness.

"But he isn't happy, Kailey. Because there's something missing. He fell in love with you. And you're clearly miserable without him, so what gives?"

Kailey stared at them both for several seconds, then held out her glass. "Could I have some more wine, please?"

Lacey dutifully topped her up, added a splash to her own glass and put the bottle down again.

Kailey took a long drink. Gathered up her courage. Looked her friends in the eyes and admitted, "I'm a coward."

Carrie snorted while Lacey smiled affectionately. "Don't be silly. You're one of the bravest people I know."

"But I'm not. And Ry's the first person to ever call me on it. Do you want to know what really happened with Colt last fall?"

She paused, and saw that Carrie and Lacey hung on her every word. "Well, he proposed. And then he presented this whole future where I'd move to be closer to his work, and I couldn't believe he was asking me to leave Brandt. His assertion was that a wife should follow her husband, and he withdrew his proposal when I said I couldn't just up and leave the ranch. But know what? I've discovered two things. Colt wasn't the right person, because when the right person comes along you should be able to say you'll follow them anywhere, right? And the other thing I learned about myself is that I've been hiding behind Brandt Ranch so I don't have to put myself out there. Ry and I really aren't that different, you know. We just hid behind different things."

She gave a sheepish smile to her friends. It was time she faced the truth: the ranch made for a fine excuse when she wanted to distance herself from the possibility of getting hurt. Or more than that…looking weak.

Weakness, she discovered, or at least the appearance of weakness, was what she was truly afraid of.

Evan started to fuss and Carrie put down her glass and cuddled him close, trying to soothe his whimpers. "But why?" she asked softly. "Why would you feel you had to hide behind the ranch? You're smart and beautiful. Fun."

It meant a lot to hear her best friend say those things. "Carrie, you know what it's like. I've had to fight for credibility in the industry, especially taking on the leadership role that I have. I'll be the first to admit that I sometimes fight against being, well, feminine."

Lacey sighed. "Men. Just because you have breasts doesn't make you any less qualified."

Kailey laughed, feeling better at the unequivocal support. "Hey, you know that and I know that, but not everyone feels that way, and it's not just men either. But I love what I do, so I deal with it."

"Right." Carrie nodded. "Which is why you and I used to blow off steam at the Dollar now and again." Her cheeks colored a little. "Which I haven't really done since I got pregnant. Shoot, Kailey. I kind of abandoned you, didn't I?"

Kailey shook her head. "Your priorities shifted, that's all. I guess the other thing is, when I did cut loose— like you and I used to do, Carrie—I became Fun Kailey. I've gained a reputation of not being marriage material. I'm the best friend or the fling but not more than that.

And over time, I suppose that I started to protect my-self by not putting my feelings out there. Colt wasn't the first person to hurt my feelings. And Rylan certainly wasn't either."

But it had been different with Rylan, she realized. Her feelings for him must have been bigger and more intense than she thought, because she'd cried more tears over him than she ever had over Colt or any man, for that matter. Tears formed in the corners of her eyes. "Crap," she murmured. "I didn't want to do this. Get all emotional and stuff."

"Maybe that's exactly what you need," Lacey said, reaching over and taking her hand. "I get it, Kailey. My ex-husband left me pretty gun-shy about ever being in a relationship again. You build walls around yourself and tell yourself no one will ever get close enough to hurt you like that again."

Kailey gave a quick nod, fighting tears.

"It took Quinn really pushing me to make me start fighting for the life I wanted," Lacey continued. "So the big question is, what do you want?"

That, of everything, was the easiest thing to answer. "I want it all," she whispered, sniffling. "I love the ranch. I've worked so hard with my dad to turn it into what it is today. I don't want to leave it. And I want a man who loves me, and a family of my own. Maybe I just…want too much."

Lacey and Carrie both smiled. "Honey, you're not asking for too much," Carrie assured her. She'd discreetly settled Evan at her breast and smiled with beatific contentment. "Ranching isn't like a regular nine-to-five gig. Working the land means having a relationship with it, a connection that goes beyond a job. Brandt Ranch is part of who you are, plain and simple."

Kailey thought about that. "Maybe it's too much of me, though. Gosh, I don't know. I've been a real mess lately."

Lacey was the one who took everything down to the lowest common denominator. "Do you love him?"

She didn't have to ask if she meant Rylan. Of course she did. The tears she'd succeeded in blinking away came back with a vengeance. "Maybe. Probably. And how dumb is that? I let myself fall for him when I knew he was leaving."

"But he's not leaving. And we hoped he wouldn't. We hoped that this would happen. That he'd come back here and see what a great place it is, that there's a home for him here. And he has." Lacey's gaze probed hers. "I truly think that he's needed to find his way back here all along. Are you going to punish him for that, K?"

"I'm scared he'll leave again."

Lacey nodded. "I know. And I can't convince you he's changed, and he can't convince you either, unless you allow yourself to believe it. To trust him."

Evan had fallen asleep and Carrie tucked him close in a soft blanket. "Sweetie, just think about it. You're miserable over here, and he's miserable over at Crooked Valley, and it's plain to all of us that you guys should be together. It might have started with a spark in February, but this summer it changed into something more. It wasn't just Rylan who changed. It was you. You changed each other, Kailey. And the beautiful thing is you never meant to. You were just yourselves."

Kailey was full-out crying now, tears slipping down her cheeks. "I was so terrible to him," she whispered. "I accused him of stuff that was just dumb, all because I was scared. How do you get the courage to really love someone?"

And then Ry's words came back to her. *Real courage isn't in loving someone. It's allowing them to love you back.*

The problem wasn't how she felt about him. She'd known for some time that she was in love with him. It was the act of letting him love her, giving him access to all her deepest secrets and desires. Letting herself be totally vulnerable and open.

Could she do it? Really? Could she not? How would she live next to him for the rest of her life knowing she'd blown her chance at happiness simply because she'd wanted guarantees that didn't exist?

"I've been an idiot," she whispered, looking up at her friends. "A real idiot."

"You can always stop doing that and make things right." Carrie's lips curved in a goofy smile. "We'll even help you."

"You will?"

"Of course." Lacey nodded. "Let's get down to business, then, shall we?" She held out her glass for a top up.

Kailey grabbed the bottle, topped off both their glasses and reached for a handful of chips.

Suddenly, the night didn't seem quite so hopeless.

Rylan sat on Duke's front porch, nursing a beer and wondering why things seemed so damned quiet.

It couldn't be because of Kailey. She belonged at Brandt, and even though she visited Crooked Valley frequently, it wasn't as though she was part of the daily routine. Maybe it was because it was fall, and things were slightly slower than they were in the middle of summer.

Either way, Rylan knew two things. Staying at Crooked Valley was a good decision. One he felt happy about. As soon as he'd said the words to Duke and Lacey, he'd felt a sense of rightness wash over him. The second thing he knew was that he missed her. And that he was both angry and hurt over how things had gone down.

Duke and Quinn came out of the house, each with a bottle of beer in their hands, and sat down in the other chairs on the porch, stretching out their jean-clad legs. "Nice night," Quinn remarked, and Duke agreed, and the three of them looked out over the ranch. Their domain. All three had a stake in it now.

"Where did your women go?" Rylan asked. "Figured at least one of them would be around, pesterin'." He tried a smile. It fell flat.

"They went out for a while. Left us on our own." Duke was close enough to nudge Rylan's elbow. "Peace and quiet."

Quinn shrugged. "I don't know. Seems too quiet around here without them around."

Rylan's mood darkened. They didn't know how lucky they were. The women they loved didn't hold one mistake against them for the rest of their damned lives.

"So," Quinn said, a little too conversationally to be coincidental. "This thing with Kailey."

"Is over." It stung even to say it.

"What'd you do?" Duke asked.

"Why did I have to do something?" Rylan retorted, swirling the beer around in his bottle.

"Because it's always our fault," Duke said reasonably. "Carrie rolls her eyes and tells me that men aren't as highly evolved as women."

Even Rylan had to give a bit of a chuckle at that. "Seems to me women appreciate a little caveman now and again," he replied, letting out a deep breath. He didn't need to take out his bad mood on his brothers. He already considered Quinn a brother, rather than a mere in-law.

Quinn took a drink, swallowed and rolled his head to look at Rylan. "You kind of blew it on Valentine's Day, bucko. You did a good job of fixing it until you ran out on her."

Rylan scowled. "I swear to God, I wrote a note, put it with the key card. It must have fallen behind the desk or something. And I texted and tried to call as soon as I knew Rattler was okay. I didn't just up and leave."

"To her you did."

"Dammit, I know that. But I explained…"

"Hey, we know you did. We're with you. But Kailey…she has a hard time trusting, period." Quinn frowned. "She's always felt she had to work twice as hard since her mom and dad had a daughter and not a son. She has high standards, Rylan. And people end up disappointing her, like that jackass Black."

"I'm not like that. I'd never ask her to walk away from Brandt. It's part of her. I know that much." He made a disgusted sound in his throat. Colt Black wasn't worth considering.

"I'm not saying she's right, Ry." Quinn let out a big breath. "But what I am saying is…don't give up. Not if you really love her. I know she's one of my best friends and I'm biased, but I think she's worth it."

"How many times do I beat my head against the wall, then?" Ry asked. "Because that's what I'm doing, and it doesn't feel very damn good."

Duke looked over at him and held his gaze. "As many as it takes," he answered simply.

They each took a long drink and stared off across the fields.

# Chapter 15

"Hey, Rylan, someone from Brandt just phoned. One of their hands spotted a couple of our calves on the property line."

Rylan looked up from the paperwork he was doing and pinned a direct gaze on Lacey. "You're telling me this why? Quinn and Duke usually take care of this stuff. Calves aren't even supposed to be near that place. You sure they're ours?"

"Quite sure. Quinn's got his hands full, and Duke and Carrie have taken Evan in for his latest checkup. That leaves you."

"Can't one of the hands go?" Just what he wanted, treading the border line between their property and Kailey's. After his chat with Duke and Quinn the other night, he still didn't know what to do about her. His brothers had both said he needed to keep trying and show her how he felt, but after a while a man got tired of always feeling wrong and having a door slammed in his face.

Lacey put her hands on her hips. "For God's sake, it's a few little calves. Saddle up a horse and get the hell out of the barn. You could use some space and air. You're starting to be a real downer."

His irritation peaked and snapped. "Fine," he bit back. "Since everyone seems to have an opinion on what I should do with every moment of my day, I'll get on a horse and bring back your stupid calves."

"Thank you." She sounded incredibly pleased, which only infuriated him more. "You know where the creek takes that right angle bend? It was really close to there."

Great. Just what he needed. In case he hadn't been thinking about Kailey enough, he now had to go to the swimming hole where they'd shared some of their most memorable moments. Today was off to a great start.

He put the paperwork aside and brought in Chief to be saddled, and then headed out to the property edge in search of the lost calves. How they'd been separated from the herd, he had no idea. At least the September weather was mild. The cottonwoods were shedding their leaves so that the trees and drying grasses were varied shades of brown and gold, gilding everything with the warm colors. Rylan exhaled, grudgingly admitted that Lacey was right. He'd needed to get out of the barn.

He scanned the rolling hills for any sign of the calves, but so far he saw nothing. As he rode along the edge of the creek, he listened to the trickle of the water, the level lower now than it had been earlier in the summer, and thought of the times he'd come here with Kailey. That first night he'd come upon her swimming in her underwear and how he'd joined her, making her blush. Other times they'd met in the mellow evening heat, cooled their hot skin in the cold water, making love in the pool and on a blanket on the bank. He'd taken it, and her, for granted, and now she was gone.

The creek slowed, widened and curved around a huge old cottonwood, glowing with golden leaves. And there, just around the bend, stood Kailey, in a pair of jeans and a gray hooded jacket, holding the reins of her favorite mare—an aging Appaloosa named Sprinkles.

He reined in, stared at her from beneath his hat. "What are you doing here?" he called out. "You looking for those calves, too?"

But even as he asked, he knew it had all been a lie. Lacey had set this up. He loved his family. Staying on at Crooked Valley wasn't going to be a mistake. But if they thought meddling in his personal life was okay...

"There are no calves," she called back. "Your herd is miles from here." A soft smile lit her face. "Actually, I can't believe you fell for that line. It was Lacey's idea. I bet her it wouldn't work."

"I was distracted," he replied, trying to understand. So, Kailey and Lacey had been in on this together? But Kailey hadn't talked to him in days. Not since he'd walked away from her place after she'd returned from Lewiston.

"Apparently. I'm glad, though. I wanted to talk to you."

"You could have picked up the phone," he said. A little part of him wanted to believe this was a good sign. But another remembered the harsh words she'd hurled at him, and he hesitated, staying firmly seated in the saddle.

The slight smile that had curved her mouth slid away. "Ry, I chose this place for a reason. It's middle ground, where your place and mine meet. Neutral territory."

Middle ground. Terms of peace but nothing more, right? Not the place where they'd begun the crazy slide into love, which was what he'd thought, for the briefest second, had been what she was going to say. His throat felt tight. He didn't dare get his hopes up one more time. She didn't trust him, and she'd made that perfectly clear the last time he saw her.

"Just say what you need to say," he advised.

Kailey stared up at the man on the horse. He seemed like such a stranger. The usual flirty half smile was gone from his face and his eyes were shadowed by the brim of his hat. Her heart beat a frantic tattoo as she wondered if this had been a big mistake. If she was too late.

But she'd been in the wrong. And it was up to her to apologize and make things right, if it was possible.

Her voice shook as she spoke, taking one step closer to Chief.

"I owe you a huge apology," she said, then cleared her throat. "For what happened after Lewiston. For jumping to conclusions. Though," she added, biting down on her lip for a moment, "the conclusions weren't that much of a stretch considering…"

That wasn't what she'd planned to say, and she stammered a bit and backtracked. "B-but I didn't believe you when you told me about the note. And I didn't forgive you and I should have. I'm sorry, Rylan. I really screwed things up."

His expression remained harsh, but she saw his Adam's apple bob and hoped he was feeling *something* right now. That he hadn't totally closed his heart to her.

"Say something," she whispered.

"You wanted to apologize?" he asked, his voice expressionless. "Make peace between the Hatfields and McCoys?"

She laughed. "We're hardly that, Rylan. I never hated you. There's no feud…"

"You sure don't love me," he replied sharply. Too sharply. She stared at him, her lips open. She'd really, really hurt him. Strangely enough, the knowledge gave her hope. Indifference was her real enemy. If he cared enough to be hurt, maybe there was still a chance for them.

"That's where you're wrong," she replied. "Please, Rylan. Won't you get down from there and talk to me?"

He hesitated for a moment, but then swung his leg over the saddle and hopped down. He took off Chief's bridle, too, setting him free. Chief wouldn't go far, and he'd enjoy grazing for a while until Rylan called him to go home.

"You know I'm staying on at Crooked Valley, don't you?"

She nodded. "The girls told me. What made you change your mind?"

The leather and hardware of the bridle dangled from his hand. "I fought it for too long. Leaving it the first time gave me such bad memories I didn't want to come back again. Then once I was back—really back—I realized I was so determined to leave that I was cutting off my nose to spite my face. This place has always been my idea of home. I can still rodeo—I love it, too—but working with the stock, helping it grow…that's where I want to be."

He met her gaze and his eyes hardened. "I suppose that makes me more attractive now. That I'm not such a drifter."

She absorbed the hit. So defensive, so…hurt. She hadn't realized how sensitive he was, but perhaps she should have. All the things he'd told her had added up to a boy and man who didn't give too much of himself to anything so he didn't get hurt. But he'd given a lot of himself to her, and she'd thrown it back in his face.

And so she said the words she knew he needed to hear. And she meant them.

"Rylan Duggan, I fell in love with you when I was convinced that you were leaving again. When you disappeared for days on end, competing, and when you came back and had to face losing your championship hopes. I loved you every moment of this summer. Otherwise I never could have asked you to go along with me to Idaho. Don't you get that? I'm sorry I overreacted. I'm sorry I got scared and stubborn. And am I glad you're staying in Gibson? Well, maybe I am. Of course, that all depends."

"Depends on what?"

She stepped forward again until they were only a few feet apart. "It depends on what happens here. Right now, today. Because if you staying here means we're not together and I have to see you every day and see what I messed up because I was a coward, that's going to be really hard to live with."

His blue eyes flickered with some emotion she couldn't quite decipher, but it definitely wasn't indifference.

Encouraged, she took the final steps and fastened her fingers around the denim of his jacket. "Rylan, I ruined everything. I know that. And yeah, I'm scared. I'm really scared. I'm throwing away my security blanket here and giving you the power to hurt me. This is me. Just me. I have no idea what I'm doing and no idea what comes next, and that terrifies me, but I know one thing for sure. I love you. And you can do with that what you will. You can love me back, which, by the way, is what I hope you'll do. Or you can break my heart. Either way, it's yours."

And offering it to him was something she'd never, ever done before. She thought it would be crippling and terrifying, but in this moment, it felt utterly right to surrender it to something bigger than herself.

He dropped the bridle on the ground, then took off his hat and dropped it on top of the tack. "K," he said softly, and something in her chest seemed to take wing. She loved how he shortened her name to a single letter, how his eyes raked over her with a hunger that went beyond the physical. This was the Ry she remembered. Larger than life. Dangerous and wonderful.

"I'm sorry," she said again, and to her chagrin she started to cry. "I'm so sorry, Rylan. I turned you away instead of letting you in. I was such a fool."

He reached out and pulled her into his arms. "No more of a fool than I was," he replied roughly, his lips close to her ear as he held her close.

She clung to him for several seconds, absorbing his strength and heat and the sheer delight of his body close to hers once more. "Oh, I missed this," she murmured, tightening her arms around him.

"Me, too," he replied. He leaned back a little and

brushed a thumb down her cheek. "But, Kailey, you were so sure you couldn't trust me. So angry. What changed?"

She looked up at him, knowing the time to lay herself bare had come and that she finally had to trust someone with everything. "I can't say it's any one defining moment," she said, staying in the circle of his arms. "Rather it's a lifetime of making the ranch my life. I'm a woman in a man's world. And the ranch is successful, so on some level that's threatening. At least that's what Colt said."

"Threatening?" Rylan laughed. "Honey, if we're talking about how capable and bossy you are, let me tell you, it's sexy as hell."

Her body warmed all over from the praise. "Not everyone is as liberated as you, Duggan. I fight for credibility in this industry, but now and again I have to blow off steam. I have no one to blame but myself. I'm the fun girl, you see. Not the keeper girl. Because the ranch always comes first."

Rylan frowned. "Do you realize how often you label yourself? Why do you do that? Why do you have to be anything other than just Kailey?"

No one in her life had ever asked her that before. "Ry, my parents are wonderful, but there has always been an unspoken ideal that I'm representing the ranch and have to act accordingly. Over time I suppose I've been afraid to show anyone the real me. Even my friends."

"And who is the real you, Kailey?"

She sank her hands into his hair and gazed into his eyes. "The real me is a rancher, a woman, someone who wants a lover and a family and a place to call home.

And that woman would have scared you to death six months ago."

He closed his eyes briefly. "You did. Scare me to death, that is. That's why I left that morning, you know. I could see all of it in your eyes and it terrified me. God, we're peas in a pod, aren't we? So determined to never let anyone close, so we never get hurt."

"Except we couldn't stay away from each other."

"No. We couldn't. And then, of course, what I wanted changed. I had to stop running at some point. Crooked Valley was as good a place as any."

"And I had to open my heart to someone. I know you were telling the truth about the note. I admire what you did, too. It was responsible, honorable. Hell, Ry, it's what I would have done if Rattler had been my horse. I'm sorry I didn't believe you. I was just…"

"Scared," he finished. "And so was I."

"I have a hard time trusting, Rylan. But I can't keep holding on to that one mistake. Everything you've done since coming back to Crooked Valley has proved I can believe in you. And the rest I'll take on faith. I believe in you, Ry."

Finally, finally he said the words she'd been dying to hear.

"I love you, Kailey. I thought I could go through life not having to risk my heart to anyone, but then there you were. Stay or go, that won't change. I love you. And you've said you love me. All that remains is deciding what we're going to do about it."

He loved her. Her heart sent up a wild hosanna and a smile blossomed on her lips. "We can talk about the future later," she replied. Right now they had more important matters to take care of. "Can you please kiss me first, Rylan? I've been dying for you to kiss me again."

He cupped his hand around the back of her neck and pulled her close, kissing her with a singular intent that sent her heart racing.

"I love you," he murmured, sliding his lips over the crest of her cheek. "And I missed you. So much."

"Me, too. Nothing was right…"

"I had everything I was supposed to want and it was gray and meaningless…"

"I thought I'd sent you away for good. Ruined everything…"

"Not a chance." His lips captured hers again and before long jackets dropped to the ground and their hands were skimming over warm skin, dying to be close once more.

"It's cool out here," he proclaimed. "I don't want this to be rushed and prickly on the grass and whatever else. I want to love you properly, Kailey. I want to make up for lost time and make things right."

She ran her hands over his shoulder blades, loving the feel of the warm skin beneath his shirt. "You're going to make me wait?"

He captured her arms and his fingers circled her wrists. "Only for a little while. I need you to listen to me first, okay? Because I don't want to be the one to screw things up this time."

"Okay," she agreed.

He twined his fingers with hers. "Kailey Brandt," he said, his gaze clinging to hers, "I was not looking for love. You weren't on my radar at all. And I was dreading seeing you again when I came back in May. I knew

I'd been a total ass in February. I definitely didn't deserve for you to give me another chance. But you did."

He squeezed her fingers. "I told myself it was fun and light and easy, but I knew exactly what I was in for when you asked me to go to Idaho with you. That night before I left…something changed. There was a moment when I looked in your eyes and I could see my future laid out in front of me. I wasn't scared anymore. I wanted to go home, look after Rattler, and figure out how everything fit together. I wasn't prepared for you, sweetheart. Not prepared, not looking. And suddenly there you were."

Her eyes stung, touched by the sincerity in his voice and gaze.

"I know you're scared. I'm scared, too. Scared to love you. Scared I might disappoint you. Scared I'm not the man you deserve."

His lip wobbled, and she sniffed, trying to hold herself together but not sure how long she could.

"I've never trusted anyone, not since I was five years old. But I trust you, Kailey. I love you. And somehow we'll make it all come together. You somehow became my everything. My reason for breathing, my light in the darkness."

How long had she been waiting for someone to say those words to her, to mean them, to love her so much he couldn't go on without her? She was deliriously happy and humbled by it, and she held tight to his hands as she responded. "You're my everything, too, Rylan. Nothing seems to work when you're not in my life."

His eyes were troubled, though, as he gazed down at her. "I can't just up and leave Crooked Valley, though. I have to stay to take on my third, which will ensure

Lacey and Duke's futures. I need to do that for them. I need to know I… I did something important. I can't be the add-on anymore."

"You're no afterthought. Especially not to me, Ry. You know that, right?"

His eyes softened. "I'm working on believing you. And I love hearing you say it."

She touched his cheek. "We'll figure it out. The most important thing is we're together."

She remembered saying to Lacey and Carrie that when a person loved another, they should be willing to follow them anywhere. Right now, in this moment, she knew that she would make that sacrifice to be with Rylan. He was *the* one. She also knew that he would never ask her to make that sacrifice, because he understood her better than anyone she'd ever known.

Which was exactly how she'd always believed it should be.

"Rylan?"

"Yes, honey?"

She tilted up her chin and smiled. "Is this a proposal?"

The sideways grin she loved crept up his cheek. "Well, shoot. It would be if you let me get to it."

While the horses grazed nearby and the creek burbled over the rocks, Rylan got down on one knee and Kailey put her hand over her mouth, thrilled and surprised and overwhelmed that her greatest hopes had come true.

"Kailey, will you marry me? I don't know what the future holds, but I promise I want to be the one standing beside you as we find out."

She nodded, tears clogging her throat and preventing her from answering. But she figured he got the answer anyway as he stood up and she launched herself at him, wrapping her arms around his neck.

*Eight months later*

The spring roundup was in full swing. Today the event was at Crooked Valley. Local ranchers, including the Brandts, all pitched in to help Duke and the rest of the crew brand, vaccinate and neuter cattle. It was busy, dusty, dirty, tiring work, and at the end of the day Lacey and Carrie put on a huge spread of food including grilled ribs, cornbread, baked beans and a smorgasbord of other delights that were guaranteed to please workers and neighbors alike.

Amber, now finishing kindergarten and ready to move into first grade, was in charge of plates, napkins and cutlery and made sure everything was replenished for the workers. Carrie spooned up the beans, Evan's head peeking out over the top of a baby backpack. Kailey grinned at the sight of the red curls and touched her tummy, wondering when the right time would be to tell Rylan the good news. She'd just taken the test two days ago, and figured they'd get today over with before he got to play protective daddy.

Lacey was working the grill, basting the ribs with her homemade sauce, and Kailey watched as Quinn stepped up behind her and wrapped an arm around her waist. He said something and Lacey laughed, then they shared a quick kiss before he moved on again. Recently they'd begun the screening process for adopting, hoping for a brother or sister for Amber.

A year and a half ago, Joe had been ill and the future of the ranch had been uncertain. Now it was full of life again, and children, and hope.

"Hello, gorgeous." A pair of strong hands came to rest on her shoulders. "Tired?" He gave her shoulders a little rub and she let out a satisfied breath.

"A little. Good day, though. Days like today remind me what ranching is supposed to be like. And community."

"Me, too. I'd forgotten for a long time, I think."

She turned her head and looked up at him, his strong jawline and twinkling eyes. Her husband for the past seven months. Their wedding had been low-key and lovely. Neither had wanted a long engagement or a big production. A month after the proposal, they'd tied the knot in the country church with only their families in attendance, and then had gone back to the Brandt house for a homemade prime rib dinner. Their honeymoon had been spent in Glacier National Park, a romantic three nights in the mountains sleeping in the cozy quarters of Rylan's camper. Since then they'd moved into Quinn's house—the bungalow was a convenient halfway mark between the Brandt and Duggan properties. Instead of selling off the bucking stock side business, they'd come to an agreement with Brandt and operated as a sub-contractor, so both ranches reaped the benefits without being in competition with each other.

"Do you need to stay late tonight?" she asked. As good as the day had been, she was tired, and could use some quiet time. Like a warm bath and a cuddle on the couch with her favorite cowboy.

"I should be good to go by eight or so."

"Sounds fine."

Duke strolled by, dirty from head to toe, and gave

Ry a slap on the back. "Hey, you newlyweds. It's about time you got on with the baby-making business, don't you think?"

Kailey saw him wink at Carrie, and with a laugh she patted her tummy and then raised her eyebrows at Rylan and Kailey.

"Wait," Kailey said. "Are you saying that you and Carrie…"

Duke's grin was huge. "We said we wanted to have our kids close together. So they'd grow up together."

He looked at Rylan as he said it, and the brothers shared a look that a year ago never would have happened. So many fences had been rebuilt within the family, all due to Joe's crazy will.

"Congrats," Rylan replied, shaking his brother's hand.

"Well, you're a healthy lookin' guy. No reason why this should be taking so long."

Kailey's heart pounded in anticipation. "Um, who said it was taking too long?"

Duke stared, but she only had eyes for her husband. All it took was a quick nod on her part and he let out a whoop that could be heard all over the farm yard. "When?" he asked her, and she laughed.

"I found out a couple of days ago."

He picked her up and swung her around. When he set her down again, she saw Duke grinning at Carrie and patting his belly to share the news and Quinn and Lacey grinning at them like idiots while Amber piped up, "Why is everyone smiling?"

It was Rylan, the man who just a year ago had driven into Crooked Valley with no intention of staying, or falling in love, or making plans for the future, who answered her.

"You're gonna have another cousin, sweetheart."

Amber was off, telling the good news to anyone who would listen, and Rylan turned back to Kailey and looked into her eyes. "Are we ready for this?"

She smiled at him and shrugged. "Rylan, when have we ever been ready for anything? We just take it as it comes. And it all works out right."

He tucked a piece of hair behind her ear. "Jeez, for someone who had trust issues, you've really learned to take a lot on faith."

"All because of you," she murmured, gazing up into his eyes. "All because of you."

\* \* \* \* \*

Award-winning author **Mary Sullivan** realized her love for romance novels when her mother insisted she read one. After years of creative pursuits, she discovered she was destined to write heartfelt stories of love, family and happily-ever-after. Since then, Mary has garnered awards, accolades and glowing reviews.

Mary indulges her passion for puzzles, cooking and meeting new people in her hometown of Toronto. Follow her on Facebook, Facebook.com/marysullivanauthor, or go to marysullivanbooks.com to learn more about her and the small towns she creates.

### Books by Mary Sullivan

### Harlequin Western Romance

#### Rodeo, Montana

*Rodeo Father*
*Rodeo Rancher*
*Rodeo Baby*
*Rodeo Sheriff*
*Rodeo Family*

#### Harlequin Superromance

*Cody's Come Home*
*Safe in Noah's Arms*
*No Ordinary Home*

Visit the Author Profile page at Harlequin.com for more titles.

# RODEO FATHER

**Mary Sullivan**

To my wonderful agent, Pamela Hopkins,
who continues to have faith in me book
after book after book. Offering you
a profound Thank You.

# Chapter 1

Travis Read stood on the outskirts of Rodeo, Montana, and stared at the sorriest excuse for a midway he'd ever encountered.

He'd pulled his truck over for a closer look.

Old rides littered the prairie like a county fair graveyard. Rusty signs hung askew.

A hint he should hightail it out of town before he'd even arrived? Maybe, save for one ride. Front and center, a spit-shined carousel stood out from the other decaying machines as though risen fresh from the grave.

Merry-go-rounds weren't usually on Travis's radar, whimsy being a stranger in his life, but he had his nephews to think about now.

He'd bet both his old Stetson and broken-in cowboy boots the boys would be tickled by the carousel. He was.

Gleaming in the meager late-October sunshine, the merry-go-round seemed like a good omen.

*No way, Travis.*

Grimly, he straightened his spine. He didn't believe in omens, good, bad or otherwise.

"You look like a man who could use a smile."

A feminine voice drifted out of the early-morning mist that shrouded the hushed countryside, carried on the faint breeze like a melody.

A young woman stepped up behind one of the inanimate ponies on the ride, materializing with a playful smile and a smear of grease across her left cheek.

One fist gripped a wrench and the other a rag, which she used to burnish a gilded saddle on a white pony. The contrast of that wrench and the small hand charmed Travis. No mean feat. He didn't charm easily.

She thought he could use a smile. Dead right.

The woman grinned and his heart stuttered. Good vibes shimmered from her like sunshine reflecting off clear water.

The corners of his mouth, rusty with disuse, twitched.

"Yes, ma'am, I sure could use one of those." No sense denying the truth she'd picked up on. "You don't see many of these around anymore."

She crossed her arms on the elaborate saddle. "Bet you've seen better looking amusement parks."

"Could use some work."

She laughed. "*That's* an understatement if I've ever heard one." As she stared around the downcast place, her expression became subdued.

Her friendliness had lightened up the gray corners of his heart.

"Nothing a little elbow grease won't cure," he ventured, clumsy in his attempt to make her smile again.

She drew herself up and grinned. Aaah. Better.

"Yes," she said. "You're absolutely right."

Unnaturally drawn to this attractive stranger, Travis leaned forward, his body pressing against a wood-slat fence that needed a hammer, a whole lot of nails and a few coats of paint.

"Someone's done a good job on the carousel." By the look of pride on her face, he'd found the culprit. "Looks great."

*She* looked great. Her smile warmed the chill in his heart.

"What's your name?" she asked.

He doffed his Stetson. His mom might not have taught him much, but she'd stressed the importance of good manners. "Travis Read."

"Rachel McGuire." Her voice rang like birdsong. "Haven't seen you around town. Just passing through?"

She rested her chin on her crossed arms, her glance flickering toward his truck and horse trailer parked on the shoulder.

"Looks like you'll be staying a while?"

He stiffened. He didn't discuss his life with strangers, a habit ingrained years ago.

Yeah, he planned to stay, but only long enough to get his sister and nephews settled in, and then he'd be moving on.

No sense telling that to Rachel, no matter how attractive he found her humor-filled eyes.

It was none of her business.

"Got hired to work for the Webers," was all he was inclined to share.

"On the Double U? You're fortunate. Udall's a good man. Uma mothers everyone for fifty miles around. As long as you're a hard worker, they'll treat you like gold."

If there were a definition in the dictionary for *hard worker* it would be his name. He'd toiled since he was old enough to shovel shit and straw.

Enough about him.

He pointed to a sign dotted brown and green with rust and verdigris, which arched above the entrance to the park: Rodeo, Montana, Fairgrounds and Amusement Park, Home of Our World-Famous Rodeo.

"Heard a rumor the town's planning on resurrecting that rodeo. Next summer?" Maybe he could earn a few extra bucks. He used to be good.

Damned if she didn't perk right up.

"You rodeo?"

"Been known to ride a bull or two."

The aurora borealis he'd once seen in northern Alberta had nothing on this woman's smile.

Rachel brushed a lock of thick hair from her face. He thought the color might be called tawny. It glowed like liquid honey and looked as soft as a calf's ear.

Her smile dazzled him and sent him off-kilter. She had some powerful mojo that had him falling like a load of bricks. Images tempted him, of cozy nights in his new home with a wood fire burning and a thick blanket on the floor beside the hearth, firelight dancing over golden skin, the two of them naked and indulging in the sweetest exercise known to man—

"Care for a ride?" she asked, eyes wide.

*A ride?* Was his face that transparent? His cheeks heated like coals in a grill.

His shock must have shown because she frowned and tapped the ornamental saddle. "I won't make it go too fast if that's what you're worried about."

Ohhhh, *that* kind of ride.

Well, hell, that was obvious, wasn't it? She was standing on a carousel in a fairground.

*Cripes, Travis, get your mind out of the gutter.*

Where the heck had that daydream come from? His dreams had been beaten out of him early on in life.

Even so... A ride on a carousel... He yearned, an ache in his chest for a boyhood that had never existed.

Dusty stirred in the trailer. Travis shouldn't leave him so long, but temptation swayed him.

He'd never been on an amusement park ride in his life. They'd never had money as kids. Later, he'd been busy keeping himself and Sammy fed and clothed, body and soul patched together with spit and determination.

With the likelihood of him still being here next summer paper-thin, this could be his one chance for a carousel ride.

*Take it,* that inner little boy who'd missed all of this in childhood urged.

Why not? How long would it take? Five minutes? He could spare that.

A laugh burst out of him. "You bet! I sure would like a ride, and you can make it go as fast as you want."

As frisky as a young boy, he put a hand on the top rail and hopped over. The structure creaked under his weight.

"You need to shore up that fence."

A waterfall of feminine laughter cascaded over him. "Ya think?" she asked. "Everything in this park needs work. It's a never-ending job."

Travis stepped up onto the carousel.

Up close, Rachel looked even better. His breath backed up in his throat, his world rocked by this one short woman.

She still stood behind the white pony. What he could see of her above its body sure looked fine.

Freckles dotted a pert nose and strong cheekbones. Flecks of gold flashed in eyes lit with an inner glow.

That her hazel eyes and some of the streaks in her hair matched was about the most striking feature he'd ever seen on a woman.

One small freckle dotted her bottom lip.

The tiniest pair of silver cowboy boots hung from stars in her earlobes.

He wondered what the rest of her looked like. With her arms crossed on top of the pony, the too-long sleeves of a plaid flannel jacket covered most of her hands. Her right hand still gripped the wrench.

Inside the collar of her jacket was a prettier shirt collar, Western, pink with white piping and small white flowers embroidered on the tips.

She caught him studying the flowers. "Bitterroot," she said. "Montana's state flower."

A straw cowboy hat with a pink band embroidered with more bitterroot flowers hung behind her on the center column of the ride.

She flung an arm wide to encompass the characters on the old ride. The pungent scent of fresh paint and turpentine wafted from the structure. "Take your pick. I've been fine-tuning the engine and oiling her parts to put her to bed for the winter. I need to test her. Might as well have a passenger on board while I do."

She smiled again. "Waste of energy otherwise, running her with no one on her. This lovely old lady was made to be enjoyed." In her voice, he heard a world of affection.

"Choose your animal and climb on," she said.

Travis walked around the carousel and rubbed his hand across the backs of the odd animals—odd for an amusement park ride, that was. Along with the usual horses were a pair of bighorn sheep, a bison, a cow, a white-tailed deer and an elk, all wearing ornate saddles. Strangest darned ride he'd ever seen.

He chose a big black bull.

"Predictable," Rachel muttered, tempering it with a humorous tone.

"Sorry to disappoint, ma'am, but I've never seen a bull on a carousel ride before. It's big and sturdy."

In her quick glance down his big body, he saw admiration, but her eyes shifted away too quickly. So was she attracted to him? Or not?

"The bull should hold your weight," was all she said.

He mounted. It did. He held on to a pair of long hard horns.

"Ready when you are," he called back over his shoulder when he heard her walk away behind him.

From somewhere near the center column of the big old thing, she called, "Here you go."

He heard a lever being moved. The ride took a few arthritic strides. Then the engine kicked in and picked up speed.

His breath caught. There was something to be said for taking your first ride as an adult.

"Hang on to your hat, mister. You're going for the ride of your life."

On this old thing? Not likely.

He liked her sense of humor. Together, they could have a lot of fu-u-u-u-u-n-n—

The carousel picked up more speed than a machine this large and heavy should. Travis gripped the horns.

A breeze rushed past his ears, filling them with whispered sighs and longings he'd thought he'd given up on years ago.

"You want music?" she called.

"Yeah!"

The toots and whistles of a calliope filled the air with the old Beatles song "All You Need Is Love."

Stress, responsibility and apprehension fell away, lifting his spirits. When had he ever been free?

Unadulterated joy filled him, the kind kids never question, but that had never had a place in Travis's childhood.

There'd been tangled bits of hope hidden in miserly corners of his world, but there had never been joy.

He let go of the horns and spread his arms wide. The cool wind worked its way through his jacket and shirt, filling him with vitality and refreshing his tired mind. The sun, having finally burned off the morning fog, melted the permafrost of his heart.

His cowboy hat, part of his head for nearly twenty years, flew off.

A huge laugh startled out of him, snatched immediately by the wind and caught by Rachel. He heard her laugh in response.

After a time, the ride slowed and he wiped rivers of tears from his cheeks. He wasn't crying. No. It was just the wind.

He smiled harder than he had in a long, long time.

"That's more like it," Rachel said as she waddled over, satisfaction tinting her tone. "That's the kind of smile I like to see on a man's face."

Whoa. Back up. *Waddled?*

Her pregnant belly stuck out a mile. His dreams of

warm winter nights, a fire in the hearth and a willing partner deflated like a weather balloon in a snowstorm.

The woman was about to pop. What was she having? Triplets?

When other people saw pregnant women, they got warm fuzzies. Not Travis.

Pregnant women made him think about being trapped, about expectations and responsibilities. He'd had his fill of those. Still did. Big time.

He had one big responsibility to handle in this town before hitching a ride on the next good breeze and heading back out.

Reluctantly, he dismounted, his dreams slow to die. But die they did. As always.

Oh, Lord, mischief lurked in Rachel's hazel eyes. Damn the woman. She'd known exactly how attracted he'd been to her and how shocked he was now.

"Nice meeting you, Travis. I'm sure we'll see each other around town." She handed him his hat.

He settled it onto his head slowly, tamping it down with a hard tug, the grown man firmly back in place.

"Thank you, ma'am." He might be disappointed in her pregnancy, but she'd given him a gift. His gratitude was sincere. He adjusted his expectations and left the carousel, his stride long and fierce.

He couldn't get away fast enough, driving without a backward glance.

He didn't believe in new beginnings. No matter where he went, he always ended up in the same old place.

Not so for his nephews. Travis wouldn't let that happen to Jason and Colt. Damned if he would let them down. They deserved a good home, and he would create one for them here in Rodeo. They would get more out of childhood than he ever had.

*Screw your head on right, Travis. Disappointment never killed a man. Get on with it.*

With purpose compelling him forward, he put Rachel out of his mind and drove straight to the Double U, where he pulled up in front of a sprawling ranch house with cedar siding and red shutters framing wide windows.

No one answered the front door when he knocked.

He'd been here once before, the day he'd been hired, put in touch with the Webers by an acquaintance, a cowboy he respected and trusted.

That day, he'd taken a tour of the town and had known immediately it would work for Samantha and the boys.

He'd chosen a house for them, one that had been put on the market just a half hour before he stepped into the real estate office. The down payment had been a result of years of having nothing to spend his paycheck on but himself...and he didn't need much.

A good, solid house. Needed some work, but it had been built well. A safe town. Meant to be.

Travis might not believe in good omens for himself, but he did for his only remaining family.

He ran his new boss, Udall Weber, to ground in the stable.

Udall shook hands with a firm grip. "Good to see you again. You get settled in all right?" A big man with a ruddy complexion, his skin had been ruined by years of hard work in the unforgiving elements.

"Not yet. Got an appointment in an hour to pick up the keys. Meantime, where can I put Dusty?"

"Last stall on the right. First, let's saddle up for a quick tour of the ranch."

"Glad to have one."

"Take the weekend to get yourself organized. Monday will be soon enough to start work. We got fences that need mending before winter."

Travis backed his horse out of the trailer. Dusty, a solid gray gelding he'd owned for a dozen years, had covered a lot of miles with him. His brief visits to get Sammy and the boys out of Vegas and settled in San Francisco seemed like a bad dream here on the stunning Montana prairie.

"Park your trailer behind the barn beside mine." Udall pointed to a spot. "Don't mind if you store it there for the winter till you get your place set up."

"Thanks. Appreciate it." His place never would be *set up*, not for permanently holding cattle.

His clothes were in a bag on the backseat of his pickup truck. His motorcycle rested in the bed. What else did he need?

Sammy's voice rang in his head. *You need a home, Travis. Put roots down somewhere and stay for longer than a year.*

Nope.

"You meet anyone in town yet?" Udall asked, breaking into his thoughts.

A picture of whiskey-colored eyes and tawny hair flashed across his memory. "I stopped at the amusement park outside of town. Met a woman named Rachel."

The corners of Udall's mouth turned down. "Rachel McGuire."

Travis frowned. "You don't like her?"

"I like her fine. Lovely young woman. She's got a

rough road ahead, though. Husband's dead and she's pregnant, with another little one already at home."

"Jeez, that's tough."

Wind knocked out of him, Travis had to admit he was one of the lucky ones. Sure, he had his problems, but that poor woman...what a future she had facing her.

His admiration grew. How she'd kept her good humor boggled his mind. Another kid at home as well as one on the way? Warning bells clanged. No matter how much he admired the woman, he'd be keeping his distance.

"What's with the carousel? It's great, but the rest of the place looks abandoned."

"We got us a committee that's reviving the park. They've set their sights on getting it up and running by next summer."

"Think they can?" Considering what he'd seen today, Travis had his doubts.

"If anyone can, it would be Rachel and her gang."

With a rough laugh, Udall strode away to saddle up, his denim jeans and shirt emphasizing his lean, hard frame.

Travis saddled Dusty, a chore he'd done thousands of times before. This was where he belonged, with horses and ranchers. Running his hand along the horse's neck, he murmured, "You survive the trip okay, boy?"

He rode out with his new boss onto land as pretty as any he'd ever seen. He'd been raised in Arizona, a state with its own brand of stark beauty, but often arid. He liked the colors of Montana.

"Monday morning, we'll get you out trailing," Udall said. "One of the hands spotted a dozen cattle holed up in the gully at the south edge of the property."

Travis followed him out onto the range.

"In his reference letter, Lester Green said you're one of the best he's ever seen at flushing cattle out of tough spots and bringing them home. Said you did real good up in Wyoming last fall."

"Yeah. Lester was a good boss." Travis loved trailing, one of his favorite jobs. "It's late to be finishing up gathering cattle for the winter, isn't it?"

"Yep. Had a couple of the hands out sick. Some kind of flu goin' 'round."

They spotted a sheep caught on a piece of damaged fence on the far side of a field of dormant alfalfa.

"You keep sheep?" Travis asked.

"My neighbor raises them and spins her own yarn."

Together, they got the distressed animal off the fence, but not before it kicked Travis in his ribs.

He hissed.

"That hurt, I bet." Udall said.

Travis rubbed the injury. "Part of the job."

Udall set the animal loose on its own side of the fence. "I'll come back with tools tomorrow and fix this."

"Let me."

Udall shot him a surprised look. "You sure? You only just got here."

"I'm sure. Just spent too many days on the road. I'm itchy to get out on the land."

Udall smiled approvingly. They mounted and rode on.

So darned glad to be back in the country, Travis breathed deeply of fresh air purer than anything he'd ever found in any city.

His worries fell away, leaving only the wind in his ears, the sun on the prairie and the warmth of the animal beneath him.

# Chapter 2

Rachel McGuire rested her head against the inanimate pony's unforgiving neck, unsure whether to laugh or have a good, hard cry.

What on earth had just happened to her poor battered heart?

The second she'd laid eyes on the new arrival, Travis Read, she'd been attracted to him.

What kind of man could melt her hardened heart with just a look from blazing blue eyes, the rustiest of smiles and so few words? And not just her heart, but also her pregnant body, waking it from a long slumber.

Could the timing possibly be worse?

What kind of poor, dumb fool was she for finding a man so attractive when she was more than seven months pregnant, and as big as that horse she'd heard shuffling in his trailer?

She'd wanted to flirt. But why would he ever be interested in her?

That smile? When he'd ridden the carousel? Oh, sweet heavenly pumpkins, pure and utter joy.

She'd given him a simple ride on a carousel, and he'd smiled at her as though she'd hung the moon.

And all of that lovely warmth and admiration she'd basked in had come to a crashing halt when he'd seen her belly.

Of course she understood why. Totally got it.

But wouldn't it be nice to be carefree and available to flirt with a man who'd found her attractive?

*Suck it up, Rachel. This is the life you chose. Live it.*

Rachel laughed at her lapse in common sense. "You so need to get over yourself, Rach."

She put the finishing touches on the carousel, preparing it for the coming winter. An hour later, she tucked away her tools, along with her unreasonable attraction to the new man.

She drove into town and stopped at the used-clothing shop.

Her wardrobe was pretty slim pickings at the moment.

She found a glittery maternity top she could wear to work. If she took off the sequins and rearranged the beading, she could remake the top into her own style. Embroidery, sewing and knitting calmed her. That she could take a five-dollar top and make it personal filled her with pride.

At the market, she shopped for next week's groceries. In the produce section, she found marked-down overripe bananas that would make an excellent bread.

She picked up fruits and vegetables on special and root vegetables in season.

A huge bag of lentils was on sale. Good source of protein. She bypassed the expensive sugary cereals and instant oatmeal to pick up a bag of rolled oats. By the time she finished, she had an economical, nourishing menu planned for the weekend and coming week for herself and her daughter.

*Maybe I should get a small steak to share with Tori.* Her mother was always on her case about eating meat for the baby, and Tori was a growing girl who needed protein.

She perused the packages, but the prices worried her. She picked up one minuscule steak, shuffling along the counter to see if there was a better deal, until she ran smack dab into a hard body.

She looked up.

Travis Read. Here. In the grocery store.

Good grief. Was her heart going to do somersaults every time she met him? Or bumped into him? Literally.

He grasped one of her upper arms to steady her, his big palm warm even through Davey's thick old jacket.

"I'm sorry!" Her heart thumped at just the sight of him let alone the touch of those long fingers. "I wasn't watching where I was going."

Rachel's skin seemed to constrict until it was a size too small for her body.

"No problem," he said. "No harm done."

The thick honey of his deep voice flowed along her nerves. Her pulse skittered a foolish teenage girl's dance in her mature woman's body.

Travis had a great mouth, finely shaped with a firm outline. How would his lips feel on hers? Would his kiss be more refined than Davey's had been? Her husband's kisses had been long on enthusiasm and short on finesse. She had a feeling Travis loved on a whole different level.

*Get a grip, Rach.*

"You okay?" Travis asked. He glanced down.

Too late, she remembered she'd opened her jacket when she'd entered the store. Her shirt wasn't maternity and didn't fit properly. Only the top three buttons were done up, and the bottom of the shirt splayed over her big belly.

Her nicer maternity jeans were hung up at home, waiting for her to put them on for work.

The pants she had on now, a pair she'd bought secondhand, were already worn out from her first pregnancy. The belly panel was stretched to the max, showing white flecks where the elastic had broken.

Good grief.

The silence went on too long. "You made it to the Double U?"

"Yeah. Made it there just fine."

A dark shadow painted his strong jawline. He smelled of citrus. His body generated heat.

She stepped away.

*Come down to earth*, she scolded herself.

She dropped the one barely there steak she'd picked up onto her discounted vegetables and lentils. His basket held seven steaks. Seven!

Her economic situation had never embarrassed her in the past. Frustrated her? Oh, yeah. But caused her shame? No. It had merely been a fact of her life. It disconcerted her now, though.

Neither of them had said anything for a while. Their silence fell into truly awkward, uncomfortable territory.

"Don't forget to add some vegetables," she blurted.

Cripes, small talk had never stressed her out before. She could usually talk the paint off a barn door, yet here she stood with her mouth gone as dry as a popcorn fart.

Travis sidled away from her, hefting the basket with a rueful kick up of one side of his mouth. "Yeah, guess I'll grab a few potatoes."

"And greens." *Brilliant conversation, Rach.*

He grimaced. "Maybe."

She managed a reasonable facsimile of a grin. "Which means you won't."

His sweet fraction of a shy smile made a brief appearance.

He doffed his hat and left. "See you 'round town, Rachel."

She watched him stride away.

The phrase *salt of the earth* came to mind. Travis Read would fit in well in Rodeo, maybe better than she did. After all, she wasn't much of a cowgirl. She didn't ride horses, and she didn't live on a ranch.

She loved Montana, though, and loved her town with all of her heart. Rachel adored its basic, varied, salt-of-the-earth residents. She was working her fingers to the bone on next summer's fair to keep the town alive and make it prosperous again.

Tamping down her wayward daydreams, she paid for her purchases.

At home, she poured a glass of OJ, taking it and an oatmeal muffin outside to soak up the rays of what might be one of the last good days of autumn.

She sat on the porch step—*porch* being a generous term for the slice of tilting wood and two steps hammered together under the front door of her mom's trailer.

Sunlight flooding the valley reflected off the tarnished white wood siding of the Victorian across the road.

Rachel sighed. She missed Abigail Montgomery, her

elderly friend. Her death, days after Davey's, had been devastating. Worst time of her life.

She'd lost too much six months ago. Thoughts of her big, irrepressible Davey… Whew! Those could still bring her to her knees.

She wrapped her arms around herself and rocked. She missed him every night.

She'd already cried a river for him, and for Abigail, but she had a life to live and children to raise. She needed her good spirits to help shoulder her burdens.

Veering away from her grief before it brought on tears, she concentrated on the Victorian.

Her every-second-of-the-day dream about owning that house perked her up, rerouting her thoughts away from devastating memories.

To everyone else in Rodeo, the aging home looked like a run-down romantic anomaly in the Western landscape, but to Rachel it was perfect.

But then, romantic notions and daydreams had always been her downfall, hadn't they?

Davey had never known about this particular dream. She'd wanted to surprise him with a fait accompli. *Look, honey, I bought us a house.*

Any day now it would be hers. She hadn't heard even a whisper about whether Abigail's British relatives were going to put it up for sale, but why wouldn't they?

It was useless to them.

She'd scrimped and saved until she had just shy of five thousand dollars in change and small bills hidden in her closet.

Dumb spot to keep her money, but she and Davey had had a joint bank account. Had he known about this money, he would have siphoned off every spare cent for his motorcycle passion…or for treating his friends to beer every Friday night…or for chewing through money like it was cereal.

Davey had had those great big hands that could love her with enthusiasm, but they were a pair of sieves where money was concerned.

She should roll the change and count the money soon and get it into the bank. Later. Right now she needed these moments of rest.

The pretty trills of a horned lark on Abigail's land floated across to her on the late-October breeze.

No one else in town would want that house.

There was no way there would be a speck of competition. It needed work.

It would be hers. It could have been hers a lot sooner had she married someone more practical.

*The heart has a mind of its own, Rach, and you just have to follow it.*

*I sure did, didn't I?*

Yes. She sure had, right back into the financial insecurity she'd grown up with.

She let out a sigh full of hot air and yearning.

The distant hum of an engine—a motorcycle—cut through her daydreaming. Her unreasonable heart lurched with thoughts of her late husband.

A big Harley shot down the old road toward her.

It wasn't Davey, of course. Never again would her husband ride home with a shit-eating grin that would light up any cloudy day.

She scrubbed her hands over her arms and shivered despite the sunshine. Oh, Davey.

The bike came close, closer, and slowed down enough to initiate the turn into Abigail's driveway. Who was it?

The noise disturbed the lark. Routed, he surged from his hiding spot, his distinctive yellow-and-black face catching the eye of a white cat crouching in the grasses along the side of the road. *Ghost.* Abigail's cat shot out toward the songbird, right into the bike's path. *No!*

Rachel stumbled to her feet. "Get back," she yelled.

The biker swerved to avoid the cat, Ghost ran back into the tall grasses and the bike tipped over. The machine flew across the road, screeching and shooting sparks, leaving the rider bouncing and rolling along the shoulder in a plume of dust.

In the ensuing silence, dirt and stones fell on his still body.

Rachel froze. Unwelcome memories of that awful day and the police officer at her door surged through her. *He's gone, ma'am, in a head-on collision with a tree. I'm sorry.*

Resurrected shock held her immobile.

The man lay unmoving.

Rachel stared. *Please, not another death. Abigail. Davey. No.*

A groan from across the small highway galvanized her.

Rachel ran over, the only sound her pounding pulse.

He still hadn't moved. *Oh, dear Lord, please don't die.*

Kneeling beside him, she checked his body for signs of injury. Hard to tell through the leather. She touched his shoulders, arms and legs, feeling for broken bones. Under layers of solid muscle everything *seemed* fine, but what about internal injuries? She didn't know how to check. With a wail of frustration, she tore into herself for never having taken first-aid classes.

One arm moved, raising the visor of his helmet.

Her frantic glance took in his face. He was conscious. Deep-set blue eyes watched her steadily, silently.

He reached up to remove his helmet. She stopped him with a hand on his wrist, feeling a strong pulse, thank God. "Should you do that? Is your head injured?"

Her voice shook. So did her hands.

"I'm good." He took off his helmet, and she gasped. *Travis?*

Of all people—What—? How—?

"Are you okay?" Her voice emerged reed thin.

He didn't respond, just stared into her eyes, then touched her bottom lip with a glove-clad finger.

"Only one," he murmured.

Huh?

His eyes met hers again, mesmerizing. She could fall into that blue gaze for hours. The moment stretched out. A smile, sweet and broad, curved the corners of his mouth.

Oh my-y-y. What did Travis use for toothpaste? Moonbeams?

He sat up slowly, his body coming close enough for her to feel his heat even through his leathers. She sat back on her heels.

She should tell him to be careful, to check for injuries, but couldn't find her voice.

His hand brushed a strand of hair from her forehead, the leather soft against her skin. Grasping the tips of his glove with his straight white teeth, he tugged it off, then did the same with the other. Still mesmerized, Rachel stared, swallowed and stared some more.

Again he reached for her hair and ran his fingers through it, massaging her scalp. Rachel almost purred like a cat.

"Soft," he said. "Calf's ear." He wasn't making sense, but Rachel was too captivated to question him while he touched her with such gentle grace. Her traitorous desire overrode her common sense.

She moaned low in her throat.

He moved his hand to the back of her neck, urging her close to his chest. As pliable as a rag doll, she allowed it. His lips touched hers with velvety moisture and a faint exhalation of coffee-scented breath.

She hadn't touched a man since Davey. Davey. Her late husband. Her eager, playful lover.

*Pull back, Rach. Don't allow this. Davey is only six months gone. You should—*

He deepened the kiss. Taking his time, he caressed her tongue with his. His skill. Oh, his earnest, deep skill. Yes, to his awesome finesse. She'd known it would be like this. Heavenly bliss.

Rapture. Joy.

Need simmered inside her. In the months since Davey's death, what she had needed most was his touch, his soothing physical support, one last endless night of blazing lovemaking.

A woman should be allowed to say goodbye to her husband. Rachel's anger wrestled with her guilt and desire.

Fireworks blazed. Buried dreams came to life. This man's touch, his mouth, soothed away aching, aching grief.

Rachel sighed and lost herself in his kiss, exploring his mouth with her ardent tongue.

She'd never kissed, had never been kissed, so slowly and intently. Her mind went blank and her body limp.

Elizabeth announced her presence with a hard kick to Rachel's belly.

She pulled back. "Ouch." She'd been kneeling too long.

"Ouch?" Travis's voice sounded lost in a sensual fog, echoing how she felt.

"The baby kicked me. I need to stand up."

"Baby?" Coming out of his daze, his eyes widened. Horror spread across his features. "Sorry! God, I'm sorry. I shouldn't have done that."

"You've had a shock," she managed to bite out, while she really wanted to blurt, *Don't be sorry. I've never been kissed like that in my life. I needed it. After all of the turmoil, and the crazy worries about the future, I needed something for me. Purely, selfishly, for just me.*

But that was a daydream that required a hasty burial. *Just me* was not possible these days.

She eased away from him and rubbed her belly to soothe Beth.

"Are you okay?" she asked, striving to pretend she hadn't been rocked by a stranger's kiss, that this was nothing out of the ordinary.

"Yeah." He nodded with a perplexed frown.

Did he understand any better than she what had just happened?

"Should I call an ambulance?"

"No ambulance. No hospital. I'm good."

The cowboy she'd met a short while ago was gone, replaced by a motorcycle rider. "No head injury? You were out cold."

"Naw. Not out cold, just winded."

"But you didn't move when I was checking you for injuries."

"No, I didn't." His jaw hardened, so briefly she barely caught it. She didn't have a clue what was going on.

He stood and winced. "This head's pretty hard. I've survived worse. Gonna be bruised tomorrow, though."

Rachel struggled to get to her feet. Travis rushed to help her. "You shouldn't be kneeling in your condition."

*In her condition.* For a brief moment, she hadn't been a pregnant woman, but a desirable one. He'd looked past her circumstances to *her*.

She stared at him. "Are you serious, Travis? I thought you were unconscious. I needed to check you. You could have been badly hurt."

"I appreciate your concern," he said, his hands strong beneath her elbows, lifting her as though she weighed no more than a sack of potatoes. "I'll be stiff the next few days, but that's all." He made sure she was steady on her feet, took her hands in his and squeezed before he released her, his rough calluses a jolting return to reality.

She needed reality, needed to get her head back onto her shoulders. So, he hadn't been knocked out, but maybe he'd been in shock. How else to account for that kiss? He hadn't known he was kissing *her*. Maybe he'd thought she was an old girlfriend. Or a current one? After all, she was nothing to him.

His leather jacket had a tear along one arm. Travis could have been killed.

On a dime, those awful memories raced through her again. Davey, Davey, Davey.

Her blood arced and swooped through her arteries. Her pulse skittered worse than on a caffeine high. "You sure you don't have internal injuries?"

"No injuries. Everything feels fine. Good thing I slowed down to take the turn."

Rachel reached down to swipe dirt and gravel from her knees. A fine tremor ran through her. Anger overtook the fright he'd given her.

She couldn't fend off images, thousands of Davey carefree and laughing, and that one horrifying imaginary picture of him broken by the side of the road thanks to his damned obsession with motorcycles. Because of them, he was gone for good, and her children were fatherless. What was it with men and their stupid, dangerous toys? *Unfair, Rachel. A motorcycle is just a tool.* Davey's reckless speed had been the real problem.

Common sense held no sway, only anger. "Maybe you should stop riding motorcycles. They're dangerous."

At her sharp tone, he shot her a hard look. "Not if you know what you're doing. Was that your cat that ran out in front of me?"

"No, it was Abigail's."

"Who's Abigail?"

Rachel pointed to the aging Victorian. "That was her house."

"Right," he said. "I thought the owner died months ago. Who owns the cat now?"

"Ghost turned feral after her death." Rachel drew a breath to steady her quavering voice. This man's decisions were no concern of hers. Who was she to judge what he did with his life? She modulated her tone. "She won't come near anyone. I'm worried about her."

"She's gonna get herself killed."

"That's what I'm afraid of."

He strode to his bike and lifted it onto its tires, the machine as light as a bicycle in his capable hands. He was strong, but then again, she already knew that.

Where Davey had been tall and lean, Travis was maybe five-eleven and heavily muscled.

He turned the bike toward the house.

Those memories of Davey still haunting her, she couldn't help but ask again, "Are you sure you're all right?"

His soft smile eased her anger, a bit. "Yeah, I'm good. Honest. How about you? You good?"

"I'm fine."

He touched a couple of fingers to his forehead in a casual salute—no wedding band, not that she was looking—and then limped up the driveway toward the Victorian.

"Wait!"

He turned back.

"Why were you riding a bike? Where's your truck?"

"Left it in the garage for a checkup. It's been running rough, and I want it ready for winter."

"Where's your horse and trailer?"

"Udall's letting me leave them on his ranch till I'm set up here."

Here? At Abigail's?

"Why are you going to Abigail's house? Won't you be bunking in the worker's quarters on the Double U?"

"Nope. I'll be living here." He parked his bike at the side of the driveway. She followed him.

Living here. In Abigail's house, which she hadn't even heard had been rented. Travis would be living across the road from her, where she would have to see him every day and remind herself that no amount of makeup or dresses could change what she was…an ungainly woman who was a month and a half away from giving birth. No amount of dolling up would make her as attractive to him as he was to her.

But he'd kissed her.

He'd been stunned, dazed, that was all. She would probably never know who he'd really been kissing while he'd put his lips to hers so sweetly.

"No one told me the house had been rented."

"Rented? No, ma'am. I bought the place." He mounted the stairs to the veranda.

Bought—? Her house had been *sold*? When had it been listed, and why hadn't she heard about it? This was a small town. Everybody's business was an open book, for God's sake, and not one person had thought to tell her the house she craved had been sold?

*What do you expect, Rach? You kept that dream close to your chest, didn't you?*

True, she had. She hadn't wanted people, not even Davey, to think poor Rachel McGuire was crazy enough to believe she could actually find a way to buy a house.

Maybe she hadn't heard him properly.

She chased after him, stood at the bottom of the stairs and stared up at him.

"You're joking, right?"

He frowned down at her from the top of the steps. "Why would I joke?"

"You're not supposed to be living here. No one's supposed to buy this house." She sounded like a lunatic. She didn't care.

Her house, the only thing she wanted more in life than her children's health and happiness, had been sold.

The air became thin.

She panted. Stars danced in front of her eyes. Her vision narrowed. A moment later, she found herself sitting on the bottom step with a hand on her back urging her head between her knees. Hard to do with a nearly full-grown baby in the way. The cowboy squatted in front of her and chafed the backs of her hands.

"Are you all right?"

She straightened, still struggling for air, but not so dizzy.

"Are you hungry or something? You fainted. Good thing I caught you."

She'd fainted and he'd caught her? The man moved fast.

"Wait a minute. Back up."

When Travis started to pull away from her, she grasped his hands, craving his solid comfort as her daydreams slid into nightmare. He squatted on his haunches and watched her with a steady regard.

"I didn't mean get away from me," she said. "I meant, back up in the conversation. Please tell me I misunderstood. You did *not* buy this house."

"I bought the house."

"No." It came out a croak, with tears clogging her throat. This house was supposed to be hers.

He watched her with pity. Great.

As if it wasn't bad enough that she was Cindy Hardy's daughter and a widowed, single mother with a bun in her oversize oven and a three-year-old daughter with no father, and that they lived in Cindy's tin can, but now she had also lost the chance to own the only house in the county she could have ever hoped to afford…and the only one she'd ever dreamed of owning.

Sure, her itty-bitty down payment would buy a small trailer, but after the childhood she'd had, the thought made her sick. She wanted more for her children. She wanted a real home.

The man who had bought her house watched her as if he was afraid she would faint again.

A terrible rage arose in her.

She didn't want pity. She wanted a knock-down, drag-out fight, to pound something hard and not stop for a good month.

Bursting with the unfairness, she pushed against the

cowboy squatting in front of her. Travis fell onto his butt in the dirt.

"Hey!"

Rachel had never touched another person with violence in her life.

She stood. Her belly might make a swift exit impossible, but she couldn't stay here.

He jumped to his feet and grasped her upper arms to stop her. "Why'd you do that? I've done nothing to you."

She kept her mouth shut because, if she didn't, she would start to scream and never stop.

His big hands still gripped her arms. She hated him. She didn't want him to stop touching her.

She put her hands against his chest to push him away, but her outrage deflated. If she could fall into the earth and disappear, she would. He was right. *He* had done nothing to her. Life had. As hard as she fought, she couldn't get ahead.

Stuff happened.

She was tired of stuff happening.

She would just have to work harder. And harder. And harder. God, she was tired.

"I'm sorry," she whispered, her palms soothed by the solid beat of his heart beneath his worn denim shirt.

Despite his confusion, despite how she had just treated him, he watched her with concern. Travis was kind and good, and she was behaving like a child.

"I truly am sorry."

"It's okay. I can see you're upset."

She started down the driveway to go home, or what passed for a home.

"You're shaky," he called. "You need some help getting across the road?"

Cripes. The day had started so well. For a short

while, he'd found her super-duper attractive. Now, he was treating her like an invalid.

"I can manage by myself," she answered with a touch of irritation.

She managed to make it inside the front door before the first tears fell.

After five minutes of the worst pity party she'd thrown for herself since Davey's death, she rinsed her face and called her friend Nadine.

Rachel brought her up to speed on everything that had just happened.

"I'm angry, Nadine. Mad to the soles of my shoes. Life has to start turning around for me sometime soon."

Nadine said, "I hear you, sweetie. You've had a rough go of it. How can I help?"

Nadine wrote for the local newspaper. She was handy with research and a computer.

A need for...something...burned inside Rachel. Vengeance, maybe? Or perhaps just to learn that Travis was *not* the perfect man he appeared to be? That he was flawed and unworthy of her attraction? That he didn't deserve her house? It would be so much easier to think of him as her enemy if she didn't like him so much.

"Find out about him," she ordered Nadine. "You're a great reporter. You do research for your articles. Find out who Travis Read really is and then let me know."

"Will do, honey. I'll get back to you soon."

Rachel wished Tori were home right now. She would give her daughter the biggest hug, but every Friday morning, Cindy and Tori had a standing date for a few hours of shopping and then lunch at the mall.

Cindy worked at the hair salon in town and had disposable income. Cindy cared more for clothes and perfect nails than she did about improving her living situation.

Every week, she gave Tori the treats that Rachel could not afford and, every week, Rachel rose above her own regret and envy to be happy for Tori.

The new mall out on the highway twenty miles away was a monstrosity into which Rachel refused to set one foot. She liked the shops on Main Street, thank you very much.

Her mom loved the mall, but then, she had no sense of loyalty to her town at all.

Rachel missed Victoria. They'd only been gone a few hours, but Rachel needed her daughter something fierce.

Tori was goodness and light and the antidote to every disappointment life had visited upon Rachel.

She took her straw cowboy hat from the hook beside the door. She'd embroidered the bitterroot flowers on the band herself, as well as the ones on the secondhand shirt she wore. She set it on her head defiantly, then sat on the porch step to wait for her daughter to come home. She shouldn't be wearing straw at this time of year, at the end of October for Pete's sake, but Davey had given it to her after their first date. 'Nuff said.

## Chapter 3

What the *hell* had that kiss been about? Travis took himself to task about as hard as he ever had in his life.

What had he been thinking? He knew only that Rachel had run across the road and had touched him with hands more caring than any he'd ever known. Her concern for him, a man about whom no one cared or gave a second thought, was a powerful attraction.

Women usually wanted stuff *from* him, as opposed to worrying about him.

After a childhood as bereft of affection as a snowball in hell, tenderness took him by surprise.

He'd been winded and shocked at losing control of his bike, flat on his back cursing himself for a fool, and then there she was like an angel, leaning over him with thoughtful concern and fear for his well-being.

His parents hadn't cared. His sister would have, but

he'd spent too many years taking care of her and their pattern was set in stone. He was the caretaker, not she.

Travis watched the woman waddle back to the sad-looking trailer across the road, stubborn defiance stiffening her spine.

She asked for nothing and offered so much. Too much.

*Have a care, Travis. You don't even know the woman and already you're* kissing *her?*

He'd never done anything like it in his life. He'd had plenty of one-night stands, but not with women with pregnant bellies and a whole barn load of responsibility.

Lying in the road with his protective shields down, this morning's attraction had flared.

Her hair turned out to be every bit as soft as a calf's ear. And she'd tasted as sweet as he'd imagined.

But what good was attraction when he could do nothing with it? She was pregnant. He had a glut of duties to fill in the coming months. He didn't need more.

He had his own life to live.

*Case closed, Travis. End of story, got it?*

He needed to back away from Rachel and *stay* away.

He unhooked his saddlebags from his bike and carried them into his house. *His* house.

Travis Read. Homeowner. He couldn't wrap his head around it.

*Home.* Lord, how did a man learn how to make a home when he'd never known a single good one in his whole life?

The challenge scared the hell out of him.

The empty rooms waited like hungry sponges to soak up the noise and chaos Jason and Colt would surely create.

Was he doing the right thing in uprooting them and

bringing them here? He had only his gut to rely on, and it was shouting a resounding *yes*.

In the old-fashioned kitchen, he unpacked his groceries and put them into the ancient fridge.

Upstairs, he chose the largest bedroom for himself and the new king-size bed he'd ordered. He'd slept in bunkhouses all his adult life. Now he owned a bed.

Soon it would be Samantha's, and he'd be back in another bunkhouse somewhere.

His bags hit the floor with a solid clunk.

Walking back downstairs, he stared around. By the time Sammy and her boys arrived, he needed to turn this house into a home.

He had plenty of work ahead of him, in cleaning up the place and renovating. Floors needed sanding and walls painting.

He had no template to guide him. He would start with whatever needed fixing and then take inspiration from the many ranch wives who'd made homes and fed him and his fellow cowboys on too many ranches to count.

There was nothing inside him to draw on.

He had plenty of longing, but zero know-how.

Moving on was all he knew, and bunking with a dozen other men was his way of life.

Travis Read. Homeowner. A home meant obligation and duty, a millstone around a man's neck…and he was damned tired of those.


Rachel sat on the porch and watched her mother pull into the driveway and park her decked-out pickup truck beside Rachel's old junker.

Cindy Hardy had no understanding of the notion *less is more*.

She had bought every chrome feature the local dealership could get its hands on.

Thank God Rachel had been able to talk her out of a lift kit.

Cindy mistakenly assumed that men drooled over her, when all they really wanted was her truck.

Too many of the men in town had known Cindy, as in *known* known, to want to have anything to do with her romantically.

To the people of Rodeo, Montana, Cindy had always been and would always be the girl from the trailer park—even if there was no park, only a trailer.

The second Cindy got Tori unbuckled, Rachel's daughter jumped out of the truck, came running toward her mom and threw herself into her arms, squealing, "Mommy, Mommy."

Rachel broke into a huge smile and hugged her little three-year-old bundle of joy. Cindy unloaded the bags. Rachel oohed and aahed over her daughter's new purchases. Cindy had bought her a lot of fun stuff. Thank goodness it wasn't all toys, but also new clothes. Another week of Cindy's wages down the tubes.

Rachel should tell her to stop, but without Cindy buying Tori's clothes, the child would have little to wear. Besides, how could she tell Tori's only grandmother to stop spoiling her?

Nope. She didn't have it in her heart to ruin Cindy's fun, even if Cindy never had understood that it would have been better to have saved at least some of her money to improve her life's situation than to wait for some man to come along and save her.

Rachel would never, not in a million years, depend on a man again where her finances were concerned. She planned to scrimp and save and work until her knuckles hurt, and then get her children into a stable, secure home life.

Tori chattered away, reminding her of what was at stake.

Davey's parents had both died when he was in high school. Ironic that it had been a car crash.

Cindy was Tori's only other relative apart from Rachel.

Maybe one day a week of being spoiled wasn't so bad.

A sound from the road caught their attention. A truck turned into Abigail's—correction, Travis's—driveway.

Rachel brushed her fingers through Tori's soft blond curls. Mother Nature had fashioned her daughter's hair out of strands of pure sunlight.

She and Tori watched the activity across the road, Rodeo's version of reality TV.

"That's a big chruck, Mommy."

"Truck," Rachel corrected automatically. "It sure is, Tori-ori-o."

With a pang of deep-seated regret, Rachel thought, *My house belongs to someone else now.*

"What's going on over there?" Cindy asked.

Cindy Hardy wore full makeup, and styled and sprayed hair. She'd tucked a sparkly, faux-Western shirt into her favorite jeans, which in turn were tucked into polished gray snakeskin cowboy boots, boots that had never seen the inside of a barn. A big rodeo belt buckle, a gift from a former lover, accentuated a still-trim waist.

Rachel suspected the guy had probably had a bunch of buckles made up expressly to give to women like Cindy. No rodeo rider worth his salt would give his own buckle away.

"It sold, but we didn't hear about it," Rachel said, not

bothering to update her mother on details. The thought of introducing her to Travis made Rachel antsy in a way she didn't want to look at too closely.

Cindy was still young and attractive, even if her style wasn't something that appealed to Rachel.

Two men got out of the truck. "Wonder if the new owner will paint," Rachel murmured. "It needs to be freshened up."

Cindy's husky laugh mocked her. "It needs a heck of a lot more than a coat of paint."

Resentment shot through Rachel. "I would have been happy to have done the work to fix it up." A fixer-upper was the only kind of house she could ever hope to buy.

A commotion across the road snagged her attention, as the two burly men opened the rear doors of the truck.

Travis didn't own much. The truck was less than half full. The men unloaded a large dresser and carried it into the house.

Tori marched her fingers up Rachel's leg, singing "The Itsy Bitsy Spider."

Rachel glanced down at her three-year-old daughter, gazing into eyes so blue they rivaled the cloudless sky, into Davey's eyes, the first thing that had attracted Rachel to him. His brilliant, laughter-filled eyes.

She was struggling to replace his laughter in their lives.

The pair of movers came back for a big leather sofa. "Too masculine. That house needs comfortable, cozy sofas and armchairs. Shabby chic. Chintz."

"Chins," Tori whispered.

The furniture looked brand-new.

Travis came outside, all traces of leather gone. The cowboy she'd met this morning stood on the front porch.

He leaned against a veranda post, a rugged movie

star in worn jeans, a snug white T-shirt, denim jacket, well-used cowboy boots and a black Stetson.

He should have looked out of place on Abigail's old-fashioned veranda. He didn't. He looked…perfect.

Cindy whistled. "Good-looking man. *He* bought that house? Wow. Who is he?"

Rachel didn't fill her in. She had never, not once in her life, competed with her mom where men were concerned, but she felt a rivalry now with a raging fire.

"What does he need a whole house for?"

Good question. "I don't know, Cindy."

Rachel had had time to cool down. Contrary to what she'd thought earlier, Travis was not her enemy. He was only a man who'd somehow managed to do better in life than she had.

His glance swept the countryside, Cindy's house, Rachel and Tori…and Cindy.

What good looks Rachel lacked, Cindy had in spades. Tori had inherited her blond curls from her grandmother, along with her charming dimples. Somehow those had bypassed Rachel.

All Rachel had were strong features and freckles, courtesy of a father she'd never met.

"I'm going over to meet him." Cindy squeezed past Rachel and Victoria and stepped down from the porch.

"No!" Rachel didn't want her mother embarrassing her. "Mom, please. Don't—"

"Don't what?"

"Don't flirt with him like you do with every man you meet."

Cindy wouldn't just be welcoming Travis to the neighborhood. She would ramp it up to see what she could get out of the man.

"He's the best-looking man we've had around here

in ages. If you think I'm going to pass him up, you're nuts." Cindy rubbed her hands on her thighs, the gesture telling. "I'm still young. I can flirt with any man I want. It's none of your business."

Cindy was pretty enough to turn any man's head, but she'd been plagued with a neediness that routinely drove her into the arms of the wrong kind of man.

Relentless, she was forever on the lookout for her next conquest.

Her sights had just zeroed in on the one across the way.

"Please, Cindy, no. You want to get your hooks into him." Rachel knew Cindy's needs inside and out. The vulnerability in the depths of her eyes was exactly the thing that had gotten her into trouble when she was only fifteen, hitching her pony to a good-looking drifter's wagon and then getting pregnant. Whoever the guy was, he'd been long gone by the time Rachel had been born.

Rachel was twenty-eight and her mother only forty-three. Rachel guessed Travis to be in his mid-to late thirties. Cindy could conceivably flirt with him, but what a load of trouble it could bring.

"Mom, he's not a drifter. He's our new neighbor. He bought the house, for Pete's sake."

"So?"

"So…" Rachel said with forced patience. "This could go wrong in so many ways."

"Everything will be fine. I'm only going over to talk to him." In Cindy's voice, Rachel heard the hints of desperation that had been growing stronger since Cindy had turned forty.

"And when the relationship goes sour, as it always does?" Rachel's displeasure bubbled over. She'd seen this movie too many times and hated the ending. "How good a neighbor will he be then? How good will *you* be?"

Cindy shrugged. "Maybe this time it will work out." She started to mosey down the driveway, but turned back. "You could always move into a place of your own, and then you wouldn't have to watch me talk to men." She walked across the road.

Mom was right. This was her mother's home, not hers. Cindy could flirt with whomever she wanted. "Come on, sugar pie, let's go inside," Rachel said, urging Tori ahead of her, unwilling to witness Cindy's performance.

Inside the house, she strode to the kitchen and settled Tori into a chair.

In the bedroom, Rachel chose one of her few maternity shirts and put it on with her good maternity jeans.

She returned to the kitchen where she put the finishing touches to the dinner she'd made to take to work with her, every action staccato and peevish.

She had no claim on the new stranger. Cindy could do whatever she wanted with him.

She packed a quinoa salad and a pint of milk, dropping them into her bag too hard.

Forcing herself to calm down, she took Tori's tiny face between her hands. Rachel kissed her forehead and her nose. "I love you, sweetie. Come sit on the porch and wave goodbye."

She picked up her purse from the hall table and left the trailer, making sure Cindy was on her way back before heading to her car.

Tori retrieved her favorite stuffed animal, a furry gray platypus. Rachel shook off dirt before she let her daughter hug it to her chest. "Stay on the porch till the car is gone, okay?"

She approached Cindy who'd moseyed back across

the highway with her ultra-sexy, phony walk that Rachel disliked.

Wary of her mom's Cheshire cat grin, she asked, "What's up?"

"I've got a date," Cindy said with a whole boatload of smugness.

Disappointment thrummed through Rachel. So that's the kind of man Travis was, a guy who kissed strangers, but liked flashy women like Cindy. Was the man a player? Had she pegged him all wrong? "When?"

"Tonight."

"Tonight? But I'm working. You're taking care of Tori."

"I know. I'll ask Laurie to babysit for a few hours." Cindy went to the porch and bent to talk to Tori. "You don't mind, do you, honey? Laurie is fun."

"She colors with me." Tori smiled with Cindy's dimples.

"But I can't afford to pay her," Rachel objected, knowing Cindy wouldn't offer to pick up the tab.

"Sure you can. You make good tips at the bar."

"But—" What could she say? *I need money to move out, to get away from you?* She couldn't bear to sound so cold and ungrateful, especially not when Cindy had been kind enough to take her in. Rachel should have never moved back into the trailer with Cindy and her resentment, but what else could she have done? Davey had left her with nothing but broken promises and hot air.

Rachel gave in to the inevitable. "Okay. I'll be home after one."

Before leaving, Rachel kissed Tori again because, while Davey hadn't been able to keep a buck in his pocket, he had made her laugh a lot and had given her the most precious of gifts, two children.

Just as Rachel opened her car door, Tori called, "See you later, aggilator."

*Ah, Victoria, my sweet divine daughter, you raise my spirits as much as your father used to.*

Rachel blew her an air kiss. "Alligator, Tori-ori-ori-o. In a while, crocodile," she sang and got into her old car and drove away laughing, but not before catching her new neighbor watching her with a strange expression on his face.

*Travis Read, who are you? The man who loved his carousel ride this morning, or the kind who is attracted to a flashy, shallow flirt like my mother?*

A headache pounded behind Rachel's left eye. The tray full of beers she carried dragged down her arms. Was the music louder than usual tonight?

Honey's Place was the only bar in Rodeo. True, there was the diner, but her friend Vy ran an alcohol-free eatery, and most people wanted beer with their fries on a Friday night.

A lot of these people were cowboys who worked the ranches in the area. They came in at the end of the week for liquor, great burgers and fun music.

Despite her aching legs and feet, Rachel hustled. She needed her tips, needed to come up with an alternative plan now that Abigail's house had been sold.

If she felt a tad desperate, well…she was.

A table called for a round of beers. Rachel headed to the bar to fill the order.

"How're you doing?" Rushed but efficient, Honey Armstrong filled orders as quickly as her servers brought them to the bar. Her mane of long, blond curls wild tonight, she peered at Rachel critically. "You look tired."

Fearful of giving Honey a reason to send her home early, Rachel put on her game face.

"I'm good."

"Rach, don't try to fool me. You know you can't."

"I'll take a dinner break soon," Rachel promised.

Honey pointed a finger at her. "You'd better. You look worn out."

It was Friday night, the bar was packed and Rachel needed to hustle. She would take care of her aching body tomorrow morning.

Off-duty, Sheriff Cole Payette, sidled up to the bar and sat on the only empty stool. His spot. No matter how busy Honey's got, the locals left it empty for him. Friday and Saturday nights often found him sitting there for hours, nursing a beer.

Rachel liked him.

As it turned out, Rachel didn't get that break she'd promised Honey she would take. Her energy flagged, but customers continued to pour in.

With every step, her feet screamed for attention.

Too bad. As long as there were customers, she would continue to work and bring in tips.

She set a heavy tray of mugs of beer onto the table next to the front door and handed them around. She was just making change when she felt a draft. New arrivals. Good. More tips.

She glanced up…and froze. Cindy walked in with Travis, the man freshly shaved and movie-star handsome, the tips of his hair still damp from a shower, she guessed.

Why couldn't Cindy have taken him to the diner for dinner?·Why come here? But Rachel knew. Her mom was showing off that she was with the handsome new cowboy in town, and Honey's would be a lot more crowded than the diner. Cindy liked an audience.

She wore even more spangles tonight and had put on her sparkly eye shadow.

When he saw Rachel, Travis raised one eyebrow as if to ask, "You work here?"

Rachel suppressed the part of herself that found him attractive.

Fantasizing about a handsome stranger when she looked like a beer barrel on legs was just the type of daydreaming she had to quit.

Anyhow, Cindy must be his type. He'd asked her out on a date pretty darn quickly, hadn't he? Which meant he wasn't Rachel's type. And why was she having those kinds of unlikely thoughts, anyway? He was dating Cindy, and he had bought Rachel's house. Cindy was welcome to him.

Rachel's dating days were long over.

Then why, in the middle of a crowded bar surrounded by people she'd grown up with and loved, did Rachel feel so lonely? So in need of someone to talk to? Of someone who would listen? Or who would just hold her hand so she didn't feel desperately alone?

Travis and Cindy sat at one of her tables, and Rachel left them with menus while she finished delivering drinks to another couple of tables.

When she returned, she pointed to the hooks lining the walls on either side of the door. "You can hang your hat there."

Travis raised his eyebrows. "I didn't notice them. No one will take it?"

Rachel's grin might have been tired, but she dredged up a ghost of this morning's sass. He needed to understand what kind of town he'd moved to.

"Not in this town. A man's hat is sacred around these parts. All the establishments in town have their cowboy hat hooks."

"Thanks. I'll keep it in mind."

"What can I get for you two?"

"A gin and tonic and a bacon burger with fries," Cindy said.

"I'll take a Corona," Travis said, "with an order of the hottest wings you got, a bacon double cheeseburger and a side of onion rings. You have coleslaw?"

Rachel nodded.

"Creamy?"

"Sharp vinaigrette."

"The way I like it. I'll take a side of that, too."

The way she liked it, too. "I'll make sure it's slurpy." She smiled.

Travis's returning smile might have been small, but moonbeams dazzled.

*Get your head out of the clouds, Rachel.*

Cindy sniffed.

After Rachel picked up the menus and walked away, she heard Travis say, "She looks tired. Is she okay?"

"She's fine. She's tougher than she looks."

*So are you, Mom. Tough as nails.* She bit down on that thought. It was uncharitable. Mom had a right to her fun, but Rachel was filled with jealousy, a mean-spirited emotion unworthy of her, but undeniable. She wouldn't mind sitting down for a carefree evening in a bar for drinks and a burger with a handsome man.

*Hey, you chose your life. You need to live it without regrets.*

A good philosophy, just hard to hold on to when she was dog-tired.

## Chapter 4

Travis delivered his hat to the row of hooks on the wall at the front of Honey's Place.

Cowboy hat after cowboy hat graced the wall, most in muted blacks and tans, but a couple in white. Seemed to be the only kind of hat here.

He glanced around at the Western decor with its twin themes of old and new. Big old wagon wheels lined the walls along with huge modern landscapes of local scenery, not overly sentimental stuff, but rugged and true to nature. Local artist, maybe?

Hundreds of white fairy lights illuminated the rafters.

The people were loud, but Travis heard not one discordant note, just a lot of folks having a good time. The huge space rang with laughter. Denim and Western shirts abounded, along with plenty of silver jewelry on the women. He didn't doubt a good portion of the hats on the wall belonged to those same women.

*My kind of town.*

A country and western band belted out hits from a small stage at the back end of the long room. He tapped his fingers on his thighs.

He returned to the small table Cindy had chosen, a table that fit only two, snugly. She'd said they were meeting up with a bunch of her friends.

"So where are the friends we're supposed to meet?" Travis asked. He had to make sure she got his message loud and clear. This wasn't a date.

He wasn't looking for romance. Besides, she wasn't his kind of woman at all.

"They'll be along soon," she said, her gaze darting about the bar and her knee doing a quick jig. "Do you dance?"

Before he could respond, she was hauling him out of his seat and to the dance floor where they joined a crowd of line dancers moving to a Brooks and Dunn cover.

Just as the second song started, he spotted Rachel carrying a tray of food and drinks to their table. He dragged Cindy off the dance floor. "I'm starving. Let's eat."

When Rachel put the tray down, it wobbled. He ran to grab it.

"I'm okay," she said, but his beer tipped over the edge and landed on the floor. The bottle shattered, sending suds all over his boots.

Rachel gasped. "I'm so sorry," she whispered. "I'll clean it up." She rushed away.

He still held the tray with the food. He spread the

plates and Cindy's drink on their table, and left the empty tray on the bar.

"Rachel's always been clumsy." Cindy looked unhappy. Thunderclouds formed on what had been a clear evening. Travis didn't know what went on between these two women. The last place he needed to be was stuck in the middle.

"The tray was heavy. No problem. A little beer never hurt a pair of boots." He waggled his eyebrows comically to ease Cindy's pique. "These've survived a hell of a lot worse."

Cindy seemed to relax.

Rachel returned with a broom and mop, her stomach leading the way. "I'll get you another beer, but I need to clean this up before someone slips and falls."

"You go get the beer. I'll do this." He tried to take the broom away from her, but she held on.

"Nope." Rachel shot him a look of grim determination. "It's my job."

"I don't mind. I can do it."

"No." The woman had a strong grip, and even stronger willpower.

Travis let go, and she swept up the glass.

"You look pale. You okay?"

Her back stiffened as though maybe he'd offended her. *Note to self. Don't show this woman pity.*

"I'm peachy," she said, struggling to smile, but tense lines bracketed her mouth.

The sexy good humor he'd found so attractive this morning had crawled home to bed early, leaving behind an exhausted shell.

Someone called from another table. "Rachel, we need another round here."

"Be right there, Lester." She rushed to the bar and placed their order, returned with Travis's beer, then disappeared into the back. A minute later, she returned with a freshly rinsed mop and finished cleaning up. Then she hurried to the bar and picked up a full tray of drinks.

Head spinning from the whirlwind, Travis asked, "You worry about her at all?"

Cindy sighed. "Yeah, I do, but she chose to marry a lazy loser. Whatever trouble she's in, she brought on herself." She pointed a French fry at him. "Before you start thinking I'm heartless, I took her back in after her husband died."

"Shame he died. Man, that's tough." He couldn't imagine how hard it would have been for his sister if her husband had died before Colt was born.

Cindy nodded. "I babysit her daughter when she's working."

"Except for tonight."

"I needed a night out." He'd put her on the defensive.

Careful to keep censure out of his voice, he asked quietly, "There are no friends coming, are there?" She'd assured him she was meeting people, and he was welcome to join them. The woman had misrepresented the evening.

"No." She smiled with the barest hint of hope in her eyes. "Being out with me isn't so bad, is it?"

"No, it isn't." Which was mainly true. Cindy had a lot of perky energy. "I gotta be honest, Cindy. I'm not looking for romance. I just need to get settled in. This isn't an official date." He softened it with a smile. "It's good to be out on a Friday night with a pretty woman, though."

Mollified, she sipped her drink.

Just after he'd taken a bite of an excellent charred

bacon double cheeseburger, a hand settled onto his shoulder. It belonged to Artie Hanson from the auto shop.

"Brought the keys to your truck." He dropped them onto the table in front of Travis's plate, axle grease ground into every crack and wrinkle of his clean hands. "It's sitting in front of the shop."

Travis had phoned Artie to make sure the mechanic could finish the work by tonight so he'd be spared the ride home with Cindy. He liked to be independent.

Travis swallowed. "That's great, man. Thanks." He reached for his wallet. "How much do I owe you?"

Artie waved it away. "Boss lets me off duty on Friday nights." The man laughed. An inside joke. He owned the shop. He could set his own hours. "You going to be in town on the weekend? Stop in and settle the bill then. Or on Monday."

Artie clapped his back and walked away.

"Is he always so trusting?"

"Most people in this town are." Cindy's tone was only half admiring. The other half sounded resentful to Travis's ear, but he wasn't about to ask why.

While he ate, his gaze roamed the bar. He stopped when he realized he was keeping an eye on Rachel.

*She's no concern of yours.*

It seemed that the habit of caring for others, after years of taking care of Samantha, was ground into him. *Quit it.*

He'd finished his burger, wings and onion rings, all while Rachel's steps slowed and her face grew paler.

*Not your business, man. Let it go.*

He couldn't. He fought the urge to help. It didn't matter. Guess he'd spent too many years taking care of his younger sister to see a woman go so far into a bad case of hurt without helping her. He had to do something.

He excused himself and walked to the bar where he squeezed in between two old guys drinking whiskey. Behind the bar, a beauty hustled to fill drink orders. This town sure had a lot of pretty women. A mass of curly blond hair flowed down the bartender's back to her waist.

"Hey, you're Travis, aren't you?" she asked. Laughter lurked in her china-doll blue eyes. At his surprised look, she answered his unspoken question. "It's a small town. Everyone knows your name by now. I'm Honey, by the way."

Ah. The owner.

Friendly smile as well as pretty. Nice. He handed her a twenty. "Can I order a burger or something for Rachel? She needs a break."

Honey's gaze sought out Rachel. Her lips compressed.

"She still hasn't stopped? Honestly, that girl. Talk about being stubborn." Honey removed a towel from her shoulder and tossed it onto the bar. "I told her to take a break well over an hour ago. If she's not careful, she'll hurt my future godchild."

While Travis went back to the table, she slipped from behind the bar into the back hallway.

"Honey's gone to get Rachel some food," he told Cindy. He figured he should explain why he'd left.

Cindy cocked her head to one side. "You're a nice man, aren't you? That was a real kind thing to do."

Since he'd told her it was good to be out with a pretty woman, Cindy's mood had mellowed some. The second gin and tonic helped, too.

A guy got up from the bar and walked behind to pull mugs of draft and fill orders while Honey was gone.

"Who's that customer who's serving drinks now?" he asked Cindy.

She checked out the bar. "Cole Payette. He likes to help Honey sometimes."

"I hope I didn't get Rachel into trouble with her boss." He finished his beer.

"Honey's her friend," Cindy said. "She won't fire Rachel."

A few minutes later, Honey returned to the big room with an order of chicken fingers and fries and handed them to Rachel. She pointed to Travis, probably telling Rachel who'd paid for them.

Rachel shot him a look full of brimstone. Oh, shit. Clasping her hands behind her back, she refused to take the plate from Honey. The gesture made her stomach stick out a mile.

She stormed over to their table. "I don't know why you think you can tell me when I should be eating. I can figure out my own breaks."

"Sorry, I—"

"Of all the paternalistic, presumptuous things to do. I don't need your charity. Go buy dinner for someone else."

He shot his hands in front of himself, palms out. "I didn't mean to offend," he said. "You're looking more exhausted with every step. Considering how early it was when I saw you at the carousel this morning, you've put in a long day already and this bar doesn't close for another few hours."

Beside him, Honey gasped. She planted a fist on her hip. "You were out there this morning? You get one morning a week to sleep in, and you spent it at the fairground?"

Rachel's mulish expression turned chagrined. "I put

the carousel to bed for the winter." She shot Travis a look that said, "Thanks a lot for snitching on me."

Honey forced the plate of food into Rachel's hands. "We'll have our fund-raising dance in a couple of weeks, and then we'll forget about it until spring. Got it? I know the fairground is important to you, but take it easy for a while. Take care of yourself." Her voice had softened. "Go eat."

"Ma'am," Travis said to Rachel, "I'm real sorry I made presumptions where I shouldn't have. I don't make the same mistake twice." He wouldn't do it again. She had a valid point. He had no right to tell her anything. She wasn't his baby sister.

"Would you consider eating the meal because it's hot and ready to go? No sense wasting it." Travis watched the moment she realized he was right.

"Okay. Thanks." She sounded begrudging, but took the food anyway, and that was the important thing.

Honey pointed toward the back where Travis assumed the restrooms were. Rachel headed there with the plate of chicken. Honey took Rachel's tray and filled her orders.

Rachel disappeared around a corner.

The guy named Cole kept filling orders at the bar while Honey took trays of drinks around.

Travis asked where the washrooms were and Cindy told him. He used the restroom, then returned down the hallway toward the bar. He stopped when he passed an open doorway and backtracked. Inside a cramped office, Rachel sat on a plastic chair, wolfing down the food. He hadn't noticed her the first time through the hallway.

"I hope I didn't get you into trouble," he said from the doorway.

She startled, her gold-flecked eyes huge and framed by gray bruises of exhaustion. The poor woman wasn't just tired. She was plumb worn thin enough to see through.

"No. Honey's a good friend." She took a bite of a chicken finger. "You were right. Both of you. I was struggling. Thank you for the food."

Travis hid a smile with one hand. She was saying all the right things, but her tone said she still resented being told what to do.

He could relate to that.

Beside her sat a pint of milk and a plastic food container filled with something beige dotted with bits of color.

"What's that?" he asked.

"What's what?"

"That stuff." He pointed to the plastic container.

"Quinoa salad."

Shaking his head, Travis leaned against the doorjamb. "You and my sister. She likes that weird California health stuff, too."

Rachel laughed, a musical counterpoint to the noise from the bar behind him.

She had a good laugh, clean and without guile. "Quinoa's not from California. It's South American, but yeah, it is healthy."

"It's beige. Does it taste as bland as it looks?"

She shook her head. "It's good."

Her worn brown cowboy boots sat on the floor next to the chair. Cracks in the leather attested to their age.

Through her thin socks, her ankles looked too big for such a small woman. "Your feet swell up?"

"When I'm on them too long. It's the pregnancy."

If she were his sister, he would massage them for her. He used to when Sammy was pregnant with the boys and her husband was too busy navel-gazing to pay her much attention. He sensed Rachel wouldn't appreciate a stranger touching her feet, or offering sympathy.

Nor did he have any desire to touch her again after the foolishness of this afternoon's kiss.

She looked hesitant and then seemed to gather courage. "What's it like inside these days?"

Huh? He stared at her. "What's what like?"

"The house. What shape is it in? I haven't been in for a long time. The owner was in palliative care for the past year."

She liked his house that much? "Not great. I've got a lot of work to do to bring it up to scratch."

"That bad?"

"Nothing impossible." Her wistful tone puzzled him. "It's just a house."

"Just a house?" she squeaked. "It's beautiful. It's got great bones and huge potential. Even with the work that needs to be done, it's perfect." She looked so damn cute with her warm eyes and thick eyelashes and tawny braid with wisps of hair floating around her cheeks. They were filling with color now that she was off her feet and eating.

He didn't like this attraction. It made him antsy and tense. He started to back out of the room, but she asked, "Hardwood floors still in good shape?"

"They need refinishing. Oak. Three-quarter inch. They'll be incredible once they're done." Travis had a good feeling about this house for his family, if he could get the work done by Christmas. "You should see the fireplace with the carved wooden mantel."

In her smile, he saw longing. "Still beautiful?"

"A work of art. Looks like I've got to strip off about twelve coats of paint, though. From all of the moldings, too." He cocked his head. "You seem to know the place well."

She smiled, and it was sweet and wholesome. "The owner was a special friend. Before she became ill, we had tea together a lot."

She swallowed and looked away. He thought it was sadness choking her up.

Unsure what drove him other than a need to reassure her about himself and her mother, because it felt weird to be attracted to the daughter, even if he didn't want to be, while having drinks with the mother, he said, "It isn't a date."

Her hand paused on the way to her mouth, one lonely French fry dangling from her fingers. "What?"

"With your mom? Cindy? Tonight isn't a date. She said we were meeting other folks. I thought I could get to know some townspeople."

She chewed her fry with a small, thoughtful frown furrowing her brow. Another aspect he liked. She had depth, this one.

"I'll meet ranch hands while I work, but not enough of every kind of person living here. My family—"

A gasp from the doorway caught his attention, and he glanced behind him. Cindy.

"What are you two doing?" Disappointment hovered beneath her suspicious anger.

Travis really didn't have time for drama.

"Shooting the breeze," he said in the most casual tone he could muster. He owed this woman nothing. He could talk to whomever he wanted, but he didn't want to make trouble between mother and daughter. "Just getting to know one of my neighbors."

Cindy spun away and slammed into the women's washroom. Talk about being high maintenance.

"Am I in trouble?" he asked.

Rachel's animation about the house leached out of her. "We're both in trouble. Cindy can hold a grudge for days. You'd better go back to your table and make it up to her."

Travis sighed. Was one night of peace and innocent fun too much to expect?

Just as he left the room, Rachel stopped him. "She's not a bad person, honest. She's just…" She shrugged.

Just real needy. "Got it."

Throughout the rest of the evening, he managed to smooth Cindy's ruffled feathers, not really sure why he was bothering. He didn't know the woman and didn't care whether she nursed a good pout, but he thought of Rachel and wondered how Cindy's anger would affect her.

Shortly after ten, a fight broke out. Travis didn't know who the two guys were, or what their beefs were, but they came too close to his table. When one of them bumped into Rachel serving nearby, he got up and steadied her, holding a hand up to let the guy know to keep his distance.

The guy could barely stand upright, wavering on his drunken feet and grinning idiotically.

The man who'd taken over for Honey earlier at the bar came running, grabbing the second guy by the scruff of his neck and propelling him against the wall with one of the guy's arms shoved behind him and half-way up his back.

"Goddamn it, Clint," Cole yelled above the driving beat of the music. "I told you before. You and Jamie need to keep your fights out of public places. You want to fight, take it home."

He whipped a pair of handcuffs out of his back pocket and cuffed the guy. Travis stared.

Cole turned to the man Travis held off with his raised right hand. Three sheets to the wind, he burped up a lungful of beer and chicken wings.

"Do I need to cuff you, too, Jamie?"

"Naw. I'm okay now. I'll go home peacefully."

"And you, Clint? Should I call out one of the depu-ties? You wanna spend the night in jail?"

Clint shook his head. "I'll leave."

Cole unlocked the cuffs, then watched the pair of them stumble out, leaning on each other like the best of buddies.

The man stuck out his hand. "Cole Payette. I'm sher-iff here. You're the new guy."

Travis nodded and shook his hand. "Travis Read. What was their problem?"

"Brothers from different mothers. Every so often they take potshots at each other, but only when they're drunk. The rest of the time, they're good buddies."

Payette righted a chair that had been knocked over, watching Travis with an odd smile.

"Good to meet you, Travis. Welcome to Rodeo. Usually we're a peaceful town. Thanks for your help." Cole's eyes slid off to Travis's left and then back to him. He grinned and returned to his stool at the bar.

"Um… Travis?"

The voice so close beside him startled him. Travis looked down at Rachel. "Yeah?"

"You can let go of me now."

Cripes. The whole time he'd held off the guy named Jamie, he'd held Rachel with his other arm, tucked against his body and out of harm's way.

"Oh…sorry…ah, I—" He didn't know what to say because he didn't know what he'd been thinking.

A small handful, a perfect fit, her belly hard and warm against him, she belonged in his arms.

It felt natural and good to hold her.

No! No, no, no. He didn't need a woman in his life right now, especially not one laden with burdens he didn't want to bear.

He didn't want to like her.

A funny smile curled her lips. "I truly can take care of myself, Travis. I deal with stuff like this most nights."

At least she wasn't mad at him.

"I really didn't know I was doing that."

"I know. I could tell."

The feeling of well-being, and the sense of rightness she engendered in him, shook him so badly he rushed to let her go.

Before he could, the softest of touches flitted across his ribs. Wonder filled him. The touch had come from Rachel's big belly.

"What was that?"

Despite her obvious fatigue, this morning's mischievous grin made an appearance.

"That was the baby," she said. "Beth."

"No fooling?"

"No fooling, Travis. Guess she was saying hello."

It happened again. Wild. Amazing. That little crea-ture inside that big bump was real and moving. "What was it? A hand or a foot?"

"Could have been. Or an elbow. Maybe a knee." She ran her hand over her belly. "It's pretty awesome, isn't it?"

The baby moved again, some incredibly tiny part of her body brushing across him, like maybe the little thing was communicating with him. Saying hi. Touch-ing. Reaching out. Whoo.

"It's…it's incredible." He didn't have words to de-scribe the feeling. Whoo-hoo. It was about the most magical experience imaginable.

He released Rachel by increments, because he was also letting go of another creature, her baby. He'd never much thought about how real babies were before birth.

He'd only met Rachel a mere twelve or so hours ago, but she'd now bestowed on him two wondrous gifts—a child's dream ride on a carousel, and an unborn baby's touch.

"I'd better get back to work," she said.

He bent to pick up the tray she'd dropped, handing it to her with his mouth open and searching for words. There were none.

Had Cole's funny smile been about Travis holding Rachel as if she belonged to him? She didn't. No woman did. Uh-uh. No way, no how. He had one priority—to take care of his sister and nephews and then hightail it away from here.

While he might be filled with awe, he would never think to take on the encumbrance of parenthood for himself. More power to her, but he was hunky-dory on his own.

He returned to Cindy. It was time to head home.

It took them a while to leave the bar because everyone and his uncle wanted an introduction. Friendly people. Considering the night a success, he left knowing that Sammy and her boys would find a community in Rodeo where they could belong.

He caught a last glimpse of Rachel, who was too busy to notice him leaving.

Cindy dropped him off at the garage to pick up his truck. He scooted out of her pickup the second it stopped. He wasn't about to give Cindy ideas about kissing good-night.

Once he'd driven himself to the house, he wandered the too-quiet rooms. The echo of his boots in the stillness set up an emptiness in him that rankled.

Boots. On a wood floor.

He needed to become more refined. No carting of muck and God knew what else into his new home. This wasn't a bunkhouse. It was Sammy's new home.

He returned to the front door and took them off.

Tired, he entered his bedroom and made up his new bed with the sheets he'd had delivered. He unpacked his saddlebags, his belongings paltry enough, his lifestyle so simple it took him all of ten minutes to put away his clothes. He stared at the freshly made bed. He might be bone weary, but his mind wouldn't quit. He knew he wouldn't sleep, so there was no point trying.

He unloaded a bunch of new kid's books onto the new bookshelves.

The house was too quiet. He hated the hollowness of the place. He'd have to get a TV soon, or a radio— anything to fill the emptiness until the boys arrived.

Christmas and his nephews couldn't come soon enough.

## Chapter 5

At seven on Saturday morning, Travis walked down Rodeo's Main Street, humming with energy and feeling so darn lucky that he'd found this town for his family.

Despite Cindy's subterfuge, last night had been good. He'd met a few people and had fun.

Passing one small shop after another, with names like Jorgenson's Hardware and Hiram's Pharmacy and Nelly's 'Dos 'n' Don'ts, unpretentious and without a trace of neon lights or razzle-dazzle, he knew he'd made the right choice in buying a house for Samantha here.

He had simple needs. He'd had nothing much to spend his paychecks on once he'd put Samantha through school. The money was just sitting in the bank. He'd put it down on a house for Sammy and the boys.

They were his only family.

Funny that he'd never thought to discuss repayment

with Sammy. If she did, she did. If she didn't, well, hell, so what? What did he need a house for?

When he felt a trace of yearning on his own behalf, he ignored it.

He returned his attention to the town.

Cowboy hats and worn-in denim were everywhere, on both men and women. Not a single pair of designer jeans could be found.

Pickup trucks lined the road—not urban warriors, but real honest-to-God working vehicles covered with rust, dust and dirt. This was a working town.

He nodded to an old man passing by with the bow-legged gait of a retired cowhand.

Travis stepped into the Summertime Diner for breakfast. He'd picked up a few groceries yesterday, but he wanted to be out among people. Eating breakfast alone in the house didn't appeal to him. He was used to eating in farmhouse kitchens surrounded by ranch hands or cooking up bacon and eggs in a bunkhouse with a bunch of other men. Udall vouched for the diner, so here he was.

Busy place, even this early on a Saturday.

Looking to his left, he spotted wooden hooks lined with cowboy hats. He added his to the mix. It was a funny tradition this town had, but seeing his hat hanging with so many others made him feel like he was part of something.

If that also struck a chord of loneliness in him—the awareness that he really had no community—so be it. Part of his life.

All of the stools at the counter were already occupied. Too bad. That was usually a good place to strike up a conversation and get to know people.

Spotting an empty booth near the back, he headed for it, catching a waitress's eye and pantomiming that he wanted coffee. He fell into the booth facing the street. Might as well get a look at the local color.

A small voice in the booth behind him said, "Mommy, I want pamcakes."

"Okay, sweetie-pie. Pancakes it is. Blueberry?"

He recognized Rachel's upbeat voice. She must be here with her daughter. Awfully early for her to be out, considering she closed the bar last night.

"Yeah. Booberry," the pip-squeak said.

"*Blue*berry."

The child giggled. "I said *boo*berry." That childish voice, that high-pitched laugh made him ache to see his nephews. Soon.

A family entered the diner and searched for an empty table. There were none left, and here he sat hogging an entire booth to himself.

He didn't want to sit with Rachel. He didn't like that he found her attractive. He didn't like that he'd thought about her as soon as he woke up in the house she'd been angry with him for buying.

The family's kids looked antsy, as though maybe they were hungry.

He couldn't invite them to join him. There were too many of them.

He gave in as graciously as he could, unsure whether Rachel would even agree, and peeked around the back-rest.

"Good morning," he said.

Rachel didn't look surprised to see him. She must have seen him enter the restaurant.

"Hi," she said.

"Place is filling up." He gestured over his shoulder. "There's a family looking for a booth. You mind if I give them mine and share yours?"

She didn't bat an eye, as though this kind of thing happened regularly. "Sure thing," she said. "Tori, scoot on over along the bench. Travis is going to join us."

Travis gestured to the family standing by the front door that they could have the booth. They dazzled him with their gratitude.

In Rachel's booth, the little one moved over and Travis joined them.

"I'm Tori!" the pip-squeak said. "I'm having pamcakes."

"Me, too."

"What kind are you having?"

"Booberry!" he said, feeling foolish, but gratified when she giggled.

"Mommy," she squealed. "Travis calls them booberry, too."

Rachel caught his eye and smiled. It did wonders for her face, softening that strong jaw and warming the whiskey highlights in her eyes.

The child picked up a raggedy plush animal. A platypus?

"This is Puss. You can kiss him." She held the thing up to his face. He kissed it on the nose while his cheeks heated like hot tar on an August afternoon.

Watching his discomfort, Rachel grinned, some of yesterday morning's sass returning after a night's sleep. Travis settled back against the bench and steeled his heart, or libido, or whatever it was causing this strong unwanted appeal.

She looked younger this morning with her hair pulled up in a high ponytail.

The waitress arrived with a coffeepot and orange juice in a plastic cup for Tori.

Rachel put her hand over her cup. "Vy, when you have a minute, can you bring decaf?"

"Sure thing, Rachel. I forgot. What'll you folks have to eat?"

After the waitress left to place their orders, Travis asked, "Does the owner make her dress up like someone out of the forties because it's a diner or something?"

Vy wore a kerchief on her head, black eyeliner that curved up at the corners and bright red lipstick to match a red-checked shirt. Her black skirt flared out like a bell, swishing around legs accentuated by a pair of wedged heels. Or he thought that was what they were called.

"Vy *is* the owner, and that's just her style. She likes to dress retro."

"Seems out of place in a boots and denim town."

"Yeah. She likes the surprise value. Tourists think it's fun."

Travis drank half of his coffee and started to feel human again. "You worked late last night. What brings you out so early today?"

"Gramma doesn't like noise in the morning," Tori answered. "Mommy brings me here for brekfest."

The child rose up onto her knees, picked up her OJ and took a sip. "Only sometimes, though." She set the juice down with exaggerated care, without spilling a drop.

"Only Saturday," Rachel confirmed. "It's too expensive to eat out every day."

So, Cindy was sleeping in while the woman who'd worked until 1:00 a.m. was up at six with her child. He had to hand it to Rachel. She took her job as a mother seriously. She didn't seem resentful or angry, just took quiet responsibility for her daughter.

What did she do for herself? Besides give strangers rides on a carousel she'd fixed up?

Or was she like Sammy, a single mother so fixated on doing the best for her kids that she put her own needs last?

Rachel wiped a dribble of juice from Tori's chin. "Don't let Cindy hear you call her Grandma. She doesn't like it."

"But she is my gramma."

"She is. She just doesn't want to be called that."

"But Carol-Sue can call *her* gramma *Gramma*. Why can't I?"

"Who's Carol-Sue?" Travis asked.

"A character in one of Tori's books."

To her daughter, she said, "Everyone's different. Cindy doesn't like being called Grandma."

Rachel caught his eye. "Cindy loves being a grandmother."

"Gramma loves me."

"Yes, she does, sweetie-pie, but being called Grandma makes her feel old."

Vy returned with pots of both regular and decaf, topping up Travis's mug and filling Rachel's empty cup.

"Thanks, Vy."

Tori hummed beside him and colored on her paper place mat with three crayons.

"May I ask you a question?" Rachel asked.

"Go ahead," he answered. "Won't guarantee I'll answer it, but ask away." He craved privacy, especially after a childhood of being on the receiving end of too much gossip.

"Why would a single man buy that Victorian? I would have pegged you for a ranch house kind of guy."

"You'd be right about that, but I bought it for my sister and her two sons."

She smiled suddenly, brilliantly. "That's okay, then."

"What do you mean?"

"That house deserves a family. It should be full of children and happiness."

Her selflessness—she even put a house's needs before her own!—rattled him, maybe because she accepted her burdens with grace while he itched to be free, with nothing more on his mind than a good ride over a green field.

Even if he wished that he and Sammy had had a mother half as committed as Rachel, resentment bubbled. Was the woman a saint?

"It's just a house, Rachel."

She didn't seem to notice the hard edge to his voice.

The longing, the wistfulness he'd seen in her last night when they talked about his house painted her cheeks pink.

"Children will live there. That's all that matters."

A burst of intuition hit him, or maybe it was the slight hint of rancor in her tone.

"Should have been your children? Right?"

"Yeah." She sounded bitter. "In a perfect world."

The flash of unhappiness on her face vanished in an instant. The woman was resilient.

"Again, why the Victorian?" she asked. "Why not the Podchuk ranch house? It's up for sale."

Not usually a man for introspection, Travis had asked himself that question a hundred times. "I can't rightly say. It's old-fashioned. I guess it looks like it could make a nice home."

She nodded.

He sipped his coffee, then said, "Can I ask you something?"

Rachel nodded.

"How did your husband die?"

"A accident," the pip-squeak piped up.

He glanced down at the child. Damn. He'd forgotten she was there, or he wouldn't have asked. "I'm real sorry about that."

"He rided a motorcycle and wented too fast and hitted a tree."

Aaaahhh. Hence the deep concern he'd seen on Rachel's face when he'd tipped his bike yesterday. He'd recognized something more, though. Anger.

"Motorcycles is bad," Tori said. "Really bad."

Travis glanced at Rachel but she'd shut down, her hazel eyes blank, as though she'd pulled blinds down. The windows to her soul weren't sharing anything with him. Both resentment and anger at her late husband churned through Travis. It was all well and good for him to ride, but he didn't have dependents. Rachel's husband should have behaved more responsibly.

But was Travis truly free? What about Sammy and his nephews? Now that Sammy's husband had farted off to the Himalayas to *find himself* and she had a crook like her former boss on her tail, weren't she and the boys his responsibility? Wasn't he the only person they could depend on? Was *he* being careless when he rode his bike? What if something happened to him? What would Sammy do?

Maybe he'd park it in the garage for a while and just use the truck. Next week, he'd take out a life insurance policy on himself with Sammy as the beneficiary.

Man, why hadn't he thought to do it months ago?

"Tell me about your sister," Rachel said.

Travis rubbed the back of his neck. He didn't share, not like Sammy who blurted out every thought.

Still, Rachel seemed genuinely curious, not prying, and not one to spread gossip.

"She's six years younger than me. Thirty-one. Our Mom died of cancer when she was only twelve. Dad had died the year before. I was eighteen, so she never went to a foster home."

No need to mention he figured the big C had been floating out in the atmosphere looking for the most tired, sorriest woman around and had found Cerise Read. Once it took hold, she'd succumbed quickly. Dad had died the year before of cirrhosis of the liver.

"But it did mean you were a teenage boy taking care of your sister." Rachel cut to the heart of the matter. "Must have been hard. No time for yourself, I'm guessing?"

Travis nodded. "It was just the two of us for years until Sammy got married and had her two boys, now nine and five."

"She and her boys are coming here? Husband, too?"

"Nope. Sammy's divorced. Her ex is off in a Hindu temple in the Himalayas somewhere." For all intents and purposes, Travis was their stand-in father.

When their breakfasts came, he dug in, but put down

his fork when Rachel reached across the table to cut up Tori's pancakes.

"Let me," he said. "It's easier from this side of the table."

Having spent time with his nephews, he knew how small to make the pieces and how much syrup to pour on, or how much *not* to. "My nephews like to drown their pancakes in syrup and their fries in ketchup."

"Mommy, Travis got sausages. I don't got sausages."

"I didn't order any for you, honey. I didn't know you would want them. Besides, you won't be able to finish your pancakes if you have something else with them."

"Uh-huh. I can. I want sausages."

"Okay." Rachel raised her hand to flag the waitress, Vy, but Travis stopped her.

"Why don't I give her one of mine? She won't eat a whole order of sausages. If she can't finish her pancakes, I'll eat them."

"You don't mind?"

"No, ma'am. I'm used to sharing with my nephews."

"What's nephews?" the pip-squeak asked while Travis sliced a sausage first lengthwise, then crosswise into small bits and put them on her plate.

Rachel explained the concept of nephews.

"What's their names?" Tori stuffed two pieces of pancake into her mouth. Travis wiped the syrup from the corners of her lips.

"Jason and Colt."

"Do they like Carol-Sue books? She gots a dog *and* a cat."

Travis smiled. "Somehow I doubt those boys are reading about a girl named Carol-Sue."

"What are they like?" Rachel asked, and Travis was off and running on his favorite subject outside horses.

He exhausted the subject of his nephews. To her credit, Rachel didn't look bored. Neither did Tori, who kept asking questions about them. Curious kid.

After breakfast, they stepped out of the restaurant. Remembering last night's fiasco with Rachel's dinner, Travis didn't make the mistake of denting her pride by offering to pay for breakfast. They settled their own bills.

Before Travis could go his own way, the pip-squeak took hold of his hand and started to drag him down Main.

"Travis, come on. I got to show you something."

"Tori, no," Rachel protested. "I'm sure Travis has stuff to do."

"But, Mommy—"

"No, Victoria. Leave Travis alone."

The child looked so crestfallen that Travis asked, "What does she want to show me?"

Rachel sighed. "A pair of boots she wants. She checks every Saturday to make sure they're still there."

"Okay," he said. "Let's go."

"Are you sure?"

"It's only five minutes out of my day. Where are they?"

Tori saw which direction the conversation was heading and took hold of his hand again. Rachel shrugged. They followed Tori to the window of a shop that sold Western clothes.

Tori let go of him and pressed her hands and nose against the glass.

"My boots," she whispered, and Travis leaned close.

"Which ones?"

She pointed to a pair of bright pink cowboy boots, probably the tiniest pair he'd ever seen. So damned cute.

"Those sure are pretty cowboy boots."

"Yeah," she breathed. "I want them, but Mommy says we don't got the money."

He heard Rachel groan behind him. "Thanks for airing all of our secrets, Tori," she said with a gentle laugh.

"We got to save our money for Beth." Tori sounded so adult and so accepting that his heart went out to this little girl.

"Your mom is a smart woman," he said.

They parted ways, with Rachel driving out of town while Travis paid Artie for his truck repairs.

Before returning to his truck, he made one more stop, his feet overtaking his better judgment, but there was a method to his madness.

Yesterday morning on the carousel, Rachel had given him a gift unlike anything he'd had in a long time— five spectacular minutes of freedom from weight and responsibility. He'd been carefree and filled with joy.

He needed to balance the scales. He didn't like being beholden.

More than that, he hadn't liked how resigned Rachel's little girl was already to the realities of life. He remembered the same resignation in Sammy when she was little. Give Tori a few more years, for God's sake.

He stepped into the store and asked how much the pink boots in the window cost.

The low price surprised him until he saw them up close. They weren't real leather, but would that matter to a girl who would outgrow them in four or five months?

"You think these might fit a little girl about this tall?" He gestured with his hand in the vicinity of his knees.

"Probably," the clerk responded. "If they don't fit, bring them back. No problem."

He bought them and tossed the bag into the bed of the truck.

Not ten minutes into the drive home, Travis noticed Rachel's car on the side of the road. Empty. Out in the middle of nowhere.

His gut did a nervous jig. He might not want to care too much, but the woman was pregnant and had a small child with her. He remembered last night's swollen ankles. If her car had broken down and she was walking, her feet wouldn't thank her.

In the distance, two dark shadows, one short and the other shorter, trudged toward the horizon. Travis drove on until he came alongside them, slowed and then passed to pull onto the shoulder far enough ahead that he wouldn't cover them with dust.

He got out of the truck and approached.

He didn't like the begrudging acceptance on Rachel's face, a lack of surprise that something had gone wrong for her, or the way Tori's little feet, clad in pink rubber boots with bright purple flowers, scraped the gravel.

"Car broke down?" he asked.

Rachel nodded.

"We been walking *forever*, Travis." Tori's bottom lip trembled. "Mommy can't carry me 'cause Beth is in the way."

Tori spread her hands to be picked up. "Can you carry me?"

"Sure." He settled her into his arms, her weight, her

slim limbs and her tiny wrists fragile compared to his sturdy, rough-and-tumble nephews.

"Any idea what's wrong with your car?" he asked Rachel.

"Old age. It does this regularly. I'm pretty sure I need to replace the battery."

"You need to consider getting a new car."

"Yeah." Behind him, she sighed.

He settled Tori into the backseat of his truck and strapped her in.

"She's too tiny to ride without her car seat," Rachel objected.

He knew that from taking care of his nephews, but they were still a ways away from her home. "We're not going far. I'll be careful."

Rachel climbed into the passenger seat, Travis giving her a gentle boost with a hand to her elbow.

Once behind the wheel, he pulled onto the road and Tori immediately observed, "Travis, you don't got no music."

"Don't have, sweetie," Rachel corrected.

"I know, Mommy. Travis don't have no music."

"Any music."

"I *know*. That what's I'm saying, Mommy. He don't have any music. Where's his music?"

Travis laughed, silently, because he didn't know whether Tori's emotions were as fragile as her tiny body. He flicked the radio knob and Taylor Swift's voice filled the cab.

"'Love Story!'" Tori squealed. A second later, in a high sweet warble, she sang, "'Baby, just say yes.'"

He shot an amused glance at her mother. "She knows this song?"

"She knows all the Taylor Swift songs. She loves music. We have the radio on in the car all the time."

Travis studied her tired profile. "You working tonight?"

"Yeah. People are generous on Saturday night. I'll make good tips."

He pulled into the driveway directly across from his own. Cindy stepped out of her front door, dressed to kill with sparkles galore on her Western shirt, and made up to within an inch of her life. Travis glanced at his watch. Not quite ten. Must be gearing up for a hot lunch date or something.

"You took my daughter out this morning?"

Travis didn't miss the bite in Cindy's tone. "No, ma'am. Her car broke down on the highway. I'm just giving her a lift home." No sense mentioning they'd actually had breakfast together. Even if it wasn't by design, Cindy might not like it. He did his best to avoid drama in his life.

He rounded the truck to help Rachel from the passenger seat, but she was already out and lifting Tori from the back.

"Careful!" he admonished.

A rueful grin tugged at the corners of her mouth. "I can lift her. I just can't carry her."

"What are you going to do about your car?"

"Call Artie at the garage and have him tow it."

That would cost her. "I'm handy with an engine. I'll take a look at it."

"I've got some sense with engines, too."

He smiled. "Yeah. The carousel."

When she answered him with a smile, they seemed to share a sweetness he wasn't used to. It unnerved him.

It seemed to do the same for her. The smile slowly fell from her lips. "I'm sure it's just the battery. It's time for a new one."

Travis addressed Cindy. "You think you could watch the little one for a minute while I take Rachel back to her car?"

Cindy nodded. "C'mon, Tori. Let's go inside."

Rachel climbed back into the truck. When they arrived at her car, Travis popped the hood and retrieved jumper cables from the bed of his truck.

"You're a regular Boy Scout, aren't you?"

He checked for sarcasm, but all he noted on her face was appreciation.

"Get in the car and turn it on when I tell you to."

After he'd lined up the truck with her car, he hooked up the cables to the two batteries and got her car started. He instructed her to drive it for twenty minutes before returning home.

"Thanks, but I know that much."

"Yeah, sorry. I guess you would."

He leaned his forearms on the open window well of the driver's door. She smelled like coconuts. Her shampoo, maybe? "You going to be able to catch a nap before you head to work?"

Her smile showcased even white teeth with one slightly crooked eyetooth. The imperfection didn't detract from her looks. Not at all. Her laugh tinkled on the fresh sunny air. "Not likely."

She drove away.

He waited until her car disappeared and he was sure the thing was still running before driving home and putting her out of his mind.

Neither she nor her daughter nor her unborn baby were any concern of his.

He changed into work clothes and headed out to the Double U to give Dusty a ride. He brought tools with him and picked up a couple of steel posts from Udall's supply. He located and repaired the fence where yesterday's sheep had gotten tangled, pounding the posts deep into the ground. Felt good to have a hammer in his hands again, to use his muscles, to work.

He worried about Rachel.

"Stop it." His voice echoed across the fields.

Dusty snorted as if in agreement.

"Right," Travis said. "I need a woman and a couple of kids like I need a hole in the head."

After a good long ride across the land that left both him and Dusty satisfied, and during which he'd pinpointed a troublesome spot close to a creek, he returned to his house. He made a note to tell Udall where some of his jackleg fence had been flattened by something big. Moose or elk, maybe. It would need to be repaired before the snow set in for the winter, which could be any day now despite the unseasonably mild weather. You just never knew when winter would roar in this close to the Rockies.

He lunched on tuna sandwiches while those tiny pink cowboy boots sat on the sofa, asking him when he was going to give them to the child. What was appropriate?

Confused, he stepped outside and surveyed his land.

*His* land.

Lord, what a responsibility.

## Chapter 6

"Travis," a tiny voice called from across the road. Tori stood on the front porch of the sorry-looking trailer.

Rachel stood on the shoulder, putting out a bag of yard waste.

Travis sauntered over. "Hey."

"Travis! You came to visit!"

Tori jumped down the steps of the porch and fell, landing on her hands and knees in the dirt. She let out a hurt wail.

Rachel started toward her, but Travis was faster. He picked her up and brushed dirt from her pants.

"I hate this place!"

Startled by the vehemence of Rachel's tone, he spun around to stare at her. She looked undone. Defeated.

"I'm sorry," she said, her lips pressed into a thin line. "I shouldn't have said that. It just sure would be nice to live somewhere with a lawn." Her voice took on a wistful note. "And flowers."

Yeah, he guessed maybe this wasn't the ideal place to raise a kid.

"Travis, look." Tori held out her hands with a little sob. The palms were scraped. Gently, he smoothed off the dirt.

When she rested her head on his shoulder with a weary hiccup, his heart just about broke. He thought of those tiny boots. Now was as good a time as any, he guessed.

"Listen," he said to Rachel, "do you have time before you head into work?"

*Don't do this,* he warned himself, but his heart refused to listen.

"A few hours." Rachel watched him with a furrowed brow.

"Come to the ranch with me," he blurted because, apparently, he didn't have a speck of prudence left. "Let me take Tori for a ride."

"Ride?" He'd caught Tori's attention. Her head shot up. "What kind of ride?"

"On my horse."

Both Rachel's and Tori's eyes widened as though he'd handed them a bouquet of stars. His five-eleven grew to ten feet tall. It warmed him head to toe.

"Do you mean it?" Rachel asked.

"Yeah, I do. Just a gentle ride in the paddock up on Dusty. It won't be dangerous."

"Yes," Rachel answered lickety-split. Maybe she was afraid he'd change his mind.

"Come over to my place. We'll take the truck."

"No, I need to put Tori in her car seat."

Oh, yeah. He should have remembered that himself. Her husband had died on the road.

He raised his shoulders, thinking. "I guess we could all go in your car?"

Rachel smiled. "Yes. Let's."

He lifted one finger. "Can you give me a minute?"

Returning to his house, he snagged the pink boots and stared down at them, so small in his callused hands. He missed his nephews. The house was too quiet, too empty. He needed to fill his day.

Justifications for his impulsive actions complete, he went back outside.

He crossed back over the road and Tori squealed. "Mommy, look what Travis got!"

A grin split his face, cracking muscles he hadn't used in a good, long while.

"You want to sit down on the step and we'll get these on you?"

Tori rushed to the porch and yanked off her rubber boots. Travis squatted in front of her and helped her on with the cowboy boots, her feet tinier than he ever remembered his nephews' feet being.

"She'll need thicker socks if she's going to walk far in these. They're still a bit big."

Rachel didn't respond. He glanced over his shoulder. She stared at him like she didn't know what to make of all this, or maybe she just didn't trust him.

Yeah, he understood. Why would she?

They'd met...what?...thirty hours ago? She didn't know him from Adam.

He set the little one upright and stood. Tori ran around the yard, taking the boots for a test drive.

Travis shuffled his feet. He didn't know how to talk

about anything personal. "Yesterday morning? That carousel ride?"

She nodded.

"It was a gift." Lord, he felt foolish and awkward saying that.

Her shoulders rose. "It was only a ride, Travis."

"These are only a pair of boots, Rachel," he responded. "I know you have trouble taking stuff, but I want to thank you."

He rested his hand on the roof of her car. "I know you don't like owing people anything. I already figured out that much about you. I'm the same. The boots and the ride are my way of balancing the scales."

She seemed to understand that. She relaxed, a bit, and buckled the child into her car seat then climbed into the driver's side.

Travis folded himself into the passenger seat. Rachel, looking thoughtful, switched on the radio before backing out of the driveway.

At the Double U, they found both Udall and Uma in their front yard, Uma as compact and weathered as her husband.

"You mind if I take Dusty out in a corral to give Tori a ride?"

Uma grinned, sending one set of wrinkles on a collision course with another. "Of course not. Make yourselves at home. Hey, Rachel, how's the pregnancy going?"

"This baby can't come soon enough." Despite the sentiment, Rachel laughed.

A man would never tire of that laugh.

Travis took them to the stable and introduced them to Dusty.

Tori grasped his pant leg at the knee and sidled against him. "He's big, Travis."

Dusty wasn't some cute pony from a book. Travis picked her up. "Not when you're way up high like this. That better?"

She nodded, but still looked trepidatious, if that was a word.

"Here." Uma's arm appeared from behind him holding a carrot. "Give him this."

Tori took it and held it out in her tiny hand. Dusty, perhaps sensing how scared she was, took it as gently as Travis had ever seen.

"His chewing is loud." Tori seemed to be coming around.

Travis turned to Rachel. "Take her outside, and I'll saddle Dusty and bring him out through the far doors to the corral. I'll get in the saddle, and you hand her to me, okay?"

Once Dusty was ready to go, Travis walked him out and mounted.

Tori sat on top of the fence, with Uma keeping her steady. Travis reached down and took her into his arms, turning her to face forward. He locked his arm across her small waist and scooted her back against him so she'd feel safe, those ridiculous miniature pink cowboy boots sticking out from her splayed legs.

"Okay? You ready to ride, Little Miss Cowgirl?"

She giggled. "Yeah. Just a bit, Travis. Not fast, 'kay?"

"You got it." He urged Dusty into the most sedate walk imaginable. The horse looked back over his shoulder as if to ask what the heck was going on.

"Easy, Dusty, we got precious cargo." Dusty plodded around the corral.

Tori clapped her hands. "Mommy, look, I'm riding a horse. I'm a cowgirl!"

When Travis glanced at Rachel, her full-fledged happiness knocked his socks off. Her eyes looked suspiciously damp. *Thank you*, she mouthed. Apparently, anything was all right with her as long as it made her daughter happy.

He smiled back because this was one spectacular ride. He and Dusty loved to burn up the prairie, loved to ride to race the wind, but even his horse seemed to sense how important this moment was.

The happy bundle in his arms and the grateful woman on the other side of the fence sent his pleasure through the stratosphere.

God, he'd been lonely.

Late that night, Travis had no idea why he couldn't sleep. His shoulders and biceps ached from the renovations he'd started today after returning Tori and Rachel to their trailer. He should be exhausted from washing the walls and prepping them to be painted. He was, but damned if he could get to sleep.

No sense lying in bed, staring at the ceiling. He got up and went downstairs.

He'd seen the white cat hanging around the front yard. Poor creature was going to get herself killed if she wasn't careful. He wondered what she was living on. Field mice?

In the kitchen, he opened a tin of tuna and put it on one of the saucers from the old set of dishes he'd found in the cabinets he'd scrubbed down today. He grabbed a cold beer from the fridge and the bag of licorice whips he'd picked up at the general store and headed for the front porch.

Snagging a thick, fleece-lined flannel jacket, he donned it before sitting on the veranda steps. He deposited the tuna at the foot of the stairs. Quietly he waited, taking an occasional sip from the bottle and chewing on licorice.

Eventually, Ghost appeared, as pale in the moonlight as her namesake. She sniffed the tuna. With a low growl, she tucked in.

The rough sputter of an engine approached and the Focus pulled into Cindy's driveway. Home from work, Rachel stepped out with her purse and a thermal lunch bag.

She glanced around, doing a double take when she noticed him sitting on the steps and Ghost eating at his feet.

She crossed the road and walked up his driveway. "How'd you get her to come out?"

"I opened a tin of tuna."

The blond highlights in her caramel hair shone in the dim moonlight. "Her favorite," she said. "Abigail used to feed it to her instead of cat food."

"It was the only thing I could think to give her. Got lucky, I guess."

"You sure did."

Travis held out the bag of licorice. "Whip?"

"Red! My favorite."

His, too. She took one and bit into it. He scooted over so she could sit down.

"How was work?" he asked, voice low and soft. Not that he would wake anyone out here in the back of beyond, but it seemed a shame to disturb the peaceful night.

"Busy! Whew." Rachel whuffed out a breath of air that stirred wisps of hair. "You'd think the state was about to put a ban on beer. Honey's was packed."

"Good for tips."

"Yeah," she said, her voice as quiet as his own. "Good for tips."

Suddenly, she leaned forward and peered at the saucer Ghost was licking clean. She yelped. "You used Abigail's Royal Doulton for the *cat*?"

"Her what?"

"Her Lady Carlisle china?"

Lady *who*? He shrugged. It was a saucer with flowers on it. "So what?"

"So…it's worth a fortune. It's one of the prettiest patterns ever made."

It was too fussy for him. "I've got a whole set inside."

Rachel pressed a hand to her chest, drawing his eyes to her round bosom. Hard to tell what her natural bust would look like. Must be bigger than usual because of the baby. He shook his head. Why was he thinking about that? Why was he even looking?

"You've got the whole set?" She sounded breathless.

"Yep. It came with the house."

"Don't ever throw it out or give it away. Ever. I'll save from now until Doomsday and buy it from you."

"Okay. I need to use it for now, though. I have nothing else. I'll buy a plastic bowl for the cat."

After that, they said nothing, just chewed on their licorice and watched Ghost.

Rachel's silence was restful. From the moment his sister became a teenager, Samantha had started to talk nonstop, big on air and slim on depth. She could talk the ears off a field of corn. Travis loved his sister, but it bordered on too much.

Finished with her meal, Ghost mounted the steps and sat beside Travis to lick her paws.

"You've made a conquest." Humor hummed in Rachel's voice. "All these months I've been trying to feed her, I made the mistake of buying *cat* food instead of people food. What *was* I thinking?"

Travis chuckled. For a while, they settled into silence, and he felt himself relax, Rachel being an easy woman to spend time with.

Sammy and the boys would do well here. They would be safe. No worries.

His curiosity got the better of him, and he broke the silence.

"Why is this house so important to you?"

He sensed her stiffen beside him. Damn. He hadn't meant to make her uncomfortable.

"I…um…didn't always have the happiest childhood." A sigh that sounded like it came up from the soles of her worn cowboy boots gusted out of her. "My mom and my grandparents fought a lot."

"Why?"

"They were all the same. Stubborn. Not one of them would ever give an inch." She squeezed one hand inside the other. "Mostly, it was about me. My mom had me when she was only fifteen. Her parents never let her live it down."

"And your dad?"

"Gone before I was born. I never knew him."

"I'm sorry." He knew it wasn't enough, but he wasn't used to giving solace. Didn't know how.

She shrugged. "I've learned to live with it."

Sounded to Travis like maybe she still carried that loss inside her.

"The trailer is small. Even with only four of us, it felt crowded. When the fighting got bad," she went on, "I would come over here to visit Abigail. She was sweet and loving. She would make me tea and homemade cookies. Only time in my life I had homemade baked goods."

At least she had some good memories.

"I grew to love the house as well as Abigail. It was big, without a bunch of people crammed into two bedrooms in a trailer surrounded by dirt. It was always calm here. I loved the romance of the refined Victorian design on the rugged prairie."

They were quiet for a while, settling back into the earlier easiness.

Finally, she said, "It's time for me to head home. Thanks again for your help today with the car, and for taking Tori out on your horse. She was still chattering about it when I left for work."

Good. Favors and gifts balanced and reciprocated. He'd given her something in return for that magical carousel ride.

With the scales balanced and the slate wiped clean, he owed no one a single thing.

She stood to leave. "You've made yourself a friend in Ghost. Enjoy."

"Good night," he said, while the cat deigned to allow him to pet her.

Travis watched Rachel take her time crossing to her own house with the slightest waddle. Not a pretty term, but that's what it was. What was most surprising to Travis was that he'd never noticed before that a pregnant woman's walk could be so feminine.

For several minutes after Rachel silently entered her own house, Travis remained on his dark porch, running his fingers along Ghost's knobby spine, pondering womanhood and the many attractive forms it could take.

"She's home," he whispered to the purring cat. "Safe."

Travis picked up the Royal Lady Somebody china saucer and entered his house, thinking that he'd better head into town tomorrow to pick up a flea collar for the cat. He had the feeling they were going to be buddies, but no way was she bringing pests into the house he was getting ready for his boys. He closed the door behind himself, leaving the cat outside complaining.

He lay on his bed and, moments later, the nervous energy that had dogged him earlier was history…and that was a bad sign.

Sure, through years of ingrained habit, he was used to helping women who needed help, but this thing with Rachel, whatever it was, was dangerous.

He didn't want her making him feel better about himself. He didn't want her making him feel restful instead of restless.

He didn't want to be lured, seduced, lulled into taking on more than he wanted in life.

Starting tomorrow morning, he would guard his heart better and keep his distance.

He owed the woman nothing.

Sunday morning found Rachel behind the back of the trailer clearing out the rest of the old plants she hadn't managed to finish pulling from the garden yesterday.

It should have been done in late September. With November breathing down her neck, Rachel still hadn't finished.

Tori sat at the small plastic picnic table Rachel had bought for her that summer. She drew pictures of animals and colored them in, currently working on a purple-and-black tiger. Or what she said was a tiger. It looked like a blob on legs with stripes, sort of like Rachel herself these days. Without the stripes.

Despite the coolness of the day, she wiped sweat from her forehead with her sleeve.

Cindy came out of the house with a jug of iced tea and three plastic glasses.

"You going to finish cleaning out your vegetable garden today?"

"I should be able to, yes."

"Why?" Cindy put the items she carried onto Tori's table. "We can buy all the vegetables we want from the grocery store."

"I know, but I like organic and can't afford to buy it, so I grow veggies. Besides, the cost is a lot cheaper than even the regular vegetables at the store."

Rachel raked out the portion of the garden she'd already cleared. Economizing was important to her. She paid Cindy rent and bought all of the groceries for herself and Tori. No one, least of all her mother, could ever accuse her of being a freeloader.

And then there were those boxes of Mason jars hidden in her closet into which she put every penny she could spare.

"It's a lot of work, Rachel. You should be keeping the weight off your feet today. Relax. Take care of that baby."

"The baby's fine." Sometimes she got tired of people fussing about the baby. For once, she would like people to see her, just her, and not her pregnant belly. Like Travis often did, looking past the baby to her.

*Oh, stop that, Rachel. He sees your pregnant belly as much as anyone does. Doesn't he?*

"If we want vegetables planted come spring," she said, "I need to get this year's plants out. I can't leave them to rot over the winter."

With another mouth to feed, next year's garden would be even more essential. She planned to make her own baby food for Beth, just as she had for Tori.

"It's your funeral." Cindy filled a plastic tumbler with iced tea. "Here, have some of this while I finish up."

"No, Cindy, it's my job." It was a matter of pride that Rachel should pull her own weight.

"Sit. Drink." She handed Tori a smidgen of tea.

Cindy grabbed the rake from Rachel, who hung on, and they grappled for it.

"Oh, for God's sake," Rachel said. The two of them let go at the same time and ended up on their backsides in the garden.

Tori pointed and giggled. "Funny!"

Cindy picked up a handful of leaves Rachel had already raked together and tossed them at her daughter. Rachel threw a bunch back. Tori joined in, and it turned into a glorious free-for-all.

They ended up lying on their backs on the grass staring at clouds scudding across a blue sky, spent from laughing hard.

It brought back memories of when Rachel was small and Cindy still so young she used to sit on the floor and play with her daughter as though she were her friend instead of her mother. They'd loved dressing dolls together.

"Is the baby okay?" Cindy asked.

Lazily, Rachel nodded. "She's fine. I'm pregnant, not sick." Even so, she reached out and squeezed her mother's hand. It was nice for Cindy to actually *be* motherly.

Cindy stood and picked up the rake. "Even if I don't agree with all the work you put into this, I'm not the Wicked Witch of the West, you know."

Rachel sat up and took a sip of tea. She hid a smile behind her plastic cup. Yeah, some days Mom was the Wicked Witch of the West, but not today, and it was nice to work beside her in harmony.

After Rachel finished her drink, she carried two bags of yard waste out to the curb for pickup in the morning.

The Victorian caught her eye, as it always did.

The house with its cockeyed periwinkle-blue shutters, gap-toothed white gingerbread scrollwork and wraparound veranda basked in the Montana sunshine like a forgotten wedding cake.

Overdone and civilized amid the simple wild splendor of the valley in the shadow of the distant Tendoy Mountains, it was a house only a lonely girl would fantasize about. Rachel loved every overly decorated inch of it.

Her phone rang. She pulled it out of her pocket.

"Hey, Rachel." Nadine's voice drifted over the airwaves.

"Nadine, what's up?"

"I investigated him just like you asked me to."

"What? Who?"

An exasperated sigh filled the line. "Travis Read."

Rachel had forgotten. In her disappointment on Friday, she had asked Nadine to dig up dirt. Now she regretted that rash decision.

"You work quickly," she told her friend.

"With the internet, it's a heck of a lot easier to find things than it used to be."

"What did you learn?" While she waited for Nadine's response, Rachel held her breath. She liked Travis. She really liked him. She didn't want dirt. She didn't want to know his secrets.

"Surprisingly, there isn't that much to tell outside of the man being a wanderer. He sure does move around a lot, every year as far as I can tell. He's had a lot of different addresses in the past ten years."

Rachel's heart sank. She had been fathered by a drifter. Cindy's dating life had been littered with them.

After Rachel had been raised without a dad, she'd vowed to never do that to her kids. Then she'd fallen for a guy who had died too young through his own foolishness, and her children were left without a father after all.

The only man she needed was one who was dependable, reliable and who would love Rodeo as much as she did. A man who wouldn't mock her town as some of those drifters passing through had or who wouldn't laugh at how hard she worked to get that old amusement park up and running again to save this town. She needed someone who would stick around.

Not that it mattered. No man would be interested in her. She came with too much baggage even for the most dependable man.

She had no one to lean on but herself.

"Thanks, Nadine," she murmured.

"Anytime, hon. Take care of yourself. Remind me when you're due?"

"First week of December."

"Let's get together before then."

"You bet."

She ended the call and sat on the porch step, shaken. Travis Read might be a decent guy, but he was a wanderer.

She stared at the beautiful Victorian that had been a beacon of safety all of her life.

He'd bought the house for his sister and nephews, not for himself. She'd known that but had assumed he would be staying there, too.

She'd been a fool to let him get under her skin. She had also been a daydreaming fool to think that last night's quiet, friendly conversation meant anything.

Terrifically awful premature flickers of feeling had developed in her and kept her awake last night.

She would have to guard her heart with a ruthless hand.

Even aware of the differences in their situations, she had dreamed anyway, so unwisely.

Already, she'd fallen far enough into a bad state of infatuation when nothing would ever be returned. Worse, the man would probably be moving on soon after his sister arrived.

Rachel might be a daydreamer, but she was *not* her mother, falling for one dissatisfied wanderer after another.

She pulled herself under control. *No more dreaming. Face reality, Rachel. Accept it and live with it.*

At least there might be someone for Tori to play with in that house. After all, her children's happiness was more important than hers. Just once, though, she would like a little something for herself.

Rachel tugged on the hem of Davey's old, fraying sweatshirt and stood. *No self-pity, Rachel. It's a waste of time.*

"Mommy, can we play in the leaves again?"

Yep. Tori was more important. How could a woman possibly feel sorry for herself when she had an amazing child to spend time with? So what if Tori wasn't a man who could offer support and warm arms, filling her with affection and sating her yearning body?

That would have to wait until after she'd finished with the responsibilities she'd taken on with wide-open eyes.

On Sunday morning, Travis headed into town for breakfast again.

He wanted to get to know more of the townsfolk. He managed to snag a stool at the counter beside Cole Payette.

They had a good conversation about everything ranging from ranching, to next year's rodeo, to their favorite sports teams.

Cole filled him in on plenty of details about Rodeo. Seemed like Travis had done well in choosing this town for Samantha.

They chatted through breakfast, and Travis came away with a positive impression of Cole.

Good. Travis just might need the man on his side if Manny D'Onofrio ever found out where Samantha ended up. Not that he would. Travis had been ultra-careful.

Even so, Sammy's former boss in Las Vegas was a

man of means who fostered a dangerous loyalty in his more fanatical employees. Who knew what that might mean if Manny located Sammy?

He filled Cole in on some of the details of Manny's trial for embezzlement. Sammy, who'd worked briefly as an accountant for Manny, had blown the whistle on him and had testified in court. Manny held a grudge.

Hence, Travis's need to get Sammy settled out here in the back of beyond using her own name instead of her husband's.

As sheriff, Cole needed to know.

After breakfast, Travis drove out to the big mall on the main highway to get pet supplies because the stores in town were closed on Sunday. Along with a flea collar, he also bought a plastic bowl and a cat brush to get the mats out of Ghost's fur.

Back home, he slowed to turn into his driveway.

Rachel and Tori stood in theirs.

Before he caught himself with his new resolve to stay aloof, he waved.

The little one smiled and waved back, but Rachel offered only a brisk nod.

He got out of the truck with his purchases and walked across the road.

Rachel didn't smile, didn't wave, didn't greet him with anything remotely akin to her normal goodwill.

Something had changed this morning.

"What's that?" Tori pointed to the pet-store bag.

Yesterday, he and Rachel had been friends. Last night, they'd spent precious moments sitting on his veranda in a state of harmony he'd never felt before.

Friendship with a woman other than his sister had

been as foreign in his life as carousel rides and boyhood dreams.

Sure, he'd decided to keep his distance, but what had changed in Rachel since last night?

An iceberg separated them. He didn't have a clue why.

He answered the child's question. "A flea collar for Ghost."

"Look, Travis. I'm wearing my new boots."

"I can see that. They sure do look good on you." Knowing how much her child's happiness mattered to Rachel, he glanced at her. Once again, her gaze flitted away. No smile. No shared enjoyment of Tori's joy in a flimsy pair of boots.

Nothing. Nada.

Awkwardness settled over him.

She turned and directed her daughter into the trailer without saying goodbye.

Travis shook his head, at sea.

Only a couple of days after meeting the woman, he cared about the potential friendship that had seemed to be building between them.

He walked to his own place, but stopped on the veranda to glance back.

Sure, he'd recognized the danger in finding her so appealing, but he'd had it under control. He'd flat out just liked talking to her. That's all. Just talking. Just relaxing with a friend.

Now that was gone.

The distance between their homes might be only a few yards, but the distance between their hearts was a whole universe long.

## Chapter 7

Throughout his first week on the ranch, Travis worked hard. He'd never been a slacker, but making a good impression on Udall and Uma seemed to be more important to him than with any other employer.

He liked them. He liked the town.

He wanted his family to fit in after he left.

In return, he wanted to be respected, to be the kind of man his father had never been.

It seemed that, at the ripe old age of thirty-seven, he was growing into himself and becoming his own man.

All it had taken was his sister's crisis for him to realize how fragile life was, and how fleeting peace could be.

The first couple of days, all he did was chase down cattle hidden in the most remote, thorniest spots, riding through the roughest terrain on the ranch.

"They always pick the worst spots to hunker down in," he commented to Udall after they'd found yet another one grazing on the side of a small mountain. "That isn't even the sweetest grass on the prairie."

"Ain't that the truth? Don't know why." Udall turned his horse toward the hill. "Let's get him."

Twenty minutes later, they'd routed the animal and trailed him back toward home.

Day after day, Travis rode the Weber ranch, getting to know its contours, its beauties and its tough spots.

When he was out on his own, he radioed one of the hands, Bill Young, with observations about broken fence lines and whatever else needed attention.

Bill would come along later on an ATV, what most cowboys called a Japanese quarter horse, and mend as needed.

In the evenings, even as he had a hasty dinner and stripped woodwork, he kept half an eye on the trailer across the road.

Unsettled by his last encounter with Rachel, and her cool reaction to him, he had an urge to see her, to find out what had happened. What had he done to offend her?

His chance came on Thursday night. Already tired of his own cooking, he headed into Honey's Place for a beer and burger.

He showered, shaved, donned fresh jeans and a clean shirt and headed back out.

Rachel was at the bar filling an order.

The place wasn't as packed as it had been last Friday night, but a good crowd filled probably two-thirds of the tables.

He searched for a table near where he'd sat with

Cindy last week, hoping it would be in Rachel's serving area.

When she approached, he knew he'd hit the jackpot.

She didn't return his smile. He'd expected that.

Until he sorted out what the problem was, he figured he'd get more of the same treatment. How to approach her, though?

"Hey," he said.

"What can I get for you?" she asked. He guessed she had to be polite. He was a customer. She had no choice.

He decided to test her. "Same order as last week."

"Okay," she said and walked away with the unopened menu and no questions asked.

She returned with a Corona.

Fifteen minutes later, out came his dinner, a perfect replica of last week's meal. She'd remembered. She was one hell of a good waitress.

She set the burger and onion rings on the table in front of him without making eye contact.

"Rachel," he said.

She added the plate of hot wings.

"Rachel, please."

She put down his coleslaw and made to leave, but he grasped her wrist. He could feel a fine tremor beneath his palm.

"Tell me what I did wrong."

"Nothing. Everything's fine."

"It isn't and we both know it. I just can't figure what I did."

At last she looked at him. What he saw in her eyes puzzled him. She wasn't angry, but hurt. He recognized more of that quiet acceptance of less that he'd seen when her car broke down.

What did that attitude have to do with him?

How was he asking her to expect less from him? He'd never offered her anything, so how could she expect little?

"What did I do?"

Her pulse beat rapidly against his fingers. "You did nothing wrong."

"Then what changed? On Saturday night, we were almost friends. On Sunday morning, you were treating me like an enemy."

"I wasn't." Her eyes flashed.

"Okay. Maybe not that badly. But you were warm and friendly until then. Since then, you've been cold."

Talking so much, delving into problems, was out of character for him, but he wanted to know.

His eyes dropped to her belly. The last thing he needed was a ready-made family. So maybe it was best that things were rough between them. Why did he care?

The answer hit him in the solar plexus. He *liked* her. It wasn't a case of wanting to take her to bed, though under different circumstances, he would sleep with her in a heartbeat.

The important thing here was that he just plain *liked* her...and had enjoyed her high regard of him.

It hurt that he'd lost her respect.

If he couldn't get it back, so be it, but he at least wanted to understand why.

He squeezed her wrist gently, noting that she hadn't pulled her hand away. She could have. He would have let go at the least resistance.

"Tell me what happened."

She relented, eased that rigid backbone a fraction, and signaled to Honey she was sitting down for a minute.

* * *

Rachel wasn't a coward, but tonight she felt like one, for one simple reason. Embarrassment.

She didn't want to tell Travis that she'd spied on him.

How was she supposed to explain that she didn't want him to be a drifter when that fact shouldn't affect her at all?

She peeked at him. He watched her steadily.

She counted herself a good judge of character, mainly because of the revolving door of Cindy's love life. She'd learned a lot growing up in Cindy's trailer, strictly by virtue of watching, listening and keeping her mouth shut.

Beyond a shadow of a doubt, Travis was a good guy.

Too bad he liked to move around.

Again, that had nothing to do with her.

First to break the silence, he said, "What's up, Rachel?"

She ran a fingernail along the seam of the wooden table. What could she say? *I'm attracted to you? I like you? I'm pregnant and already a mother, but I want a relationship with you? And why shouldn't you want to leave when you hear that?*

Might as well get this thing started. "I might have asked my friend Nadine at the newspaper to check you out."

"Check me out? Why?" A frown furrowed his brow. He wasn't happy about this. If the tables were turned, she wouldn't be, either.

"You just seemed too perfect. I was angry that you'd bought the house. I wanted to find a reason to dislike you."

He perked up. "You thought I was perfect?"

She sent him a lowering look. "Maybe. Anyway, that was last Friday. I forgot I'd asked her. I really didn't want to spy. I was just upset that the house was sold to someone else."

"So? Why the cold shoulder?"

"Nadine called on Sunday."

"And?" He moved his hand in a circular motion, urging her on.

"And she said you never stay in the same place for more than a year."

He was silent for so long she wondered what he was thinking. She glanced up. He watched her without flinching, his expression shuttered.

"Why would that make you angry?" When she didn't respond, he continued, "Why would you be angry with a guy you've known only a week just because he might leave town next year?"

She chose her words carefully. Crushes were for teenage girls, not grown women with children. It was too, too embarrassing to admit to Travis that she *liked* him, especially so quickly.

Suppressing memories of that incredible kiss they'd shared when he was injured on the highway, she forced herself to deal in generalities.

"First, let me apologize for being cold. It was an unreasonable response."

She gathered her thoughts.

"Cindy's had an endless string of boyfriends, mostly men passing through because she's already dated all the eligible men in town. And some who were ineligible. Nothing good has ever come of those relationships."

She motioned for him to eat. No sense in letting all of that good food to go to waste. "It was hard to grow up with that, seeing all of those men use my mom and then leave town. Cindy has her faults, but she doesn't deserve to be treated so callously."

"No, she doesn't. She has a good heart even if she is too needy."

"Yeah, that's the right word."

"So you think I might use Cindy and then leave?"

She hadn't given Cindy a single thought.

"No. It's just that I've developed a dislike of drifters."

His spine stiffened. "I'm not a drifter. Yeah, I move on after a while, but I don't take advantage of others. I earn my own keep. I'm a hard worker."

"Dear Lord, I know that, Travis. I can see that. All you do every night is work on that house, and that's after putting in a day of hard work for Udall."

A tiny smile kicked up the corners of his mouth. Her gaze darted away because it set her nerves humming. "You've been talking to Udall about me?"

"No!" Okay, maybe she had run across Uma in the grocery store and had possibly asked her how Travis was doing on the ranch, to which Uma had responded with a resounding, "Boy, that man can work!" But she'd hadn't talked to Udall, so she wasn't lying, was she?

"My response to what Nadine told me wasn't logical, Travis. It was emotional. I've seen too many men come and go over the years for me to trust a traveler."

"What does that have to do with me?"

*Dear Lord, don't let him guess how much I care already*, she prayed.

"It's just my response to all new people in town."

He nodded.

"I'm not a drifter, Rachel," he stated emphatically, again, as though that were all she needed to know.

Thank goodness Travis didn't bring up how friendly she'd been on his first morning in town, giving him a ride on the carousel and all.

Her aim was to get out of this discussion in one piece without plopping her heart out on the table like a sacrifice.

A family came in for dinner, and that ended the conversation. Rachel stood to welcome them and take their orders. She'd managed to keep it general. Travis would never suspect how much she liked him, and how much she wanted him to be the staying kind.

She walked away knowing she hadn't gained anything from the conversation. She hadn't heard the only thing she'd wanted to, the most *unreasonable*, improbable, impossible thing she could ever wish for.

He hadn't said, "I would stay for you."

*McGuire, you are such a daydreamer.*

Travis was still awake hours later, going over his conversation with Rachel. He was glad they'd talked, but still didn't understand why his comings and goings mattered to her.

He wasn't about to become involved with Cindy, so what difference did it make if he left in a year, or less?

He heard a car turn into her driveway across the road and glanced out the window, but it wasn't Rachel's car.

He threw on a coat and stepped outside.

Rachel approached her door as a car driven by Honey backed out of the driveway and took off.

"What happened to your car?" He didn't need to raise his voice. In the stillness of the night, she would hear him. He walked down his driveway.

Rachel turned. "It wouldn't start."

"Again?" He crossed the road. "Want me to go boost it for you?"

"Not at this time of night. You need to get up early. Why are you still up?"

He wouldn't tell her the truth. *Because our talk kept me awake. Because I still can't figure out why it matters to you if I stay or go, or why your opinion of me matters to me.*

"Couldn't sleep," was all he admitted to. "Let's go start your car."

*Cripes, Travis, what are you doing? You've got a whole shitload of crazy going on right now. You do* not *need to help this woman.*

"Tomorrow's Friday. Mom takes Tori to the mall for their girl-bonding. I'll get into town somehow and get the car started then."

"Let's do it now."

"Why are you pushing this so hard?"

"I need…"

"You need?"

"To know you're safe. That you can get around tomorrow if you need to. That you have a working vehicle."

"Travis, I'm not your responsibility."

"I know." Even to his own ears, he sounded confused. "Please get in the truck and let's get this done."

"Okay," she said, but looked as puzzled as he felt.

The second they were both buckled in, she started to talk, all about independence and going her own way and being a capable woman, thank you very much. She didn't need any man to take care of her. She was fine on her own.

And yet, here she was in his truck.

He figured she could give him a piece of her mind all she wanted. It beat the hell out of the silent treatment she'd given him this past week. He didn't ever want to be on the receiving end of that again.

When she wound down a mile shy of town, he said, "Rachel, I know you're capable." To his surprise, he realized he meant it. He worried about her when he shouldn't. Her business was her own.

He scrubbed the back of his neck.

"You're right," he said, and meant it. "You are independent. You're doing a great job with your daughter. You did a great job with the carousel. You are a kick-ass waitress. The townspeople love and respect you."

Next, he said something he'd never found easy. "I'm sorry."

She took her time, but eventually nodded. "Thanks. I appreciate the apology."

A moment later, she asked, "What was it for?"

"I've been high-handed at times."

He sensed her nodding beside him.

"Know what I need from you?"

He'd piqued her curiosity. He felt her watching him. "No, what?"

"I need a friend. You're the best person I've met in this town. We both know I'll be leaving at some point. I have no designs on your mother, so she won't get hurt. You've got a whole barrel of responsibilities that have nothing to do with me, and you're independent as you said, so you won't be demanding a lot of me."

Whew, an entire speech. What was it about this woman that had him opening up and talking so much?

Something in the honest, straightforward way she dealt with people demanded no less from him.

"You want me to be your friend?"

She seemed a mite disappointed. He didn't know why.

To his mind, friendship was the best gift a person could offer. It was worth all the gems in the world.

"Yeah. I didn't like when you weren't talking to me."

There he went spilling his beans again.

"It hurt when you were cold."

His admission seemed to please her.

"Okay. We can be friends."

"Okay, then. Don't friends help each other out in times of need?"

"Yes."

"And this is a time of need."

"For me, yes. Here's the problem, though." She shifted in her seat. "When will there ever be a time for me to give something back to you?"

He cast a startled glance at her. "You don't know?"

"Know what?"

"The carousel ride, to start."

"You already paid me back for that."

"I know. I guess I can't stress enough how huge it was. Sammy and me—"

He could feel her eyes on him.

"Sammy and you?"

"We didn't have anything. Dad drank too much and Mom was…" He shrugged, trying to minimize what they'd gone through. He wasn't looking for pity. "Best way I can describe her is weak. She wasn't a bad person, but she didn't have a lot to give. Sammy and I were on our own. Then they died."

She rubbed one hand on her thigh. "I'm sorry."

"I don't want you to feel sorry for me. I just want you

to understand how it was. We had nothing. No money. No stuff. I kept us together by working every waking hour I wasn't going to school. After Mom died, I had to drop out."

They arrived in front of Honey's. He pulled up beside Rachel's car.

"There were no extras, no movies, no county fairs, no music. That ride you gave me was…" He had to stop talking because he'd become emotional. He wasn't an emotional man.

A moment later, he cleared his throat. "When I was growing up, there was no joy." He turned in his seat to face her, desperate for her to understand. "You gave me joy."

Her whiskey eyes looked suspiciously moist. She tucked a strand of tawny hair behind her ear. One silver cowboy-boot earring winked at him in the dim light from Honey's front door.

"Travis, that's the best thing anyone's ever said to me."

"There's more. When I felt your baby talking to me…" When her eyes widened, he amended, "I mean when I felt her moving, it was like she was communicating with me. Acknowledging me, or something. Strange, huh?"

"No, not strange. I feel the same way. Sometimes when she moves, it feels like she's playing with me already."

"You've given me two gifts the likes of which I could never repay. My point is that you have to understand why I need to help you out when I can. Okay?"

"Okay. Just be less bossy about it."

"I can do that."

They got out of the truck. Rachel sat in the driver's seat of her car.

Travis boosted the battery, closed her hood and came around to her open driver's window. "Consider scraping together enough cash to get yourself another cheap clunker. There's got to be a better one out there."

"I'll think about it." She smiled, not one of her dazzlers, but a quiet, thoughtful one. He found it no less attractive than the bright, shiny ones.

"Thank you, Travis. Thanks for explaining things to me."

The wind picked up, and he tamped his hat more firmly onto his head. "I'm a lot more than just a macho dude, you know."

"A bossy macho dude."

"I'll try to do better."

"Promises, promises."

# Chapter 8

Weekdays, Travis spent long hours on the ranch, collecting cattle and mending fence before the snows set in.

Weeknights, he'd spend longer evenings working on the house, getting it ready for his sister and her boys.

Sometime before Christmas, they would be driving in from San Francisco. He didn't want them here while he renovated. He wanted to give them a perfect house.

Friday and Saturday nights became a pleasure for him, a break away from the endless work. He'd spend them at Honey's, getting to know his neighbors and dancing up a storm.

That Rachel worked there was an added bonus he didn't look at too closely.

Cole Payette was becoming a good buddy. More often than not, Travis found himself on a stool beside Cole at the bar getting to know the man better. Saturday mornings found him having breakfast with the guy on stools at the counter in Vy's diner.

It might seem like they had little in common, Cole being a one-town man and Travis a nomad, but they never lacked for conversation. And their quiet moments were companionable.

It had been a long time since Travis had had a good friend, someone closer than a mere acquaintance.

When he arrived home after a night out, he would say, "Come on, Ghost," and walk into the house, followed by the newly clean cat.

As it got colder, Ghost took to spending more time inside than out.

She became a permanent resident and his new companion. He sure hoped Sammy wouldn't mind keeping the cat.

"Who would have thought," he murmured to her one night, "that I'd take on not only a house, but also a pet."

He shook his head and kept on stripping the floors. Later, while enjoying a beer in front of the fire, Ghost jumped onto the sofa and curled up beside him. He liked the feel of her warm weight against his leg.

In mid-November, the town held a Thanksgiving dance in the elementary school auditorium.

Brown, orange and red construction paper leaves covered the walls along with the obligatory rows of hooks for cowboy hats. He'd come to learn the town took its hat hooks seriously.

Good thing, since Travis took *his* hat seriously.

In the middle of the evening, five women took to the stage.

Rachel stood in the middle, with Honey to her right and Violet from the diner to her left. Standing beside

Travis, Cole leaned close and identified the other two for him.

"Nadine and Max. The official park committee. They're the ones who've spearheaded the revival of the amusement park."

"Think they'll get it done on time?"

Cole grinned. "No doubt in my mind at all. They're driven."

They were an attractive bunch, all in their late twenties. Honey wore her trademark turquoise and silver jewelry. Her mass of blond hair hung in curls to her waist.

Violet wore her distinctive forties and fifties retro style. In the diner, she pinned her hair up beneath a kerchief, but tonight her straight blue-black hair hung down her back in striking contrast to her violet eyes.

Nadine had beautiful red hair every bit as straight as Vy's.

The last woman on stage, Max, stood out by how boyish she looked compared to the other women—Rachel womanly in her pregnancy, and Honey with her masses of curls, Vy with her hourglass figure and Nadine with her perfect manicure, makeup and sparkly party dress.

Max wore a boxy plaid shirt, torn jeans and broken-in cowboy boots.

"Folks," Rachel began, "you all know who we are and why we're here tonight. We're the reason you paid for tickets to the Thanksgiving dance for the first time ever."

Her microphone squealed, and someone adjusted the sound.

"I love this town," she continued with an emphasis on *love*. "I don't want it to die. Our young people are leaving in droves. If we get the rides fixed and offer great deals on unique entertainment, we can bring in tourists. We'll top it off with a first-rate rodeo. Our goal is to open for three weeks next August and later expand into something that will last longer."

Her passion for the project shone through, and Travis saw a glimpse of the woman he'd met on his first morning in town.

The world would be a pretty awesome place if all of Rachel McGuire's burdens could be eased and this Rachel could be present all the time. She was magnetic.

"We thank you all for your generosity," Honey said. "Many of you bought more than one ticket, and it's appreciated. The money will go a long way toward revitalizing both the amusement park and our town."

Travis heard something that sounded like a sigh from Cole, who stared at Honey. He nudged him with his shoulder.

"How many did you buy?" Travis asked.

"Only ten."

"Only?"

Cole shrugged. His cheeks turned suspiciously pink. "Let it go, Read."

"Sure thing, Payette."

A moment later, Cole asked, "How many did you buy?"

"Only a dozen."

The corners of Cole's mouth kicked up. "Only?"

"Let it go, Payette."

"Sure thing, Read."

They stood in companionable silence throughout the speeches.

When they ended and music started up for dancing, Travis sought out Rachel.

"Tell me about the women you've teamed up with to resurrect the fair."

"You know Honey. She'll be in charge of entertainment."

"She'd be good at that." Travis grinned. "What will Vy be doing?"

"Food."

"Makes sense."

"And Nadine? I haven't met her. What will she be doing?"

"Promotion and hospitality."

"And last, the one on the far end. What was her name?"

"Maxine Porter. Max. She'll resurrect the rodeo that started it all and gave the town its name."

"Sounds like you have everything covered."

"I think so. We'll have to work hard, but we're all up for it."

Rachel glanced around the room.

"I love this place and these people." She turned her gaze to him, her eyes luminous and sad. "I couldn't possibly ever leave. I love my friends. I want my children to grow up here. My own childhood might not have been ideal, but the town is. It's worth preserving."

"What is it, Rachel? Why so sad?"

"I feel like this is our last chance. What if we can't make this happen? What if tourists don't come? There's nothing else here. No industry. No manufacturing. The ranching is good, but it can't keep the whole town afloat. Beef prices rise and rise and people eat less and less of it."

Someone bumped into them, and Travis pulled her

close. They ended up slow dancing with the flow of the crowd.

"I'm afraid we might fail. Then where will the town be?"

"Why wouldn't you succeed?" he asked.

She shook her head, clearly suffering a lack of confidence. First time he'd seen that in her.

"Know what I saw when I watched you five women on stage?"

"No. What?"

"A smart, determined group of women. Starting with you."

"Really? Starting with me?"

"Yeah."

They stopped speaking and stopped moving. The air around them seemed to become rarefied. The coconut scent of her shampoo drifted around them. While Rachel turned her brilliant golden eyes on him, Travis lost the ability to breathe, let alone think or talk.

*Move, Travis. This isn't what you want. Friendship, remember? Only friendship.*

The song changed, but Rachel stayed in his arms until a moment later when she gasped, breaking the spell.

Travis followed the direction of her gaze. Cindy was dancing with a man Travis didn't recognize.

"Who's that?" he asked.

"A stranger. He was in the bar the other night asking about job prospects in town."

Travis studied her keenly. "You didn't like him." He didn't need her to answer. He sensed the tension in her.

"I thought he was less than honest. He bragged about all the places he'd been."

"Ah, I see."

"What does that mean?"

"The man's a drifter. That's an automatic strike against him."

"That was some of it." He liked her unflinching honesty, even about herself. "Not all, though. It was more than a knee-jerk reaction on my part. I don't know what his game is. The only thing I feel for certain is that there is a game."

Travis checked him out. Other than the slicked-back dark hair and shiny gray suit, there wasn't much to distinguish the man…except that he appeared to like Cindy, and she liked him.

There wasn't an inch of breathing room between them.

He returned his attention to Rachel, who hadn't stopped watching the pair.

"You think Cindy will get hurt."

"No doubt in my mind."

"There's nothing you can do about it. Cindy's a grown woman and can date anyone she wants."

"I know." She said it grudgingly. It took a moment, but she rallied and showed him her game smile. "I'm okay, Travis. Really."

He led her off the dance floor.

"You need a drink or anything?"

"I'm good. I'm going to head to the ladies' room. Thanks, anyway."

When Rachel stepped out of the washroom, she nearly collided with Nadine.

"I nearly forgot. I have news for you," Nadine said. "I've been doing more digging into Travis."

Rachel's heart sank. "I didn't know you were going to keep looking."

"You know me. I do a job till it's beaten to death. I love doing research."

"You mean you love digging up dirt."

Nadine's broad smile was dazzling. "That, too."

They made room for a couple of women to pass by.

"Seriously, though," Nadine said. "I have news you need to hear." All traces of her good humor had vanished.

"You're scaring me, Nadine. What is it?"

"It's about Travis's sister."

"What about her?"

"Apparently she worked in Las Vegas for some big criminal named Manny D'Onofrio and testified against him. He's in jail now for embezzlement. The scuttlebutt is that he vowed to get revenge."

"Jeepers, Nadine. That sounds like something out of a bad movie."

"I know, but the source was impeccable. Apparently this Manny guy could be quite vicious."

Rachel shivered.

Travis was bringing his sister and her two boys to live in Rodeo, along with whatever danger this *vicious* Manny guy was threatening.

Rachel felt as though she had chips of ice in her veins. Travis had bought the house right across the street from Rachel and her children for his sister. She was coming here to live.

Was she a criminal, too, like her boss? Had she cut a deal to testify against this guy so she wouldn't have to go to jail herself?

Bile rose into Rachel's throat, not morning sickness, but fear.

Travis was bringing danger to her town, to her backyard, to her family.

She knew he wanted them here by Christmas. How close was his sister now?

Was trouble looming on Rachel's doorstep?

Travis was a nice man, a good one, but she would never forgive him for this. None of the kindness he'd shown her in the past could make up for bringing this here.

If she had to fight tooth and nail to protect her family, she would.

If Travis or his sister got in her way, God help them.

"Thanks." Chilled to the bone, she marched away from Nadine to fetch her coat and then to find Travis. "Gotta go."

She located him at the bar set up in the far corner. He nursed a beer.

"Could I talk to you for a minute?"

He raised his eyebrows at her hard-edged tone, but dutifully followed her outside.

In the cool night air, she rounded on him. "What's this I hear about your sister having something to do with a crime in Las Vegas?"

He reared away from her. His expression flattened. "How is that anyone's business but mine?"

"If you bring danger to this town, I have a right to know."

"I'm not bringing *danger*. I'm bringing my sister and her two little kids."

"Your sister worked with a criminal." She'd raised her voice, and a pair of smokers nearby stared at her.

"Did she get some kind of deal? What kind of crime was she involved in?"

"She wasn't involved. Only her boss was. She—"

"He said he would come after her."

"He's in jail. Everything will be fine."

She heard defensiveness. Was he protesting too much? She tried to get in his face, but Beth got in the way.

"If any harm comes to my family, I will never forgive you. I will personally boot you and your sister out of my town."

He glowered and hovered over her. She'd never seen him angry and, boy, was he fierce. She stepped back.

He pointed a finger at her. "You know, I thanked you for putting me on that carousel my first day here, but I didn't sign on for a roller-coaster ride. You need to get your emotions together."

"I have every right to defend my family."

He talked over her. "I don't know what's wrong with you, but I don't need this. I'm outta here."

He strode to his truck and drove off. Only once she sat in her own cold vehicle did she realize he'd left without his jacket.

Tough. He could come back for it himself tomorrow.

She no longer cared.

Driven by a need to see Tori, to make sure she was safe and sound, she made it home in record time, following Travis's taillights in the distance.

By the time she turned into her driveway, he was already inside his house.

She paid the babysitter and watched her drive away.

Only after the sitter's car had disappeared down the road did Rachel go to her bedroom doorway to stare at her sleeping daughter.

Tori was safe and sound for now, but how long would that last?

The weight of her duties pressed down on her. Without Davey, she had only herself to rely on to keep her children fed, clothed and sheltered…and to keep them safe.

In this moment, despite all of her constant pep talks to keep her spirits high, she was overwhelmed.

*Davey, what have you done to me?*

Travis couldn't remember ever being so mad at a woman.

No, that wasn't true. There'd been his last girlfriend, Vivian, who'd turned out to be dishonest and using him. He'd been furious with her, but this was a different anger altogether.

This was based in fear, in utter terror that Rachel was right—that somehow Manny would find Sammy here. And that Travis truly had brought danger to a town he really liked, and to people he respected.

In his darkened living room, he watched Rachel storm into her trailer. Moments later, the babysitter drove off.

Spooked, he sat watching her home for hours. Nothing moved. No one drove out of the still Montana night to wreak havoc in Rodeo.

In the wee hours of the morning, he forced himself to go to bed.

The following week passed uneventfully. He spent his time alone. On Thanksgiving Day, he stood in his empty home and craved the mayhem of his nephews.

Nothing hollowed out a man like knowing his Thanksgiving dinner would be something pulled out of his freezer. Cardboard turkey, reconstituted mashed potatoes, gluey gravy and cranberry sauce awaited him later this afternoon.

His mood matched the chill wind blowing across the fields. Once the cold had settled on the land in earnest, both color and leaves had been quick to disappear.

There was weather coming in. Travis could feel it.

He stared across the road at the gray metal box hunkered down against the wind. It looked too flimsy to survive much.

Since the dance on the weekend, Cindy's car hadn't reappeared in the driveway. Travis wondered where the new man in town was staying 'cause he was certain that's where Cindy would be found.

How was Rachel doing today?

What kind of Thanksgiving was she having? How was Tori? Was Beth moving a lot?

Travis wouldn't intrude. She'd made her feelings about him clear. She wanted to have nothing more to do with him.

He should want nothing more to do with her.

In his anger he'd been nasty, but he... Well, hell, he might as well admit it. He missed them.

He liked Rachel. He liked her company and her conversation and her smile.

Sick of his own company by eleven in the morning, he made a decision to reach out. He would either be welcome or he'd get a kick in the teeth.

Either way, he'd get a break from himself.

Besides, Ghost needed the company, too.

He shrugged into his sheepskin coat and stepped out into a cold landscape, the unseasonably mild weather of three weeks ago a distant memory.

At Rachel's front door, he screwed up his courage, took a deep breath and knocked.

Travis stood on her doorstep, big and handsome and uncertain of his welcome.

No wonder.

Her emotions were all over the map where this guy was concerned. She could blame it on hormones and the pregnancy, but her basic honesty compelled her to admit the truth.

She liked Travis far more than she should, and it killed her that there was no hope for a future with him.

She was pregnant, he would soon be taking care of his sister and her children, and she didn't want to be anywhere near him if criminal elements came to town.

She'd fumed about it since Nadine had told her about his sister, but today, alone in the trailer with Tori, with nothing but a small turkey breast for their Thanksgiving feast, Rachel was rethinking her stance.

Her mom had been AWOL all week. They might not always get along, but Rachel missed her, especially on this special holiday.

For all intents and purposes, Rachel and Tori were alone. Travis was alone. His sister hadn't arrived yet.

"Would you do me a huge favor?" Travis asked.

He needed a favor? He hadn't yet figured out that she'd give him anything he asked as long as it didn't hurt her or her children?

"What do you need?" she asked.

He ran his fingers through his hair and rested one hand high on the side of the trailer, looking anywhere but at her. His coat gaped open to reveal just a denim shirt underneath. He wore neither hat nor gloves, despite the drop in temperature.

Obviously he'd just run across the road for a brief visit.

"It's a strange request." He picked at a piece of flaking paint with his thumbnail. "Would you and the little one feel like coming over for a couple of hours to help me decorate the house for Christmas?"

*Would she?*

He was offering her the opportunity to decorate the Victorian for Christmas? He might as well hand her happiness on a silver platter and tie it up with a big red bow.

Would she? Heck, yes!

"Of course." What else could she say? She might have promised herself she would keep her distance from Travis, but turn down the chance to get inside that house and gussy it up? No *way* would she pass that up. "I'd love to help. So would Tori."

"Help what, Mommy?"

Rachel glanced down. Tori had joined her at the door.

"We're going to help Travis decorate his house for Christmas. Would you like that?"

"Yes! We help Travis." She sat on the floor and pulled on her pink cowboy boots. She stood on tiptoe, but couldn't reach her coat. Rachel really needed to hang some low hooks for her.

She handed Tori her winter coat, hat and mittens before donning her own winter gear. The Victorian might be only across the road, but neither Rachel nor Tori was as hardy as Travis seemed to be.

After pulling the front door closed behind her, Rachel followed Travis and Tori across the frozen dirt yard. When crossing the road, Travis held Tori's hand.

Rachel approved. She might be trying to keep her emotional distance, but the guy made it hard. He did too much that was right and good.

She stepped into a toasty house. Travis had a fire going. It smelled woodsy, warm and inviting, and so, so much better than the trailer.

Glad to be out of the tin can for a while, she hung her coat and Tori's on the hooks beside the front door.

"You did a beautiful job with the renovations, Travis."

He came to stand beside her in the living room doorway. "Thanks. I tried to keep it true to its roots while modernizing a bit."

The floor was freshly sanded and finished. "I like the color you used on the oak."

"Come in. I want you to see what I did in the kitchen."

She smiled up at him. "If I didn't know better, I'd say you're proud of the house."

A sheepish smile grew on his lips, those beautifully defined lips she'd actually dreamed about.

"Yeah, I guess I kind of am. I've never owned a house before, or a single acre of property."

"You've been caught by the pride-of-ownership bug."

"Maybe. It's for Sammy and my nephews, though. I want them to feel pride. And happiness." He took her elbow to drag her to the kitchen, but she stopped him.

"Wait. I'm savoring all of the changes in here first."

He'd taken all the old layers of paint from the wood trim. Stained dark, it provided a wonderful contrast to the lighter oak of the floors.

She touched a wall. "How did you decide on this sage green for the walls?"

"A woman in the shop helped me."

"Nancy?"

"That was her name."

"She's good with her advice. I like this." She still didn't much like his overstuffed leather couch and armchair in this space, but hey, it was his house. Not hers.

Nonetheless, it was an inviting space. He'd stripped the mantel and wood around the fireplace and had painted it a glossy white. It worked, really brightening the room.

"You did a good job, Travis. I like it."

He towered over her, his heat a source of both balm and sexual irritation, and a real danger to her peace of mind. Good thing he didn't know that.

"That means a lot to me, Rachel. Your opinion matters."

It did? Would wonders never cease? This man kept giving her the sweetest of gifts. Now he offered her his high regard.

Disconcerted by the happiness he brought her, she stepped farther into the room, away from Travis, avoiding trampling her daughter where she sat on the floor, rubbing Ghost's belly.

"Where did this come from? Have you been sewing in the evenings?" She pointed to the rag rug on the hearth, knowing full well he hadn't made it, but it amused her to tease him.

"It came with the house. You wouldn't believe the stuff I've found in different cupboards and nooks and crannies."

"I'll bet Abigail made it. Blue, ivory and rose were her favorite colors."

"That explains all the quilts in those colors."

"She left you quilts?"

"Her family did. At least, they didn't take them when they cleared out the furniture. It seems there was a lot of stuff they didn't want."

"They're distant relatives from England. She didn't have anyone close left. I guess they didn't feel like carting the stuff across the ocean."

"Probably not. In the meantime, I don't own a lot, so I've been using her stuff to fill in the gaps."

Rachel nodded her approval. "You need to update the paintings to your style."

"Trouble is, I don't know what my style is. I know what I don't like, but haven't figured out what I like."

*I can help with that.* Thank God, she didn't blurt the thought. Travis's life was his. This house was his. Neither had anything to do with her.

And yet…here she was about to help him decorate this house for the holidays. The honor warmed her.

"I'm sure your sister will have ideas of her own. Let's look at your kitchen and then start decorating."

He seemed to like that.

In the kitchen, she pulled up short. Red cupboards dominated white walls.

"Why the red?"

Travis frowned. "Again, Nancy's idea. I told her I wanted color, and she suggested the red. I like it. Don't you?"

He sounded less than confident. Did her opinion matter that much?

"Yes, I do. It surprised me, but you know what? It works."

His frown eased.

To match the cherry-red cabinets, he had placed a

few red-and-white-checked items around, a tablecloth and napkins on a large pine table and a couple of dish towels hanging on a rod.

Other than that, very little cluttered the countertops. A toaster designed to look like an old-fashioned radio sat beside a swan-like stainless-steel kettle.

The clean lines served to balance the frivolity of the ornate wood trim, again stained dark here in the kitchen. Surprisingly, it all worked.

She would gladly cook and bake in this kitchen… and that surprised her. She would have gone more traditional to suit the house, but Travis had gone 1950s and had pulled it off.

"I love it."

He exhaled as though he'd been holding his breath.

Tori stepped into the room. "When are we going to decorate?"

"A better question is," Rachel said, "what are we going to use for decorations?"

"I've been looking online for ideas. I never had much of an example when I was a kid." He tucked his hands in his back pockets and, again, Rachel had the sense he was looking for approval. "I thought I could go a little old-fashioned. Plus I don't want to spend a lot of money."

He jerked his chin in the direction of the cabinets. "This renovation stuff is expensive. I need to put a lid on it for now."

"So, what do you have in mind for decorating?"

He opened the plain white refrigerator and pulled out a couple of bags of fresh cranberries. From a cupboard he took a bag of popcorn.

Rachel perked up. "Popcorn and cranberry chains? I love it. So unusual these days."

"Not too old-fashioned?"

She shrugged and held her hands palm up. "Who cares? It's your house, Travis. No one else's. Do what you want."

The side of his mouth quirked up. "Glad it meets with your approval. C'mere."

He left the room, talking over his shoulder. "You liked that Lady Whoever china so much, I think you'll like what I found in the attic."

Small, yellowed boxes sat on the dining-room table, a plain black rectangle with leather parson dining chairs. Again, it wasn't her style, but it wasn't her house, either, was it?

He opened one of the small boxes, and Rachel's breath caught in her throat.

"Ooooh, Travis. You have glass ornaments?"

Jewel-toned balls decorated with hand-painted sparkles nestled in bits of tissue paper.

With his attention on her reaction, Travis said, "It gets even better."

"How can it possibly get any better?"

"Look at these." He lifted the lid from a box, and she was speechless.

Delicate glass birds were nestled into paper muffin cups inside the sectioned box. The intricacy of the painting on the birds left Rachel in awe.

"Travis," she whispered. "Do you realize what you have? These things are worth a fortune."

"I figured since they're so old. I don't want to sell them, though. I want to use them."

Oh, this man. His head was screwed on so right she could hug him. She smiled instead.

"Right answer, Travis. These will be amazing on

the tree." She frowned. "You *are* going to have a tree, right? I didn't see one."

"Bought it yesterday. It's thawing in the back porch. Figured you could help put it up."

Again he seemed to be proud of himself, but stumbled when he glanced at her belly.

"On second thought, if you want to start popping corn and stringing it with cranberries, I'll do the heavy lifting with the tree."

She grinned. "I can do that."

She put out her hand, and Tori took it. "Let's go make popcorn, honey."

Travis's kitchen was warm, not drafty like the trailer's, and a pure delight to work in. Every element on the new stove worked.

Tori ate more popcorn than she threaded and broke too many popped kernels when piercing with the blunt needle Rachel had given her. Her lower lip trembled.

"Know what I need you to do, honey?"

"What?"

"What do you see on Travis's walls?"

Tori studied them. "That painting." She pointed to the old-fashioned oil of golden fields.

"What else?"

"Nothing, Mommy."

"Right and that's a real problem. Know why?"

Tori shook her head. "Why?"

"Don't you think it would be nice if Travis had a few pretty drawings to decorate the place?"

"Like in our house?"

"Yes, exactly. Do you feel like coloring a few angels for him?"

"Yeah!" She ran to Travis. "Do you gots paper and crayons?"

"I have computer paper. No crayons, though."

Rachel stood and donned her coat. "I'll get some stuff and be right back."

"It's a bit icy out there. Are you okay crossing the road?"

"I might be eight months pregnant, but I can still walk."

Travis grinned ruefully. "Sorry. I'm working on doing better, Rachel."

With a jaunty wave, she set off for the trailer.

Minutes later, she returned with construction paper, children's scissors, crayons, glue and glitter. Travis was going to hate her for that last item, but what were Christmas decorations without glitter?

After removing her coat, she entered the living room and stared. Like something from a Christmas painting—or from one of her daydreams—Tori sat in the big armchair beside the fire, eating popcorn with Ghost curled on her lap, while Travis, tall and capable, put the finishing touches on the Christmas-tree container. He turned the tree this way and that to find the best aspect.

"What do you think? Is this best?" He turned to her with a smile, and just like that she lost the last of her heart.

She was a goner, completely head over heels in love with a man she couldn't have.

Shaken and stirred, she gripped the back of the sofa and tried to smile.

## Chapter 9

Frowning, Travis took a step toward her. "Are you okay?"

Rachel raised a hand to halt his progress. If he touched her, she might disintegrate into a puddle. She wasn't strong right now. Vulnerable and yearning, she needed to get on more solid footing if she were to survive this day. Or, even more, if she were going to enjoy it.

Travis had given her this gift, and she refused to squander it.

Tamping down on rampant emotions and her most unreasonable desires, she said, "I'm okay, Travis. Just a bit of indigestion. Beth does that to me sometimes."

Didn't that just underscore how unprepared she was for romance…talking about indigestion and pregnancy, of all things. If all of her unrealized daydreams hadn't pierced her heart so badly, she might have laughed at her foolishness.

She smiled, albeit shakily, but rallied and said, "You're right. That is the best aspect of the tree. I like it."

He rubbed his hands. "Okay. Now what? What goes on first?"

"You usually start with threading the lights through the branches, and then we'll add decorations afterward. Do you have lights?"

He picked up a pair of bags from the corner of the living room. The local hardware store's logo graced the sides. "I'll show you what I bought."

Like a magician with a bottomless magic hat, he pulled out boxes of Christmas lights one after another, smaller boxes of white fairy lights, big red pillar candles, a fake greenery wreath and fake snow for the windows.

"Fake snow? Really, Travis?"

She might as well have crushed him. A crestfallen expression crossed his face.

"Oh, hey," she said, rushing to reassure him. "I'm joking! This is going to look awesome in the windows."

He brightened, leaving her to wonder why her opinions were so important to him.

"Here," she said, handing him the lights for the tree. "Start with these."

While he did that, she settled Tori on the floor with the construction paper.

She drew and then cut out a couple of angels, pink and yellow, and handed Tori the crayons to color them.

"Okay," Travis responded. "What do you think of the lights?"

He was on his knees plugging them in, his behind sticking out through the bottom branches. Rachel didn't usually notice men's butts, but Travis had a good one. A great one. Maybe the best male butt on the face of the earth.

Rachel picked up a piece of Tori's construction paper and fanned her face. What was she to do with herself and her inconvenient desire?

The lights on the tree came on, and all thoughts of sex and heat fled.

"Oh, Travis," she said, pressing a hand to her chest. "It's enchanting."

There wasn't a better word for it. Blue lights twinkled in the greenery.

Tori jumped up and ran to him, wrapping her arms around his legs.

"It's pretty, Travis!"

He ruffled her hair. "Glad you like it, sprout."

"Here." Rachel carried over one of the strands of popcorn and cranberries, and they hung it across the front, looping back once.

"Let me get the other strand."

Travis was there ahead of her. When he returned, they looped it across the tree twice below the first strand.

They all stood back.

Blue lights winked behind the red-and-white strands. Even without further decorations the tree was already pretty.

"Let's start adding birds," Rachel said, as excited as a child to see the finished tree.

They were attached to small clips that hooked onto the tree.

"Me, too, Mommy. I want to hang birds." Tori reached for one, but Rachel held back, torn. She didn't like to deny her daughter new experiences, but the birds were fragile, old and valuable.

Travis must have noticed Rachel's hesitation and understood the reason, because he said, "I have a special job for you, Tori. Look."

From one of the hardware store bags he pulled a large gold angel. Tori squealed and clapped her hands.

"Putting this angel on the top of the tree looks like the kind of job you would do just right." Travis asked her to hold it.

She handled it with reverence.

While Rachel clipped birds onto the tree, Travis lifted Tori so she could place the hollow angel right onto the top spire.

They stood back and admired it.

Rachel had finished the birds and had started on the equally delicate glass balls.

To preempt Tori from touching them, Travis asked, "Hey, weren't you making angels for me? Where are they?"

"Here!" She gathered her angels and handed them to him.

"Well, now, these are beautiful, but you've left me in a real quandary."

"What's a quand?"

"In a real jam. I don't know where to hang them. Help me out here and show me the best spots."

Tori rose to the occasion and had Travis hang them around the room. The fact that every spot was only three or four feet off the floor, in other words, at Tori's level, didn't seem to bother Travis one bit.

The way he valued Tori and considered her opinions was another of the things that Rachel lov—liked about him.

Oh, who was she kidding? She loved him.

There was no denying her heart's desire, but boy, did it hurt that life hadn't turned out differently.

Why her life had ended up the way it had was a mystery to her. All she could do was hold on tightly to her belief that she would survive, and she would raise her daughters to be the best people they could possibly be.

One way or another, she would give them a good chance. She hadn't figured out how yet, but their lives would be better than hers.

There would be no fighting in their home. It might be only a tin can, temporarily, but with Cindy shacked up with the new man in town at the moment, there was peace.

By late afternoon, they'd finished decorating.

"I guess it's time for us to go home." Rachel didn't want this glorious day to end. Not yet. Soon enough she could return to the reality of her life alone.

Travis glanced out of the window toward her trailer, sitting in the falling darkness. Dusk came so early at this time of year.

"We could, you know, maybe have supper together," he said.

Was it possible that he didn't want things to end so soon, either?

"I could pick us up a pizza." Travis interrupted her thoughts. "What would you think of that?"

"Pizza! Yeah!" Tori clapped her hands.

How much did she have in her wallet? Could she offer to help pay? Payday wasn't until next week.

As though reading her mind, he said, "It's my treat. You helped me decorate." He glanced around his living room. If she weren't mistaken, Rachel would almost think he looked emotional. "The least I can do is spring for pizza."

He pulled up short. "Darn. It's Thanksgiving. Everything will be closed."

"The pizza shop next to the new mall is open every day."

"Good." Travis rubbed his hands together.

"How about if Tori and I go home and get her bathed for the night while you drive into town? That way she'll be ready for bed when I get her back home later."

"Perfect. I'll leave the front door open. C'mon back when you're ready."

They discussed toppings and Travis drove off.

Rachel and Tori went home and did their thing. With Tori clean and dressed in warm flannel pjs, they put on their coats and headed back to Travis's house.

Kneeling by the fireplace in the living room, Rachel stirred the ashes to life and built the blaze back up again.

They'd done a great job of decorating the mantel with fake greenery threaded with fairy lights and red pillar candles. A good day's work. Satisfaction and happiness flooded her.

Travis had given her a real gift today.

Whistling, she carried the milk and hot chocolate she'd brought over to the kitchen to make hot chocolate for Tori.

Ensconced in front of the fire and covered with a colorful afghan from the back of the sofa, Tori curled up with Ghost.

Just as Rachel put the half-full mug of warm chocolate into Tori's hands, the doorbell rang.

"Who on earth?" Maybe Travis had his hands full and couldn't turn the doorknob.

Rachel opened the door and stared. A beautiful woman stood on the veranda.

Tall and slim, in a long, white, wool coat, she might be the most sophisticated visitor to ever come to town.

A white scarf shot with gold thread cradled a firm jawline and a white-fur hat framed a heart-shaped face.

The only color, her bright red lips, popped against all of that stunning white.

She looked like a model from a magazine.

Rachel combed her fingers through her hair, aware that she came up short in comparison to this goddess.

"Oh!" the woman said. "I thought this was the address for Travis Read."

"It is. This is his house."

A tiny frown formed between dark brows. "You live here?"

Rachel shook her head. "We're visiting."

"Is Travis home?"

"Not at the moment. He'll be back soon." Should she invite her in? Rachel liked to be polite, but this wasn't her home.

"I'm a friend of his," the woman said.

When Rachel vacillated, the woman continued, "A *very* good friend. I'm anxious to see him again. It's been a couple of months."

Rachel understood immediately, but Travis hadn't mentioned a girlfriend.

A light bulb went off. Her thoughts traveled back to

the day Travis had kissed her so sweetly and thoroughly after crashing his bike.

This paragon of womanly sophistication must have been who Travis was really kissing, not Rachel with her late husband's clothes and big belly.

She stepped aside and the woman entered.

"I'm Rachel McGuire. I live across the road."

"Vivian Hughes." She took off her coat and hung it on one of the hooks. Next, off came the hat. Long, straight, jet-black hair hung down her back.

Beside her Rachel felt gauche. Funny, until Travis had come to town, she'd never worried about her appearance. These days, it seemed that was all she did.

The realization bothered her.

*Pull yourself together, Rachel. You aren't that shallow.*

No, she wasn't, but sometimes her pride smarted.

"This is my daughter, Victoria."

Tori stared wide-eyed and lifted her hand in a tiny wave.

On closer inspection in the living-room lighting, the woman wasn't so perfect, after all.

She was older than Rachel had thought at first, closer to Cindy's age than to her own. Tiny wrinkles radiated from the outer corners of her eyes. The black of her hair was just a shade too dark for the woman's eyebrows. So not real.

Vivian sat on the sofa and checked out the room, her eyes resting on Tori's crude but colorful angels hung around the room.

"Cozy," she murmured, and Rachel wasn't sure whether she referred to the room or to a perceived relationship between her and Travis.

Travis entered the house.

"Hey, who owns that sleek little BMW in the drive-way?"

"Travis," Tori called. "You got comp'ny. We been taking care of her."

Rachel heard him toe off his boots. She held her breath. Just who was this Vivian to him? Just how *very* close were they?

Travis entered the room and, to Rachel's satisfaction, did not look happy to see Vivian.

*So small, Rachel. So mean-spirited.*

*So honest.*

"Viv," he said, voice flat. "What are you doing here?"

Vivian stood and, for the first time since arriving, did not look cool and collected.

"We need to talk, Travis."

His lips thinned. "We already said everything that needed to be said. There's nothing else."

Okay, this was uncomfortable. Rachel did not want to be here for this kind of conversation.

"Tori and I should go," she said.

"No. I got pizza. You're not going home without din-ner."

"This kind of conversation should be just between the two of you, Travis."

"There isn't going to be any of *that* kind of conver-sation, is there, Viv?"

"You're right, Travis," Vivian answered. "This isn't about us."

"Why are you here, then?"

Vivian twisted her fingers, the red of her nails an exact match to her lipstick. She bit her bottom lip for a second. "It's about Manny."

Everything inside Rachel froze. *Manny.* The criminal Travis's sister had worked for was Manny D'Onofrio, Nadine had said. He was *vicious.* He vowed revenge.

"What about him?" Her hard-edged voice could cut through steel.

Both Vivian and Travis stared at her.

"He's the criminal from Las Vegas, right?"

Vivian nodded.

"What attachment do you have to him? Who *are* you?"

"I'm Travis's girlfriend."

Travis stepped forward. "Not for well over a year, Vivian."

"But I hoped—"

"No, Viv. There is no hope. I made that clear months ago in Vegas."

"I thought you seemed open to starting over."

"Telling you I was ready to forgive you for your betrayal is not the same as saying I want to start over."

Rachel didn't care about any of that. She had only one concern.

"Is Manny coming here?" Her granite tone rattled them. Rachel sensed Tori's bewilderment as she watched the adults.

"He's in jail," Vivian said.

Rachel looked at Travis.

"He has men, employees who are loyal to him," he admitted.

He turned his attention to Vivian. "Are they coming here?"

She nodded.

Blood frigid, Rachel scrambled to get her daughter

out of this house before a band of criminals with guns landed on the doorstep.

"Mommy, I want more hot chocolate," Tori complained.

Fingers numb, she buttoned Tori into her jacket. "You'll have some more at home."

"But the pizza…" Travis's expression pleaded with her to…what? Stay? Ignore the danger?

"But what if someone shows up to…" She trailed off. She didn't want to scare Tori.

"It isn't going to happen this second, Rachel."

"How do you know?"

He opened his mouth. Closed it. How could he know when these guys planned to arrive?

"I can't stay here, Travis." Frantic to get away, she shoved her arms into her coat and opened the door. Crossing the road, she made herself slow down for Tori's sake.

Once inside her own home, she locked the door and shoved a kitchen chair under the knob. Her teeth chattered.

"Mommy?" Tori's lower lip trembled. "What's wrong?"

Rachel forced herself to get control. The very last thing she wanted was to scare her daughter. All she asked for was that her children be safe and have enough to eat.

She made herself smile. "Let's watch TV, okay?"

Tori immediately said, "'Kay," and ran to her favorite chair, a child-size blue plush armchair, one of Cindy's purchases. Some of Rachel's fear must have transferred, though, because Tori picked up her platypus and held her extra tightly.

Rachel flipped through the channels until she found a sappy Thanksgiving movie suitable for family entertainment.

Aware of Vivian across the road bringing bad news, Rachel jumped at every sound the gusting wind made. Again, she felt the full weight of her responsibility.

For the first time since Davey's death, she let go of her grief and gave in fully to her anger. She'd loved Davey, but he should have been careful. He should have thought of his family.

He should have loved her and Tori more than he loved his fun.

All of the joy drained out of Travis's hitherto amazing day, leached out by this lousy excuse for a woman. What the heck was Vivian doing here?

Where Rachel was comfortable in an oversize men's gray sweatshirt, round in pregnancy and as honest as the day was long, Vivian was thin and fashionable... and the most dishonest, betraying woman on the face of the earth.

The sound of the front door closing behind Rachel and Tori angered him even as he was filled with remorse.

He should have never come here and brought his troubles with him, so close to her and her kids.

Oh, jeez. Damn it all to crap. His heart ached like he'd lost something precious and rare.

Travis turned to the woman he didn't trust and might possibly hate more than Manny D'Onofrio—at least Manny had never hidden who he was. "Stay put," he ordered. "I'll be right back."

He deposited the smaller of the two pizzas in the kitchen and carried the larger one across the road.

He knocked, but no one answered. Figuring Rachel might have been spooked, he called, "Rachel, it's me. I brought pizza."

He heard noise on the other side of the door, and then it opened.

Rachel stood beside a chair she had obviously slid in front of the door to protect them. The hollow, fearful look in her eyes worried him.

"You didn't have to bring that over."

He shoved it into her hands, not giving her a chance to resist. "Yes, I did. You and Tori worked hard. I promised you dinner. Here it is."

"Okay."

"Rachel, I'm not going to let anything happen to you."

Her backbone kicked in. "I can take care of Tori and me. You just worry about yourself and your girlfriend."

"She's not my girlfriend."

Rachel held up her hand. "Please, Travis, just go. I'm too tired for this."

He could see she was. "Okay, but call me if you need me."

"Yeah." She closed the door firmly, and he knew she wouldn't call him for any reason.

He stomped back across the road to confront Vivian Hughes.

He'd thought he'd loved her once, but there was a huge leap between lust and love. He'd certainly trusted her, but that was before he'd found out she was working for Manny, keeping an eye on him, hoping to find

out anything about Samantha that Manny could supply
to his defense team.

How on earth any of that intelligence could have
helped Manny's embezzlement case, Travis didn't understand. Trying to find dirt on Samantha to discredit
her as a witness, perhaps? Maybe he just wasn't devi-
ous enough to figure it out.

To say he was mad put it mildly. Furious was more
like it. And terrified.

"How did you find me?" he demanded.

Vivian's gaze slid away from his. "Remember when
we said goodbye last year? How angry you were?"

He nodded.

"You made me so mad. When I asked to see you
three months ago to apologize for betraying you to
Manny, it was really to betray you again."

He couldn't speak, not for the life of him, or he would
spew all kinds of filth.

"I was only pretending to be sorry," she said. She
looked sorry now, but he didn't care. "I really went there
to stick a tracker onto your truck. I've been monitor-
ing your travels. When you remained here for a while,
I figured maybe this was where you planned to settle
and bring Samantha."

"What? *Why*?"

"Manny asked me to." She shrugged, and the gesture was delicate and feminine, but at the moment, he
could gladly throttle her. He shoved his hands into his
pockets. "I told him where you are."

"Did his men come with you?"

"No. I left right after I told Manny. He said good job,
paid me and told me to leave."

He had to warn Sammy not to come. Where could he

send her? Fury flooded him, chasing out the ice with a white-hot flame. All of his work in finding this town, this house, had gone up in smoke because of Vivian.

Travis couldn't get his phone out of his pocket fast enough. He fumbled, dropping it onto the carpet.

"Travis, I—" She approached, but he held up a hand.

"Keep away from me, or so help me God I won't be responsible for my actions." He dialed Sammy's number. "Betraying me the first time was bad enough when it only hurt me. This time you'll be hurting my sister and her boys."

Sammy's phone rang, but she didn't answer. Travis cursed. "You're lucky I'm not a violent man."

Travis cut the connection. He dialed Cole Payette's number.

"Hey, Travis." Cole answered on the second ring. "What's up?"

"I got a person here at the house who needs to be escorted out of town."

"But—" Vivian interrupted.

Travis shushed her.

"Does this relate to the situation with your sister?"

"It sure does. I'll call her and tell her not to come to Rodeo. In the meantime, the woman in my house is a danger to me, to my family and to everyone else in town."

"No, I'm not." Vivian no longer sounded scared, but she was starting to heat up. Too bad. He didn't care about her feelings.

"I'll be right there." Cole disconnected. Great sheriff. Great town.

He thought of Rachel across the road, angry with him for bringing danger to her home. She was good people.

The best. And he was so damned sorry he couldn't be the type of man she needed. Instead, he was the kind who attracted people like Vivian and Manny.

He phoned Samantha again. Still no response. Where was she?

She wasn't due to leave San Francisco yet. Maybe her battery was dead. Sammy could be impulsive. It would be like her to come early to surprise him.

He prayed to God she wouldn't cross paths with Manny's men.

Cursing, he turned his attention to Vivian.

"Why?" he asked.

"Why what?"

"Why did you betray me to Manny not once, but twice?" He'd thought he'd buried the hurt, but seeing her again brought it flooding back.

"For money, Travis. Manny gave me a lot of money. Tons. I'll be secure for years to come."

*Money.* Worse than the anger was the grief.

She'd killed a love he'd thought was special, strong enough to inspire the most momentous decision he'd ever made.

He'd never contemplated marriage before Vivian. He had never believed it was for him. But for a brief time, he'd thought the two of them could make it work.

*Hold on. Be honest. You were leading up to asking her, but you never did, did you? Why did you hold back? Was it really love?*

Had he known on some level that there were problems, with Vivian or himself or the relationship?

Travis called Sammy again. No answer. He tossed the phone onto the sofa.

Brooding, he stared at Vivian.

She watched him silently. What did she want from him?

He thought of a question he should have asked at the start. "Why are you here?"

"To warn you." She spread her hands as though to say, Isn't it obvious?

It wasn't. Where Viv was concerned, nothing was as it seemed.

"Why? You betrayed me to Manny, twice now, and all of a sudden you're on my side warning me?" He startled and headed for the door. "Are they here? Are they waiting outside for me to lead them to Sammy?"

She rushed after him and grabbed his arm. "No, they aren't anywhere near here yet. I was telling the truth."

He stared at the well-manicured hand on his sleeve. "I don't understand."

"All along I felt bad about the way I was using you."

"You slept with me. Did your job description include whoring for your boss?"

She shrank from him. "No. I liked you. I was attracted to you. I wanted to sleep with you. Manny gave me hell for it after you left, along with a black eye. He was jealous."

"Is that supposed to make me feel sorry for you?"

"No. Just understand. I truly cared for you, Travis. You're a good, good man." Her voice deepened with intensity. "You're a better man than Manny will ever be. After I told him where you were now, I was so ashamed. Your sister did the right thing when she testified against him. You're innocent. Your sister had no idea what she was getting into when she went to work for him. Neither of you deserve Manny's revenge."

Was she telling the truth? Hard to say. She'd seemed sincere in the past, too.

The sound of tires on gravel alerted Travis. He peeked through the window and breathed a sigh when he saw it was the sheriff.

Had it been Manny's people, he would have fought to the death rather than tell where Sammy was, but then who would be left to protect her and the boys?

A split second before Cole knocked on the door, Travis opened it.

"Thanks for coming."

Cole nodded. "No worries. This her?" He gestured toward Vivian.

"Yeah. Vivian Hughes. She works for Manny D'Onofrio."

Cole turned a cold eye on her. "I did some research after our talk. He's a nasty piece of work. You work for him?"

Vivian lifted her chin. "Not anymore. I quit. I came to warn Travis about his men coming here."

"I have no way to verify whether you're telling the truth. Travis says you're a danger to the town and its people. I believe him. I'm going to ask you to leave."

Vivian turned her gaze to Travis. Her eyes shimmered like jewels behind her tears.

He wasn't moved. The thing about trust was that once broken, it couldn't be repaired.

"That's it?" she asked.

"What were you expecting?"

She shrugged, but this time he wasn't fooled. She wasn't indifferent. She wanted him back. She'd actually thought this would be enough to fix things between them.

She'd thought she could take Manny's money *and* have Travis.

There wasn't enough glue in the entire state of Montana to fix what Vivian had broken. She just didn't understand that.

"It's over, Vivian. There's nothing between us. Are you telling the truth about the people coming to town?"

"Yes."

"Then, I thank you for that. You did the right thing. But I hope to God I never see you again."

"Fine." She swallowed hard. At the front door, she looked back once before heading to her car.

Cole said, "I'll see that she leaves. I'll follow her for a while to make sure she doesn't double back."

Travis shook his hand. "I appreciate this, Cole. We don't need her kind in Rodeo."

The sheriff turned up his collar against the rising wind. "Batten down the hatches, Read. There's a major storm moving in."

"Will do." Travis agreed, recognizing that the menacing sky on the horizon was a harbinger of more than just bad weather. It also represented the havoc Manny had let loose in sending his men to Rodeo, Montana.

## Chapter 10

With the weather forecast on her mind, Rachel bundled up Tori and took her into town to buy groceries.

There was a storm coming in, due any minute. Rachel wanted the fridge and pantry as full as she could afford.

She owned a small wind-up radio in the event of a power outage so she could keep on top of news and weather reports. In her bedside table, she kept a flashlight.

When she got home, she'd pile the bed with her blankets and all of Cindy's, in case of a power failure. She and Tori could snuggle together, and Cindy wasn't home to use them anyway.

Rachel still hadn't seen her mother since the dance. She'd called and had left a message, but Cindy hadn't returned her call.

It hurt that her mom wouldn't even check in to see how they were doing. Sure, Rachel had always been independent, and possessed more common sense than the thimbleful rolling around in Cindy's brain, but why couldn't Cindy exhibit the least bit of motherly concern?

Rachel bought mostly dry goods. If they lost power, she wouldn't be able to cook anyway. She stocked up on bread and rolls, peanut butter and jam, and cartons of shelf-stable almond milk. Dry cereal would do for now.

They drove home with Tori warbling away with the songs on the radio. Rachel never tired of her sweet high voice.

In the unrelenting dull gray of the day, the trailer looked abandoned when Rachel drove up.

She carried the groceries inside with Tori trailing behind.

She didn't bother jamming a chair under the front doorknob. What were the chances of anyone coming to her crummy little trailer after finding Travis in his own house?

Last night's panic had given way to common sense.

She set the bags on the kitchen counter.

Rachel got Tori set up in front of the small TV and put away the groceries.

After every last item was in its proper place, she headed to her bedroom to put away the three pairs of thick socks she'd gotten on sale for Tori.

In a space as small as the trailer, everything had to be put away the second after you were finished using it.

But when she opened the door, she stopped dead. At the sight of her bedroom turned upside down, with everything topsy-turvy, her jaw dropped. It had been trashed.

Oh my God, they'd been robbed.

She started back to the kitchen to call the sheriff, but halted in Cindy's doorway, caught by the sight of empty drawers.

Not trashed or turned over drawers, but *empty* drawers.

She stepped inside.

This was no robbery. This was Cindy leaving. Rachel checked the closet. Cindy's one suitcase was missing.

Her mom had—

Rachel's legs gave out, and she sat heavily on the bed.

Her mom had left.

There was no other explanation. She had packed her bag and had headed out of town without a single word to her family.

In the bathroom, all of Cindy's toiletries were gone, including the expensive creams she'd taken to using lately.

Why had she ransacked Rachel's room? Cindy owned a lot more clothes than Rachel did, and they were a lot prettier.

Back in her own room, the truth hit her like a wrecking ball, sending shards of Rachel's life flying.

Rachel had been robbed after all, by her own mother.

The items from the top shelf of her closet, behind which Rachel had hidden her boxes of Mason jars full of the change she'd scrimped and saved over the years, were strewed on the floor.

Her money, five thousand dollars' worth of sacrifices, was gone.

Dizzy, she stumbled before realizing she'd been holding her breath. She lay down on the bed. Stars danced behind her closed eyelids.

Before she could stop them, tears leaked from her eyes, little bits of ice shaking free of the iceberg her heart had become.

Rachel would have expected betrayal from a lot of people, but never her own mother. Not Cindy.

What on earth was she going to do?

She should have rolled every last coin and counted every single small bill and deposited it all in the bank. She'd gotten into the habit of hiding the money from Davey and had never changed that after his death.

She'd been a fool.

After Davey's death, it hadn't taken her long to realize she would need to use some of her down-payment money to support herself and her children after Beth was born.

Now Cindy was gone and had taken her money.

How would she buy food? How would she pay the hospital after she gave birth to Beth? Her limited health insurance wouldn't cover everything, and her credit rating was still recovering from Davey's extravagant spending habits. Would the hospital even accept her credit card?

Her head stopped spinning, but her breathing was still shallow. She made herself breathe deeply, evenly. She couldn't manage normal, though. Not when her life had just been shattered.

It would never be normal again.

At least there was no mortgage on the trailer.

Her heart clenched.

Or was there?

Would Cindy have borrowed against the trailer before leaving? Surely the bank wouldn't be that foolish.

But she'd had a week since meeting that man to plan all kinds of weird and foolish things.

Was she even with him anymore? After all, that was only an assumption on Rachel's part and the product of gossip in town.

A swift kick to her ribs alerted her to Beth's discomfort. She stood carefully and paced, sidestepping the clothes and mess on the floor.

Thinking over Cindy's actions at the dance, running away with the stranger was the only explanation.

A spot of bright pink on her bedside table caught her eye. A note.

*It's time for me to live for myself. You're strong. I'm not. I need a man. Gerry's good to me. You know how to live on less money. You'll be okay.*

Oh, Mom. Yet again, she was making a fool of herself over a man. The more things changed, the more they stayed the same.

Rachel swiped tears from her cheeks fiercely. She had to stop crying for Tori's sake. Tears accomplished *nothing*.

Angry with herself and her mother and life, Rachel's pacing changed to stomping.

With no other outlet, without the option to scream until her grief and rage ran dry, she stomped.

Oh, how she stomped.

If the floor of the trailer caved in, tough.

She stomped out to the front doorway, where she'd set a baseball bat in case she needed it. She clutched it and tramped back to her bedroom, closing the door so Tori wouldn't hear.

This crappy trailer, this hollow life, Cindy's dishonesty, Davey's carelessness, came crashing in on her.

With the bat as her weapon, she pounded her mattress, keening low in her throat. She hit it again…and again…and again, over and over until her arms ached.

She'd been good. She'd been kind and thoughtful and giving. She'd been the best person she could possibly be, yet these people and this life had dumped all over her. And she was furious.

She pounded the mattress until her rage died, until she fell limply against the side of the bed.

Since his death, she had grieved Davey, had cried buckets with the pain of missing him, but hadn't fully acknowledged her anger. What kind of woman would be angry with a man who had died far too young? Her. She'd been enraged, but had buried it.

"You should have cared more about me and Tori," she whispered, swiping tears from her cheeks. "Now, we're alone."

If tears were bad, self-pity was worse.

*Buck up. You have a beautiful daughter here and another on the way. Count your damned blessings.*

What she wanted more was to count the money she'd put away for the next few months. What was she supposed to do now?

Drained, but strangely cleansed, she rested the baseball bat in the corner and trudged to the kitchen to make a couple of grilled cheese sandwiches.

Rachel tried to pull herself together for Tori's sake.

Even though she didn't know how they would survive, Rachel understood she had to do her best for her child. She stroked her belly. Correction, her children.

Outside, the wind howled and snow beat against the windows. The storm had hit fast and hard.

After cleaning up the mess Cindy had made of her bedroom, Rachel put Tori to bed.

Giving Tori an amazing Christmas became her top priority, but how? How could she buy presents?

She stiffened her resolve. There was always a way. She couldn't purchase gifts, but she could make them.

Scouring the trailer for ideas, she found a stash of yarn left over from one of Cindy's failed attempts at domesticity.

Rachel sat on the sofa and cast on to knit a pair of bright pink mittens for Tori. Cindy might not have had a talent for crafts, but her mother had. Rachel had learned many things from her grandma. Knitting was one of them.

The first mitten went quickly because Tori's hands were so tiny. A couple of hours later, Rachel had finished it and was casting on to start the second one when a bad case of indigestion hit.

Funny. All they'd had for dinner was grilled cheese sandwiches and tinned tomato soup, a simple meal she'd eaten hundreds of times before without problems.

She rubbed her tummy. "Beth, honey, you're messing with Mommy's body."

Her discomfort slowed her down.

A while later, it got worse. When her first contraction hit, she panicked.

The problem wasn't her tummy. It was Beth. The baby wanted to come.

*No.*

Not now. No. The timing couldn't possibly be worse. She was a week early. The storm was vast, moving down from the north across the entire state.

Another pain and she dropped her knitting.

In her bedroom, she woke Tori. Scrambling with fumbling hands, she dragged her own small suitcase out of the closet, packed and ready for the trip to the hospital.

Another contraction tightened her belly, and she gasped.

"Hurry." She nudged Tori. "Wake up, honey, please. Beth is coming."

Tori sat up and rubbed her eyes. "From where, Mommy?"

"From my tummy. Remember I told you about it? It's going to happen now."

"I'm sleepy. Tell Beth to wait until morning."

Despite her nerves, Rachel laughed. "I wish she would wait, too."

Nervously, she glanced out the window. The wind lashed a solid film of snow against the glass. By morning, the storm might have abated, but the roads wouldn't be any clearer. It would take days to clean up this mess.

Still, she had to brave the drive. She had no choice.

What to do with Tori now that Cindy was gone? Surely, she could depend on one of her friends. Maybe Honey? Yes. Honey would take her in a heartbeat.

Okay. First, Rachel would drive into town to drop her daughter off with Honey above the tavern.

Next she would drive to the hospital, but that was a twenty-minute drive on a good day. Tonight it would take—

Snow beat against the thin walls of the trailer. It could take hours, if she made it there at all.

She wasn't too proud to admit she was scared. Terrified.

She tried to phone Honey, but there was no signal.

Another contraction hit. She bent over and held her breath until it passed.

"Please hurry, Tori. We need to go."

"Go where?"

"I'm taking you to stay with Honey before I go to the hospital."

Reacting to the tension Rachel couldn't hide, Tori climbed out of bed and dressed.

Rachel threw her clothes into her little knapsack. "Do you want Puss?"

"Yes, Mommy, please. Puss likes Honey."

Translation... Tori liked Honey. Rachel breathed a sigh of relief. Everything would be fine.

Her optimism lasted through getting them both into their winter clothes and stepping out through the front door, where the wind knocked them back into the trailer.

Dear Lord, it was a bad one.

With Tori's knapsack on her back and her own suitcase in her left hand, she grasped Tori's hand firmly and pushed them both against the wind.

"Hold on to my pant leg while I close the door." The wind whipped the words out of her mouth. "Tori? Tori, can you hear me?"

Rachel bent over and wrapped Tori's tiny fingers around her pant leg. Against the side of her hat, she yelled, "Hold on tightly. Don't let go. Okay?"

Tori nodded.

"Look at me, Tori."

Her daughter looked up, but closed her eyes against the snow buffeted by the relentless wind. "Don't let go at all. Do you understand?"

"Yes, Mommy." The wind carried off her voice, thin

and sounding scared to be outside in a raging snow-storm, but Rachel was assured Tori understood.

Only then did she pull the door closed and retrieve Tori's hand and hold it tightly.

Not only the wind, but also contractions robbed Rachel of breath. She figured they were only three minutes apart already—so much faster than with Tori.

How could this be happening?

She could only barely make out the car through the swirling snow.

The drive would be bad, slow and treacherous. Even if she managed to stay on the road, it would take her two, three times longer to get to town, never mind to the hospital miles away.

Did she have that long?

Another contraction hit, answering with a resounding no.

She looked around wildly. She couldn't possibly give birth alone in the trailer. No way was her daughter starting her life in that tin can—but if not there, where? Rachel really had no choice. But what would she do with Tori? She didn't want her daughter more frightened than she already was.

A light flickered across the road, hardly visible.

Travis was home.

Tori would be safe with him in the Victorian while Rachel gave birth in the trailer.

Rachel's independence had carried her far, but it was time to ask for help for her daughter's sake. She couldn't think of a single person she would rather run to for help at this moment than solid, dependable Travis Read.

"Change of plans, Tori," she shouted. "You're going to stay with Travis."

"'Kay." Tori huddled against Rachel's leg. "I like Travis. So does Puss."

"Let's go."

By hook or by crook, Rachel was getting Tori safely across the road to Travis and into the Victorian where she had always found safety and solace.

They trudged across the road. It took forever. Rachel's focus never swayed from that one yellow light in the living room window. She knew, even if her daughter couldn't understand, that they were perilously close to getting lost out here in the storm. Without that light to guide them, they could easily veer off course and freeze to death just feet from shelter.

The snow was thickening and the wind becoming worse.

She didn't relish the trip back to the trailer alone.

At last, they reached the porch. Rachel knocked, the wood hurting her frozen knuckles through her gloves.

The door opened and there he was, the man she knew would protect Tori with his life. Relief flooded her.

She'd been wrong to say all of those nasty things to him. Travis would never knowingly hurt another human being. He never would have come here if he'd thought trouble would follow him.

His dear face registered surprise followed by alarm when she gasped and grasped her belly.

"Rachel, what the hell?"

"Travis, I'm cold," Tori said.

"Get in here."

He lifted Tori into his arms, then grabbed Rachel's hand and dragged her inside. When the suitcase banged against the doorjamb and she dropped it, he ordered, "Leave it. I'll get it."

Once he had them safely indoors, he went back for the suitcase and slammed the door against the wind that was forcing snow inside, even with the deep porch attempting to offer protection.

He carried Tori into the living room where a glorious fire burned in the grate.

Undressing her with care, he said, "What on earth are you doing out in this weather? Only a fool would leave home in this."

"Then I'm a fool." Rachel was so far past tired she didn't have the energy to quarrel with him. The stress of her mother's betrayal weighed on her like a ton of bricks, and she still had to get back across the street to give birth.

"You got that right." Travis sounded angry, but he handled Tori with a gentle touch. He set her up in an armchair and hauled it right in front of the fire.

Ghost ambled over and jumped up beside her.

"Kitty!" Tori said around a huge yawn.

His startled gaze took in Tori's pajamas.

To Rachel, he said, "You got her out of bed. Why?"

Rachel couldn't answer, but leaned on the back of the sofa and breathed hard through a contraction.

In an instant, Travis was by her side rubbing her back. "What's wrong?"

His hand felt so good, she ordered, "Harder."

"What?"

"Press harder. Right there. Yes, that's good. Press harder! Yesssss."

"Rachel." She caught a warning note in his voice. "What's going on?"

"Can you take care of Tori for a little while?"

"Of course, but why? Where are you going?"

"Back home for a while."

"Back home? Whoa. Wait." He watched her double over. "Are you—? Is the baby—? Sweet Jesus, you're in labor, aren't you?"

Rachel panted. "A bit early. Can't drive to hospital in this. Don't want Tori to hear if…it gets bad."

"It already looks bad."

She shot him a small smile. "This is nothing, Travis."

"Does Cindy know how to deliver a baby?"

Rachel shied away from the truth. Travis didn't need to know that Cindy had left. "She's had a baby. I've had one. Everything will work out."

Oh, she didn't want to be alone—she really didn't— but neither did she want Travis pitying her, or feeling responsible for her. He might be superdependable, but the guy had his hands full with a sister and two nephews coming to town.

Rachel meant nothing to him.

"Put Tori to bed if you have a spare one. Or the sofa is fine."

She opened Tori's knapsack and handed Puss to Travis. She picked up her suitcase and headed for the door.

"I'll be back in the morning."

Fingers crossed. She hoped it would be a fast labor. It sure felt like it would be.

With a deep, fortifying breath she stepped outside and pulled the door closed behind her. She climbed down from the veranda to start the loneliest walk of her life.

## Chapter 11

Travis stared at the closed door.

What the hell had just happened?

He turned to Tori who was falling asleep near the fire and picked her up.

"We'd better get you into a bed."

"'Kay."

"Is your mom really having her baby tonight?"

"Uh-huh." The child nodded against his shoulder. "She said Beth is coming."

"Cindy knows what to do, right?" he asked, though why he expected a sleepy three-year-old to be able to answer that was beyond him.

"Cindy's not home, Travis. Mommy said she ranned away."

"She *what?*"

"Cindy ranned away. Mommy will be alone. Why did she putted me here and go back alone?"

Travis cursed internally. "Good question."

He would give Rachel an earful about this later, but for now he had to drag her back here with him.

He plopped Tori into the armchair, said, "Wait here," and shrugged into his sheepskin jacket.

When he threw open the door, the wind smacked him in the face. Why did this hyper-independent, ornery woman think it was all right to give birth alone in an empty trailer when she had a perfectly good friend right across the street who would do anything to help her out?

Including helping her to give birth? His gut clenched.

Yeah, including that.

He'd think about the details once he had Rachel safe with him.

He jumped down from the veranda and nearly ran into her.

A sob escaped her. "I can't do it, Travis. I can't give birth alone. Help me. Please."

Thank God! He yanked her against his chest. She was safe! She'd changed her mind.

Inside his house, he slammed the door behind her and threw his shearling jacket onto a hook. He turned to give her a piece of his mind, but halted. She looked miserable.

"I'm sorry."

"Why? For needing my help?"

She reacted to his harshness by shaking her head. "No, for all of the nasty things I've said and thought about you lately."

"Aw, hell. Don't worry about it. I understand."

He took her coat from her and hung it up. Gently,

he took her arm to lead her into the living room when Rachel gasped.

A great spurt of liquid gushed from her. Travis jumped out of the way. "What the he—"

"My water's broken. It won't be long now."

His hands started to shake. "What do you need me to do?"

"Get Tori into bed first, preferably behind a closed door."

"You got it."

"C'mon, munchkin." Tori didn't hear him. "She's already out like a light."

"She's a heavy sleeper."

He gathered her, Puss and Ghost into his arms and carried them upstairs to the bedroom he'd set up for the boys, gently placing her in one of the twin beds and covering her with ample blankets. He tucked Puss under her arm.

Ghost circled and lay beside her.

Travis closed the door.

Back downstairs he ran to the kitchen and put on a huge pot of water to boil.

"What are you doing?" Rachel asked.

"I don't know. That's what they do in the movies."

Her skin was pale and her cheeks flushed, but she smiled. "Get me some old rags and I'll clean up my mess in the hallway."

Outrage filled him. "Stop that kind of talk. I'll take care of it, but first, we need to get you settled in. Where? In my bed?"

"No, birthing's a messy business. I don't want to ruin your new mattress."

"I don't care," he said harshly.

She touched his arm. "I do. Do you have any extra blankets?"

"The linen closet is full of old quilts. I haven't touched them. They're probably dusty."

"Those will be Abigail's homemade quilts. She will have taken good care of them over the years. Let me see them."

She chose three large thick ones and a whole bunch of old towels.

Without warning, she leaned against him and breathed heavily. Panted. Moaned. "God," she said.

"Contraction?" he asked.

She rode it out and nodded. "Bring all of that to the living room. We need to get me settled in. Quickly."

He followed her, asking, "How can you be so calm?"

"Because I've done it before. If this were my first, it would be different."

He started to spread the quilts on the sofa, but she shook her head.

"No, here."

"On the floor? Are you out of your mind?"

"The floor can be cleaned up easily."

"I'm not letting you give birth on the floor."

"Travis, honestly, this is the way I'm most comfortable doing it, okay?"

He would have argued, but she started to keen. The pain on her face was unbearable to him.

When she came through on the other side, she ordered him to pile up the quilts and cover them with all the towels from the closet.

He did what she asked, doubling the quilts. The pile added a buffer against the hard floor in front of the fireplace.

Travis built it up. "Good?" he asked.

"Yes, that's good." She took his hand in hers. "Travis, you need to get up close and personal with me right now."

"What do you mean?"

"You need to check me out, make sure everything's okay."

"You mean…" He tried to swallow, but came up dry. "You mean check down *there*?"

"Yes."

He'd never looked at a woman down there in any way but sexually. "I'm not a doctor. How will I know if anything's wrong?"

"You won't. Or maybe you will. I don't know. I just need you to look."

"Is there any way around it?"

"None."

His harsh breathing filled the room, but he helped Rachel to lie down. She bent her knees, and he lifted up her dress.

Her underpants were damp and stained pink from her accident in the hallway. Correction, not an accident, but a natural part of childbirth.

"I can't take my undies off. Can you do it for me?"

Before he could respond, she let out a groan that seemed to come from the depths of her soul. She gritted her teeth and arched her back.

When she finished, she was panting. "They're coming closer."

"That seemed like a bad one."

"Yeah. They'll get worse."

*Worse?*

"I don't know what to do."

"That's okay." She arched with pain again. She panted, "My body does. The birthing will take its course."

"What if something goes wrong?" He was scared shitless. He knew nothing about this. He was a capable guy and wasn't used to feeling useless.

"Everything will be fine. Things feel fine."

This torture was fine?

He wiped her forehead where sweat dripped in what seemed like an unending torrent.

Sure, this was a natural occurrence that had been happening since the dawn of time, but did women have to suffer so damn much?

During the next contraction, with Rachel's back bowed and her hips off the floor, he managed to get her underpants down to her knees. While she relaxed to rest and wait for the next one, he hauled them off.

He checked, even though he didn't know what he was looking for. Not seeing any obvious problems, he focused on trying to keep Rachel calm.

He held her hand, tiny in his, but she squeezed until he thought she would break his fingers. As small as it was in his big palm, why weren't her own fingers breaking?

He knelt between Rachel's legs while her body worked to birth her baby. He marveled when the head started to show…and even more when the baby's body turned to allow the shoulders to come through.

Travis was there to catch Beth.

A sense of wonder flooded him. He'd never known anything to feel so good in his life.

In the second it took to ease her from Rachel's body and hold her, he lost his heart.

This little girl had been talking to him before she was born, and now he held her for real. She in her tiny, red newness had a power over him that he'd never imagined.

She was real. Awesome. Amazing.

Travis held the tiny, as-yet-unspoiled creature in his hands and thought, *I could get used to you. I could get used to holding you. I could certainly spoil the day-lights out of you. I could love you, almost as much as I love your moth—*

He halted that thought with the veritable screeching of tires. No way would he go there. Not true. Not true at all.

This was a temporary aberration, this business of having a woman and kids in his home.

Even once Sammy, Jason and Colt got here, he'd be moving on.

This house might be the beginning of Sammy's dream, but it wasn't his dream. They were the reason he'd bought it. Without them, he would still be a wandering cowboy looking for the next job and the next bunk.

His priority, his sole purpose in being in this town, was them—not the widow who lived across the road, even if she did give birth to splendid creatures on his living-room floor.

He used one of the towels to wipe Beth clean.

"You're one tough cookie, Rachel."

"No. Just determined to have healthy babies."

"This one's healthy, all right. Her lungs are, at any rate."

"Give her to me, Travis." She raised her arms to him, but she looked tired.

"Are you sure you're strong enough?"

"Travis, you can seriously ask me that after what I just went through? Give me my daughter."

He rested the baby on her chest. "You look all done in."

"I'm exhausted, but I want to get to know my baby. Can you unbutton my top and my bra? I want her skin to skin. It's good for her to get to know her mama."

He did as she asked, revealing breasts that were heavy and blue-veined. He'd never seen anything more beautiful in his life than this red, wizened baby on her mother's pregnancy-ravaged, perfect body.

Rachel reached her hand to him. He took it. She squeezed, though not as hard as when she was giving birth, thank God.

"Thank you, Travis. I was terrified."

"You didn't seem it."

"I was. I've never been happier than when you came out of your house to get me so I wouldn't have to do this alone."

"I was scared, too."

"I know, but you rose to the occasion."

"I didn't do anything. You did all the work."

She chuckled. "Yeah, I did, didn't I?"

"Thank you, Rachel. This was a gift. Something special. I'll never forget tonight."

He touched Beth's hand. She curled tiny, perfect fingers around his thumb, or tried to. His fingers were huge and clumsy compared to hers.

"Imagine," he said. "Five minutes ago, she didn't exist. It's a wonder."

"Yep. The best wonder on earth."

"What about that?" He pointed to the umbilical extending from her body and still attached to the baby.

"The afterbirth will come out in a minute." She winced. "Soon, I think."

He swallowed hard. "Is it going to be bad? Please tell me you don't have to go through that again."

She closed her eyes, briefly, then said, "No, it won't be that bad. It'll be sort of like aftershocks following an earthquake."

"So we survived the earthquake. Now, your body finishes up for you."

"Yes. You'll have to cut the cord. Wash some scissors in that water you put on to boil, okay?"

"The water!" He raced to the kitchen to find it full of steam. Fortunately, the pot he'd put on was huge and had been filled to the brim. It was still half full.

He dropped his scissors into it and retrieved tongs from a drawer to fish them back out of the boiling water.

Back in the living room, he crouched beside Rachel.

"You have any string?" she asked, her exhaustion clear in her reed-thin voice.

"Should I boil it?"

"No."

He got it from a drawer in the kitchen. By the time he returned to Rachel, the afterbirth lay on the towels between her legs.

He'd seen plenty of farm animals being born and had a rough idea of what needed to be done now. He used the string and scissors to sever the connection between mother and daughter.

He put it into a garbage bag beside the back door. He'd deal with it in the morning. He wasn't going out in this snowstorm.

The howling wind still rattled the old house.

After helping Rachel tidy herself as much as possible, he built the fire back up.

"You warm enough?" he asked into the silence of the room.

She didn't answer. He glanced at her. In the few moments that his back had been turned, she'd fallen asleep. He pulled the quilt up more securely over the baby and the sleeping woman's shoulders.

He stood to pick the two of them up to carry them to his bed when the lights went out.

"Damn. Power outage." In truth, given the severity of the wind, he was surprised it hadn't happened earlier. He lit the kerosene lamps he had ready and waiting on the mantel.

He nudged Rachel's shoulder. "We need to get you off these wet towels and quilts," he whispered.

The whiskey highlights in her eyes that fascinated him were dimmed by fatigue, but her spirit flashed. "Why?"

"Because the power just went out, and it's too cold to put you in my bedroom. I need to make up a bunk for you down here."

Her gaze flitted around the room. "Tori?"

"I'll take care of her, no worries. First, I'll get the bedding from my room."

He dragged the king-size duvet from his bed along with his pillows.

Back downstairs, he said, "Hang on to Beth."

He lifted both of them onto the sofa, then checked out the state of the blankets that had been underneath her. The towels were drenched along with the top two quilts. The bottom quilt could be salvaged.

He left it where it was and spread his duvet on top of it a couple of feet from the fire.

"Hold on tight." Picking them back up, he put them onto the side of the duvet closest to the fireplace and folded the other half over them.

Getting his sheepskin from the hallway, he covered them with it.

"Travis, we'll die of heat."

"If the power stays out, it will be frigid in here by morning. I'm going to get Tori."

He put the child onto the armchair he'd moved close to the fire earlier. Ghost followed and curled next to her again. He covered her with the duvet from one of the twin beds. She slept through the whole thing.

He lay down fully clothed on the sofa with the duvet from the other single bed and settled in for the night, the only sounds the popping of logs in the fire and the howling of the wind around the old house.

The house had felt empty since he'd moved in. Tonight it was full of loved ones and joy.

Travis had never been happier.

Throughout the night, Travis got up several times to stoke the fire and add logs.

He'd never had more precious cargo to protect.

In the morning, through bleary eyes, he noted that the storm seemed to have abated outside.

A thin wail tore at his heart.

"Rachel," he whispered. "What does she need? To be fed?"

"Already working on it, Travis," Rachel whispered back, and he was engulfed by such a powerful wave of intimacy he wanted the moment to last forever.

He'd never, not once in his life, not even through everything he'd shared with Samantha, felt this close to another person.

He saw her hands move beneath the quilt and then the baby quieted.

In the armchair, Tori still slept, curled up like a kitten under her duvet.

Peace, and a profound sense of happiness, washed through Travis. He loved these girls.

He got up and stoked the fire. Just about to return to his bed on the sofa, he stopped. *Whoa. Go back to that last thought.*

*I love these girls.*

He returned to his bed on the sofa, laying down with the stunning realization that here in Rodeo, Montana, was a treasure worth more than anything in the world.

He'd traveled all over the western states and up into Canada, not knowing that all the while he'd been searching for this. For them.

*You sure? Maybe it was Beth's birth, Read. Maybe this is only leftover emotion from last night's drama.*

He searched his heart. His soul. The feeling was deep. True. Since he'd arrived in Rodeo, he'd been steadily falling in love with Rachel.

He'd found paradise and perfection here in Rodeo. But how did Rachel feel about him?

He fell asleep pondering that all-important question.

An hour later, he awoke again to hear Tori stirring.

"Mommy? Where are you?" she asked with a hint of uncertainty in her voice.

She sat up in the chair and rubbed her eyes.

"Easy, Tori," he said gently. "You're okay. You came to my house last night. Remember?"

She nodded. "I'm cold."

Travis stood to stoke the fire yet again. He'd be doing this particular chore for the rest of the day. He doubted crews would get out too early this morning to get fallen wires repaired and power restored.

Rachel shifted gingerly. She poked her head out of her blankets.

"Good morning." She sounded sleepy and happy, if a tad weary.

"How're you doing?"

She peeked under the blanket. "We're good. I should get Tori and me home, though."

His expression flattened. Last thing he wanted was for them to leave. Ever. "Why? What's over there that you need?"

She took a moment to respond and then said, "Absolutely nothing." She looked at her two girls and then at him. She smiled sweetly. "I guess the power's off over there, too?"

"I would imagine."

"I'm still cold, Travis," Tori piped up.

"Take this." Rachel tried to haul the sheepskin off herself. "I'm hot."

"Okay. Here, Tori." He covered her with part of the coat. It dwarfed her. She giggled.

"If we're going to visit for a while, we'll have to put together a makeshift bassinet for Beth."

Tori perked up. "Beth? She's here? Where?"

"Right here," Rachel murmured. "Come on down and meet your baby sister."

Tori crawled out from beneath the coat and tiptoed over.

"It's okay. She's already awake."

Tori knelt on the floor and shivered. Travis crouched behind her to lend his warmth. Besides, he wanted another glimpse of the precious creature he'd delivered last night.

Rachel peeled back the duvet gently. Beth lay against her mother's breast.

Tori wrinkled her nose. "She's little. Can she play with me?"

Rachel laughed. "Not yet. She has to grow a bit first."

Beth's unfocused gaze took in her surroundings.

"She doesn't look awake, Mommy. Can she see me?"

"Not too clearly, Tori. She was only born a few hours ago."

The miracle of the experience still humbled Travis. It flat-out boggled his mind that he'd been part of that messy, spectacular event last night.

Tori knelt to kiss Beth's forehead. Travis steadied her so she wouldn't fall on the baby.

"She's soft, Mommy." Tori patted Beth's forehead.

"Gentle, Tori, like we taught you with Ghost."

The cat, still ensconced on the armchair, lifted her head. She jumped to the ground and ambled into the kitchen where she set up her morning, god-awful yowling.

In his arms, Tori startled. "What's she want, Travis?"

"Breakfast."

"Me, too."

"Sure thing, missy. I'll get right on it just so long as you don't start any of that caterwauling yourself."

Tori giggled.

Travis stood, picked her up and deposited her under the covers and sheepskin on the armchair. "Curl up there and stay warm while I figure out what we'll have.

We don't have any power for cooking, but I've got some ideas that might work."

He prodded the log in the fireplace, and the fire flared. "You ever been camping, Tori?"

"What's camping?"

"I'll take that as a no. We're going to have us some camping fun. We'll get to it in a minute. First things first, though."

He stared down at Rachel and the baby. "How do I set up a bassinet? I don't have anything like that."

"Can we use one of your dresser drawers?"

"You can use anything you think might work. I'll go get one."

She called after him. "Bring whatever spare linens and blankets you might have."

"Sure thing," he said from halfway up the stairs he was taking two at a time.

The upstairs sure was frigid. Keeping the first floor warm would be a full-time job today. Good thing he'd prepared for the storm.

He dumped the contents out of one of his drawers and filled it with the sheets from the boys' beds.

Back downstairs he dragged the afghan from the sofa.

"Let's put her over here." Setting the drawer by the end of the sofa nearest the fire, he doubled over the bed sheets innumerable times and used them to cover the pillow that fit into the bottom perfectly.

He crouched beside Rachel. "Hand her over."

With great care, he set the baby onto the sheets. She let out a tiny squawk before Travis covered her with the folded afghan.

Behind him, Rachel stood. Travis spun around. "Should you be standing?"

"I'm good." She peeked at Beth. "Hold on. I'll set her up properly. Let's get rid of the pillow and put the folded afghan on the bottom."

Travis helped her.

"I need my suitcase," she said.

He retrieved it for her. She took out a couple of small pink blankets and wrapped the baby in them snugly. She took out another blanket, knitted and thicker than the first two, and doubled it up, laying it on top of her.

"We'll have to watch her to make sure she stays warm enough. She's too young for pillows and afghans."

Travis didn't have a clue what she was talking about, but he'd watch her 24/7 if that's what it took to keep Beth safe.

Rachel glanced around. "Um…where's the…um… washroom? Did you keep the one off the kitchen?"

"Yep. It's still there. It'll be cold, though. Let's get you and Tory dressed warmly. We can't spend all day under the blankets."

He stared at Rachel. She still looked tired. "Amendment. *You* can stay under the blankets."

Her laugh belied the dark bags under her eyes. Did nothing keep this woman's spirits down?

"How do you do it?" he asked.

"Do what?"

"Laugh. Enjoy life. Keep happy when there is so much going wrong for you."

"Travis, I have my moments. I have times when I feel overwhelmed, but at this moment, I'm the most fortunate woman who ever lived. I have two wonderful, beautiful daughters."

"She means me and Beth, Travis."

"I understood that, Tori." A laugh that started deep inside his soul burst out of him. This woman with her unbeatable optimism brought out the best in him.

Rachel smiled. "I like your laugh, Travis."

Her smile warmed him from head to toe.

"Why don't you and Tori put on as many layers of clothes as you can stand and I'll rustle up breakfast?"

A few minutes later, they passed him in the kitchen on their way to the bathroom. A second later, Tori yelped.

"It's too cold, Mommy. I can't sit on it."

"You have to."

He heard Tori sob. He knocked on the bathroom door. "Can I come in?"

"Yes." Rachel sounded frustrated.

He opened the door. She *looked* frustrated. Tori hopped around and clutched herself. Clearly the kid really had to go.

"Tori, will you go if I hold you over the toilet without touching the seat?"

"But I haves to take down my pants to go."

"I know. I won't look. See that painting of the colorful fishes?"

She nodded while she hopped.

"I'll stare at that, okay?" He put his hands under her armpits and lifted. Rachel pulled down her pants and underwear, and Travis positioned her over the seat with her little butt hovering without touching. He held her there until her tinkling finished, all while staring at the abstract painting of fish left by the former resident.

He stood her on the floor and Rachel pulled up her pants.

"Better?" he asked.

"Thank you, Travis. Better."

He glanced at Rachel. "You going to need help, too?"

"I'll manage." He heard laughter in her voice. "It's going to be uncomfortable."

"That's putting it mildly. Come on, Tori. Let's give your mom privacy. You can help me with breakfast."

He closed the door behind him and Tori. In the kitchen he was just getting bacon out of the fridge when he heard a much bigger yelp than Tori's tiny one.

"Oh my Lord, it's like ice!" Even from a distance and behind a closed door, her voice carried.

Travis couldn't help but laugh, but also thanked his lucky stars he could do his business standing up.

He carried Tori and the bacon into the living room.

"Tori, do you want me to try to make hot chocolate in the fireplace?"

Her jaw dropped open. "You gots hot chocolate?"

"Yep. I felt bad I didn't have any when you were here decorating for Christmas. I went out and bought some for your next visit."

"That's today! Today is my next visit!"

"Right, but we have no power, so we're going to try to make it using the fire."

He snuggled her into the armchair under her blankets.

"Stay put. I need to get a few things from the basement."

Snagging one of the lanterns, he hurried downstairs where he rummaged in a big old box of his camping equipment and came up with a kettle and a small pot. He also found a metal stand he used on campfires.

Back upstairs, he retrieved milk from the fridge and

the tin of hot chocolate from the cupboard. He filled the kettle with water.

In the living room, he found Rachel already ensconced on the sofa beside her brand-spanking-new daughter.

"Can you drink normal coffee now? I don't have decaf."

"I don't honestly feel like coffee. May I just have hot water?"

"Sounds kind of dull."

"It will be warm. That's all I want right now. What can I do to help?"

On his haunches in front of the fireplace, he swiveled to look at her. "That walk to the bathroom didn't do you any good. You're pale."

"I just need a little more sleep. It was a long night."

"Yeah, it was at that." He smiled. "And much of it was spent working. If you need to go to the washroom again, I'll carry you."

"That isn't necessary." She craned her neck to look around him. "What are you doing?"

"This is my camping trivet. I'm putting a pot of milk on for Tori's hot chocolate. It'll scald quickly, though. I'll have to watch it."

He went to the pantry off the kitchen and returned with fondue forks. "Your neighbor's British relatives left a lot of interesting old stuff in the house."

"What are those?" Tori asked.

"Fondue forks."

"What's fondue?"

After he explained about fondue, he opened the bacon and wrapped a slice around the fork. When he held it over the flame the fire spit and hissed from dripping fat.

Once the slice was cooked, charred in some parts, he put the slice onto a plate and handed it to Tori.

"Mommy first!"

"Okay. Here you go, my lady, on your Lady Someone-or-Other china."

"Lady Carlisle. Thank you." She blew on it then bit into it. "Oh, that's so good. Why is it that everything tastes better cooked over an open fire?"

"Don't know, but it's true."

He handed Tori her cup of chocolate, but not before topping it up with a quarter cup of cold milk. "Should be cool enough for you, sprout."

"What's a sprout?"

"You ask a lot of questions, kid. Hold that with two hands."

"Travis, could I change my order from hot water to hot milk?"

"Sure."

"No, wait. Save the milk for Tori."

"This is instant chocolate. It can be made with water, too. You need the milk right now more than she does."

"True. Besides there's milk at home in the fridge. Since I won't be there opening and closing the door, it should stay fine for quite a while."

Travis took the chocolate from Tori. "Travis, I'm not finished."

"I know, but I'll hold it while you eat this bacon."

He handed her a strip of cooked bacon on a small saucer.

She chewed it and licked her fingers. "That's yummy! Can I have more?"

"Tori, Travis has to eat, too," Rachel admonished.

"She can have as much as she wants. I've got more in the fridge and the freezer. I stocked up."

Rachel stared out of the front window where snow settled in huge drifts everywhere, and where the roads were still impassable.

He handed Tori another slice of bacon.

"What about your sister? Have you heard from her?"

"No. I can't get through to her on her phone. Texts aren't making it through. I'm worried, Rachel."

He felt a touch on his shoulder. Rachel had stood to comfort him.

"I told you to stay seated," he said gruffly, because the worry about Sammy and the boys coupled with last night's experience and now Rachel's proximity left him shaken and emotional.

"Sure." She returned to the sofa and got her plate. "More, please." She looked saucy and not the least repentant for disobeying him, but he understood what she was doing. She was trying to make him feel better, and he was grateful.

He dropped another slice of bacon onto her plate. The next slice went to Tori. Only then did he eat.

"You have a bunch of forks," Rachel said. "Why don't you put on more than one slice at a time?"

Travis shrugged. "We have nowhere to go and nothing to do. Without electricity, it's going to be a long day. There's no sense in rushing."

"True."

The baby started her pitiful thin little cry, and Rachel picked her up. "She needs a change."

She moved to get her suitcase, but Travis stopped her. "What do you need?"

"A diaper and a wiping cloth."

He brought them to her, and she changed the baby while Tori watched. "What's that?"

"That's where her belly button will be."

"Mine doesn't look like that."

"No. Hers will look like yours eventually."

"What are you doing now?"

"She's hungry. I'm going to feed her."

"Does she want bacon?"

"No. She can't eat people food yet. Only breast milk."

"I got milk in my hot chocolate. You can give her some."

"That's just for big girls like you. Beth needs to stick with breast milk for now."

Behind him, Travis heard a long drawn out "ooooh" and peeked over his shoulder. Rachel had the little one to her breast, trying to get her to latch on. He spun about so he wouldn't invade her privacy.

"She drinks from *there*?" Tori said.

"Yes, my breasts are full of milk."

"Mommy, that's silly. You aren't a cow." Tori sounded stern.

"All kinds of creatures produce milk to feed their babies, including humans."

"Does Travis have milk, too?"

He choked on the slice of bacon he'd just put into his mouth.

"No," Rachel answered. "Men don't get milk. Only women do. I have it because I gave birth to Beth."

"Does she like it?"

"Yes. Very much. You used to like it, too."

"No, Mommy, I liked hot chocolate."

"Eventually. Before that, you ate just like this."

"I don't think so." Travis heard rustling and peeked over his shoulder. Rachel lay on her side facing away from him with the baby lying on the sofa, he presumed drinking from the other breast.

He couldn't see anything, so he didn't think he was invading her privacy as he helped Tori get snuggled back under her covers again. When she sat down, a cat's indignant meow sounded.

Tori and Travis both laughed. Ghost had snuck in under the blankets and Tori had sat on her.

He made room for both of them. "I'm going to make toast. Those few slices of bacon weren't enough food for any of us."

"Toast! Yes, please."

"What do you like on yours? Just butter? Peanut butter? Jam?"

"Melted butter."

"Melted butter? Does she mean just normal buttering?" He directed the question to Rachel who spoke over her shoulder.

"Yes."

He stuck a fork through the first slice and held it over the fire. Unfortunately, one side got burned. He scraped off the charred bits, but Tori looked down her nose at it.

"Travis, it's burned."

"I'll eat it while I drink my warm milk." Rachel put the baby back down in her drawer bed and covered herself up again.

"What do you take? PB? Jam?"

"Usually marmalade, but I can live with jam."

"You don't have to. Hang tight." He fetched an unopened jar from a cupboard in the kitchen, buttered the burned toast and spread it with marmalade.

After handing it to her on her plate, he made a less burned one for Tory.

Only then, again after making sure the two of them had enough, did Travis make toast for himself, plowing through a half-dozen slices of bread.

"Do you have a griddle in your camping stuff?" Rachel asked.

"I have one in the kitchen. Why?"

"For lunch we should try making crumpets on the fire." She sounded drowsy. "Do you think we'll still be here at lunchtime?"

"Oh, yeah. No doubt at all."

No response.

He glanced over. Rachel was out like a light.

Travis tucked her in.

He found Tori nodding off with a chocolate mustache. He tucked her in, too.

After building up the fire again, he snagged his sheepskin, put it over himself and sat in front of the fire with his back against the end of the sofa.

How could all of this mundane, unexciting stuff leave him so happy?

Peace, love, happiness flooded all of the cavernous spaces that had lived in Travis since his empty childhood.

## Chapter 12

Travis hadn't known it, but he'd searched his entire life for this. For her. For Rachel.

All of the miles he'd traveled, all of the ranches he'd lived on, every cross he'd had to bear were all worth it, because all had led here, to Rachel.

He hadn't known he'd been searching. He'd thought the emptiness that dogged him was just a part of life.

After years of being tied down with Sammy, he'd wanted nothing more than to avoid anything that hinted of responsibility. It was enough to keep himself fed, clothed and earn a living.

But take on others? No way.

As much as he'd loved Samantha from the day she was born, he'd also felt responsible for her. His parents had done the barest minimum. Everything else had fallen to him.

He would never tell her so, but there'd been moments, especially as a teenager who couldn't play sports or date or hang out with friends, when he'd bitterly resented his role as mother, father and caregiver.

He'd never known a carefree childhood or adolescence.

*How carefree is your life now, Read? Sure, you can go anywhere at any time, but what is it worth?*

There was no pleasure in living year after year in bunkhouse after bunkhouse with a bunch of men, many of them strangers for the first few months, and then never seeing them again after he left.

His life had become normal ordinary survival, and that was it.

Where was the joy?

He'd been on the chilly outside looking in at warm places that had never been open to him.

Here, in this living room with a woman and two children who completed him, he was finally home.

Rachel was magic, fantasy, desire and fulfilled longing all rolled into one. The joy she'd given him on the carousel ride on his first day in town was a small taste compared to this entire feast.

They belonged together.

The realization stunned him.

So how did he go about wooing her?

He'd never wanted to stay with a woman permanently before. With Vivian, he hadn't realized until too late that he hadn't been in control. She'd been pulling his strings throughout their relationship.

Even when he'd thought she was the one, he'd held back from making the final commitment, his intuition kicking in on some level. Or maybe he'd just had cold feet.

He felt none of that now. Not one iota. All he felt was a desire to move ahead, to act on feelings he'd never experienced before.

Rachel was a mother with two young children. She'd just given birth. How on earth did he make his feelings known to her?

He couldn't touch her, couldn't offer her his body. Man, after what she'd just been through, those thoughts were the furthest thing from his mind.

Her body would need time to heal. So what did he have to offer her instead?

He didn't know who to talk to or where to go for advice. Who could he ask?

The obvious answer was Sammy, but he couldn't get hold of her.

That thought sobered him and brought him back to earth and out of his amazing euphoria.

"What are you thinking?" Rachel's whisper came out of nowhere.

She was watching him, her face dark that far from the light of the fireplace. He couldn't make out her expression.

"Are you warm enough?"

She laughed. "You have so many covers piled on top of me I can barely move. Shivering isn't possible."

He smiled. "Good."

"What were you thinking about so seriously? What's worrying you? Do you need us to leave?"

"God, no! Why would you think that?"

"This is a lot of responsibility for a single man. You're used to having your space to yourself. Now we're here crowding you."

"Rachel, honey, do you know how many times I

wanted to invite you over? I've spent too many years alone. There's more space in this house than any one man could possibly use."

She raised her eyebrows when he called her *honey*.

"Okay, you might have wanted the company of a woman." She didn't say *me*, just *a woman*. As though any woman would do. She didn't get it yet. How could she? He'd never even hinted to her that he wanted her. Travis held in a secret smile. She would understand soon enough. He'd make sure she did.

"You didn't count on having two children here," she continued. "Especially not a newborn baby."

"True. I gotta be honest, Rachel. I like it."

"But this isn't reality. Reality is months of sleepless nights and diaper changes and pureed green peas."

"I've shoveled a mountain's worth of shit in my lifetime. That little thing's diapers won't faze me."

She made a scoffing sound. "You won't believe what this tiny body will be able to produce. We'll see."

"No, *you'll* see." He was dead serious. Only in hindsight, now, did he see that he'd had a connection to Rachel since the first moment he'd seen her on that carousel.

Not just an attraction, but also a deep connection, as though he'd recognized parts of himself in her. And parts of her in him.

His life, his former burdens, and the sight of her pregnant belly had held him back, along with his own fear, but today he saw everything clearly.

He might think it was the high emotion of Beth's arrival, but that was only the catalyst. He could finally see what had been happening from the moment he'd arrived in this town.

Rachel had been on his mind ever since. No amount of resistance had been strong enough to stop the train that had barreled down on him.

Somewhere along the way, he'd decided her family could also be his. *She* could be his family. He wanted that more than anything he'd ever wanted in his life.

"What do you mean, I'll see? What will I see?" A puzzled frown furrowed her brow. "What are you saying, Travis?"

Was it too soon to admit his intentions? He thought so. Best to let things develop more slowly.

The farthest he would go at the moment was, "Will you bring the children over for Christmas? Spend the day with me, okay?"

She didn't answer right away.

"Please?" he said.

Again she hesitated. "What about your sister and her children?"

"You'll like each other. I want you to meet them." *I want Sammy to get to know you.*

"The children would have someone to play with. The boys would like that. So would Tori, I bet."

"Okay. We'll come over. I'd like that."

So would he.

Many times that day, Travis paced in front of the window. Snow had drifted too high for him to drive out and get a doctor for Rachel, or to drive her to the hospital. And with the phones not working properly, he couldn't even call a clinic for advice.

She said she was fine, but even so, he worried. He wanted both her and the babe checked out.

The power stayed out for another fourteen hours.

He kept them with him until the following morning, walking them back across to their trailer, carrying the baby while Rachel rested her hand on his arm.

He'd insisted. Sure, giving birth was natural, and she was capable of taking care of herself, but cripes, it had only been a little over twenty-four hours.

He didn't know if there was ice under the snow.

The bottom line was that he didn't want to see anything happen to her. She'd become as precious to him as anyone had ever been.

"I'll bring the suitcase over once we get you settled in," he said.

"I appreciate all of this, Travis."

Tori whooped and giggled in the snow.

"It's a winter wonderland, isn't it?" Rachel said.

"Do you like winter?"

"I like all seasons, Travis. Each one has its good points."

Her optimism, that ability to rise above everything that went wrong in her life, was what he found most attractive about her.

She found some good in everything. Even when she got really low, she didn't whine, just got on with business.

The trailer felt too empty to him. He didn't want to leave her here.

He'd asked her to stay with him longer, but she'd said, "I need to get on with the rest of my life. No time like right now to do that."

Just inside the front door, she hesitated. He thought maybe she was having second thoughts about coming back. Noting the moment she stiffened her spine and moved forward, he shook his head.

Stubborn didn't begin to describe Rachel McGuire.
Fine. This situation wouldn't last forever.

Rachel didn't know it yet, but her days in this tin
can were numbered.

He perched Beth in her cradle in the corner of the
living room.

"Still a bit cold in here. It hasn't warmed up fully
yet."

"She's well swaddled and cozy. If it's too chilly, I
can put her in the carrier and wear her. She'll be fine."

He didn't bother asking what all of that meant, just
straightened and looked down at her. "You'll call if you
need anything?"

Her skin looked good. Her hazel eyes were clear. The
time at his house, getting sleep and doing nothing more
than feeding her baby, had done her good.

The bags of exhaustion under her eyes were gone.
He wished he could banish them forever.

"Yes, I'll call."

"Promise?"

"I promise. Travis, thank you for everything. I
couldn't have done it without you."

"You're about the most capable woman I've ever met,
Rachel. You would have been fine." He tucked her hair
behind her ear. He wasn't sure, but he thought he de-
tected a fine tremor running through her at his touch.

Good sign.

"I'm glad you didn't have to do it alone."

"Me, too."

Travis couldn't keep himself from giving in to an
urge that had been building for weeks.

He leaned forward and kissed her. He liked the feel

of her full lips under his and the scent of his soap on her skin and the breathy sigh that escaped her.

"Travis, you're kissing Mommy."

He pulled away slowly, that one freckle on Rachel's lower lip tantalizing at this close range, tempting him to return for seconds.

"I sure am, Tori." He smiled down at her. "Get used to it."

Rachel's eyes widened.

Travis grinned and left the trailer, whistling all the way across the road to his home.

Inside, it felt empty, though. He wanted them back here now. He didn't want them to ever leave again.

He would make a good home here, one that would put his childhood to shame.

Between him and Sammy, they could sort out where and how everyone would live.

He hadn't understood that there was no burden in love.

When he held Beth, her small weight represented responsibility. He couldn't imagine the commitment it would take to raise her to adulthood, but that responsibility would also come with tremendous reward.

Was she a burden? Never. Would she be a challenge? Yes. Was he up to it? His answer was a hands down, flat-out, resounding yes.

The same with Tori. Even when she was tired and fractious, all he felt for her was affection.

He'd always loved his sister. He loved his nephews more than anything, but the worry of keeping them safe had overwhelmed him at times.

The difference between the two families was that,

even though Sammy and her children loved him, he'd lived on the outside looking in.

He remembered thinking that all he would ever know of family life would be to live it vicariously through Sammy and his nephews.

Here, with Rachel and Tori and Beth, was hope and inclusion and possibility and love.

Especially love.

He was a capable guy. He was up for the challenge.

Somehow, he could blend the two families and make it work.

He would fight tooth and nail to make it work.

He set about putting away quilts and washing dishes and planning his campaign to win Rachel McGuire's heart.

After the snowplows came through, he drove into town and stopped in at Cole's office.

"Rachel McGuire had her baby." Travis explained what had been happening. "I need to get a doctor out to see her. Who should I talk to?"

Cole gave him a name and an address.

"He's probably her doctor. I kinda doubt Rachel was seeing anyone else. Doc Chambers does everything around here."

Travis stopped in, introduced himself and told him about Rachel. "Can I ask you to go out there to pay her a visit, make sure she and the baby are healthy? I'd compensate you up front."

"I've heard from Rachel. I'm heading out there in an hour to check on her."

"I'd still like to be the one paying for this visit." He paid and then drove home, more settled now that he knew she'd be taken care of.

Sure, it was a high-handed decision, but doctors and hospitals were expensive, and he knew he had a heck of a lot more money than Rachel did.

This way she wouldn't have to dip into any savings she might have. She could use her money for the next few months until she could get back to work.

The second his phone worked again, he called Samantha.

She answered on the second ring. Hallelujah.

"Where've you been?" He sounded angry, but cripes, he'd been worried.

"What do you mean? I'm in San Francisco. Where else would I be? We didn't plan to leave for a couple of weeks."

"I've been calling and calling and not getting through."

"Really? My phone's been on. I've been here. Did you try texting me?"

"I did everything but turn myself inside out."

"I don't know what's wrong, Travis. Maybe there's something wrong with the phone. It has been acting strangely, but I didn't know calls weren't coming through. I'll get it checked out."

"Do that. We had a storm here, but I was calling you before the weather rolled in."

"What's wrong? What's got you so upset?"

He told her about Vivian.

"That she-snake," she said. "No offense, Travis, but I never did trust her."

"Now I understand why."

"I don't think it matters what Vivian said about Manny and his men."

"How can you say that?"

"I got a letter from him. From Manny."

"He's not supposed to know where you are!" Fear settled in his belly, messing with the lunch he'd eaten a while ago.

"He doesn't. Apparently it went to his defense attorney and then to the prosecutor who sent it along to me."

"What did he want?" Talk about a snake who shouldn't be trusted.

"It was a weird letter, Travis, but…"

"But what?"

"I believe everything he wrote in it."

"Like what?"

"He's found religion. He's turning over a new leaf."

"Come *on*, Samantha. *Seriously*?"

"I worked for him for two years. Plenty of long hours. Lots of overtime. I got to know him well. This sounds different."

"All of a sudden he's a new man?"

"He said he's called off his boys. They're no longer looking for me."

"So within the space of a couple of weeks, he gets Viv to tell him where I am, where you plan to live and then turns around and calls off his goons?"

"It was a long letter. He said he gave Vivian a bunch of money to set herself up in an honest business. He gave his men what he had left. He said he won't need it anymore."

"And you believed him?"

"Every word."

Travis scratched his head. "Aren't you being naive?"

"No, I don't think so, Travis. He's old. He has no family left. I think prison changed him."

"I'll believe it when I see it. In the meantime, when are you and the boys leaving?"

She hesitated then said, "Do you mind if we come in February instead of for Christmas?"

Thank God for Rachel and the girls coming over for Christmas, or he'd be feeling hollowed out right now. "Why?"

"Remember how upset Jason was about the trial and moving so much and about his dad leaving?"

"Yeah."

"Well, he's joined the drama club at school and loves it. They're putting on a musical before Christmas and a play at the end of January. He really wants to do them."

Travis reined in the hurt that had started up in him, that his nephews didn't want to see him as much as he wanted to see them. It made sense for Jason to find something for himself.

"This has stabilized him, Travis. It's given him some peace. I'm going to uproot him again to bring him to Montana, so let him have these two experiences first."

Travis didn't respond, even though he understood.

"Okay, Travis?" Samantha asked.

Finally, he answered, "Yeah, okay," and it was. Whatever was best for Jason was fine by him.

"Sammy, one more thing…"

"What?"

"There's this woman…a really nice one…she has two children, girls, and I, well…" He didn't know what Sammy would think. "I guess I've kind of fallen in love."

"It's about *time*, bro." Samantha laughed and hooted. "What's she like?" She didn't sound disapproving. Just curious.

"The best person I've ever met."

The tension in Travis's shoulders eased. Sammy approved. She would like Rachel. "I don't know how we'll work out the living arrangements."

"Relax, Travis. We'll make things work. Can't wait to meet her."

A week before Christmas, Travis drove into town.

He hadn't seen any movement at Rachel's, no comings and goings, and it hit him. How was she getting out to get groceries when she had a newborn?

He'd heard through the grapevine that Cindy had not just left the trailer, but she'd actually skipped town.

If he went across the road and offered to pick up groceries, he had no doubt Rachel would say they were all fine.

Instead, he planned to just show up with food, but he had to be crafty about it. He'd tell her he was inviting himself for dinner…and it was a potluck and he was bringing the food.

*Clever, Travis.*

After the storm, he'd been called to the ranch to help with snow clearance and winter chores. He'd put in long days.

At night, he shoveled her driveway so she could get out if she needed to.

She might have had visitors. He was gone so much during the day he couldn't know for sure.

This foray into town to pick up groceries for her was really an excuse to go see her.

He picked up ready-made stuff. From the grocery store's small deli counter, he picked up a cooked rotisserie chicken along with a box of potato wedges.

In the meat department, he stared down entire shelves of steaks. If he picked up a couple for her and Tori, she would see it as charity.

It wasn't. It was love.

He didn't have experience in this new, fledgling love business, but his instincts told him it was too early to tell her how he felt.

*Right, then. Subterfuge, it is.*

He would just have to tell her he didn't want chicken. He wanted steak.

He chose four filet mignons.

Lastly, he got a bag of ready-made salad and paid for it all.

Next stop… Vy's diner.

"Hey," he called when he walked in. "Those look good. Are they spoken for?"

Vy stood behind the counter, frosting a batch of cupcakes. She looked up and smiled. "Nope. I just felt like baking."

"Can I buy half a dozen to take out?"

Vy's dark brows rose to the kerchief she wore when she worked around food.

"You having a party?" She turned up a cup and poured him some coffee.

He shrugged. "Sort of. I guess." He sat down and sipped the hot brew. "I'm taking a bunch of food over to Rachel."

"Isn't that baby the cutest little thing you've ever seen?"

"When did you see her?"

"I stopped in three days ago."

"Do you know if she's had other visitors?"

"Sure, the other girls came with me. We brought new

baby clothes. Some really cute stuff. People have been in every day making sure she's okay."

"I didn't know. I've been busy at the Double U. I haven't been over."

"I heard you delivered Beth."

"Nah. She delivered herself with her mother's help. I was just there to catch her."

She covered his hand where it rested on the counter. For a fraction of a second, he wondered if she was making a pass. It wasn't ego. It had just happened too many times in the past.

She cleared up that misconception when she said, "Thank you. Rachel means the world to us. We're all grateful you were there for her."

Briskly, she wiped down the counter and got out a box in which to package his cupcakes.

He listed everything he'd picked up at the grocery store to take to Rachel's and added, "I wonder if maybe she'd like some soup."

"Great idea. Whatever you all don't finish tonight, she can reheat for lunch tomorrow." She bustled into the kitchen and returned with two canning jars of soup, which she put into a big paper bag. "You can return the jars the next time you come in. I have a hearty minestrone and a lovely parsnip soup."

Travis made a face. "Parsnip?"

"Don't knock it till you've tried it. Parsnips, cream, a little fresh ginger, and a texture like silk on your tongue."

"I'll have to take your word for it."

"Try it. That's an order. You'll be back here tomorrow for more."

"Won't promise that much, but I will give it a taste."

He pulled his wallet out of his back pocket. "You know that great meat loaf you make?"

"You want some of that, too?"

"Give me enough for the girls for tomorrow night's dinner."

Vy raised one perfectly shaped black eyebrow. "The girls?"

Travis blushed. "Rachel and Tori."

"They wouldn't by any chance be *your* girls, would they?"

Travis sobered. He was full to bursting with love for them, but didn't know what to do with it other than confessing it all to Rachel and hoping for the best.

Gossip could rage through a small town like a forest fire, but Travis had a good feeling about Vy. He'd eaten in here often enough to get a handle on her. Something about the protective way she talked about Rachel inspired a trust he didn't show a lot of people.

"You gotta promise you won't tell anyone, not even those women helping with the fair. I do think of them as my girls. I love Rachel."

Vy had been leaning one hand on the counter and one on her hip, in her usual cocky pose, but now her mouth fell open and she straightened to her full height. "I was joking. I didn't know... Oooooh."

She covered her head with her hands. "I think I'm going to explode. I've wanted Rachel to be happy for so long. Davey was a great guy, but... Rachel needs someone dependable."

"I know it seems fast, but—"

"No," Vy interrupted. "It is *not* too fast. It's about time someone recognized Rachel for the gem she is."

She leaned across the counter, grasped the lapels

of his coat and hauled him toward her. She had a good grip. She laid a smackeroo on first one cheek and then the other.

"Thank you." She wiped moisture from beneath her eyes without smudging her perfect makeup, a skill that awed Travis. "I can't think of a better man for Rachel."

Hard-headed Violet was a softie. She swiped her thumbs across his cheeks to get rid of her lipstick, he guessed.

"Have you told her how you feel?"

"Not yet."

"Give her time and space. You'll know when it's the right moment."

She went into the kitchen and returned with another container, placing it in the bag on top of the meat loaf.

"These are all warm, so I'm putting the cupcake box into a separate bag. Keep them apart so the icing won't melt."

He paid for the food and made to leave, but she stopped him.

"I'm giving you something extra for Rachel from me." From a cold display case, she took out large bowls of rice pudding and custard. Spooning them into two plastic containers, she said, "Tell Rachel she needs the calcium in these. They're both loaded with cream and milk."

He thanked her and left, breathing out a sigh. He hadn't realized until now just how nervous he'd been about the town's reaction to a newcomer, a relative stranger, laying claim to one of its loveliest women.

Vy's approval warmed him through and through.

Now to see if Rachel would accept all of this food.

Instead of turning into his own driveway, he drove into hers.

He took the bags from the diner and carried them to the door. While he waited for her to answer, a crowd of nerves took to line dancing in his stomach.

The door opened. Rachel looked surprised to see him. He drank in the sight of her. She looked tired, but not that beat-down exhaustion he'd seen while she'd been working in the bar.

Her hair was mussed, and she looked both womanly and sleepy. What would she do if he slipped his arms around her and held her?

Man, he yearned. He wanted all of the things that had been missing all of his life, and he wanted them now. This moment.

She yawned.

Covering her mouth, she said, "Sorry, you caught me napping."

Damn. He hadn't thought about that. "Sorry! You want me to come back later?"

Tori squeezed between the door and her mother's legs. "Travis! What's in the bags?"

Direct as always. He laughed. He'd missed her. He glanced back at Rachel. He'd *really* missed *her*.

A gust of wind kicked up, and Rachel shivered. "Come in out of the cold."

And didn't that sum up his entire life? He'd been on the outside looking in for too long time.

He stepped into her trailer. It might as well have been the grandest home in town. He was happy to stand and stare at Rachel all day.

Again, Tori piped up, "But, Travis, you didn't say what's in the bags?"

He walked to the minuscule table they ate their meals on and set the bags down.

"First, I have to ask your mother something before I open the bags."

Tori hopped from foot to foot, staring at the bags he knew she recognized from Vy's place.

"Ask her quick, Travis."

He crossed his fingers with a smile and said, "Rachel, I know this is sudden, but I'm hoping you don't have plans. Can I stay for dinner?"

"Yes!" That was Tori. Her fingers rested on the edge of the table, clearly itching to open the bags. "Say yes, Mommy."

Smiling ruefully, Rachel answered, "I can't very well say no, can I?"

She was right. She couldn't disappoint her daughter.

Yep, craftiness paid off.

He opened the bag with the meat loaf and jars of soup. Next, he took out the rice pudding and the custard. "These two are from Vy. She says you need the calcium."

"That's so sweet of her."

"What's in that bag?" Tori asked, pointing to the one he hadn't opened.

He knew from his nephews not to bring out dessert until dinner was finished. "That's for later. Let's put it in the kitchen."

"Travis, this is so nice of you. It's kind of early, but I wouldn't mind digging in right away, if you don't mind."

"Sure, but there's more."

Her voice took on the hard edge he recognized as her streak of independence. "More?"

He pointed to the food on the table. "Rachel, how far do you think soup's going to take me?"

After a swift glance down his body, she said, "Okay."

"I have a favor to ask before I get the rest of the food from the truck."

"What do you need?"

"Can you dress the little one to play outside? You can eat the calcium-filled food while we play for a while. Okay?"

"You're a gem. She's been going stir-crazy with me."

"Good. It's cold out. Dress her warmly."

He retrieved the rest of the bags from his truck and came back. Rachel gaped.

"Now, don't get your dander up," he warned. "Once I decided I was coming for dinner, I got excited and picked up some of my favorite foods."

He unloaded the bags onto her kitchen counter.

"Can you put the hot food into the oven? Tori and I are going to grill some steaks."

"On the barbecue? Outside?" Rachel peered through the window. "It's freezing out there."

"Yep. We won't be long. Tori won't get cold."

"I'm not cold! I'm hot!" The child stood like an over-stuffed beach ball in her winter coat and scarf and big mittens and hat.

"Let's go." He picked up the steaks and left before Rachel could complain that he'd bought too much food.

Across the road at his house, he made Tori stand inside the front door while he got his grilling implements, spices and a clean plate from the kitchen.

Outside, Tori started rolling a couple of large snow-balls to build a snowman while he pulled the grill out of the garage and turned it on. He seasoned the steaks and threw them on once it had heated up.

"Travis, this is heavy." Tori struggled to put one ball on top of the other. She'd made them too big to handle all by herself. He helped her, but realized he didn't have anything to use to dress it.

He did the next best thing. He picked up the child and tossed her into a pile of snow he'd created when he'd cleared his driveway.

She shrieked. Her laughter floated on the air and filled his heart.

"Again!" She scrambled off the top and launched herself into his arms. He caught her and tossed her back up to the top.

This, *this*, was joy, and fun, affection and love. Playing in the snow. Grilling food for the girls he loved.

He flipped the steaks and continued to toss Tori around in the snow. The kid really had been stir-crazy. She had a lot of energy to expend.

When the meat was cooked, he put it on a plate, switched off the barbecue and walked back across the road with Tori.

Inside the trailer, Rachel had effected a stunning transformation.

The small table was covered with a lacy cloth and only one lamp burned. The effect was more cozy than romantic. Good thing. This was a family gathering.

He would get to the romance later.

Or maybe this was part of it.

Was romance only about flowers and wine, expensive dinners and lovemaking?

Couldn't it also be about showing love in the smallest ways? In easing burdens and sharing responsibilities? In consideration and cooperation and just plain everyday affection?

He hoped so, because he had a lot of these simple things to give to Rachel and her girls.

There were only two folding chairs at the table. That's all that would fit.

Rachel leaned over a bassinet on the tiny sofa. "Beth has been asleep for a while, but she should go a little longer."

She picked up Tori's small plush armchair.

"I'll have Tori eat in her own little chair."

"Uh-uh, Mommy. Want to eat with you and Travis."

"But there's no room."

"She can eat on my lap."

Rachel looked hopeful. "Are you sure?"

"Yep. We'll make it work, won't we, Tori?"

"Yep. We make it work."

The food lined the counters in the kitchen. Travis added the steaks to the spread.

"Let's dig in," he said. "I'm starving." He picked up Tori and settled her onto his arm and took a plate in his other hand.

"What do you want? A little bit of everything?"

"French fries!"

"That's all?"

"Yep."

"Nope. You'll eat meat and salad, too."

"'Kay."

Beside him, Rachel hummed low. It sounded like a laugh lurked in there somewhere.

"Funny," she murmured. "She never agrees with me that easily."

"Must be my charm."

The sassiness he'd encountered on his first morning in town shone through in her laugh. "No doubt."

He liked sharing jokes with her.

While he held a plate, Rachel filled it with a bit of everything, except soup. He wasn't a soup kind of guy. He'd bought it for her.

He sat on a chair with the little one comfortable in his lap.

Rachel placed a small mug on the table beside his plate.

"What's that?" he asked.

"Parsnip soup."

"Um. I'd rather not."

"Vy said you'd say that. She said you made a face when she mentioned parsnips."

Surprised, he asked, "You talked to her?"

"She phoned and said—and I quote—'Make sure macho man tastes the soup.'"

He took umbrage. "Macho man?"

"I think she was joking. You've made a conquest there."

"Why would you say that?"

"Vy's not easily won over. She can have a really hard edge. When she talks about you, though, I can hear affection in her voice, especially when she called you macho man."

Travis stopped chewing. Was that—? Did he hear *jealousy* in Rachel's voice? Did she think there was something going on between him and Vy?

That could screw up everything he wanted to build.

In a rush to set her straight, he opened his mouth, but pulled up short. Nah. This felt good, too good to end so early.

Rachel McGuire had feelings for him, no doubt about it. Oh, yeah, she sure did.

She liked him. She really, really liked him.

He cut bits of chicken and steak into pieces for Tori then dug into his own meal, feeling at peace with the world, in the finest state of contentment he'd ever known.

He tasted the soup. Vy was right. It was excellent. Smooth as silk, just as she'd said. He'd have to tell her that next time he visited the diner.

They ate in silence for a while until Rachel asked, in a tone he knew was meant to be nonchalant, "Is there anything you want to share?"

"Share?" he asked, playing ignorant.

"About you and Vy?"

While he might be enjoying Rachel's jealousy, he didn't want her to be unhappy.

He set down his fork and laid his hand over hers. Startled, she glanced up at him. In her gold-flecked eyes, he saw both defiance and hope.

"I'm here. With you. With your girls. I'm here because I want to be." He turned her hand over and placed a kiss on her palm. "I'm here because I want to be with you."

She stared at him and licked her bottom lip.

He leaned forward to kiss that tiny freckle, but Tori put her little hand up to his face.

"Here! Kiss my hand, too, Travis."

Ha! The joys and complications of having children around.

Throughout the rest of the meal, he watched Rachel. She looked flustered, but happy and that made him happy. Her cheeks were red. A good sign?

The baby fussed, and Rachel left the table to sit in an old armchair to feed her.

"Did you have enough to eat? I could bring your plate over to you."

"I'm so full, Travis. That was a lot of food." She sent him a shrewd glance. "I'm on to your tricks, you know. This is far, far too much food for one dinner."

He grinned, unrepentant. "I know, and before you say it, no, I'm not taking any of it home. It's for you and Tori."

"Thank you." She said it quietly, and he knew it hurt her pride, but he also heard relief.

"You had enough, Tori?"

She nodded and he set her on the floor. She ran to a box in the corner, pulled out some Legos and started building.

"I'll put the leftovers away. Where do you keep your plastic containers?"

She told him, and he packaged up the leftover chicken, steak, salad and soups.

When he opened the refrigerator door to put it all away, he got a shock. There was next to nothing in there other than a few condiments and a carton of milk. What would she have done for dinner if he hadn't come by?

He damned Cindy to hell and back for leaving her daughter in this situation. Just when Rachel needed her mother the most, the woman was gone.

Cindy should have been here buying groceries, or babysitting so Rachel could get out.

"I'll get you some more groceries when this stuff runs out. You need more milk for Tori for tomorrow?"

"Just milk, Travis. Nothing else. No, wait, a loaf of

bread, as well. Can you get my wallet? I'll give you money for it."

"I'm not taking mon—"

"Travis, please." Her jaw jutted as she dug in for a fight.

There came a time when you just had to allow a person her pride. He carried her purse to her. She took out her wallet and handed him a five-dollar bill.

He managed to get a quick peek inside. It was all she had. So the problem wasn't just not being able to get out to get food. It was also not having money, unless she had oodles in the bank.

Somehow, he doubted that.

Otherwise, there would be more in the cupboard than peanut butter.

Anger raced through him, but he held it in check.

What Rachel and her children needed most right now was not high emotion, but simple acts of support and kindness.

If he ever saw Cindy again, though, he'd tear a strip off her hide.

"Anyone want a hot drink with dessert?"

"Dessert!" Tori abandoned the Legos and wrapped her arms around his legs. She did that a lot.

The spontaneous act filled him with wonder.

He could get used to being part of a family.

That sign of jealousy in Rachel could be a start. He knew she found him attractive. He knew she liked him.

Could she ever love him?

He made tea for Rachel and hot chocolate for Tori and put out the box of cupcakes with small plates from the cupboard.

They sat in the living room because Rachel still

held Beth, who had finished her dinner at her mother's breast.

Tori made it only halfway through her cupcake before lying down with her head in Travis's lap and falling asleep. All that playing in the snow had worn her out.

After he'd finished his dessert, Rachel said, "Beth is sleeping. Would you like to hold her?"

"Yeah."

Her brows shot up. "I'm surprised. I thought infants would intimidate you."

"I held my nephews a lot when they were little. Their father was AWOL most of the time."

Rachel brought the baby to him and snugged her into the crook of his arm.

"Did your brother-in-law travel for business, or something?"

"Yeah. Something. He was always running off to different ashrams and yoga retreats and meditation conferences."

Rachel covered Tori with a blanket. "Sounds like a man who is trying to find himself."

"That's all fine and dandy, but he should have done it before having kids. Once you've made that commitment, those kids are more important than anything else. Kids don't ask to be born."

"True."

Of course she would understand. Her own father had run off and left her behind.

Silence settled over the trailer.

Tori slept soundly, as did the baby in his arms.

Again that sense of peace that this small family brought with it came over him.

In time, he gave Beth back to Rachel and carried Tori to bed, tucking her in fully clothed.

At the front door, Travis pulled on his boots and coat.

"Thank you, Travis. You gave us a real gift today. It was wonderful to have more than just our own company."

She pointed one stern finger his way. "But don't do it again. I can take care of myself and my children."

"Yes, ma'am." He leaned forward, kissed her gently on her lips and smiled.

Just before stepping out of the trailer, he said, "See you on Christmas Eve."

"What? I thought we were coming on Christmas Day."

"You are. Sammy and the boys aren't coming until February. They won't be here for Christmas. I want to have you all over for supper on Christmas Eve, too."

When she didn't respond, he leaned in. Her eyes dropped to his lips. Obviously, she thought he meant to kiss her again.

She didn't step away, and in fact, seemed to move closer.

So, she liked him *and* she desired him. Perfect.

"You have any plans for Christmas Eve?"

She shook her head.

"Good. Bring the kids over at five."

He left his truck where it was and walked across the road. After cleaning the barbecue and putting it away in the garage, he closed the front door with a big smile on his face.

# Chapter 13

Rachel bundled up the children and drove into town.

She needed to get the last of her money out of the bank.

What she would do after Christmas when it was all gone was still a question. She wondered if she could get an advance from Honey.

But then what would she do when she was working and not getting paid because she'd already borrowed it and spent it?

Her stomach roiled. Her mind balked at applying for welfare or any kind of public assistance. Grimly, she thought, *I will if I have to.* It would take a while to come through. What would she do in the meantime?

In town, she parked and got Tori out of the car, then Beth.

In the bank, she talked to Ethel, the aging teller who'd been there all of Rachel's life.

"Can I withdraw a hundred, Ethel?" That would leave another forty to last through Christmas.

Dear Lord.

For now, she needed a hundred to get more groceries, oatmeal, powdered milk and more diapers for Beth. She was just about out of the supply she'd put by before giving birth.

Ethel frowned. "Didn't you know, Rachel?"

"Know what?"

"Oh, dear, I'd hoped it was okay. I'd hoped she'd asked first."

Dread weighing on her shoulders, Rachel didn't need to ask who *she* was. Cindy. Rachel had put her onto the account after Davey's death, for when she gave birth and Cindy would have to buy food for Tori.

Obviously a foolish move, but she'd thought she could trust her own mother.

"What is it, Ethel?"

"Cindy cleaned out the account before she left town."

Rachel locked her knees to keep herself upright. She breathed through her nose so she wouldn't get light-headed.

"I see. Okay, thank you, Ethel."

She left the bank quickly, with her dignity intact.

She would get through this. She would survive.

Dear God, how?

In the days after their meal together, Travis hadn't made the mistake of taking more food across the road. He'd known Rachel wouldn't accept more even if he invited himself to dinner.

In another few days, he'd be feeding them all on both Christmas Eve and Christmas Day.

Sitting in the diner one morning, he perked up when he recognized Rachel's car pull up and park across the street.

She got both children out of the car and went into the bank. A short while later, she came back outside. She didn't look happy.

"Vy, come here," he called.

When she did, he said, "Sit down." She slid into the window booth across from him and followed the direction of Travis's intent stare.

"What do you want?" she asked.

He pointed. "Does she look happy to you?"

Rachel finished strapping both of her children into the car. She rounded the hood and got into the driver's seat, sitting there without starting the engine.

There was no missing the deep unhappiness on her face.

"No," Vy said, and Travis glanced at her. Her mouth drooped in a grimace. "What's going on, Travis?"

"I think Rachel's out of money."

"Impossible. She's worked hard at Honey's. She had to have been saving to get ready for this time. She has a good head on her shoulders."

"I would have thought so, too." He explained about the empty refrigerator and cupboards. "I caught a look at her wallet. She had nothing."

"Look." Vy grasped his arm. "She's driving back out of town without stopping at the grocery store. Would your groceries have lasted this long?"

"Nope. We have to do something." He corrected himself. "*You* have to do something. She won't take any more from me, but if her friends stopped in, each a few days apart, with supplies, she might accept that."

"That's only temporary. What about after Christmas?"

"Vy, I hope to God I will have convinced her to change her living situation permanently by then."

A broad smile split her face. "Yeah?"

"Yeah." He threw forty bucks onto the table. "That's to cover my sandwich and some food for Rachel. Can all of you work out a schedule between you?"

He stood and retrieved his hat. Before leaving he said, "Leave Christmas Eve and Christmas Day open for me. I'll be taking care of things then."

"You got it, Travis." She took off her apron.

"Will!" she hollered to her cook. "I need to go to the pharmacy for diapers and wipes. Oh, Lord, what else would she need for the baby?"

Travis shrugged. He knew stuff about babies only second hand.

"Don't worry," Vy said. "I'll raid my stores here and bring her eggs, milk, flour. All kinds of stuff."

To Will she hollered again. "Wrap up a bunch of that fried chicken and mashed potatoes and a container of the pasta carbonara to take out. I'll be back in a few minutes to deliver it personally."

Christmas Eve arrived. To Travis, it seemed to have taken forever to get here.

He fussed with the food, more nervous than he could ever remember being. He had a lot riding on tonight's dinner.

The evening started at five o'clock in deference to the two children. They arrived on time.

At the door, Travis took Beth so Rachel could take

off her coat. She hung it with Tori's beside his. Travis liked the look of their coats hanging together.

He wanted to see them there from now on.

"Travis, look. Mommy curled my hair."

"She did a good job. It's beautiful." He noticed that Rachel had taken care with her own appearance, as well. Her hair was full and curly. From the first moment he'd set eyes on Rachel, he'd wanted to run his fingers through her hair. That urge was even stronger now.

In the living room, he noticed something else. She'd lost much of the weight she'd had when she was pregnant. He'd never seen her normal figure before, and he liked what he saw. A lot.

"I'll take Beth and undress her." When Rachel took the baby from him, the side of her breast brushed his forearm, and his desire for her shot through the roof.

*Quit it, Travis. This is a family night.*

He had to get this relationship settled before his unrequited lust sent him 'round the bend.

Not only that, he just plain wanted these girls in his life forever.

"Where's that drawer we used for Beth before? Can we use it again?"

"You bet. I emptied it earlier just in case." He brought it to the living room, and Rachel put the baby into it. They covered her with the receiving blankets Rachel had brought over with her.

"She's cute as a button, Rachel." It was no lie. The child was beautiful.

"Me, too. I'm cute as a button, too, aren't I, Travis?" Tori tugged on his pant leg.

From his nephews, Travis knew all about sibling rivalry.

He picked up Tori and twirled her around. "You bet! You're the cutest button in the jar."

She giggled while he twirled her until they were both dizzy.

Dinner was beef stroganoff and crusty bread. Vegetables weren't his thing, but he'd included steamed green beans.

They ate in the dining room on the Lady Carlisle plates that Rachel loved so much.

They had one of Uma's homemade apple pies for dessert only because she'd put Travis to work peeling a mountain of apples. She'd made ten pies for Christmas and had given him one to take home.

After apple pie with vanilla ice cream, they sat in the living room. Tori sipped hot chocolate while the adults drank decaf coffee.

Deep satisfaction filled Travis.

The evening ended too soon.

"Travis, can you come over in the morning to see what Santa left for me?" Tori asked at the door.

He'd be honored. Life with these girls brought joy on top of joy on top of joy. "Sure thing, sprout."

She slammed herself against his legs and yelled, "You're my best friend."

With a quiet smile, Rachel left with Beth in her arms. They made their slow way across the road and the snow-covered ground in front of the trailer bathed in the cool winter glow of a full moon.

Only after they'd made it inside their front door did Travis close his door.

The following morning, he awoke early as excited as any kid on Christmas morning.

He dressed with care and walked across the road in

the darkness. They were in for a few months of dark mornings. Some of the ranch hands minded, but Travis didn't. He liked mornings. The sun hadn't yet crested the horizon. His breath frosted in the early-morning air. He knocked on the door.

No answer.

He knocked again.

Finally, the door opened and Rachel stood in an old plaid robe belted at her waist. Her rumpled hair begged to have his fingers untangle it. He wanted to bury his face in it.

"Am I too early? I thought Tori would be up by now."

She started to laugh, couldn't seem to stop, and he stared, bewildered.

"Rachel, what is it? What's wrong with you?"

She wrapped her arms across her waist and kept laughing. He frowned and got exasperated.

"If you don't tell me what's so funny, I'm leaving."

Laughing too hard to say anything, she threw her arms around his neck so he wouldn't leave.

He hadn't bothered to button his coat for the short walk across the road, so her full breasts flattened against the white shirt he'd put on. Only a couple of layers of fabric separated them.

He clung to her as though his life depended on it. In a sense, it did.

In his arms, she quieted and stopped laughing.

"Um, Travis, you should let me go."

"Never, Rachel," he whispered fervently. "I've wanted you from the first moment I set eyes on you."

"Impossible. I was more than seven months pregnant." Her breath brushed his ear.

He kissed her neck.

She moaned. "Don't do that, Travis. I'm a mother."

He chuckled. "Mothers don't like to be kissed?"

"Mothers love it." The sentiment seemed to have popped out almost against her will, and Travis chuckled again.

He kissed her neck and ran his tongue along her jawline.

She pushed against his chest and stepped away, straightening her hair self-consciously.

"We can't do this."

"Yes, we can. I care for you, Rachel. I have since the day of the carousel ride. Hell, I'll admit it. I love you."

She stared with a deer-in-the-headlights shock. "You can't."

"I do."

When she didn't respond, he tucked her hair behind her ear. "Do you have any feelings for me in return?"

"It doesn't matter what I feel. I come with two kids, Travis."

"I'm aware of that, Rachel. So?"

"So...we're a complete package. You can't have me without them."

"I'm aware of that, too, Rachel. I love those two little girls already."

"This isn't possible. Stuff like this doesn't happen. Men don't fall in love with pregnant women and take on ready-made families."

"This one did and will."

"Okay, that's what you think now, but what about next year? You don't stay anywhere, Travis. You travel around. I can't do that."

"I'm not doing that anymore, either. You give me

more than I thought was possible. Joy. Happiness. Stability. An end to loneliness. Did I say joy?"

They stared at each other, a showdown of wills, Rachel still unbelieving.

She looked away first. "I need coffee. Make us a pot while I get dressed."

"Why were you laughing at me?" He knew he sounded hurt, but what on earth had been Rachel's problem when she'd answered the door?

From halfway to her bedroom, she started to laugh again.

"It's five-thirty in the morning, Travis."

Feeling like a damned fool, a hyperactive little boy in a man's body, he cursed himself for not checking the time before he'd left home.

His cheeks heated.

Midway through making the coffee, he started to laugh, too.

Christmas Day turned out to be the most perfect day he'd ever lived.

Dinner was perfect, and both Tori and Rachel loved the presents he'd picked out for them—a pretty mauve sweater for Rachel and a tiny pink cowboy hat for Tori. He could imagine it hanging on a hook at the diner with all the adult hats.

He hadn't expected anything in return, but Rachel had knitted him a black scarf. He would make a point of wearing it often.

The only fly in the ointment was that she refused to talk any more about his loving her. Worse, she refused to admit that she cared for him in return.

He walked them back home, Tori with her pink cow-

boy hat perched on top of her winter hat, but Rachel
scooted inside before he could kiss her good-night.

He had no idea what was holding her back.

Did he have to *prove* his love somehow? Okay, sure,
he would do anything, but *what*?

When Travis visited the following afternoon with
containers of leftovers, Rachel didn't know what to
think, or what to do.

She already knew she loved him, and he claimed to
love her, but she'd chosen the wrong man before.

Davey had been fun, enthusiastic and as likable as
all hell, but he hadn't been dependable.

Travis seemed dependable, but had a history of moving every five minutes. How on earth could she trust
that he would stay put?

Thank goodness the children were napping because
he got down to business right away.

"What's holding you back?"

She'd already broached the subject of his nomadic
lifestyle yesterday, so she told him what else bothered
her. "Since this is a serious topic, I'll be honest, but this
is hard for me to talk about."

Travis leaned forward and rested his elbows on his
knees. "What can be that bad? You're strong, honest,
attractive...just about perfect."

Although touched by his flattery, she resisted it.
"When Davey and I started dating, he told me he'd
also been interested in another woman, but chose me
instead. I knew the woman. She was pretty. Gorgeous,
actually. After Tori was born, I asked him why he chose
me over her, and he said it was because so many other

men were attracted to her that he could never be sure she wouldn't be tempted by someone else."

She stared out the window. "I, on the other hand, he had complete faith in. I was, in his words, like a worn-in pair of cowboy boots, always ready and waiting by the front door."

A laugh burst out of Travis, and Rachel frowned. "What's so funny?"

At her combative tone, he sobered. "The man was a fool. Yes, you are steadfast and loyal, but I don't want you in my life for that. Not solely for that. I want you physically. A lot. I want your affection. I want to be treated with love and respect the same way you treat those kids of yours. And I want to give you that in return."

He knelt on the floor in front of her.

"When I look at you, I see the woman I want in my life for always." He grasped her face in his hands and kissed her, not a head-spinning, gymnastic-type of kiss, but a slow and deep and earnest promise.

He pulled away and she stared into his deep blue eyes. This couldn't really be happening. Travis Read loved her.

"Rachel, you are so damned attractive. Did growing up with your vain mother leave you feeling plain? You aren't. I was attracted to you from the first second I set eyes on you."

He stood and put on his coat. "Just as soon as it's possible to leave Beth for a couple of hours, I'm taking you out on a date."

"But—"

He left without waiting for an answer.

Rachel brushed her fingers across her lips, because

that promise in his kiss had been tempting and so, so sweet.

To dream about possibilities or not to dream? That was the big question for a woman who'd been burned by dreams in the past.

Travis called Vy and arranged for her to babysit Tori and Beth for a couple of hours in two weeks. He'd done an internet search to find out when it was okay for a woman to be able to make love after giving birth, and that seemed to be the earliest.

He couldn't think of another way to convince Rachel of his love than to show her with his body.

She wasn't believing his words.

He went straight to Rachel after he hung up and told her in no uncertain terms that they were going to have a date and that Vy would take care of the children.

He knew the women had continued to drop off food and supplies periodically since Christmas. He didn't know what Rachel thought of that.

That Saturday night, mid-January, rolled in cold and clear.

Rachel drove off, presumably to take the children to town. She came back soon afterward and parked in his driveway.

He opened the door and watched her walk up to his steps and up onto his veranda, remembering the times she had waddled here. He'd found her attractive then, but this version of Rachel knocked his socks off.

She stepped into his house and did something unexpected.

Without warning, she grasped fistfuls of his shirt and

dragged her to him, kissing him as though only tonight existed, as though there were no tomorrow.

He didn't resist, but fell into it with all of his heart.

"No dinner, Travis. Let's go upstairs now."

"Rachel." She wouldn't let him look at her. He forced her to step back. "What's going on in that head of yours? Why the rush?"

She wouldn't meet his eye.

"Are you—" He tilted her chin up with his hand. "Rachel, are you nervous?"

She nodded.

"Why?"

"You've known a lot of women. I don't have a lot of experience. There was a brief friendship with a guy in high school and then only Davey after that."

"What does experience have to do with anything? It's about feeling good with each other. I love you. Do you feel anything for me besides desire?"

She nodded, but didn't say anything. How much did she feel, he desperately wanted to know.

"Are you sure you want to go upstairs before dinner?"

"Yes. I really do. Travis, it's been so long, and I've wanted you since I saw you that first day."

He smiled, wonder coloring the moment. "You have?"

"Yes. I'd really like to get over being so nervous. I won't be able to eat a thing."

He took her hand and led her upstairs to his bedroom where he lit one candle. "That okay?"

He kissed her gently, soothing more than arousing. She seemed to like it so he kept it up.

In time, she melted against him.

He unbuttoned her blouse and slipped his hand inside.

Her breasts were full, ripe. He slipped her blouse from her shoulders and reached around her to unhook her bra. In his wildest dreams, he never imagined they would be awkward with each other.

He let his desire guide him.

He took one nipple into his mouth, keeping his touch gentle. A quiet moan slid up her throat.

"Is that okay?"

"Yes," she whispered. "Travis, I've wanted to see you for so long. Let me."

She undid his shirt and slid it off his shoulders. "Oh, Travis, I do like your shape. So much."

"And I like your body. Let's undress and get into bed."

"First, Travis, wait. I have to do this." She undressed fully and stood in front of him. She looked nervous.

He drank in the sight of her. She had a pretty body, with a tummy still soft and full from having carried a baby. Lines crossed it horizontally. No wonder. That skin had done a lot stretching.

"You hate my stomach, don't you?"

"What? No." He finally figured out what was worrying her. "Did you think I was looking for perfection? Rachel, this body has nurtured two beautiful girls. Why do you think that can't be attractive?"

The worry fell from her like a dark cloak gliding to the ground.

"Couples expect that their partner's body will change over the years, but this is the first time you're seeing me, Travis, and it's right after I've had a baby."

"Rachel? Do me a favor?"

"Anything."

"Get into bed so I can love the daylights out of you."

She smiled and scrambled into bed.

He undressed while she watched him. Once under the covers, they reached for each other.

He took his time arousing her, first because he was nervous about hurting her so soon after the birth. Secondly, he wanted to soothe her nerves.

She, in turn, seemed to want to please him, reaching for him while he was reaching for her.

They got in each other's way.

Rachel threw herself onto her back and laughed. "We're trying too hard, aren't we?"

Travis rose above her and grinned, leaning on one elbow so he could watch her reaction while he touched her.

He circled her nipple with one finger. "Yeah. I want to make you happy."

Her breath hitched. "Oh, you do, Travis. You make me so happy. I want to make you happy, too."

"So, let's go with the flow. Let's take as long as we need to, and make each other happy." He replaced his finger with his lips.

"You're right. Oh!" She made a cute little noise in her throat. "That feels good. This isn't a race. We have a little time." Her words became breathy. "We can take turns loving each other."

"Right. Let's do that."

That sentiment lasted all of two minutes, and they were all over each other again.

He kissed. She licked.

He tasted. She savored.

They got in each other's way again.

"Don't remember this ever being a problem before,"

Travis murmured while he paid homage to her other breast.

"Me, either."

Self-conscious, Travis set himself the task of losing himself in his senses. Flowers had nothing on the way Rachel smelled. Her skin felt like the softest of flower petals under his fingers as he stroked her everywhere.

Her moan brought him relief. They were going to be okay together.

He entered her and found bliss. Holding himself still above her, he watched for signs of pain but saw none.

He'd never in his life made love to a woman he loved, and it changed everything. Every touch sizzled, every word sparkled, and every high dazzled.

He could do this every night for the rest of his life and never get enough.

Rachel ran her palms over his chest. "Oh, Travis," she breathed. "You are so beautiful."

So was she. Breathtaking. He began to move.

When she came, he sighed. When he came, he roared with pleasure.

Rachel lay in Travis's arms sated and relieved.

Their lovemaking hadn't been sexy or lusty or passionate, but awkward and sweet, and about as satisfying as anything Rachel had ever experienced.

It had been lovemaking on a deeper level than ever.

Intense contentment washed over her, along with thoughts of possibility. Travis couldn't be more earnest if he tried.

She knew deep in her soul that Travis had changed profoundly since his first day in town, that what he was offering her was true and real.

That this might, against all odds, turn out to be permanent filled her with hope. What more could he possibly give her but hope for a secure, happy and loving future?

She laughed, filled with happiness.

"Are you good?" he asked, his voice rumbling in his chest beneath her ear.

"Yes," she whispered. "I'm euphoric. And you?"

"Yeah, that word says it all. I want you in my life forever, okay?"

"Yes. I want that, too. Remember the day you had us over to decorate the tree?"

She felt him nod.

"I knew for certain that day that I loved you."

"You did?" His voice filled with wonder. "I had no idea. We'll work out living arrangements somehow. We have some time until Sammy and the boys arrive."

"What are you saying, Travis? Are you asking me to live here with you?"

"I'm asking you to marry me." He cursed. "I don't know how to be romantic. I should have bought a ring and champagne."

"Travis, you're giving me love. I don't need champagne. I'm drunk on love for you."

His eyes widened and he kissed her deeply.

She told him about Cindy stealing all of her money and anger flashed on his face. "Let's not talk about it now. There will be no negatives in this bedroom, only love and wonder and happiness."

With long languid strokes, Travis learned the contours of her body.

She caressed his chest, his body strange and new,

yet the man achingly familiar already. She wanted him again. And again.

"Sorry that was so awkward." Travis nuzzled her shoulder. "I'm usually more skilled."

She moaned softly. "Travis, if you turn more skill on me, I'm not sure I'll survive, because that was wonderful."

She touched his cheek. "Yes, it was new, but I loved that. That was our first time and it was perfect, in all of its getting-to-know-you glory."

"Nice way to put it." He held her jaw. "Know what I think?"

She stared at his mouth, fascinated by it. "What do you think, Travis?"

"The second time's going to be even better."

She stared wide-eyed for a long time and finally whispered, "I can't wait."

"Know what else?"

"No. What?"

"We don't have to wait."

She reached for him and said fervently, "Thank God."

Vy called a little after ten.

Rachel's children missed her and wanted to come home.

Travis and Rachel hadn't even eaten, but had stayed in bed and had played with each other endlessly, their love being made manifest finally and irrevocably in more than just words, but also in the sweetest, and sometimes hottest, of gestures.

Travis loved how responsive Rachel was, and how inventive.

He didn't question how all of this was possible. He

just thanked his lucky stars he'd found this town and Rachel. The joy she'd given him that first day on the carousel, that stunningly simple gift, was nothing compared to the universe of honest, unbridled feelings she bestowed on him now.

The lost wandering cowboy had found his home.

Travis drove into town with Rachel to pick up the children, sated and thrilled and filled with giddy delight. Rachel was well and truly his future. "Rachel, why didn't Vy just come out to the trailer to babysit? Everything would have been easier."

Rachel squirmed. "I can't share Vy's history, or her confidences, but she only comes to the trailer when she has to and doesn't stay long. She…um…has a problem with trailers."

Despite the curiosity raging through him, Travis said, "Fair enough. The woman has a right to her privacy."

When they arrived, Vy looked upset.

"I don't know what I'm doing wrong," she said. "I can't get Beth to settle."

The second Rachel took the baby into her arms, she stopped her pitiful crying and closed her eyes.

"I think it was too soon for me to leave her."

"I guess," Vy said, but Travis heard the doubt. She glanced at him while Rachel urged Tori into her outdoor clothes.

"And you, Travis?" Vy whispered. "Was your night better than mine?"

He leaned close. "Vy, it was the best night of my life. Know what else?"

"No, what?" she asked.

"I expect every night after this one will get better and better."

"I'm glad. For both of you." Her soft smile might look sad around the edges, but he didn't doubt her sincerity.

"Come on," he said to Rachel, "I need to take my family home."

They stepped outside of Vy's apartment and approached the car. "We're your family?" Tori asked.

"Yep. You're my family now. What do you think of that?" He held his breath. He had no idea how the child would react.

"Yeah! Are we having a sleepover at your house?"

Travis shot a questioning look at Rachel.

She smiled, all womanly and soft around the edges. Then she laughed and said, "I don't know. Do you think he might serve us bacon cooked in the fireplace again?"

"I'll cook you whatever you want. Anything on this earth."

"Can we sleep in front of the fireplace again?" Tori queried. "I liked it!"

"Sure, sprout." Travis shot Rachel a rueful grin. There'd be no more lovemaking tonight.

"We'll have to get married as quickly as humanly possible," he told Rachel.

"Sooner!" Rachel said, grasping his hand and squeezing.

"Are we going to live with you, Travis?" the pip-squeak asked.

"Yep, from now on and forever and ever. I'm marrying your mom."

Tori clapped her hands. He switched on the radio and

Tori started her high-pitched warbling with the music. It would take a lifetime to get tired of this family.

*His* family.

He thought back over his life and his journey from lonely little boy to burdened adolescent to wandering man to this perfection here in Rodeo, Montana, with his new family.

He imagined days spent turning his land into a ranch and little Tori into a cowgirl. Little Beth could be anything she wanted to be and he would support her. And, oh yeah, he wanted more kids.

That thought led him to the nights he and Rachel would share, and the perfection of the lovemaking they'd shared that evening, and loving the daylights out of her for the rest of their lives.

He couldn't help but smile.

"That's exactly what I like to see on a man's face," Rachel said just before kissing him and making his dreams come true. "A smile."

\* \* \* \* \*

# WE HOPE YOU ENJOYED
## THIS BOOK FROM

**⟨H⟩ HARLEQUIN**
# SPECIAL
## EDITION

*Believe in love. Overcome obstacles. Find happiness.*

Relate to finding comfort and strength in the
support of loved ones and enjoy the journey
no matter what life throws your way.

**6 NEW BOOKS AVAILABLE EVERY MONTH!**

"Actually, I think I'll try a pint of Wild Horse tonight."

She moved the mug to the appropriate tap and tilted it under the spout. "Eleven whole words," she remarked. "I think that's a new record, John."

He lifted his gaze to hers, saw the teasing light in her eye and felt that uncomfortable tug again. "My name's not John."

"But as you haven't told me what it is, I can only guess," she said.

"So you decided on John...as in John Doe?" he surmised.

She nodded. "And because it rolls off the tongue more easily than the-sullen-stranger-who-drinks-Sam-Adams, or, after tonight, the-sullen-stranger-who-usually-drinks-Sam-Adams-but-one-time-ordered-a-Wild-Horse." She set the mug on a paper coaster in front of him. "And I think that's a smile tugging at the lips of the sullen stranger."

"I was just thinking that next time I'll order a Ruby Mountain Angel Creek Amber Ale," he said.

"Careful," she cautioned with a playful wink. "This exchange of words is starting to resemble an actual conversation."

He lifted the mug to his mouth, and Sky moved down the bar to serve a couple of newcomers, leaving Jake alone with his beer.

Which was what he wanted, and yet, when she came back again, he heard himself say, "My name's Jake."

The sweet curve of her lips warmed something deep inside him.

*Don't miss*
The Marine's Road Home *by Brenda Harlen,*
*available August 2020 wherever*
*Harlequin Special Edition books and ebooks are sold.*

Harlequin.com

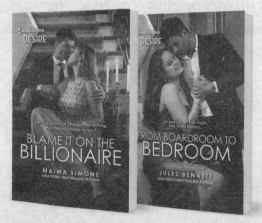